FORGET THE GLORY

FORGET THE GLORY

Elizabeth Darrell

This first hardcover edition published in Great Britain 2003 by
SEVERN HOUSE PUBLISHERS LTD of
9–15 High Street, Sutton, Surrey SM1 1DF.
Previously published 1985 under the pseudonym *Emma Drummond*.
This first hardcover edition published in the USA 2003 by
SEVERN HOUSE PUBLISHERS INC of
595 Madison Avenue, New York, N.Y. 10022.

British Library Cataloguing in Publication Data

Darrell, Elizabeth, 1931-
    Forget the glory
    1.   Crimean War, 1853-1856 - Participation, British - Fiction
    2.   British - India - History - 19th century - Fiction
    3.   Historical fiction
    I.   Title II. Drummond, Emma, 1931-
    823.9'14 [F]

    ISBN 0-7278-5657-X

C406655230

Printed and bound in Great Britain by
MPG Books Ltd., Bodmin, Cornwall.

Author's Introduction

While researching the Crimean War for my novel *Scarlet* Shadows I came across an entry in the diary of a regimental officer that I found highly intriguing. It referred to the arrival from India of two cavalry regiments to replace the Light Brigade lost in the famous charge the year before. The diarist commented on the splendour of their horses compared with the worn out beasts that had survived battle and a freezing winter in Balaclava.

Several years later I decided to investigate further and uncovered details of an amazing military undertaking. I felt this little known story deserved greater recognition. Troops today are flown to war zones swiftly and in reasonable comfort. *Forget the Glory* is my tribute to our ancestors, who did it the hard way!

Author's Note

With the drama of Alma and Inkerman, the tragic Charge of the Light Brigade, Florence Nightingale and her intrepid nurses, storms, snow and agony, one aspect of the Crimean War has been overshadowed and barely recorded. At the turn of the year 1855, two regiments of British cavalry, their vicious Arab stallions, equipment, weapons, wives, children and servants travelled from India to the Crimea as reinforcements for the lost Light Brigade.

The journey entailed covering six thousand miles, well over a thousand on foot, and crossing two continents and two oceans. They embarked highly-strung animals into makeshift floating stables, marched across desert where the nearest drinking water was ninety miles away, suffered excessive heat, violent weather, epidemics and loss of life *en route*. And they did it in thick serge uniforms, with their ladies in crinolines. At the end of the journey the prospect of savage battle awaited, but they obeyed their orders with the stoicism, loyalty and patriotic fervour of the day.

Forget the Glory is based on the personal accounts and regimental records of those who undertook this incredible journey. Although the 43rd Light Dragoons is an entirely fictional regiment, it covers the route actually taken and experiences situations similar to those encountered by the illustrious 10th Hussars and 12th Lancers. This story is humbly dedicated to their endeavour.

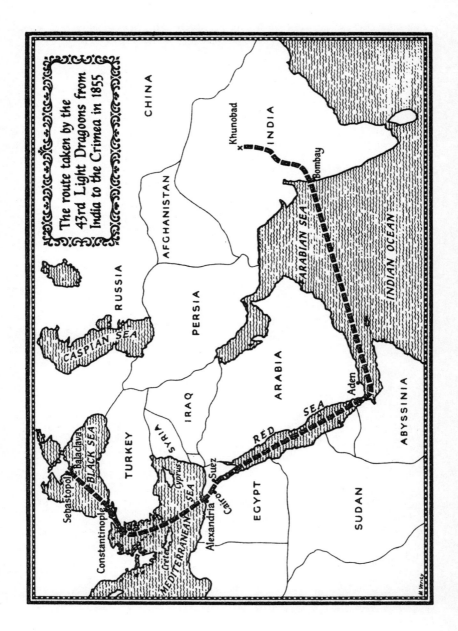

The route taken by the
43rd Light Dragoons from
India to the Crimea in 1855

CHINA

RUSSIA

CASPIAN SEA

AFGHANISTAN

Khunobad
x
INDIA

Bombay

PERSIA

ARABIAN SEA

INDIAN OCEAN

IRAQ

SYRIA

ARABIA

Aden

TURKEY

Cyprus

Suez

RED   SEA

ABYSSINIA

Sebastopol

Balaclava

BLACK SEA

Cairo

Constantinople

Crete

Alexandria

MEDITERRANEAN SEA

EGYPT

SUDAN

M Hardy

CHAPTER ONE

Captain the Honourable Rowan Gerard De-Mayne, youngest grandson of the Earl of Drumlea, was a hero who declined to behave like one. In Victorian Anglo-Indian military circles men of valour were expected to be noble of features and character, God-fearing, steady of nerve and straight of eye, clean-limbed and scrupulously moral. Regiments wished to lionize their heroes. The 43rd Light Dragoons were exasperated by theirs!

Rowan DeMayne was certainly clean-limbed, with nerves so steady he diced with death at every possible opportunity in the confidence that he would win. Coming from an aristocratic line traceable to Henry III, his features were noble enough despite the insolence that tinged his smile and the strikingly dark eyes that looked out on the world with sleepy amusement. But there was a marked lack of nobility about his character, his morals were deplorable, and he apparently feared God no more than he feared anyone or anything.

In that December of 1853 his reputation as one of the most valiant officers in the service of Queen Victoria was undeniable, but in the breasts of his fellows burnt the secret desire to see the regimental daredevil brought to his knees. In the breasts of the fair sex burnt the same desire, except that they wished him to be brought to only one knee—at their feet, declaring his unquenchable passionate devotion.

Rowan's knees remained unbent as he continued along his merry path, however, and his thoughts were far from considering what emotions he might arouse in others one morning prior to Christmas, when he and his friend Captain Gilmour Crane entered the palace of Khairat Singh, Chieftain of Khunobad Province in which the military cantonment was situated.

Dismounting in the courtyard and handing their horses to palace grooms, the two British officers trod through an archway into an inner courtyard where two servants in baggy trousers of purple silk and overdresses of gold cloth salaamed as they passed. The ruler of Khunobad surrounded himself with Persian servants taken as slaves in raiding parties by Afghans, and bartered for ammunition stolen from military supply columns. Khairat Singh had less need for weapons of defence. He maintained a close friendship with the British and the large garrison was no more than three miles from his palace, ever ready to rush to his aid. Its proximity also offered excellent opportunities for purloining guns and bullets when he needed fresh supplies. Small wonder visitors from the cantonment were always treated with great respect.

This day was no exception. Crossing the courtyard, the military men skirted a square pool on which water-lilies floated, then walked through an avenue of trees that led to a multi-domed citadel of white and red stone. Unseen watchers opened carved latticed doors with precise timing, and they continued over a floor of mosaic studded with semi-precious stones, their ringing footsteps matching exactly and their spurs jingling. In full dress uniform to impress their host, the two captains looked splendid enough to grace such surroundings. They presented a picture of military perfection in skin-tight dark-blue overalls, pale-blue tunics faced with yellow and heavily braided in silver, tall black shakoes rimmed with silver and topped with nodding yellow and black plumes, silver-tasselled sashes, elaborately embroidered sabretaches and heavy swords in scabbards embossed and looped with yellow.

By the mystical method with which such people received news of visitors, a silk-robed official managed to appear through purple hangings at the far end of the lofty chamber just as the tall dragoon officers reached a spot where corridors branched to left and right. Proceedings then followed a known and elaborate protocol until the Englishmen were face to face with a resplendent gentleman empowered to convey messages to his exalted master.

Rowan concentrated on the task of passing on the desire of his commanding officer to discuss with Khairat Singh the growing frequency of raids on villages in the province, and the failure of the Chieftain's own troops to assist in the protection of the inhabitants. As he translated Colonel Daubnay's message into the obligatory recital of elaborate phrases, he reflected that the visit was a total waste of time. The brigand bands robbing the peasants were doing so on behalf of Khairat Singh's illegitimate half-brother; a generous gesture by the Chieftain to stave off any desire by a greedy blood-relative to take over power at the palace.

During the replies by the Chieftain's spokesman, Rowan studied the erotic paintings on the walls with interest. He decided that several must be meant as sexual jokes, since even the most determined man could never perform in such manner. He discussed the subject with his friend as they left the palace for the return ride.

"It's damned impossible, Gil," he said from the side of his mouth as they marched in unison, ramrod stiff and staring straight ahead through the tree-lined avenue. "I know it for a fact, because I tried it after my last visit. Can't be done, I promise you. As for those two naked goatherds in the far corner of the west wall, what they are meant to be doing defies my imagination no matter how often I study them."

His friend cast him a glance as they broke into the last

of the courtyards where the horses were waiting in the shade
cast by the massive walls of the palace.

"I trust you found time to take in what was said to you
in reply by that fellow in green silk," he said dryly.

"Oh that! Yes. Daubnay is invited to The Presence on
Thursday next, when he will be presented with a cageful of
rare monkeys after partaking of a banquet, and then treated
to entertainment the like of which you and I would fully
appreciate, but which will embarrass a man like him into
accepting silence on the subject he has gone expressly to
discuss. The whole visit has been a waste of time. I told him
it would be."

With that declaration Rowan nodded to the servant who
had been holding his stallion and swung up into the saddle,
glad to be on the move again. He found duties of this kind
irksome to his restless spirit, but his proficiency in native
tongues plus his status as the son of a viscount made him a
natural choice.

They set off through the walled city, where the narrow
mud-baked lanes were thronged with people and laden pack-
animals. The clamour made conversation impossible as they
skirted the bazaar filled with multi-coloured wares and bar-
tering customers, then continued past narrow offshoots
where houses of mud-sealed stone and flat roofs huddled
together. The citizens of Khunobad took little notice of the
foreign soldiers, but many a covetous glance was fixed on the
showy chestnut thoroughbreds they rode. Great strong animals with glossy coats and flowing tails left undocked by
regimental tradition—the whim of a byegone colonel who
had mounted his regiment solely on chestnuts—such horses
had immediately earned the 43rd the nickname 'The Ginger
Boys'. Now, they were coming to be known as 'The Ginger
bread Boys'.

As the two men passed beneath the massive arch of the
West Gate which allowed them a distant view of their
cantonment on the far side of the plain, Rowan spoke bitterly on the subject of their reputation.

"I had hoped we should get a new man with fire and dash

when old Stapleford gave up the regiment, but it's already plain as a pikestaff Daubnay don't see further than a smart turnout and precision riding. Under his command the 43rd will never shake off that damned contemptuous nickname."

"Give him a chance," said Gil quietly. "He has been with us only three days."

"More than long enough to see that he puts pretty uniforms before regimental glory," Rowan replied in disgust. "We've been on a fools' errand today, Gil. Khairat Singh and his infernal bastard brother are laughing at us. What we should do is post spies in Khunobad and Mhoud so that we have wind of when they mean to raid the villages. Then we should attack in force. That would put an end to it."

"It would also put an end to our good relations with Khairat Singh," pointed out Gil. "We are pledged to go to his defence, not attack him." He mopped the sweat from his brow and blond moustache with a handkerchief. "By George, it's hot dandied up like this! I wish there was a straighter route we could take."

"There is," responded Rowan immediately, goaded by the frustration of knowing his friend's argument was sound, and longing to give vent to his pent-up restlessness. "If we go through the village we can knock half an hour from the journey."

"You know we can't. To jump those nullahs is an impossibility."

Frustrated even further by Gil's solid common sense, Rowan rode beside him for a few minutes in silence, the only sounds being the soft thud of hooves on the dust road, the jingle of harness and the squeak of leather as they swayed in their saddles to the rhythm of the walking pace they had adopted. The sun beat down on them from a brassy sky, and the plain had begun to move and dance with atmospheric images so that it was possible to imagine that trees and shrubs were spinning around like skaters on a frozen pond. Suddenly, Rowan could stand inaction no longer.

"I'll wager my roan steeplechaser I reach the main gates

at least thirty minutes ahead of you," he challenged, turning to Gil.

His friend drew rein and stared at him. "I'll take no wager on that madness. They'll scrape your remains from the bottom of that first nullah."

"Will they just? Then I charge you with laying them to rest in fitting manner," he said lightly, excitement already filling his limbs at the thought of the two chasms he would attempt to leap. "Adieu, Gil."

Deaf to any further protests, Rowan turned his horse and set off at a tangent from the main track, riding toward the village at a trot, no thought in his head other than the thrill of facing a dangerous challenge once more. He had a stallion that was second to none in the regiment. With precise timing and skill it should be possible to jump it across those nullahs. If not, he would break the beast's neck along with his own.

He passed the village and approached the first great cleavage in the flat plain at a gallop, bending low in the saddle and encouraging his horse with urgent words in his ears. As always, dark memories filled his mind, driving him to achieve impossibilities and prove himself a better man than any other. The thundering of his mount's hooves matched the thundering anger that filled him again; the air rushing past his ears became the whispering voices that had condemned him six years ago; the looming chasm became the depth of his humiliation and helplessness at that time.

Then he was across, flying through the air with the power of the beast beneath him adding to his own sense of power as a man. But a second nullah now faced him and his stallion, who had been injected with the same wild bravado after the success of that first leap. Together they raced on, aware of hovering death yet in mutual satanic disregard of it, until the ground fell away and all they could see was the glisten of water rushing below.

It was almost the end for them both as the horse landed short and fought madly for a foothold with its back legs on loose earth. But Rowan was out of the saddle and dragging

the beast to safety before it slipped too far. They both stood
fighting for breath, Rowan sweating heavily, the stallion
flecked with foam. But they rejoiced together in that un-
matchable fraternity between superb horse and brilliant
rider as Rowan laid his cheek against the glossy chestnut one
and told the beast they were invincible.

For a while Rowan walked, carrying his shako to let the
breeze cool his hair, and leading the horse to allow it to
recover. Away in the distance he could see the tiny figure
of his friend taking the track that wound in horseshoe bends
to avoid the nullahs and added several miles to the journey
from Khunobad city to the military cantonment. Breaking
into exuberant laughter at the thought of Gil's probable
expression, he snatched his pistol from its holster attached
to the saddle and fired six shots into the still air. His amusement increased as he realized the consternation the sound
of gunfire would cause amongst the men on watch at the
cantonment walls.

"That'll keep you on your toes, lads," he shouted through
his laughter, all anger and bitter memories suppressed by the
elation of risking life and limb a few minutes before.

He cantered through the gates fully half an hour before
his friend was likely to arrive, and he instructed the man on
guard to inform Captain Crane of the precise time of his
entry when he finally came. Then he trotted the horse along
the tan beneath an avenue of trees, heading past the race-
track on the northern perimeter and skirting the elegant
bandstand that could have been transferred direct from
Brighton as a reminder of that far-off seaside resort. The
road leading between official residences was wide and
straight, which allowed Rowan to see the pale-blue of a
muslin crinoline on one of the verandahs when he was still
some yards away. The girl wearing it was the shy, youthful
daughter of a major of Native Infantry recently arrived in
Khunobad, who had artlessly told him whilst on a picnic the
day before that her papa had warned her against associating
with the infamous Captain DeMayne. Rowan's natural
promiscuity heightened by the elation of his recent feat

prompted him to approach the bungalow calling a greeting to her.

She spun round and blushed scarlet at the sight of him, seemingly rooted to the spot. But when he smiled, swept off his shako and bowed exaggeratedly from the waist in her direction, she decided on retreat. With smile broadening, Rowan set his horse at the low fence surrounding the residence and continued riding up the path and onto the verandah beneath the overhanging roof.

"Why are you running away, Miss Parrish?" he asked in caressing tones, hoping her father was nowhere near. "I shall not eat you, you know."

She came to a frozen halt, but appeared unwilling to turn and face him. Rowan was enjoying the situation immensely.

"I am determined on conversing with you," he continued in the same tone, "and would prefer not to take my horse into your parlour in order to do so."

That made her turn, and he discovered that she was prettier than he remembered, with bright colour in her cheeks and eyes made rounder with alarmed excitement. He did not think she would heed her papa's warning for long.

"You would not dare to ride that huge creature into the parlour, sir," she declared in a breathless voice.

"You know very well that I would," he replied lightly. "So you had much better do as I ask."

Martialling more resistance, she stood twisting her hands nervously as she said, "You are being quite absurd, Captain DeMayne. If you do not leave this instant I shall be obliged to tell Papa of your behavior when he returns. Be sure he will speak of it to Colonel Daubnay."

Putting his hand over his heart he adopted a mournful expression. "Better that than despair of receiving even one kind word from you."

"Please go!" she urged in trembling tones. "If anyone should pass this way!"

"They will see a poor fellow begging a haughty young woman to take pity on him and promise to stroll around the bandstand with him tomorrow evening," he said, the full

curve of her breasts beneath the muslin reminding him of
the erotic paintings in Khairat Singh's palace. For a female
of no more than seventeen she was delightfully mature.

Glancing round in agitation the trapped girl blurted out,
"But Papa warned that you are . . ."

"So I am," he inserted smoothly. "But you could persuade
me to mend my ways very easily. Do I have your promise?"

"I . . . I have not yet decided whether or not to visit the
bandstand tomorrow."

He sat back in the saddle and folded his arms. "Then I
shall wait until you have done so."

"*Please* go," she implored, knowing the sight of a young
girl being held at bay by a mounted officer on her own
verandah would make her the subject of titillating gossip if
anyone should pass by. "I might be present at the bandstand."

"*Might?*" He inched the horse forward.

"I will," she amended quickly, her blush deepening further.

He gave a slow smile. "Good. I shall look forward to
offering you my arm." Then, before she could guess his
intention, he bent in the saddle to kiss her swiftly on the lips.
"Until tomorrow, Miss Parrish." Then he backed along the
verandah, laughing in delight at the way in which she rushed
indoors with her hands to her hot cheeks.

He was still full of elation when he tied the horse to the
rail outside the office of his commanding officer and ran up
the steps to give his report on the mission to the Chieftain's
palace. It faded a little when he was made to wait for fifteen
minutes in the outer room. He was hot, dusty and in need
of a drink. He reflected that he would have done better to
go to his quarters first, but the verbal report was short and
conventional. He had hoped to deliver it knowing the rest
of the day would be his own. While he waited, the Adjutant
chatted with him about the coming race meeting in which
Rowan intended riding a new stallion he had bought.

"That Satan is a brute. We are all agreed upon it, save

you," said the slim, greying man. "What persuades you to think otherwise?"

"Instinct, old fellow. I know horseflesh. Which is more than I can say for some," he added, nodding toward the CO's door. "Those showy geldings of his are fit for nothing but military reviews. I cannot see any one of them excelling itself in a full-blooded charge against the enemy . . . Not that there is the slightest chance of that in this regiment. Small wonder we are called 'The Gingerbread Boys'."

He grew aware that the door had opened and a short thickset man with a sparse moustache and sparser hair stood looking at him.

"I am ready to hear your report now, Captain DeMayne," said Colonel Daubnay in a reedy voice.

Rowan got leisurely to his feet and went into the office in the certain knowledge that his comments had been overheard. It would do the old boy good to know what his officers thought.

The older man stopped beneath the swaying punkah and turned to face him. "Can you give me any good reason for deserting Captain Crane this morning, and for firing your pistol in a manner that would be taken as a warning to the piquets or a signal for help?"

Taken unawares Rowan said, "How the devil did that news arrive ahead of me?"

"The Sergeant of the Guard reported to the Officer of the Day, who reported to me of course. It was only after some minutes of observation through the telescope that it appeared there was no need for the men to stand-to. May I now have an explanation from you?"

Frowning slightly Rowan said, "I fired my pistol as a signal to Captain Crane that I had successfully jumped the nullahs."

"*Jumped the nullahs,*" repeated the Colonel softly, as if to satisfy himself that he had heard aright. "Am I to take it that you were indulging in one of the immature escapades for which you are famed whilst on special duty for me?"

Rowan decided to ignore that question, and said instead,

"I have to inform you, sir, that Khairat Singh will be delighted to meet you on Thursday to become acquainted and discuss the raids on his villages. His spokesman said they were the cause of great anguish to his venerable master but, as I told you earlier, the old devil turns a blind eye to placate his bloodthirsty bastard brother. *Great anguish*, be damned."

Colonel Daubnay's small bright eyes grew even brighter. "You have already given me your unrequested opinion, Captain DeMayne. Let us get straight from the outset of our association that I will *ask* for my junior officers' opinions if I ever desire to hear them. Colonel Stapleford put me in the picture before he left, and I have been in the army long enough to assess a situation perfectly well." He looked Rowan over from head to foot before adding, "I think it would not come amiss to get a few more things straight while you are here."

He turned to stroll to his desk and sat down slowly, still studying Rowan with an expression of distaste. "I know of your past history—how could I not when it was such a public affair? But I am not a person to hold such things against a man forever, least of all when he has proved beyond all doubt that he is as courageous and daring as anyone in the Queen's service. Colonel Stapleford told me of your ready aggression in a skirmish, your valour in holding off a group of tribesmen single-handed whilst your wounded were collected. He had little need to tell me of those sole missions into the wilder areas of this land, disguised as a native, in order to gain important information for the Political Branch. They have made you into a living legend both here and at home."

With every compliment Rowan grew more and more wary. Mention of his past had stirred up the old feelings again, and this plain-speaking man was rubbing salt in the wound with every word, in some strange way. Already parched from his long ride, his throat stuck together preventing him from speaking. The tight ceremonial uniform did nothing to ease his discomfort.

12

"What I feel I should make clear at the outset to you are my plans for the 43rd Light Dragoons," Colonel Daubnay continued. "I fear they are vastly different from yours."

Certain now that his comment about 'The Gingerbread Boys' was at the root of this extraordinary interview, Rowan smiled. "I'm confident they are not, sir. Every man of the 43rd feels as I do on the subject."

"Hmm, a comforting philosophy, no doubt. But I now give you an advance hearing of what I intend saying to those under my command when the appropriate moment arises," came the cold response. "The task of an army, Captain DeMayne, is to defend crown and country. If it is small and inefficient it will do so by dying wholesale on the fields of lost battles. If it is powerful and held in awe it will succeed in discouraging any prospective enemy from taking on its might in armed conflict. I gather you deplore the fact that this regiment has accrued no battle honours through the circumstances of not being posted to the right place at the right time and, as a result, has earned the soubriquet suggesting its members are no more than men made of sweetmeat. I do not intend to let that fact turn this regiment into a subject for further derision by allowing dilatoriness, a casual attitude toward manners and discipline, and ridiculous escapades by its officers in a bravado attempt to endow the 43rd with the distinction it feels itself to be lacking. Do you understand me?"

Rowan bridled at his tone. "I understand the words, sir, but not the meaning behind them. Am I to believe that you do not *care* that the 43rd has had the infernal bad fortune to miss every war and campaign engaged in by Britain and the Empire since its formation forty years ago?"

"You may believe what you wish," said Colonel Daubnay, supremely at ease and radiating satisfaction from every pore in his stocky body. "I have spent my adult life in the army and this command is the culmination of my ambitions. It is my intention to turn this discontented rabble of men into a regiment that will knock into a cocked hat any other in India. We are here to protect the ruler and citizens of

Khunobad Province, and we shall best do that by ensuring
that we are held in total awe by friend and prospective foe
alike. I mean to instruct the regimental tailor to re-clothe
the troopers in uniforms that fit without a single crease, and
insist that the men keep them in spotless condition. I shall
inspect the horses, weed out those unfit to grace this regiment and replace them with prime horseflesh. When I am
satisfied with the appearance of my men, I shall concentrate
on riding manoeuvres in preparation for the reviews and
parades that will advertise our presence to those who know
nothing of us beyond the distant sound of our bugles." He
got to his feet again with the verve of his future visions and
pointed to the window. "Out there lies a huge open plain.
It will become the stage for the most spectacular military
shows in India. There is not a man, woman or boy who does
not thrill to the sight of rank upon rank of immaculate
handsome troops, glossy horses, gleaming harness and ban-
ners flying." His bright gaze fastened on Rowan with intensity. "We do not need battle honours, sir. We need to make
our presence known in such splendid fashion no one would
dare to provoke us into action." He came round the desk and
up to his captive subordinate. "The men will engage in
athletic training to build up their puny bodies; the officers
will do the same. I mean to put a stop to the disgusting
habits of the average trooper and teach them manners. My
officers will pull themselves together in every respect. They
are dissolute, rowdy and lacking in pride. By the time I have
finished, they will be gentlemen who distinguish themselves
equally in the saddle, in dainty parlours or in the ballroom.
The 43rd will embark on a programme of entertainment fit
for a cavalry regiment on service abroad. There will be balls,
soirées, dinners, garden parties, and race meetings. Khairat
Singh and his dignitaries will be invited whenever suitable,
and we shall accept his many return invitations."

He looked Rowan over again with a touch of disparagement. "Due to your knowledge of local dialects, and the fact
that you are the social superior of any gentleman of the 43rd,
I have no choice but to make you my Social Liaison Officer.

But you will not do as you are. No, not at all. You are a libertine, Captain DeMayne, a dissolute lecher who believes the world and all that is in it to be his oyster. You are also a warmonger, too quick to draw a sabre against another man —even a brother, as your sorry past demonstrates." Flitting from that devastatingly wounding remark to one quite trifling, he added, "Whilst on the subject of sabres, I must request you to wear yours on the correct hip. I know you are left-handed—a deplorable laxness on the part of your tutors —but you must learn to draw with your right. Practice relentlessly until you are proficient, sir. I cannot have the immaculate turnout of my dragoons marred by one of my officers wearing a scabbard on the wrong side."

He appeared to have concluded his fervent speech for the present. Rowan stood looking at him with a fury of protest boiling within him against all that had been said. Finding it impossible to control his feelings, one outraged sentence burst from his lips.

"By God, you'll turn us into a *toy* regiment!"

The eagerness vanished from the full face before him, and was replaced by icy dislike. "Another of your faults is intolerable arrogance, Captain DeMayne. You must work on that along with the rest if you wish to remain here. It is universally known that you do not consider the 43rd good enough for you, but you will henceforth cease your attempts to make it so with bizarre solo escapades. A toy regiment is better than none . . . and no other will have you, as you found to your cost!"

The following evening heralded the first of the garrison pre-Christmas parties. It was being given by the commanding officer of one of the two Native Infantry regiments stationed at Khunobad, and the officers of the 43rd had not needed Rowan's darkly-muttered warnings of their new colonel's plans to turn them into ballroom beaux to persuade them to attend. Colonel and Mrs Spry were renowned hosts who provided the best suppers in the cantonment, which accounted for the fact that Rowan, despite being Officer of

the Day, determined to put in an appearance at their bungalow.

But the pleasure of anticipation was diminished by what
had happened the previous day. As he rode through the
cantonments with Sergeant Clarke on evening rounds, he
reflected grimly that there was no doubt Daubnay had
meant every word of his proposal to turn the 43rd into a
regiment of faint-hearted popinjays. The man's stunted stat-
ure and mild appearance cloaked a personality verging on
the eccentric. One had to admit that the outrageous Lord
Cardigan had dressed his 11th Hussars in gorgeous uniforms
designed to present them as the epitome of manhood, but
there was no question *he* intended to send them into battle
at every possible opportunity, despite the restrictive qualities
of gold-encrusted waist-length tunics and crimson overalls
that fitted so indecently close to the wearer's figure the
regiment had been nicknamed 'The Cherrybums'.

As usual, the thought of the 11th Hussars sent anger and
remembered humiliation coursing through Rowan. His
brothers, Bel and Monty, looked excessively handsome in
that distinctive uniform, never more so than when each had
received a medal from their young queen. No one would
ever dismiss them as toy soldiers, however pretty their uniforms!

The night was bitterly cold. Both Rowan and Sergeant
Clarke wore heavy cloaks over their uniforms as they walked
their horses along the well-known paths. Cold nipped in
their nostrils and iced their breath as well as that of the two
horses, who were glad to be on the move on such a night.
The Sergeant respected Rowan's mood and offered no conversation as they circled the outside perimeter of the race-
track and headed toward the accommodation-blocks.

Social Liaison Officer, thought Rowan in disgust. Did
Daubnay have no idea what he had been doing on those
journeys into the interior, alone and dressed as a pedlar? He
dwelt on thoughts of his last such mission, which had taken
him over the border into Afghanistan. For more than four
months he had painstakingly inserted himself into villages,

bazaars, marriage-parties, merchants' caravans and any group that would accept him in their midst, in order to eavesdrop and gain information. He had borne the kicks of those who cleared the way for persons of eminence to pass through the streets, dodged missiles thrown at a lowly traveller who dared to lean against the walls of a chieftain's house and risked discovery with its consequent torture by listening at window apertures during the hours of darkness. He had eaten revolting messes, copied degrading habits and heartily reviled the British infidels, with only the deeply locked away determination to return to keep him sane.

There had been three other such occasions during the six years that the 43rd had been in India, and Rowan had many times been asked to join the Political Branch and make his future in India. He had always refused. They did not understand why he did what he did, and he had too much pride to enlighten them.

The 43rd Light Dragoons was a comparatively new regiment, one which had been denied all opportunity of distinguishing itself yet. Its officers were mostly youngest sons—like himself—or men from county families unable to afford the price of a commission in one of the élite cavalry regiments like the 11th Hussars, which already contained two DeMaynes and boasted a long line of them throughout its history. Rowan knew it was generally believed that he held the 43rd in contempt, and its undistinguished officers along with it. Because he had been denied his rightful place in the 11th Hussars, society thought his readiness to face danger was due to a desperate bid to make the regiment illustrious enough for a man of his social standing. Society was only partially right. He did passionately long to raise the 43rd to the same ranks as all those proud regiments who had snubbed him six years ago. But it was not because he held it or its men in contempt. It was because the rest of society did.

Rowan's most fervent prayer was for a war—preferably against one of the great western armies of Europe. Given a chance, the 43rd could be as gallant as any other on the field of battle. But its members had grown indolent, resigned and bored by year after year doing little else except simply existing in distant peaceful garrisons. Daubnay had seen the problem soon enough, but his solution was guaranteed to take away what little heart was left in the men.

Gazing up into the immense star-filled sky Rowan felt his longings as a pain in his breast. There was so much in him that could find no outlet. The blood of a warrior was hot in his veins, put there by a long line of valiant ancestors, yet he could not satisfy the inbred instinct. The blood of a lover ran with it—the DeMaynes had always been lusty men— and yet he had never come across the woman who could truly satisfy him. Once, perhaps, he had come very near to it, but he had been little more than a boy and had mistaken passion for love.

He put back his head to study the infinity to which he would eventually journey. Time was inexorably passing, and he had achieved nothing. He was bound hand and foot by the consequences of his own youthful folly. Would he ever be able to break from those bonds?

Next instant, he changed from starlight dreamer to soldier as he straightened, drawing gently on the reins with his right hand and reaching for his pistol with the left.

"What is it, sir?" whispered Sergeant Clarke, slowing his own horse.

"Sounds of a struggle at the end of D Block," he said in a low voice. "It's those devils from Khunobad after our guns again. Approach with the utmost care. If there are more than two or three, I'll do my best to engage them while you ride to call out the guards."

Edging their horses gently alongside the wall of the block assigned to D Troop of their own regiment, they reached the spot where scuffling and an occasional grunt could be heard. When they were almost at the corner and protected by a buttress, Rowan reined in and issued rapid commands in the local dialect, ending in English with, "Stand still, or I fire!"

The response was immediate and surprising. A voice cried

in feminine terror, "Don't shoot! For pity's sake, don't shoot!"

Disappointment flooded him on being thwarted of even a small piece of action, and Rowan told the Sergeant in some irritation to investigate the reason for a brawl between the women of the regiment at such an hour.

"Tell them I'll arrange for them all to be locked in at nightfall if they cause trouble again," he called after the NCO who had dismounted and walked across to dark figures near the entrance to the old stone building.

Clarke was away for some minutes, and Rowan began to grow even more irritable as the cold crept into his bones. "Come on, man," he instructed sharply. "You have had long enough to sort out a parcel of females—or must I fire my pistol over their heads to get them moving?"

But the Sergeant came out of the darkness leading a woman by the arm. "Not quite what we thought, sir. It's Rafferty, drunk as a beanpole. Bin taking it out on Mrs Rafferty here. She seems a bit shocked, sir."

Rowan had a vague view of a tangle-haired slattern with the coarse dress torn from her shoulder. Her skin appeared to have dark areas on it, but it could just as well have been dirt as bruises. His irritation began to verge on anger. The women who had accompanied their husbands when the regiment sailed for India six years ago were luckier than those left destitute in England, but most of them seemed to have tied themselves to the drunkards and bullies in the ranks. However, the women themselves were notorious bottle-tippers and looked generally so unsavoury their men probably needed a drink or two inside them before wanting any kind of intimacy with them.

He looked away in distaste. "Is she in need of attention?"

"No, sir. It's more fright than anything. I've given Rafferty a straight word on the subject, but it's my guess he won't give her no further trouble on account of he's just passed out."

Rowan sighed audibly. "This is acutely annoying. I am due at Colonel Spry's bungalow as soon as possible, and the purpose of 'rounds', Sergeant, is not to sort out marital brawls between drunken couples." He steadied his stallion, which was growing restless. "Get Corporal Parker to deal with Rafferty. He should have been out at the first sounds of a disturbance. I trust he is not also drunk!" Turning his mount's head he urged the animal into a walk. "I shall finish alone, Sergeant, and meet you at the Guard Room in ten minutes. And for God's sake see that that woman returns to her quarters at once, so that I shall not have to endure her snivelling. She most likely deserved all she got."

"Yessir, ten minutes," called the Sergeant after him. "Now, come along, Mistress Rafferty."

Rowan sighed again as he moved away. Sergeant Clarke was an honest man and an excellent NCO but since his tragic injury last year, he had grown a little too sensitive to the misfortunes of others. A grog-swilling slut would not appreciate his fatherly concern.

There were the usual people gathered in the Sprys' large airy salon. If Rowan had not known a whole month had passed, he could well have imagined this evening to be a continuation of the last soirée he had attended there. He halted for a moment in the doorway to allow his eyes to grow accustomed to the bright lights after the starlit darkness he had left behind.

The men present were those with whom he communed and ate day after day; the women were wearing their bright-eyed, feverishly-eager expressions as they tried to be entertaining. God knew, they had little enough to stimulate them out at this isolated station, but Rowan felt they would find life a little more bearable if they did not try so hard. Perfectly pleasant, respectable married matrons who greeted him daily from their carriages and commented on the heat or cold, inexplicably turned into ogling courtesans once they donned evening gowns, and countered his every remark with shocked excitement that suggested he was making improper advances to them. It was the *un*married ones to whom he made improper advances!

The first person on whom his glance lingered was a young matron who tried harder than most to gain any man's interest. The vulgar wife of the Quartermaster had found an easy target tonight. Kit Wrexham had joined the 43rd from an infantry regiment only that week and now stood, stocky and red-haired, enjoying every dazed moment of optical seduction.

"Ah, there you are!" Gil approached, smiling a greeting. "Duty done?"

Rowan nodded. "For the moment. I see Wrexham is doing his with bemused diligence."

Gil followed the direction of his glance. "I fear no one warned him about the lady. But give him credit for making himself agreeable after a hellish journey to reach us. You know most of his baggage was stolen while he slept. That uniform is borrowed."

Rowan raised dark brows. "He looks in imminent danger of losing *that* before long."

"Many a true word, et cetera," chuckled his friend.

"He'll soon get another, I imagine. I hear his father is a cloth merchant."

Gil turned back to him. "So he is. What is wrong with that? Must you always sound so damned superior?"

But Rowan was occupied in taking two glasses from the tray of a passing servant and downing the contents of them both as he surveyed the throng of guests through sleepy eyes. Miss Parrish was on the far side of the room, looking across at him with the anticipation he was used to seeing on females' faces. He had not been at the bandstand earlier that evening, after all, due to the demands of Officer of the Day. It was no bad thing; her eagerness would be doubled now.

Replacing the two empty glasses as the servant returned, and taking a third, Rowan turned to explain to his companion. "I have to down two to your every one, in order to equal the conviviality of those who arrived an hour ago. Do you really find me damned superior, Gil?" he finished with amusement.

"Not excessively so. But others do, and I swear you culti-
vate it."

His amusement increased. "One of your most delightful
traits is your acute perception. Your most annoying is that
you never cease to preach to me." He put a hand on Gil's
shoulder. "I see Miss Herriot attempting to rid herself of
Major Mettlethorpe's unwelcome company. Let us go to her
aid." They began to cross the room. "By God, she is dashed
alluring with angry colour in her cheeks. If you don't go on
one knee before her soon, I shall forget you are my friend
and take up her gauntlet."

"You are hardly the best person to give advice on when
to propose marriage," growled Gil.

"How true," responded Rowan smoothly. "My prowess
lies in the reverse direction. But the incomparable Sophie is
a very severe test to my resolve."

"You had best keep your resolve under control unless you
want a contest on your hands," warned Gil with semi-seri-
ousness.

"A contest—with *me!*" ejaculated Rowan. "You would
be the first fool to attempt it since . . ." He broke off, his
mood ruined by memories.

"My joke," put in Gil diplomatically. "I agree with you
that Miss Herriot is very handsome however."

Major Mettlethorpe backed away at their approach, and
it was then possible to see that Sophie Herriot had beside
her a plump damsel of no more than sixteen, with fluffy hair
that was so fair it was almost white.

" 'Pon my soul," murmured Rowan from the side of his
mouth, "your beauteous Sophie has found a walking marshmallow clothed in what I can only believe is an unwanted
shroud."

Gil was so engrossed trying to disguise the laughter threatening to choke him, it was left to Rowan to make the
opening greetings after giving a small bow. Sophie's cheeks
grew faintly pink as her expressive eyes gazed up at him,
ignoring his companion who was her accepted suitor.

"Captain DeMayne," she exclaimed breathlessly, "we

had given up all hope of seeing you this evening. But duty has relented, it seems."

"Not for long, unfortunately," he said with a slow smile. "So you must make the most of me while I am here. I am all yours."

Sophie was thrown into confusion, but the plump friend was overcome with giggles. Rowan regarded her through narrowed eyes.

"You appreciate wit, Miss . . . ?"

"Theobald," provided Sophie in brittle tones. "Captain Hallam presented you to my friend at the picnic two days ago. Can you have forgotten so soon?"

"Regrettably my memory is shocking, Miss Herriot."

"Shame on you, sir," cooed the pink-and-white Miss Theobald. "I have heard that your memory is excellent. You remember every detail of what you see and hear on those dangerous missions you undertake." Her pale eyes grew rounder with admiration as she looked him over from head to foot. "It is quite beyond my comprehension how you manage to disguise yourself as a filthy beggar and be readily accepted as one when sitting on corners with a begging-bowl."

Rowan's eyes narrowed further. "It is quite simple, ma'am. I roll back and forth on the floor of my stables for half an hour before setting out. When I approach upwind, no one has doubts of what I purport to be. Should you ever need a beggarly disguise, I can recommend the process to you."

The young girl gasped at such audacity, but was saved from total and everlasting capitulation to the wicked Rowan DeMayne by their hostess approaching to ask if she would entertain the guests with a ballad, if Miss Herriot would accompany her on the pianoforte.

Sophie looked up at Gil at that point, and smiled. "Would you consent to turn the music for me, Captain Crane? It is useless to ask your friend. He has made his opinion on musical entertainment quite clear on more than one occasion."

"Ah, that was before Miss Theobald graced Khunobad with her presence," murmured Rowan, determined to get as far from earshot of the salon as he could in as short as possible a time. Females singing ballads sounded, in his opinion, like a chorus of mules complaining of loads upon their backs.

The marshmallow maiden giggled in delight. "I shall win you over, sir, by singing expressly for you."

He bowed. "I am honoured, Miss Theobald. But if I should drag myself away from the bliss of your voice, it will be for the sole reason that some emergency has arisen that requires the presence of the Officer of the Day."

As he expected, the entertainment fell on his unwilling eardrums to produce the usual urgency to drown it, and Rowan made his way into the other salon where every man who had managed to avoid the social trap had gathered to help himself to the excellent festive supper laid out on the long table and to drink mulled wine. Rowan was amused to see even his host among the number, talking to Colonel Dunwoodie, Political Officer of Khunobad. Colonel Daubnay had noticeably remained in a prominent seat amongst those enduring the entertainment, as were most of the more timid officers to whom Rowan had passed on the gist of the CO's plans.

He was not long left in peace to enjoy the supper. The Political Officer strolled across to greet him, his full cheeks flushed with wine and crumbs of cheese on his moustache.

"Ah, on duty, are you? Wondered why I didn't see you earlier amidst the damsels. Wanted a word, as it happens. Rode across yesterday but you were over at Khunobad on some damned fruitless visit. Told Daubnay so."

"So did I," said Rowan. "Khairat Singh knows well who is raiding his villages, and must also know we are aware who is raiding our cantonments and outposts for guns. I thought I'd caught the devils at it just now, but it was a trooper's woman, drunk as a mollie and giving her husband no end of a problem. I almost put a bullet through her." He grinned. "Might have done the fellow a service, at that."

The other man laughed. "So you might." He took another gulp of wine. "On the subject of raids to steal our guns, must tell you we have a little problem. Thought you might be able to help us. Pettigrew is already out, and Haslam has not yet returned from Nepal."

"What about that new man?"

"Brevington-Smythe? Only speaks Pushtu. No use in this instance. We are getting reports of a build-up of men around Multan. Our agents say the populations of villages have swelled amazingly, and they can't all be relatives visiting for weddings. We suspect that bandit groups are assembling there. There appears to be no obvious motive for it, but you know as well as I do they never do anything without good purpose. We'd like to know what that purpose is."

Excitement and fear heated Rowan's blood simultaneously. He knew what was coming. "Yes, it would be interesting," he murmured, taking a pull at his own warm spiced wine.

"I'll approach Daubnay officially, of course," the other man went on. "But I thought I'd take this opportunity of sounding you out on your feelings regarding making another of your little jaunts for us."

And that was the Political Officer's way of asking Rowan if he was prepared to undertake a dangerous solo journey on a broken-down mule miles from the help of his countrymen, playing the part of a simple pedlar and knowing discovery of his true identity would mean hideous torture and death.

CHAPTER TWO

Mary Rafferty lay on her straw pallet in the corner of D Block, curled beneath the rough blanket and wide awake. The night was bitter, but she was hardened to cold. The coarse mattress was lumpy and needed fresh straw. It eased the chill and hardness of the mud floor, however, and was the regulation bed for the women of the regiment in Khunobad. They were lucky to have it. On the march they had to sleep on the ground beneath a waggon. The women never complained to the officers. It was not that they were afraid of them—quite the reverse, in fact. But their husbands cut up rough with them if they caused trouble. A tough trooper could manfully endure flogging, but wept tears of humiliation if he were lashed by an officer's tongue over something his wife had done.

As the night hours crept past, Mary stared into the darkness. Her thoughts subdued the throbbing ache of her body, the pain of the bruises caused by Jack's blows. The snores of fifty men became merely a murmur in the background; the turning of the restless women and the fretful whimpering of the Corks' baby went almost unnoticed by her. She could still hear that voice saying, "For God's sake, see that

that woman returns to her quarters at once, so that I shall
not have to endure her snivelling. She most likely deserved
all she got."

She had known that voice. It was unmistakable, and identified its owner even though he had been no more than a
dark outline way above her on a great tall stallion. Rowan
DeMayne, Captain of C Troop. He was an 'Honourable',
and the only real aristocrat in the regiment. Undisputed
hero of the 43rd, he was nevertheless resented by every one
of its officers, and chased by every woman he came across.

Mary knew all this. There was hardly a thing that happened in the regiment that she did not know about. It was
not surprising, since she had been with it from the day of
her birth. Her mother had been in service until she had
fallen in love with a smart trooper and joined the ranks of
the women of the regiment. Disillusionment had soon set
in. The sight of the 43rd's elaborate uniform on handsome
Michael Tookey had not compensated for a blanket on the
floor, the scrapings of food left in the base of a greasy pot
and married life lived in the presence of an entire barrack-
room full of men. Their husbands created a little privacy for
the women by hanging sacking over a rope stretched across
the room, and there the women lived together and had their
children. The intimacies of married life had to be performed
in fields, cellars, horse-stalls, or any other semi-private place,
unless a couple wished to take their pleasure beneath the
eyes of all those in the barrack-room.

Children were born and mostly died of fevers or malnutri-
tion, but Emily Tookey had used her years in service to
advantage by making extra money through her skills at laundering and mending. With that money she had bought
left-over or rejected food from the cooks in the Officers'
Mess, so keeping herself and child in reasonably good
health. Looking back on those days when her mother had
been alive, Mary could not remember when she, herself, had
first begun washing and mending too. There seemed to have
been no time when she had not. But it had been profitable,

and her mother had taught her the basics of reading and writing as a reward for her labours.

The peaceful pattern of Mary's life had been broken when the regiment travelled out to India, and Michael Tookey had been killed by a horse running amok in the stables. Her mother had then been forced to marry again immediately in order to survive. After that, Mary had often caught her mother in tears, the brightness having gone out of her. Soon, Emily was spending her laundry money on raw grog available in the native market, and Mary's new 'father' began fondling her swelling figure and stroking her thighs when he thought they were alone. Before long, he was not the only man to do so, and Mary began to be afraid to leave the company of her mother grown half-witted through drink.

When Emily was found to be dead one morning, Mary advertised herself as a prospective wife in order to gain protection. Jack Rafferty of D Troop had been first off the mark with his offer, and she had taken it thankfully. That had been four years ago, when she was twelve. But they had told the Padre she was sixteen, and the lie had been accepted. Age was unimportant amongst the women of the regiment.

Life had settled into the old pattern, with the addition of those visits to fields, horse-stalls, or even the back of an isolated waggon. To Mary it was an adjunct of life on a par with washing and mending, and Jack Rafferty was a kindly enough man who would defend her with his life if any man tried the old game with her, she knew. He was rough and boisterous when he tumbled her, but she soon had learned how to avoid anything painful.

The one marvellous thing about him was his ability to tell stories. An Irishman, he had a ready wit and a way with words that could conjure up all manner of wonderful visions. When in the mood for yarning he could keep his listeners entranced for hours with tales handed down by his forebears, or plucked from his own lively imagination. He could neither read nor write and had no wish to learn. But Mary would painstakingly attempt to copy down some of the stories he told so that she could teach her children. Because Jack had not put a child in her during their four years together, she sometimes wondered if she was barren. Perhaps it was better that way. A child of the regiment had little chance in life.

Compared with some, Mary Rafferty was fortunate. Yet she was constantly looking beyond the horizon to where the air was sweeter and cleaner, the colours were sharper and paths went in a multitude of directions, inviting a person along them. She yearned to make her way there and discover all that was along the way. But who she was and how she lived were such weights on her eager feet that she could not even make one step. Lately, Jack's stories made her restless, increased the yearning to break free from the person she was forced to be.

Last week she had plucked up the courage to approach the Padre and ask to borrow a book. He had given her a battered volume that could hardly be spoiled, and she had hidden away on the racecourse in order to study it. Disappointment had been total. Most of the words had been very long, and even when she had spoken them aloud in sections they had not sounded like any word she had heard before. The story the book had told had been incomprehensible to her, making her sense of frustration so great she had actually cried—something she had not done since a child.

But the main cause for her recent restlessness was Jack's growing addiction to native grog. He was not the only trooper who had taken to blotting out his anger and unhappiness over the dull life they led—but it turned him into a quarrelsome stranger, too ready with his fists. Mary remembered the way her mother had deteriorated after drinking the poisonous stuff, and worried about her own fate if her husband went the same way. The regiment took no responsibility for widows, and India was a savage country for an Englishwoman left destitute.

Tonight, her worries had increased tenfold. When Jack had returned from visiting the native quarter in a drunken state, she had remonstrated with him and asked if he intended turning his bones to pulp and drowning his wits until he could no longer call himself a man. She had meant it as a jibe at his virility, thinking it would have more effect than a pure scolding. Instead of shaming him her words had released a fury she had never seen in him before. Flying at her he had hit her again and again, saying he would not have a sluttish child telling him what he was sick of hearing from the men of other regiments. That he had not choked her to death with his hands around her throat had been due to the arrival of Captain DeMayne and Sergeant Clarke. *"For God's sake see that that woman returns to her quarters at once, so that I shall not have to endure her snivelling."* She had not been snivelling, but fighting for breath through a bruised windpipe. *"She most likely deserved all she got."* What reason did he have for thinking otherwise?

She lay gazing into the darkness hearing that voice again. It was fascinating and beautiful to her ears, deep without being gruff, slow without stumbling over the words, making the most ordinary phrases sound exciting. All the officers spoke that same way, but Captain DeMayne's voice was unforgettable. Mary was a simple girl who could not always define her own feelings and reactions in exactly the right words. So it was now. If it did not seem ridiculous she would say hearing that voice was like listening to music. Of course, it was not in the least like a regimental band with its trumpets and drums, nor was it the same sound as that which wafted on the still air when the orchestra played at balls and receptions. But it rose up and down in attractive patterns, with a hint of sleepy arrogance and a wide range of tone that revealed the speaker's changes of mood. Tonight he had begun by being excited then, when the unknown had been identified, had grown short-tempered with disappointment. He had dismissed her as if she were not there; had spoken to Sergeant Clarke about her as if she could not hear and reply for herself. He had regarded her as a nuisance, an annoying delay to his plans for the evening. He had thought her a worthless drunken slut.

The other women lying around her behind that piece of sacking separating them from the men would have made vulgar signs to the back of the officer and poured out vituperation on him and all his sort as he rode off, then returned to mutter obscene curses on his manhood. But Mary lay there burning with shame. What evidence did he have—did anyone have—for thinking of her as anything other than a low vulgar creature with a mind that accepted poverty and brutishness without protest? No, Mary Rafferty did not call down curses on the head of Rowan DeMayne. Her curses were for her lack of determination to fight her way up from the level to which she was condemned.

Yet how could she? If this were England she might leave the regiment and enter service, like her mother. But, here, the servants were mostly Indians, save for a few personal ladies' maids brought out from England with their mistresses. Even had there been a vacancy for one, Mary knew she was not fitted for such an elevated position. As a laundry-maid she would probably excel, but she had had no experience of high-class life, knew nothing of the ways or homes of ladies. All she had ever seen of them had been from a distance, and when the extremely white-skinned creatures dressed in crinolines of the most beautiful cloth and colours vanished inside those huge beehive homes, the visions ended. What lay inside those homes and what the occupants did whilst in there constituted a complete mystery.

For some time she lay thinking of those mystic people. What did they say to each other all the time; how did they occupy themselves when not riding, strolling around the bandstand arm-in-arm, or dancing at balls? Mary could do an Irish jig that Jack had taught her, but ladies did not pull up their skirts and leap about until they were exhausted. And what about pleasuring? Most of the officers had a native woman for the purpose, in special rooms at the rear of their bungalows, and some had been seen tumbling camp followers in the stables amongst the straw or in distant hollows of the walled cantonment. But they had been the rougher of the officers when they had been as drunk as troopers. How did married officers manage it with their high-born wives? They did, because children were born. But Mary could not visualize those pale dainty creatures treated with such respect and gentleness by gentlemen being thrown on to their backs and used for sport whenever the fancy took them.

Those ladies Mary saw about the cantonment were mostly very beautiful, but had strangely expressionless faces even when deep in conversation. The officers were constantly dancing attention on them, but their expressions were hidden by the deep peaks of their shakoes and the broad chain strap that was universally worn *not* under the chin, but just beneath the mouth. This left very little of their faces visible to betray their feelings, even when they inspected the barracks and were no more than a few feet away. Mary never saw officers without their shakoes, except when they rode in the races. Then, they wore flat caps and were bent so low over their horses it was no easier to see faces.

Contrary to the views of the other women with whom she lived, Mary did not despise and ridicule 'the toffs'. Neither did she resent their obvious contempt for those like herself. She knew it was largely deserved, and longed to change herself—not to earn the approval of her betters, but to satisfy her longings for a sight of what lay beyond the present confines of her life. She was not silly enough to dream of becoming a lady. A girl did not *become* a lady, she was born to be one. But Mary did hope most fervently to own *two* dresses, a bed, a place she could go to and be alone, and to be able to read a whole book without difficulty.

Her thoughts returned to that voice that had come out of the darkness. The Honourable Rowan DeMayne would be able to read any book ever written and say the words without stumbling over them. Did he realize just how lucky he was? There was nothing a man like him could not do. How wonderfully free and happy he must feel; how full his life must be. It was well known the other officers resented his high-born status and the fame of his exploits; the ladies resented his universal popularity amongst their ranks. But Mary resented none of his good fortune. She wanted, more than anything, to have even a tiny part of what he had been blessed with, and hoped he made the fullest use of all possessed.

Bugles were beginning to echo across the chilly air, signalling the end of a night during which she had not slept at all. She could tell from the volume and tone which bugle was which. The faintest, like a child's toy trumpet, summoned the Native Infantry from their beds; the next, the troopers of Kingsford's Horse quartered next to them. The fuller sound of the Artillery bugle overplayed the others, to be drowned by that of the 43rd just outside the walls of D Block.

Mary usually liked the sound of that morning symphony, but on this particular dawn it deepened her frustration. If only the regiment could return to England! There might be hopes of improving her lot there. But the 43rd had been in India only six years, and it was not uncommon for a posting to last as long as twenty-two. She would be past thirty by then!

On the other side of the curtain she could hear the men falling from their beds with curses before stumbling to the urine tub to relieve themselves. While they were on parade it would be emptied by a native, and the floor swilled down. That was if the man was diligent. All too often it would be left to stand through the heat of the day.

Corporal Parker was now roaring orders at them, apparently in one of his bad moods because he was certain to get a severe trouncing from his captain over the incident last night. The Officer of the Day was not likely to keep quiet about it. Boots were beginning to ring on the stone floor as troopers finished dressing and moved around folding their blankets to regulation requirements at the heads of their beds. Before long there was silence instead of confusion as the men departed for the lines where the regimental horses were tethered. Only officers' chargers had stables.

The pattern of the day never altered. Up at dawn to parade and answer roll call, then eat breakfast before attending morning 'stables' to feed and water the horses before grooming them. Leather and harness had to be polished and checked over, necessary visits to farrier and Veterinary Officer made, and the horses exercised. By then it was noon, and all except those on piquet duty returned to their quarters to attend to their elaborate uniforms, which had to be kept spotless ready for inspection by the troop commanders. Then there was supper followed by evening 'stables'. Every other day there was riding practice and manoeuvres. Once a week the whole regiment indulged in rehearsals for reviews and durbars in full dress uniforms.

The men of the 43rd had been doing all this with lack of enthusiasm or pride, and were constantly grumbling. The fact that they had never gone to battle rankled deeply, especially when they were taunted by others that their regimental standard bore no names of famous victories embroidered in gold thread. As if to rub salt in their wounds, the war against the Sikhs which had flared up just as they had arrived in India, had been fought by regiments with long experience of native enemies, while the 43rd had been retained in Calcutta on ceremonial duty. The nearest they had ever come to drawing swords against a foe had been at the end of that war in the Punjab, when the regiment had been on the march north. C Troop had suddenly been confronted by bandits after weapons whilst they had been acting as rearguard to the column. In the ensuing skirmish Captain DeMayne had earned further laurels by holding the tribesmen at bay while his wounded were collected. But it had been a trifling incident, arousing further derision from other regiments, who had dubbed it 'The Battle of the Biscuit Boys'. Every one of the troopers longed to show their mettle in a bloody fight, but Mary wanted no war. Jack might be killed in it, and then where would she be?

The women around her were beginning to stir now. Flo Cork wearily dragged her baby to her bosom, saying, "Come on, yer little bastard. Get yer gob round that and shut yer row, fer Gawd's sake. I've 'ad no bleedin' sleep all night fer yer bawlin'."

Several of the others got to their feet, scratched them-

selves fully awake, then pushed aside the sacking to go inside
the main part of the building to collect the soiled drawers
and socks the men had slept in and replaced with clean ones
before going on parade that morning.

"Come on, Mary Rafferty, 'oo d'yer think yew are? A
bloomin' lady?" cried a coarse voice beside her. "This fire's
got ter be lit and it won't be done by bleedin' magic." Rosie
Thomas looked down at her for a moment, then squatted
down to take a closer look. " 'Ere, are yew orlright? You
don't 'arf look a mess, me gal."

Mary discovered she could not speak for the weight of her
feeling of helplessness. She simply put her hand on the other
girl's and gave it a pat of reassurance before struggling to her
feet, aching from head to foot and shivering in the chilly
dawn air. It was then she discovered her only dress was torn
beyond further repair because the much-washed material
had been unable to withstand Jack's attack. It seemed the
last straw, and she understood even more why that voice had
been so dismissive last night.

Looking up quickly into the gleaming eyes of the woman
who had been her friend for some years, she tried to tell her
distress. But no sound came from her swollen throat, and she
realized Jack had rendered her temporarily speechless. With
signs that were hardly visible in the faint light, she made
Rosie understand and the older girl put an arm round her
shoulders sympathetically as they went out to fetch wood for
the stove that would heat water for washing.

"Never mind, ducky, yew'll be orlright in a while. Men!
It's that grog that makes 'em turn nasty. Jack ain't a bad
sort, reely."

They collected the wood in their skirts, Mary using her
petticoat to hold it. The state of it was not a lot better than
the dress had been, but the material was coarser and took
the weight. They got the fire under way while others staggered in with the heavy buckets of water to fill the iron pots
in which they would boil the clothes, each woman dealing
with her own customers' garments. The men preferred to
pay the women to launder their clothes, since some of the

native cooks had been caught boiling meat in the same water to save heating a fresh lot. The daily tough mutton was unappetizing enough as it was, without adding vile flavours to it.

Inevitably, a quarrel broke out between two of the older women, and they set about each other with shrieks and clawing fingers. The rest crowded round to watch and shout encouragement to the one they championed, as the pair fell to the floor and rolled around in furious combat. Mary took advantage of the diversion to put her own batch of laundry into the hot water and stir it around with a stick for several minutes before bringing it out, dripping and steaming, to lay on her piece of board. Then she drubbed it with hands that were used to the task.

It was all done automatically. Her thoughts were rioting through her brain, and emotion was scalding her throat and breast as the laundry scalded her hands. Every day of her sixteen years had been the same as this, and had been lowly enough, heaven knew. But she had sunk lower than ever before now. The growing light revealed dark bruising on the arms pounding the laundry, and her knuckles were skinned and red. Her mouth tightened in despair as she listened to the cackling laughter of those around her. They thought nothing of her bruises. Drunken men regularly beat their wives, and the older the women grew the more cunning their methods of avoiding the worst of the blows. Would she be like the two wrinkled harridans on the floor before long? They did not know how old they were—nobody did—but they were still capable of child-bearing and could not be as ancient as they appeared.

Suddenly, she could take no more of their company and burst from the building into the freshness of a cool, perfect sunrise. Leaning back against the wall she gazed at the lemon-yellow sky to the east through desperate eyes. Out there lay a whole world she could never reach. She had been born lowly and accepted the fact. But even the lowliest person should be free, surely? Mary Rafferty was not. She was trapped forever with no prospect other than turning into a squabbling, shrieking crone like those others.

As her fists clenched beside her, the beauty of that sunrise made her swallow painfully. Jack had degraded her last night. He had truly made her a creature to earn the contempt of people like Captain DeMayne. She had been born lowly, but not contemptible. Her mother had entered the trap by marrying Michael Tookey and giving birth to a child of the regiment. Jack Rafferty had now snapped that trap shut around her, and all she could do was run around and around in it, seeking escape for evermore.

Flinging herself away from the wall, she rushed back into the barrack-block, past the noisy group of women to Jack's bed and locker. She knew where he kept his grog-money hidden. Clutching it in her purple-marked hands, she left by the door at the far end that the men used and began walking towards the native bazaar where she planned to buy material for a new dress and a piece of soap to wash herself clean.

In the distance she could hear shouted commands that signified the closing stages of the morning parade. Soon the men would be returning for breakfast. She must hurry if she wished to pass the parade ground before they were dismissed. Running was too painful for her stiff joints, but she increased her pace as she reached the stables where Indian *syces* were already grooming the officers' spare chargers. The ground was wet and muddy where they had scrubbed down the stalls and filled the drinking troughs, so she picked her way through the puddles.

Then, before she knew it, two riders were rounding the corner at a flat gallop, plainly indulging in a lighthearted race. They were officers of the 43rd and both were laughing with the exuberance of their headlong pace. The pair thundered by, sending a shower of mud flying up to cover Mary's face and torn dress with great brown splatters of liquid. It stopped her in her tracks as the horsemen disappeared around another corner. They could not have failed to see her there, but she was so insignificant they counted her as nothing.

For a moment or two she stood staring at the spot where they had gone from sight, the culmination of all her desperation causing her to tremble. From that moment on she would start to be *something;* a person in her own right, a woman who would never allow herself to be hit by a man ever again, drunken or sober. She would remain no longer so worthless that she was seen as part of the background by people who passed.

Turning, she hurried on toward the bazaar. When she had made the new dress she would go back to the Padre and ask to borrow another book. Today would be a turning point in her life . . . and she had Captain the Honourable Rowan DeMayne to thank for it. He had put new heart into her just now when he had galloped past calling laughingly to his friend. She had recognized that voice, and it had told her what she must do.

Three weeks later, on New Year's Day, Jack Rafferty died of apoplexy. Mary was stunned. There was the usual hasty burial, and she stood by the graveside at sundown reflecting that she had still been a wife at dawn. There had been no time to think what she would do. Jack had dropped from his horse at morning parade, and his few belongings had been given to her in a bundle when they had collected his uniforms and blankets from the bed-space he had occupied. The Troop Captain had sent a corporal to tell her the time of the burial—and that was that! Jack was gone, and she was a widow on the same day that she became seventeen.

It was a small group that stood at the graveside while the Padre read the service in bored tones. There were no tears. All Mary felt was a sense of betrayal by the man who had died so young and left her unprotected. She stared downward as they began to shovel earth on to the simple box, seeing nothing but the wood of the coffin vanishing beneath the growing weight of soil. Neither she nor anyone else at the funeral noticed the passing of a robed pedlar on a mean-looking mule, who headed for the cantonment gate and followed the route to Multan.

The service was over, and those who had been present to honour their comrade began straightening up. A hand touched Mary's arm. She looked up in numbed response to find Sergeant Clarke of A Troop standing beside her. She remembered how kind he had been on the night Jack had knocked her about and saw that same kindness in his expression now.

"Mistress Rafferty, would you oblige me with your kind attention for a moment or two?" he asked in quiet tones. "Mayhap we could walk over to the gate."

Without waiting for a reply he put his hand beneath her elbow and coaxed her to walk beside him to the churchyard gate. The sun was rapidly sinking behind the distant hills, leaving the chill that signified a frosty night ahead. Mary felt the cold eating right into her bones in a way she had never known before. The gate, painted white, had taken on a hellish hue from the setting sun, which made her feeling of unreality increase. In that moment she did not know who she was, or who she would ever be.

They stopped, a girl in a dark-blue dress wearing a borrowed black shawl over her head, and a tall weighty man in his forties resplendent in the showy uniform of the 43rd.

"Mistress Rafferty," began the Sergeant in self-conscious formality of tone, "I am a much older man than the one we have just laid to rest, but I am sober, honest and mindful of the plight of those placed in the situation you find yourself facing. You must take another husband straightway, and there's many'll be lining up for the privilege. First, though, I wants to put a proposition before you. My age is forty-six, and I'm due for promotion again before too long passes. I drinks a spot of porter now and again, but no more than that. As a boy I was school-taught and I keeps my hand in by studying from books. I'm clean and tidy about the place, and mostly of a quiet disposition. As a sergeant I earns enough to be comfortable, and my quarters is shaded by trees so it don't get too plaguey hot. I've watched you, Mistress Rafferty, and it seems to me you're a hard-working girl with fingers that are nimble and a disposition that's livelier than most. I wouldn't ask nothing of you save housekeeping and a mite of companionship. In return, I offers you the quietness of my quarters, the use of my books, and a trusty protection. You can have a bed of your own behind a curtain, and the freedom to make the place suitable for a female to occupy." He shifted from the stiff pose he had adopted and fingered his brown moustache nervously. "I'm a lonely sort of man, Mistress Rafferty, and I'd be a dutiful husband. Oh yes," he added quickly, as if remembering something he had left out of the rehearsed speech, "I won't fill the place with the smoke of my cigars to upset you, but step outside when I lights one."

With a tweak of his tunic to pull it even straighter, he took his cane from beneath his arm and gripped it between his hands as if ready to accept orders from a superior. "I'll be obliged for your answer, Mistress Rafferty, and shan't trouble you further if you've no heart for it."

No heart for it! Mary gazed up at him unable to believe her good fortune. A shady room apart from the barrack-block, a *bed*, freedom to make the place homely, and books to use whenever she wished. Sergeant Clarke was one of the 43rd's longest-serving members and a man of immense loyalty. Two years ago he had been detailed as one of the escorts to a consignment of treasure making its ponderous way north. The column had been attacked, and he had been shot between the legs. His emasculation had caused ribaldry around the cantonment, but he was respected by most of the troopers as a fair man, and only a few made serious attempts to belittle him. They only did it once. His ferocity had markedly increased since his injury, but his violence was no more than verbal. Providing she did not thirst for ravishment, the girl who became Mrs Clarke would be fortunate indeed!

They were married the following day, and Mary took up residence in her husband's quarters immediately. It was the end room in a block of five, all of which housed troop-sergeants. Stone walled and stone floored, it was whitewashed, and ventilated by a small window to the rear and a door opening on to a verandah running the length of the block. It contained a table and two rough chairs, a bed and a low chest. On the day Mary moved in, Samuel Clarke took her to the native bazaar and bought for her a bed, a second-hand travelling chest, some decent cloth for a Sunday gown, a shawl and some striped weave to make a curtain for her part of the room. As a wedding-token he led her into the premises of the only gem merchant who could be trusted and bought her a ring with a tiny blue stone. She was ashamed to wear it, not only because her hands were not right for such daintiness, but because she felt her new husband was getting nothing in return for his generosity.

But, as the days lengthened into weeks, Mary found her misgivings vanishing. Sam was delighted with the way she kept the place clean and sweet-smelling, the skill of her laundering and mending, her growing knowledge of how to make him contented and comfortable. Together they went through his box of books, and he showed her how to read longer words by piecing them together, then write them out for herself. Gradually, she was able to take in the meaning of what she was reading, because there was no need to concentrate so hard on the composition of each word. Even so, she often had to ask him to explain things that were beyond her experience, and it was at those times that she realized how much there was in the world and how little she knew of it. But she soon had the ability to retain all the information he gave her, and pestered him for more and more.

They grew very close in a relationship that made nonsense of its limitations. Sam soon abandoned the practice of stepping outside to smoke a cigar. It wasted time, and Mary declared she liked the aromatic smell of the tobacco. Sam's off-duty periods they spent with their heads together over the precious books, playing at cards, or sitting quietly on the verandah to take advantage of the cool breeze. Occasionally Sam invited the other sergeants in for a mug of porter and a yarn. But he always asked Mary's consent first, and she

would slip outside with her mending in order to leave the
men alone. On the first such occasion she had intended
retiring behind her curtain, but Sam had been shocked.

"T'wouldn't be right, girl," he said sternly. "I can't be
sure one of them might not let slip an oath, forgetting your
presence."

Her blithe assurance that there was not an oath or blas-
phemy that she had not heard a hundred times over was met
with an even sterner comment that she had put all that
behind her now, and he would not have his wife listening
to soldiers' ribald conversation. So, to please him, she sat on
the verandah until his friends left. At those times, more than
any other, she would gaze out over the cantonment and the
wonder of the good fortune that had fallen into her lap
almost overcame her. She had soap to wash herself with, a
comb and pins for her hair, four dresses and a shawl, *underdrawers*, of all things, good boots and two white pinafores.
She ate from a plate with a knife and fork—it had taken a
while to master that—and slept on a bed. Sam was a dear,
gentle man who told her in the very kindest way when she
slipped forgetfully back into her old habits, and never made
her feel she did not have every right to all he had given her.

Others did, though. The women of D Block had shouted
vile abuse at her the first time she had gone to see them.
Even Rosie had turned her back and uttered in loud tones,
"Oh, lordy, we ain't scrubbed the floor fer milady's feet ter
tread on terday." Mary had left in a rare fit of anger and,
when one of her former companions had flung a handful of
mud at her in passing and called her a barren cow, she had
abandoned any further thought of those who were less lucky
than she. She was treated little better by the wives of other
sergeants at Khunobad. A barrack-block whore was how they
regarded her, and always would. If Sam was angered by their
attitude he never showed it. The pair were happy with each
other and needed no other company. Their quarter often
rang with their laughter. Mary had had her wits sharpened
by Jack Rafferty's Irish blarney, and Sam's chuckle was infectious.

The only thing that upset his normal good humour was the new colonel's sweeping changes to regimental life, which the 43rd hated to a man. It was true discipline had grown slack and some of the men rebellious. The rate of desertions had increased, and so had the number of suicides which, unlike the desertions, more usually took place in the hot season. There was a tendency to lack pride in appearance; in truth, a lack of pride generally. The reasons for all this were obvious enough but, instead of bombarding higher authority for a posting to a frontier station where there was always plenty of action, or a move to somewhere like the China station which provided opportunities to take on the warlords' fanatical warriors, Colonel Daubnay was sending men aching for war to the tailor, marching them back and forth like mechanical toys in endless parades, subjecting them to long sessions of physical exercise, doubling the hours devoted to grooming the horses and arranging concerts, theatricals and *dancing lessons!* The regiment had always been the butt of military derision; now it was fast becoming the laughing stock of the Army.

Sam Clarke was the first to admit that now there was probably no better dressed body of military men in India, that the troop horses were the finest collection he had ever seen, and both men and officers were kept on their toes in a way they had never been before. But, to the inevitable grumbling of the troopers had been added a new edge of savageness that had never been there before, and the officers went round nowadays with strained expressions to accompany their clipped tones. If the 43rd had been bored and restless before, it was now growing dangerously mutinous. Tempers were short, and Sam had noticed that during sabre-practice the men galloped headlong at the dummy heads on poles, slashing at them with such viciousness that the two halves flew apart to land a number of yards distant from each other.

It was apparently no better amongst the commissioned ranks. A rumour was rife that a hot-blooded young cornet of the 43rd had become so aggressive during sabre practice with the fencing master he had opened the man's arm from shoulder to elbow with a wild unorthodox slash. There had also been an incident between a major and a captain when a fickle lady had promised a dance to one, then gone off on the arm of the other.

Sam told all this to Mary knowing the information would go no further. Their great fondness for each other had fostered complete understanding, and Mary became as fiercely loyal to Sam as he was to Queen, country, regiment and her. Besides, who could she pass the information to? The only friend she had in the world now was Sam Clarke. Her contentment and delight in how her life had changed so dramatically occupied her totally. She listened to all Sam said, and sympathized with his worries over the inability of Colonel Daubnay to see that he was courting disaster if he did not ease up on the games he was playing with his fancy regiment.

The constant longing for battle which plagued the whole regiment did not trouble her in the least as spring arrived in Khunobad. Peace was wonderful; she wanted it to go on and on forever. Battles meant killing, and killing meant Sam might be taken from her.

There were no battles, but she lost him all the same. Cholera ran through the cantonment at the start of April. Ironically, the hated physical exercise the men had been forced to take since the advent of their new colonel resulted in there being fewer deaths from the virulent killer fever in the 43rd than the other regiments at Khunobad. But Sam Clarke, weakened by his abdominal wound two years earlier, fell victim very quickly and died, with Mary beside him, as the sun came up on April 10th. They had been married less than four months.

For the first time in her life Mary experienced deep sorrow. Sam had been father, teacher and friend in one. He had shown her not only a wider appreciation of the world, but a wider span of emotions. She had grown to love and respect him. During the swift violence of cholera she had ministered to him with calmness, but when the regimental surgeon came to pronounce him officially dead she gave way to helpless sobbing. Sam had been her world. How would she survive without him?

Surgeon Captain Winters was a widower with three grown daughters in England that he had not seen for six years. Like most regimental doctors, he was a man whose family had been too poor to establish him well in society, and the army had been his only hope of using his limited medical skills. In common with the others he was regarded with slight contempt by the regimental officers, although those of the 43rd were less dismissive than the highly aristocratic members of more élite cavalry regiments, who regarded doctors as *tradesmen* and therefore unfit to grace an officers' mess.

Harry Winters was a susceptible man when it came to young girls. He had raised three of his own, whom he loved dearly, and it made him very uncomfortable to see poor little Mrs Clarke in such distress. He knew all too well the plight of women who married into the ranks of a regiment. There were two alternatives facing them at times like this—to marry anyone who came forward, or be cast out to survive for as long as possible through prostitution. Mary Clarke had done well to get where she was now. She was clean in person and habits, and plainly willing to learn, as Sergeant Clarke had proved. If she had to go back to being the wife of a trooper, the other women would give her a bad time of it. Yet he doubted if another sergeant would take her on. Sam Clarke had done it out of loneliness, knowing his sexual impotency freed the marriage from unwelcome barbs, but most sergeants would have too much pride to take on a trooper's widow.

His thoughts on that score were soon banished when the distraught girl looked at him across the body of her husband and cried that she could and would not marry a third husband, and begged him to help her find some employment as a laundress, declaring she would work for no payment in return for a room where she could sleep, however small.

They both knew that what she asked was impossible. So

Mary was left to attend Sam's funeral at sunset that day, knowing she would have to vacate on the morrow the quarter that had become a home during her short months of happiness.

She received three proposals of marriage before nightfall, but turned them all down. Sam had lifted her from the level of trooper's woman, and improved her reading, writing and simple sums. Nothing would make her take a step back now she had advanced so far. With optimism that had little foundation she told herself she could sell her bed and the travelling chest, which would fetch enough to keep her going if she could find shelter for a while. The men bivouacked on the march, so there was no reason why she could not copy them, and become a travelling seamstress once she had got herself established. Her fingers were nimble with needle and thread, and native tailors found accommodation on the verandahs of their clients as they moved around. That life would solve her problem nicely and give her the freedom she craved. It sounded ideal—until the middle of that first night alone in Sam's quarters. The truth would no longer be held at bay. She was a young unprotected female in a wild foreign land. The only profession open to her was as a whore.

At dawn she was ready to leave. Sam's personal possessions had been put in a box to send to his family in England. All she had kept were his books, because she felt certain he would want her to have them. They were tied with string and standing beside the bundle containing her dresses and underclothes. They would only go if the situation became desperate. The bed and travelling chest were on the verandah awaiting a native trader from the bazaar, who would give her a quarter of what they were worth.

She stood bravely enough as her symbols of pride were wheeled away on a rickety cart, and even when one of Sam's fellow sergeants gave her a written receipt for the effects that were to be shipped to his mother in England. But when the sweepers came in to scrub out the room ready for its new occupant, Mary picked up her bundle of clothes and the books tied with string and went down the steps on to the dust road leading to the gates of the cantonment. She had absolutely no idea where to go; she just walked.

"Mrs Clarke! Mrs Clarke!"

Mary became aware that a voice had been calling her name for some seconds, and her steps slowed.

Surgeon Captain Winters arrived beside her on an ageing horse, and climbed from it, mopping his brow. "Dear me, I feared I was too late." Then he saw her luggage and asked, "Have you already found a place for yourself?"

She shook her head numbly. Her brain seemed unable to work any longer.

"Then I have come to offer you some solution to your predicament. Colonel Daubnay has given me leave to place at your convenience a space in one of the small storerooms adjacent to the hospital. There is no question of employing you, of course, but in return for the accommodation you may make yourself useful in any manner I deem suitable." At her complete silence he went on hastily, "I would not normally consider exposing any female to the sights of a hospital, but you were born into the regiment and are used to the roughness of troopers, I understand. It might be that you could send letters to the families of those too ill to do so themselves. You are able to read and write, are you not?" He cleared his throat noisily. "I am sure there are many ways in which you can occupy yourself without feeling . . . you see, Mrs Clarke, Colonel Daubnay is a very punctilious man. His very proper sense of honour will not allow him to see any woman of this regiment cast out into the wilderness."

Mary swallowed and picked up her bundle of books ready to follow the medical officer. The men of the 43rd might hate Colonel Daubnay, but Mary thanked providence for his proper sense of honour, whatever that might mean. It had saved her from unimaginable hazards.

Hardly a month had passed before both Mary and Harry Winters realized they benefited greatly from the arrangement. In no time she was fully occupied during the mornings and evenings in the hospital. Sights that would have overcome most women were accepted by Mary with compassion and calmness. She knew exactly how to talk to rough soldiers, give as good as she got and spot malingerers. Mistress Clarke became a popular and respected figure amongst those suffering the horrors of the hospital.

The doctor found she was also helpful with completing forms, writing labels for medicines and keeping his notes tidy. Her ready diligence coupled with her awe for his work gave him a sense of dedication the disdain of his fellows had long discouraged. Soon, he was finding pleasure in her company, especially when he discovered there was a great deal more liveliness to her disposition than many of the highborn ladies at Khunobad.

Gradually, Mary recovered from her initial grief over Sam and adapted to her new life. She enjoyed her work in the hospital, and spent her rest time in the afternoons making a start on her proposed future trade as a seamstress. With the money from the sale of her bed and travelling chest she bought a child's nightgown and yards of fine cloth with which she could copy it. Knowing she was not skilled enough to work on the elaborate gowns worn by wealthy ladies, she decided it would be profitable to start with baby clothes. When she had made enough, she might set up a stall in the bazaar and pay an Indian girl to sell them on her behalf. The sooner that came about the better. There was no guarantee how long her present situation might continue, and recent events had shown her she must be able to stand on her own feet.

Her new home was very cramped, although she knew she was very fortunate to have it. A tiny stone floored annexe attached to a store containing bales of blankets, and wooden crates containing lime or acid, it was a far cry from Sam's nice room. But Captain Winters had given her a thin straw-filled pallet to sleep on after a few nights spent on the floor, and there was a cluster of trees nearby where she could sit during the hot afternoon hours to do her stitching.

Outside the hospital her only companions were Sam's books, and they were all she needed. During her first few

48

days at the storeroom she had been visited by groups of bedraggled women, who taunted her and shouted obscenities about being the Surgeon's lightskirt. It was then she fully realized how she had looked when she had been Mary Rafferty, and surveyed her tiny private home thankfully. She had also been visited by men who imagined her refusal to marry again meant she was willing to be tumbled by them all. They soon departed with no doubts as to her opinion on their premise. In truth, she had no desire for any man's lust. A woman was a great deal luckier without it.

One morning in the middle of July she had just walked across to the low white building that housed the patients when there was a commotion at the far end, where officers ill enough to require constant ministrations were kept in a long area opening on to an airy verandah. Mary watched in curiosity as several orderlies carried in a native in filthy blood-covered robes, and looked set to carry him into the officers' section. There was no one in there at present, Mary knew, and her first thought was that the man had a sickness so deadly it was essential to separate him from others. But, in that case, surely it was foolhardy to bring him into the hospital at all.

Her curiosity deepened when Captain Winters snapped at the orderlies to have more care with the way they carried the sick patient, and appeared to be extremely agitated over the situation. When the group disappeared round the dividing wall, she thought nothing of hurrying through the room that was already stiflingly hot in order to look into that other section for some clue to the mystery. The native was either dead or in a faint, for his eyes were closed and he was perfectly limp as they put him on to one of the beds covered in brown blankets.

It surprised Mary that Harry Winters himself began to strip off the native's robes, using such care it almost seemed he was afraid to touch him. It was not an easy task, for the material had stuck to the patient's body in places, and orderlies had to bring a bowl of water to wash away the encrusted blood and pus. After some minutes the job was done, and the man lay naked on the bed, as his ministrators stared down at him in momentary silence.

Then the Doctor exclaimed in shocked tones, "My God, poor devil! Whatever have they done to him?"

Mary put her hand to her mouth as she saw the deep wounds across his chest, running round to his back. She had seen men flogged on the wheel enough times to withstand such a sight, but the reason for her shock was the desperate rambling sentence that burst from the man's swollen mouth as pain began to revive him. She would know that voice anywhere. Impossible though it seemed, the brown-skinned native on the bed was Rowan DeMayne.

CHAPTER THREE

The news that the 43rd Light Dragoons' regimental daredevil had returned from his latest bizarre mission more dead than alive was around Khunobad Station almost before the victim had been washed clean of body-dye, the lice-infested beard cut close to his face and matted hair disinfected. That he was dangerously weak and too delirious to give any report on his findings—if, indeed, there were any —was the cause for some smugness by his fellows. Had Rowan DeMayne come a cropper, at last? Could he possibly have *failed* in his mission?

While the officers found the mysterious circumstances surrounding the discovery of their aristocratic captain in an unconscious state several yards from the cantonment gates when dawn broke a subject for somewhat malicious conjecture, the ladies were driven into a state of excitement ranging from the melodramatic to the ecstatic. Heroes were greatly admired; *wounded* heroes were worshipped!

In two residents of Khunobad Rowan DeMayne's return after an absence of almost six months aroused feelings of vastly different natures, which brought about a quarrel between proud, stubborn men. Maurice Daubnay was more concerned with training his officers to be perfect gentlemen than encouraging them to be unnecessary heroes. If they were both at the same time, then so be it. But the notion of a noble dragoon captain covering himself with filthy brown dye, dressing himself as a native pedlar and setting out on a skinny mule in order to *spy* on tribal insurgents was totally abhorrent to him. Such tactics reduced the army of the Crown to the level of those they were fighting, in his opinion, and would do nothing to enhance the example they were there to set. Let the officers of the Indian regiments get up to such knavish tricks if they wished. It was well known they were a damn queer set of fellows, who often 'went native' themselves. But he was violently opposed to members of his own regiment indulging in capers unfitted to their standing.

He had made his feelings crystal clear when Dunwoodie had calmly declared that he had 'another little task for DeMayne.' But his instant refusal to allow one of his dragoon officers to be borrowed by the Political Branch had been overruled by his superiors, and DeMayne had departed on New Year's Day leaving his colonel with no expert translator or liaison officer between himself and Khairat Singh, just as he had intended embarking on his expansive social programme. The whole matter had been a thorn in his side, and now the infernal man had returned half-crazed and no use to anyone.

Chatsworth Dunwoodie looked at things in a different light, however. Sending spies out to mingle with a prospective enemy saved lives, and he was all for that so long as there were men willing to risk their own for the purpose. Who, in his right mind, would order out an officer in full regimentals on such an assignment? It would be asking the man to commit suicide. So would sending someone ill-equipped for the job. Since DeMayne resisted all persuasion to leave his regiment, he had to be borrowed when needed. Old Stapleford had never cut up rough over it, but the new dragoon commander wanted his men kept in a bandbox, that much was clear.

Higher authority had ruled over the plan to mount the solo mission, and marked coolness had stood between the two colonels. Now, their differences gathered heat as Daubnay forbade Dunwoodie to visit his returned spy, and Dunwoodie raged at Daubnay for preventing vital information from being disclosed.

"DeMayne is in the grip of fever and suffering from terrible mutilation to his body," Colonel Daubnay repeated to his rival's every request. "His violence has to be restrained, and he mutters only incomprehensible phrases in native languages. He will be of no help to you until he recovers—*if* he does."

"You do not appear to realize the vital nature of the information I require from him," fumed Colonel Dunwoodie. "It is imperative that I question him."

"And so you may—when he is in a fit state to give you an answer. I will inform you when I consider he has reached that state."

"Lives are at stake, sir, I'll have you to understand. *British* lives."

"And so is DeMayne's, sir."

"What is one life when a hundred might soon be forfeit?"

"That one life belongs to an officer of *my* regiment. You may do as you please with your own men, but I will not have you endangering mine."

"You have a mistaken sense of priorities, sir."

"You have a mistaken sense of importance, sir."

So it went on while the subject of their wrath fought a battle of his own. Feverish and in a delirium, the patient had to be secured to the bed with the webbing straps used to restain men during amputations, constantly doused with water to reduce his fever and smeared with foul-smelling concoctions to prevent his wounds from growing gangrenous. He was in constant pain, and possessed by such terror of betraying his identity that even in his delirium he cried out only in native tongues.

The patient posed other problems. In view of the nature of his mission, Colonel Daubnay was obliged to post a relay of officers to sit by his bedside night and day to await his return to lucidity. After seventy-two hours had elapsed with no sign of it, he declined to tie up men in such fruitless duty. Harry Winters could not undertake the watch because he had other patients, yet someone had to be there. Mary Clarke appeared as the ideal solution to the problem. She was dependable and reasonably competent, she was capable of cooling the patient with the application of ice-cubes and washing his limbs night and morning, and she was unlikely to understand anything he might mutter without knowing he was betraying vital information. Everyone, including Mary, was satisfied with the arrangement.

For the young girl, such a position of trust was a godsend. It meant she could sit in that long room shaded by tatties for long periods at a time and do her stitching in unbelievable comfort. At night, she placed her pallet on the floor of the verandah, where she could hear any movement from the patient. She had instructions to tell the night orderly to fetch Captain Winters if she thought it necessary.

This supervision of the special patient also gave her a unique opportunity to learn something about the man who had been responsible for setting her on the right path of determination. Left alone with him she was able to see, for the first time, the face that went with that voice. It impressed her considerably. Darkened by the sun, it was the only part of his body that had needed no brown dye to cover white skin. In repose, when his eyes were closed, the broad brow, straight nose and gaunt cheeks suggested he was, in truth, a native of the country. But when he was overtaken by one of the fits of feverish madness that weakened him and caused his wounds to bleed, Mary thought she had never seen such a striking appearance on a man. His eyes were as sooty-dark as his hair and secretive beneath their sleepy lids, his expression changed from haunted to haughty with many variations between, and his mouth betrayed his extremes of emotion whether shouting frenziedly or muttering almost inaudible pleas as he turned his head from side to side. In a very short while she came to realize this person she had regarded only as a distant figure with a personality likely to remain a permanent mystery was a man of strong passions and an unquiet mind.

There were other things to be learnt from that vigil. Captain Crane had been in to see his friend soon after he had been brought in, and had arranged for certain items to be collected from his bungalow. Mary had never seen sheets and a pillow with a white cover on it before, and wondered at the use of something that had to be washed each and every day because it showed every spot of dirt. Day after day she found her glance wandering to that brown face contrasting sharply against the white material on which he lay. It did not seem a very masculine habit, yet she knew Captain DeMayne must be extremely manly to undertake the things he did. Perhaps all the officers lay on sheets . . . and did they all have soap that smelt of flowers, and jars of other fragrant substances the purpose of which she had not yet discovered because the owner of them was too ill?

She was surprised to discover that Captain DeMayne did not sleep in his underdrawers, like the troopers, but had a long loose robe of white cotton so fine a person could see right through it. There were sleeves and a small collar to it, and the garment looked remarkably like a huge version of the child's nightgown she was copying to sell. It amused her to think a man so large should dress himself in such a thing just to go to sleep. It made Rowan DeMayne slightly less exalted somehow.

There was a leather box containing brushes like the troopers used on the horses, except that these had backs that gleamed like the metal parts of a harness and were decorated with a picture and some writing Mary could not read in a way that made any sense to her. The box was locked so that it showed the beauty of the contents but prevented them from being removed. Beside that was a pile of handkerchiefs —she knew what they were because Sam had given her some to use—but these were of a beautiful soft creamy material and had the same picture that was on the brushes sewn on to them in pale thread. It was splendid stitchwork, but she thought it curious to go to all that trouble for handkerchiefs and even more curious for a man to have such pretty things.

So, although she had discovered an intriguing face, a passionate nature when unbridled, and a strange collection of possessions that did not seem to match up with a reputation for extreme courage, she still knew nothing of his likes and dislikes, whether he was humorous, what occupied his thoughts during those lone journeys into the wilder places she had never seen, and what it was about him that aroused envy in his fellows and desire in ladies. As she sat beside his bed with her sewing she wondered constantly about this person from a world she could never enter. Oh, she had no illusions. While it was perfectly natural for her to be asked to do this for him, he would never be asked to do the same for her, even though she be dying. That fact only increased her fascination for this man who, in some strange way, was hers while he remained defenceless.

On the fifth morning, after a bad night during which she had had to send for Harry Winters because the patient had fought to free himself of the restraining straps, Mary saw that he lay quiet and left her chair to step on to the verandah, where it was possible to feel a slight breeze. Feeling langorous she leant against one of the stone pillars and gazed out across the cantonment. She had enough completed infant gowns now to make a decision on the best way of selling them. Money was short. The doctor allowed her a plate of the hospital food, but it was very poor quality, which needed to be supplemented from stalls in the bazaar. Sam had introduced her to better eating, and she did not want to slip back, even in that respect.

While she stood lost in thought, letting the breeze cool her face, an orderly poked his head around the wall dividing that section from the main part of the hospital, and called to her to ask if she knew where he could find Captain Winters.

"Back in his quarters, I shouldn't wonder," she called back. "He was up here best part of the night, and I just see him go past the end of the road."

The orderly vanished, and she looked away again.
"Saw!"

It was said quietly and with a hint of weariness, but it gave her such a start she spun round quickly.

"Eh?"

Dark, dark eyes regarded her through lowered lids. "I just *saw* him go past."

Feeling nervous she walked slowly back into the area where Rowan DeMayne lay tightly strapped down. He looked dazed but lucid, and she was suddenly afraid of him as she stared down at the face so deeply etched by the horror he had experienced.

"You spoke in English, at last."

His gaze wandered slowly over her dark-blue dress covered with a pinafore, and her face framed by brown hair. A frown creased his forehead. "Who the devil are you? Isn't this Khunobad Hospital?"

Even more nervous now that rich voice was addressing her directly, she nodded. "That's right. I've been watching out for you. You've been ever so ill. At one time we wasn't even sure you'd come out of it."

He seemed not to hear half she said as his frown deepened. "Fetch Captain Winters."

"I can't. I've orders to stay with you," she said quickly. "I could send an orderly, I s'pose."

"Then *send* one," he countered wearily, adding as if she were a native servant, *"Jaldi, jaldi!"*

She went, hurrying down the stone floor and round the corner into the main part of the hospital, hardly able to marshal her thoughts. She had watched him through daytime and moonlit hours, through long periods of peacefulness and short, violent spells of terror. She had washed him, put water to his lips, calmed him, and all that time remained remote from him because he had not known she was there. She had been able to study him, watch the expressions of a face that had previously been only an impression beneath a shako, listen to that voice uttering foreign languages with emotion. Now he was conscious of his surroundings and able to see her. When he spoke it was directly to her and requiring an answer. Everything she said and did now was noticed by him, and she felt strangely exposed after their one-way relationship.

Seizing the arm of a passing orderly, she said urgently, "Run quick for the Captain. He's asking for him."

The long face registered curiosity. "Is 'e orlright, then? We all fort 'e was gorn barmy."

"Well, he hasn't," she snapped. "And you'd better hoppit quick, or he's likely to dust up rough. It'll be me gets the blame for it. *Jaldi, jaldi,*" she added for good measure.

"Keep yer skirts down, missus. You've bin wiv *'im* too long, that's your trouble. Fancy yerself as a toff?" He guffawed loudly as he turned to go. "You might 'ave bin a sop to pore old Sam Clarke, but you won't never be a hofficer's lady, for all yer wantin'. There's only one thing Captain Winters wants from you, and they're takin' bets on 'ow soon that'll be."

He went out still laughing, and Mary swung round in a flurry of skirts to return to her post. Taking bets were they? Well, it was money thrown away!

When she got back she took one look at the patient and her heart sank. His face was covered in beads of sweat and working with emotion; his eyes were full of wildness once more. All she could think of was the orderly saying he was ready for Bedlam.

Growing aware of her he said in strangled tones, "Unfasten these bonds!"

She looked at his condition dubiously. "I don't know as I ought. You've been that restless."

"*Do as you're told,*" he exclaimed with such suddenness that she jumped. "Release me, damn you!" Moving his head from side to side on the pillow he appeared to be growing frighteningly agitated, and his voice broke to a desperate plea that could have been made to anyone within earshot. "For God's sake, free me. *Free me!*"

Her fingers that were so nimble with a needle and thread grew clumsy as she hastened to loose the webbing straps that secured him to the bed. As she did so, she reminded herself that this man had collapsed outside the cantonment gates in a condition of agony and exhaustion. What must his thoughts be now to open his eyes in this place and find himself bound so that he could not move, and no one in sight save a strange girl in a pinafore? He had been desperately ill; his mind had wandered in bizarre realms. She must show him understanding and gentleness to calm his fears.

"There now, there's no need to go on so," she murmured soothingly, praying he would grow calmer once she had unfastened the restraints. "The Captain only did this to stop you hurting yourself more when you was tossing and turning. Now you've come normal, it'll be all right."

It did, indeed, appear to be all right once the straps had fallen to the floor, for he lay calmly enough despite the remnants of wildness in his expression.

"I'll get you a drink," Mary declared. "You must be very thirsty."

Pouring water from the jug that stood in a bowl of ice, she returned with the cup. He took it from her, but his feeble attempts to raise his head failed.

"I'll help you," she said, preparing to slip her arm under his shoulders.

He reacted with some violence. "No! Don't touch me!" In a return of agitation, sweat beaded on his face once more. "Get the doctor here! Go yourself, but get him here at once."

Mary fled. The sound of Harry Winters' horse approaching sent her running along the verandah to beg him to hurry. But he sounded calm enough as he dismounted, and even gave her a smile.

"I am sure there is no need for such concern, Mrs Clarke."

"But I've let loose them straps," she admitted. "He seemed perfectly all right at first. Then he got angry, all in a flash, and started off like before—sort of mad—when I tried to give him a drink. Lordy, I hope I haven't done wrong," she continued, hurrying along the verandah in his wake. "He looks real queer."

Greatly relieved that the patient was still lying as she had left him, Mary hung back on the verandah as Harry Winters stepped down into the main area and went up to the bed.

"Ah, DeMayne, fever broken at last, has it?" he asked cheerfully.

"How long have I been here?" It was almost an accusation.

"Five days, all told. How do you feel?"

"What a damned silly question," was the weary response to that. "I have to speak to Dunwoodie, or someone on his staff."

"Yes, yes, they'll be along presently. Plenty of time for that."

"There is *not* plenty of time. If I have been here five days already, they'll be damned anxious for my report by now."

"You are hardly in a fit state to hand in a reliable report, in my opinion," stated the medical man firmly.

"To hell with your opinion," raged the patient in a way that gave support to Winters' assessment. "You know nothing of what is at stake here."

"Your mind is at stake, DeMayne," was the bald reply. "No one doubts your courage, but the past five days have cast doubts on your sanity, believe me."

All fight left the man Mary had watched through those tortured five days and, even from her place on the verandah, she could see he was holding on to consciousness with an effort.

"My sanity is my own affair," he slurred.

"It is mine while you are in my hospital. You need rest."

"Then, for pity's sake, let me hand in my report and I'll be glad to rest for as long as you wish."

Surrendering rather uncertainly, Harry Winters nodded. "I'll get a message to Dunwoodie's office. They can act on it as they think fit, but I shall insist on a very brief interview." He began to move away toward Mary. "Meanwhile, I'll arrange for some tea to be brought to you."

"Not by that girl, whoever she is," came the instant response from the patient now blocked from Mary's view by the medical man.

"She's extremely capable, old fellow."

"I won't have her!"

"Has she done something to upset you?"

"Winters," began that haunting voice, "if you were lying here in this state, would *you* want any woman to see your helplessness?"

Mary moved along the verandah toward the main part of the hospital, strangely moved. That a man could endure torture and face death over and over again, yet be afraid to let any female see his natural weakness somehow made him infinitely human. Perhaps Rowan DeMayne was not so very different from other men, after all, and she understood *them* well enough.

True to his word, Captain Winters allowed the officer from the Political Branch no more than fifteen minutes with the patient before insisting that the questioning cease. The man seemed less than satisfied—even though the returned spy declared he had nothing more to report—and went off vowing to come back for further information. But it was Colonel Dunwoodie himself who arrived later that day, having just returned from a conference.

From her shady seat beneath the trees it was Harry Winters' raised voice that first caught Mary's attention, and she could see the figure of another, more senior, officer beside him as they exchanged heated words. Her intention to eavesdrop was unnecessary, for the voices carried on the still air well enough for anyone in the vicinity to hear.

"I know your rank can override my request to wait until he feels able to speak on the subject without distress, Colonel Dunwoodie, but I think you really should not disregard medical objections. Captain DeMayne's physical wounds are healing, albeit slowly, but something was done to him that must have been so hideous it will not allow him any peace of mind to face it."

"Are you trying to tell me he has lost his nerve?" snapped the large red-faced man.

"Sir, death has held him by the hand for some days. A man does not shake free of such a hold easily. It is my professional opinion that DeMayne is very close to losing control of himself, and I would not care to vouch for what he might do, under such circumstances."

"Go on!"

"Well, I think it is well enough known that he is a man of . . . er . . . some wildness of character at the best of times, and that he keeps his true thoughts well hidden. Most of us would find a six-month sojourn under the conditions he has endured taxing in the extreme, I feel you must agree, but he has been additionally burdened with unimaginable pain from wounds which will leave scars upon his body for life. You did not see the extent of his punishment, I believe."

"DeMayne is a military officer. He must expect that . . . and worse," was the uncompromising retort.

"It is the 'worse' that is the source of the trouble, sir. Of course, I am no expert . . ."

"Quite right," snapped the Colonel. "You are no more than an army sawbones, Winters. Your job is merely to keep soldiers on their feet . . . or cut them off if they are no longer of any use to them. Pray do not preach me a lot of airy nonsense about DeMayne losing control of himself. He is forever doing it, and it will be nothing new. Stand aside!"

Mary gripped her hands together angrily as she watched the senior officer stride smartly down the steps to where the patient lay and, with no sense of shame, she sidled across to the wall enclosing the verandah to stand, hidden from view of those within, by one of the pillars as she listened further.

"Glad to see you have emerged from your fever, De-Mayne," Dunwoodie began in a hearty voice. "Feeling more yourself, no doubt. Chaplain showed me your report just now, which follows up the information you smuggled to Beezley at Ludhiana two months ago. He has already alerted the garrison, but this latest information regarding dates and numbers of gathering tribesmen suggests reinforcements be sent without delay." The heartiness faded abruptly as the voice went on: "But what's all this nonsense about refusing to tell Chaplain when you were taken captive and by whom? Unless we know at what stage this happened we cannot judge the reliability of your report and decide whether or not to act upon it."

There was a short silence, then Mary heard the patient say, "You have never doubted the reliability of one of my reports before."

"Never," came the brisk agreement. "But you have never before returned under such conditions. You must see that it raises any number of queries. Your disguise was plainly penetrated . . . but by whom, and at what stage in your mission? It is your duty to disclose every detail of those months you were working for us, however praiseworthy your results. We are all aware that you underwent torture of a very severe nature. That is the price a man knowingly faces on missions such as yours and, as you know, a number of our officers have paid it in full. Their mutilated bodies have invariably been sent into one of our outposts as a warning." After a significant pause, the relentless voice added, "You returned alive, however."

Mary felt herself growing cold at the sound of that other voice as it asked, "What, in God's name, are you suggesting?"

"That you complete your report without delay. It is imperative that we know the identity of your captors, at what stage in your journey you fell into their hands, and how much information they gleaned. There will be no question of sending a column of reinforcements if they are liable to march straight into an ambush."

"Damn you, Dunwoodie, your inference is unforgiveable!" cried the victim of cross-examination. "I demand an apology from you."

"If you broke under torture, DeMayne, attempting to deny it will only earn you further contempt. Are you man enough to confess what happened?"

That rich voice Mary so admired cracked under the strain

of trying to control his anger. "By God, you sit in your damned office sending men out to something you can't begin to imagine, then ask them if they are man enough to describe it. Go to the devil, and get enlightenment from him!"

"Don't take that tone with me, man, it is close to insubordination deserving of a court martial. Although you have constantly refused to join us, you know enough of our affairs to endanger our activities. I told you where our other men were operating when I sent you on this mission, and it has been necessary to acquaint you with certain political ambitions for the future to assist your understanding of the information you have been asked to obtain. Any of this knowledge in the wrong hands could endanger our plans."

"Because of those ambitions you have used me ruthlessly, Dunwoodie. You have exploited me to the full, knowing I would have to double any other man's courage in order to earn half his recognition. How dare you accuse me of betrayal?"

"Because you returned. Silence would have cost you your life . . . like those other poor devils."

"So would treachery," came the cry. "Just how much do you know about the men of this country, from your chair in an office? They torture a hero, but honour him as he dies. A traitor breaks under pain, and they reserve an even more agonizing and humiliating death for him before throwing his carcase to the dogs. My disguise was not broken, and I told them nothing . . . *nothing.*"

"You were captured, tortured and remained silent? Then you were released and allowed to return?" came the sneer. "Despite your insulting inference, I know enough of tribesmen to treat your story with the derision it deserves. You are finished, DeMayne. Whatever pact you made with them in return for your life, you will never be trusted again. For six years you have attempted to obliterate your past by indulging in every kind of bravado scheme imaginable. It earned you a veneer of gallantry that almost hid the man beneath. Now the truth is revealed for all to see. You were right to decline to join us. You are not up to our standards. Our men would die with their secrets still locked within them."

The next few seconds consisted of the sounds of a scuffle, grunts and a final cry of pain that brought Mary from her hiding place before she could stop herself. The patient was lying face down across the bed, clutching the sheets so tightly his knuckles were white. Colonel Dunwoodie, puce in the face and with his tunic hanging open at the neck, was breathing heavily as he looked down at him in disgust.

"What more would you have me do; how much more do you think a man's mind will accept?" gasped Rowan De-Mayne. "The only thing that enabled me to reach Khuno-bad was the determination to hand over the information I had been ordered to get . . . to prevent the loss of our troops' lives."

"And the loss of your own," came the condemnation. "If you had had a spark of courage left you would have saved your family and regiment further dishonour by vanishing with your guilt to take your chances in this heathen country. Your report will be disregarded, and your movements will be watched from now on. Any attempt to communicate with natives outside the station will be frustrated. My department severs every connection with you. Your own regiment will do whatever they think necessary . . . and I hope they do it very publicly."

Mary waited only a few seconds after the Colonel had left, then she could stand the patient's distress no longer. But despite her encouragement to get back into the bed, his hands held on to the sheets as if to a lifeline, and his body began to tremble so violently the bed rattled on the stone floor.

"Lordy, he's got the shakes now," she muttered. "That Dunwoodie ought to be flogged at the wheel for this."

The sound of her voice brought a violent reaction from the man who appeared to have returned to his earlier state. Registering shock he began chattering non-stop in a native tongue, interspersing words with laughter that had a touch of insanity about it.

Half-afraid of him Mary began trying to calm him. "Come on, dearie, there's nothing'll happen to you if you lets go, I promise. Just get up and lay quiet, like a good lad," she said, as she had on other occasions when troopers had gone berserk during hot weather.

At that point, the medical officer arrived beside her, his face having turned greenish-white after the departure of Dunwoodie. He needed no word of explanation from her, but his attempts to prise open the fingers clutching the sheets were no more successful than hers and he straightened up, frowning over the paroxysms of the afflicted man's body. Mary suddenly remembered that they used to throw pails of water over troopers to bring them out of it, and crossed to snatch up the jug standing in a bowl of ice.

"No, that won't help," said Harry Winters, seeing her intention. "This is something quite different, I'm certain." His worried glance met hers. "What happened, do you know?"

Mary nodded, unashamed of admitting that she had been eavesdropping, and recounted all she had overhead. Repeating it sounded like a renewed condemnation, and she sighed as she looked down at the man still shaking uncontrollably. Could he be the same person who had galloped past her, laughing and so full of confidence, scattering mud over her and making her see what she must do? Whatever could have happened to reduce him to this?

"Colonel Dunwoodie said the regiment would sort him out good and proper," she said sadly, glancing up at the man beside her. "What will they do to him?"

"Nothing, if I have my way," was the grimly determined reply. "I'll never believe this man could be a coward. Surviving what he must have suffered, then getting himself back here in a state of agony is one of the most heroic acts I have come across." Nodding at her he said, "You may go now, Mrs Clarke, and on your way out send two orderlies to help me will you? Thank you for your assistance."

"It wasn't much," she said, wishing she could stay. "What he needs is someone who could really help him."

* * *

There was such a person, in the unlikely form of Maurice Daubnay. Not only was he extremely jealous of his six hundred-and-sixty strong regiment, he had come to loathe Chatsworth Dunwoodie. When he heard his rival had charged into the hospital to interrogate a sick officer without asking the permission of his colonel, Daubnay was overcome with rage. He might well berate and bully the members of the 43rd on every score, but he would have no one else so much as criticizing them, much less browbeating them.

In a storm of retaliation he galloped around Khunobad station registering righteous protests in every quarter, wrote reams of indignant requests to higher authorities for official word on the correct procedure for 'borrowing' officers for specific duties, and took the unprecedented step of posting a guard on the hospital verandah with orders to prevent anyone from visiting Captain DeMayne unless willingly accompanied by the regimental surgeon.

These actions caused great amusement, a deal of excitement over the whole bizarre affair, and even greater curiosity about the tarnished hero hidden away under guard. Rumours were rife. One had it that Rowan DeMayne had gone out of his mind and was awaiting shipment to an English asylum; another that he had been so hideously mutilated it was impossible for him ever to appear in public again. A third, and most popular with the fair sex, maintained that the solo mission in which he had miraculously escaped his torturers, had been so successful there was now a reward for his delivery, alive, into the hands of those who wanted exquisite revenge. Hence the guard outside the hospital. But his fellow officers, apart from Gil, who knew very well the ruthlessness of tribesmen, preferred to agree with Dunwoodie that his reputation as a hero had come to an ignominious end and he was hiding failure behind feigned illness. He had been brought to his knees, as they had long hoped.

Relieved of her vigil, Mary went back to her old routine which did not entail entering the officers' section of the hospital. But she, along with the orderlies, knew everthing that went on in there during the following few weeks, and also knew of the rumors flying around. They made her very angry. Rowan DeMayne was neither a lunatic, nor hideously mutilated, apart from his torso. As for the idea of his being a traitor ready to impart information to tribesmen as part of a pact to free him, she thought all men who believed that were fools. That seemed to include most of the officers at Khunobad, while the soldiers scoffed at the idea to a man. The hero of the 43rd remained a hero to the rank and file, who had always displayed fierce and devoted loyalty to him. In contrast to the gentlemen who did little more than dress in their fancy outfits for parades, and lounge in their quarters for the remainder of the day, Captain DeMayne had shown his readiness to face hardship, filth and the threat of hideous death time and again. Now he had met agony face to face they admired him even more for enduring it with such stoicism. In their opinion, he deserved a medal for what he had suffered.

The ladies of the station could not give him a medal, but did the next best thing. In the following weeks the officers' section of the hospital began to resemble a garden as posy after posy arrived for the patient, and Mary could not resist wandering on to the verandah to take a peep at the wonderful spread of colour. She knew the flowers had been sent by females, but flowers seemed a strange gift to a man. She could imagine a trooper being nonplussed if any of the women offered him a bunch of flowers picked in the fields. He would be an object for ridicule from his pals. Rowan DeMayne's posies were edged with lacy frills and tied with ribbons, which seemed even more unsuitable. Besides the flowers there were baskets of fruit tied with ribbons, pots of special foods, watercolours of romantic subjects and scented letters.

Often, the ladies would bring the gifts themselves, walking in pairs with a servant in tow. They would halt a short distance from the hospital and give their gifts to the servant to take into a building they would not dream of entering themselves. While they waited, their glances would be fixed on the verandah and they would laugh and chatter in great animation. Mary was amused by their antics. It was plain they hoped to be overheard by the man they could not see, and she wondered what he thought about it all. That was something she was unlikely to discover.

It was those visiting ladies that brought about a stroke of luck for Mary, however. One late afternoon when she was sitting with her sewing, two visitors arrived to send in a gift and moved across to within a few feet of her, their attention so firmly fixed on the verandah they apparently did not see her there. At first, Mary was absorbed in studying the details of their gowns, one in palest green, the other deep pink with a hem of paler frills. Then their conversation took precedence in her mind because they appeared to be having a mild quarrel.

"I think you would soon tire of his amours, Fanny, for you must be sure he would not change the habit of a lifetime even after taking a wife. Imagine sitting alone night after night until he chose to favour you with his company. I would not wish to subject myself to such indignity, though the gentleman in question might be the veriest Apollo."

"Ha, it is easy for you to be so expansive and haughty, Lydia. You have not yet made the acquaintance of Captain DeMayne. We shall see if you are still in as great a command of your wits and sensibilities when you have."

"Indeed, my dear, I assure you I have not the slightest wish to have this arrogant gentleman presented to me. But be sure I shall give him very short shrift if I should be unfortunate enough not to avoid it. As if Uncle Chatsworth had not warned me in advance of his libertine ways, I must tell you I am acquainted with the sister-in-law of Lord Paule's wife—poor Elizabeth Verwood, who suffered so dreadfully over that affair between the two brothers six years ago. The scandal nearly finished her, I believe. There is very little I do not know about Rowan DeMayne, and it is all of a nature which leaves me in disgust of the esteem in which he is held by almost every female in India. It is quite plain to me that he must be laughing behind his hand at you all, and your ridiculous susceptibility."

"What of your susceptibility," snapped the other. "The few weeks you have been in Khunobad have shown you are not averse to accepting overtures from a great number of gentlemen. Have a care you do not gain the reputation of being a shocking flirt."

"Better that, than pine for a libertine who treats one with contempt for dancing on his string. I prefer to make them dance on mine, Fanny dear."

The green crinoline swayed from side to side as its wearer turned away petulantly, then caught sight of Mary. "We are overheard, Lydia," hissed the girl significantly.

Mary thought her very beautiful until the pink crinoline twirled, and she saw the face of her companion. Shaded, as it was, by a parasol it was so startlingly lovely Mary could only stare at it entranced. She had never seen skin quite so white with an extraordinary blending of delicate pink in the cheeks. The curls hanging to her shoulders were as dark as the hair of an Indian woman and a striking contrast to her face. But it was her eyes, very large and as blue as the sky, that caught Mary's greatest attention.

"Dear me, whoever is she?" said this vision to the other.

"Come away, Lydia."

"No, stay," came the gentle reply as the beauty approached. "Look, she has some infant garments here that she is stitching. They are really very fine." She turned back to the other. "Do look, Fanny."

Her companion joined her as she picked one of the night-gowns from the grass beside the place Mary sat. For several seconds the pair studied it in detail, discussing its merits as if she were not there.

"Do you think she has them for sale, Fanny?"

"Why else would she be sitting here surrounded by so many? They can hardly be for her own children, for she looks little more than a child herself."

"If it would be of some help to her I might purchase several for my cousin." That striking face angled downward and Mary found herself gazing full into it as it was further enhanced by a smile. "Do you do all this stitching yourself, child?"

Scrambling to her feet, her cheeks burning with nervous excitement, Mary said, "Yes, mum, I done them all during these past few weeks. And they are for sale," she added breathlessly.

"I have a mind to purchase some," the prospective customer confided to her friend. "I wonder what price she places upon them."

"Give her a handful of coins," was the careless reply, half the speaker's attention having gone back to the verandah of the hospital. "She will be grateful enough for that."

Thinking her chances of making money on the sale of her work were fading Mary spoke up bravely. "I'm going to put them on a stall at the bazaar. They'll fetch a lot there."

Her words brought a reaction that was one of amusement more than anything, and she was asked, "Who are you, and what are you doing right down here at the limit of the cantonment?"

"I'm Sam Clarke's widow, mum, and I helps in the hospital. This is where I live," she explained indicating the storeroom.

"Do you hear that, Fanny?" was the shocked question. "This child is already a widow . . . and she lives in that terrible place behind her. I can scarce believe it. I have found so much in similar distressing vein since arriving in India. It is really quite extraordinary to see the manner in which the authorities expect the common soldier to live. Have they no sensibility?"

"You betray your limit of experience of the military with every word, Lydia," she was told in smug tones. "The common soldier is a ruffian of the lowest kind who would encounter far worse if he did not take the Queen's Shilling. I would advise you to have a care in expressing opinions whilst in Khunobad. They will not be viewed very kindly by those who have spent a lifetime with the army."

Mary could hold her tongue no longer. "I was born into

the 43rd, mum," she said energetically. "My father was a good man . . . and so are most of them. It's only when they go on native grog they gets a bit nasty."

The response was not quite what Mary had been expecting. A light laugh matched the amused expression as the vision said, "I believe we have a firebrand here, Fanny. I wonder if those who have spent a lifetime with the army would care for *her* opinions. She is one of their number, in every respect, despite her appearance."

The servant returned from delivering the gift at that point, and both ladies turned away. But Mary had not been forgotten. The one in pink said carelessly over her shoulder, "If you will deliver six of the gowns to the residence of Colonel Dunwoodie and tell the servant they are for Miss Moorfield, you will be given the payment I think your work deserves."

As they strolled gracefully away along the track, the hems of their fragile gowns dragging through the dust, Mary wondered what Miss Moorfield had been told by Colonel Dunwoodie, in whose house she was apparently staying. Was he the cause of her wish never to meet Rowan DeMayne? Confirmation came with her words, which travelled on the still air.

"There, Fanny, the object of your unrequited passion does not even deign to acknowledge your kind gift. He thrives on foolishness such as yours. There is no gentleman would drive me to dote on him to such an extent—least of all an all-round backguard." Rowan knew nothing of what was being said about him during the three weeks in hospital where he tried to master something that threatened his sanity. It filled his mind, every waking and sleeping thought; it drove him to the limit of his reserves. It was so dark it shut out all light without or within him. For a very long time that darkness threatened to be permanent, until he was left in blessed peace to conquer it.

On the day he returned to his quarters and regimental duties he told himself that conquest was total, but it was still there deep inside him ready to rise up and engulf him on any unguarded occasion. Gil arrived to accompany him from the hospital with their bearer to supervise the transfer of his possessions, and a *syce* leading his favourite horse.

"I tell you, Gil, it will be wonderful to be free of this place," he said as he put his arms carefully into the sleeves of the jacket held for him by the servant. Movement was still painful from the wounds to his torso, and fashion dictated that men's coats should fit the figure so closely it was a slow business getting them on. "I have never known a more uncomfortable, vile-smelling, hothouse as this," he continued, as they left the bearer with his tasks and set off to round the corner into the main section where Harry Winters was found in his office.

After expressing his thanks in cursory but courteous manner Rowan rejoined Gil to walk through the rows of beds to the far door.

"By George, it is a veritable hellhole in here," exclaimed Gil, wrinkling his nose at the mixed odours of blood, suppurating sores, vomit, urine and boiling mutton heightened in the airless low-ceilinged room at mid-morning. "I cannot believe that any man's illness would be improved by entering these walls."

"They cannot be left in barracks," Rowan pointed out, his thoughts more on getting clear of the place and back to normal. "And where else is there for them to go?"

There was no answer to that, and they were almost at the door when Gil said, "There is some kind of female over there giving us damned close scrutiny."

"Female?" repeated Rowan in mild curiosity, turning his head to look. "Oh, *that* female."

"Who is she?"

"Some trooper's widow, I believe. Helps in the hospital, according to Winters."

"Helps?" queried Gil, stepping out through the door into the sunlight.

"I should imagine the men in here are too incapacitated for the only kind of help she could give them," he murmured dryly, reaching sunlight himself. "Ah, Gil, you do not know how good freedom feels."

He found he could not swing into the saddle with the old élan, but it was wonderful riding a tall thoroughbred again after a mule with rickety legs, and a relief to be himself rather than a . . . but he must not think of that!

The cantonment had not changed during his absence, but other things had. As they rode to their quarters Gil brought him up to date on regimental. affairs, and Rowan was so absorbed in listening to something that bore out his worst fears he saw nothing of those who passed, or their expressions of avid curiosity. It appeared that Colonel Daubnay had pressed inexorably ahead with his plans to make the 43rd a regiment of muscular, beautifully-dressed, beautifully-mannered paragons that would dazzle enemies into submission rather than beat them.

"I will be the first to swear you will not recognize the superb turn out of men and horses, Rowan. He has worked miracles with the procuring of matching chestnuts that would be regarded with pride by any troopers, and the men do not dare to look less than immaculate at any time of the day. Their riding has improved a hundredfold," added Gil, "with such command and accuracy that an entire squadron could now turn on a sovereign with ranks so straight one would imagine them to be chained to the spokes of a wheel."

"And their swordplay is a first class display of flashing blades that have cleaved nothing save turnips," put in Rowan, his stomach churning with anger. "To what purpose does he intend putting these élite horsemen?"

Gil brushed his moustache with his hand nervously. "None of us care for it any more than you will, old fellow. He has established a weekly review when the band plays lively music and the regiment canters back and forth displaying riding skills. The ladies love to watch it, but Kingsford's Horse are rather whey-faced about it, I can tell you. It don't improve their opinion of our warlike qualities, either."

"Good God, it's like Astley's Circus," groaned Rowan.

"That ain't all," warned his friend. "We are expected to

be seen at the bandstand every time the bands play there, strolling with ladies on our arms or simply parading ourselves for the only purpose of establishing our presence at Khunobad. The men are encouraged to do the same, with their women in some kind of presentable get-up. It is Daubnay's wish to improve the standard of regimental wives who, he says, are a disgrace to the regiment.

"There is a veritable spate of theatricals—Kit Wrexham has revealed great talent in that direction and is quite Daubnay's favourite—and there is hardly a night passes that the officers of the 43rd are not to be seen performing immaculate quadrilles, or turning the pages of music for ladies who are encouraged to entertain us musically."

At that point, they rounded the final corner that led to the road at the end of which was the bungalow they both shared with a subaltern called Briers, and Rowan eased his stallion from a trot to a walk as he looked at his friend suspiciously.

"If this is some kind of hoax, Gil, I warn you I am in no mood for it."

"Word of honour," swore Gil with genuine seriousness. "I knew how you would take it, but you had to be told sometime. There's more, I'm afraid. Daubnay and Khairat Singh are arm-in-arm now. Our Commanding Officer thinks him 'a very good sort of man' and has promised all kinds of help."

"As I thought," said Rowan heavily. "The man has no idea of what lies behind that sumptuous facade. But how has he managed all this friendship without me as his *Social Liaison Officer?*"

"He has found a replacement. Kit Wrexham speaks dialects like a native."

Rowan looked round sharply. "The cloth merchant's son? How is that?"

"He was reared in India. Father traded from Bombay."

"Ho, he's not a child of the country, is he?"

"What, with hair as bright as carrots?" Gil gave him a close look. "Don't like the fellow, do you?"

"Don't know him," responded Rowan, growing more and more depressed as his body began to ache with the effort of riding again after his illness.

"You soon will," promised Gil as they reached the bungalow and began to dismount. "Briers went home, and Wrexham has moved in with us in his place."

Rowan stopped in the midst of handing his horse to the *syce* and stared at the other. "Daubnay's favourite—in with us? Gil, how could you let it happen?"

"Hadn't much choice. Daubnay requested it. Ours is the bungalow nearest the theatre."

"Hell and damnation," swore Rowan in disgust. "Are we to have singing and prancing night and day to add to all else? I won't have the man here, and that is all there is to it."

"He has been here over four months and quite settled in."

Rowan stood where he was after the horses had been led away, realizing the full implications of his absence. Seven months gone from his life, and all that had been achieved was the dandifying of his regiment, the intrusion of a man he would never like, and a close friendship with a chieftain who must be laughing up his voluminous sleeves at the gullibility of his natural enemies.

"Come on, let's go inside and have a glass or two of something," coaxed Gil. "You look done in after even that short ride."

Rowan walked heavily up the steps, weighed down by frustrated hopes that appeared to be growing even further away from realization.

"Isn't there just *one* good thing that has happened in my absence?" he said to Gil's back as they entered the parlour shared by the occupants of that bungalow.

His friend turned to him with a fatuous smile. "Well, it happens that I became betrothed to Miss Herriot six weeks ago. We are to be married next spring."

"Then I wish you all the happiness in the world," he said immediately, clasping Gil by the hand. But it was an effort to put the necessary warmth into his voice and smile. The effort had to continue throughout several toasts to Gil's future, and a long description of what had prompted him to propose and how delightfully Sophie Herriot had accepted. It was not that Rowan wanted the girl for himself—far from it—but that which he had locked away deep inside him was stirring dangerously. Whilst he had been in purgatory, those he had left behind appeared to have been frittering away their time with dancing, play-acting and fluttering hearts. It put an intolerable burden on his restraint, so he quickly emptied several more glasses in an attempt to lighten it.

Because of that, he was not entirely master of himself when he and Gil became drunkenly aware of the sound of thundering hooves growing nearer, and then the noisy advent of a stocky red-haired man Rowan recognized as Kit Wrexham, his unwelcome fellow resident. He stood in the middle of the room, his fair-skinned face flushed with exertion, shooting glances from one to the other of the pair sprawled alcoholically in chairs.

"The news has just coom through," he said, his excitable state betraying his trade background in his accent. *"We are at war!"*

Rowan's heart gave a great slow lurch as the implication of those words overcame him. At last, at last, his martial spirit sang through the deadening effect of liquor. His chance had come, that moment he had been longing for for six dreary years. Here was his opportunity to obliterate humiliation and contempt, prove his worth to those who had turned their backs in well-bred disdain. Getting unsteadily to his feet, he found his elation was so great it made the words come out thickly from a tense throat.

"Whom do we fight?"

Kit Wrexham looked puzzled, then enlightenment dawned. "Ah, you would not know what has been happening at home, but it has been apparent for several months that something would have to be done about the Russian oppression of Turkey. News has just reached us that an armada has sailed to the Balkans, and our regiments have engaged them in battle in the Crimea." He shook his head and grinned. *"We* shall not be fighting anyone, DeMayne.

But your two brothers will be in the thick of it. The 11th Hussars form part of the Light Brigade." His grin broadened. "You miss out yet again, it seems."

Before he knew it Rowan was across the room and at the man's throat, gripping it with frenzied fingers that had to choke those words from it so that their meaning could not be true. He could not take that on top of all else.

CHAPTER FOUR

Rowan was surprised that the interview took place at Colonel Daubnay's bungalow rather than his office, and was uncertain what to expect as he rode there the following afternoon just as the sun was sinking. But if he hoped the atmosphere might be casual with the offer of a chair and cool drink, he was soon disillusioned. It seemed his commanding officer was merely loath to leave the supervisions for a party he was giving that evening.

As Rowan waited in the large airy salon he noticed that it held an additional number of items since the occupation of their last colonel. Assessing the paintings and *objets d'art* he concluded that Maurice Daubnay had discriminating taste, and plainly spent his limited wealth on the acquisition of a valuable private collection. Whatever was a man with underlying aesthetic passion doing in a profession such as this?

Since his superior made no attempt to sit down when he finally arrived, Rowan was forced to remain standing also. But he did his best to start on a friendly note by smiling and saying, "Good afternoon, sir. I believe I have you to thank for allowing me some peace at the hospital. I am very grateful."

There was no return smile as they faced each other across the rich red and blue carpet. "Yes, but I should not have been obliged to take such measures if you had not created the situation. Are you fully recovered?"

"Thank you, yes, sir."

"I understand you handed in a report on your mission to Colonel Dunwoodie."

Rowan felt his muscles tense. "That's right."

"Why did you not submit it through me?"

"It was extremely confidential."

"Are you suggesting that I am not to be trusted with such reports? You are one of my officers, sir."

"I was acting for the Political Branch at the time. The information was for their action alone."

"Have you never heard the word 'courtesy', Captain De-Mayne?" He strutted back and forth on the carpet for a few seconds to allow his remark to sink in. Then he stopped and cleared his throat. "I understand the report was the first of two."

Rowan tensed further. "No, sir."

"But it is incomplete. There is no explanation of how you came to return in a state of collapse and shock, or of who gave you those grievous wounds."

He stared at the man's face, seeing something quite different that made the room start to spin around him. Sweat broke on his face and the scars across his torso began to burn as he fought the nauseous giddiness that threatened to have him spinning with the room.

"You will not say—even now, to me?"

He could not say to anyone. Ever!

Beady eyes stared back at him challengingly. "Are you aware that it is being hinted that you broke under torture and offered to betray military secrets in return for your life?"

"Society will always believe what it wishes to believe, as I have experienced," he murmured, still fighting sickness.

Maurice Daubnay bristled. "Well, I, sir, wish it to believe

the truth of the matter and nothing else. This whole affair is extremely disturbing. While I do not approve of my dragoon officers involving themselves in melodramatic affairs—as I made perfectly clear at the outset—you must see that your conduct reflects on the regiment as a whole."

With his pulse thudding in his temples, Rowan cried, "Is that all you care about, your damned fancy regiment?"

"I would be a strange commanding officer if I did not," was the snapped reply. "I will make allowances for your rudeness because, unlike some others who are less astute, I realize you have been through something of an ordeal. I also pride myself on being an excellent judge of character. You are less likely to break than any other of my officers. Now, DeMayne, you have only to tell me about your terrible experience, and I will put an end to all this damning conjecture once and for all."

They stood looking at each other in silence for more than a minute before the older man let out his breath in an angry gust.

"You are a blind fool, man. What is anyone to think when you return bearing the undeniable marks of torture? If you did not break and reveal what they wanted to know, why else would they have allowed you to go free?"

With an effort Rowan managed to say, "You think they would allow a traitor to return to those he betrayed? Having got what they wanted, their contempt alone would guarantee a death sentence."

"Then what *did* happen?"

His refusal to answer appeared to remove the last of his commanding officer's patience. "You not only allow yourself to be condemned, but also the regiment you have worked for six years to bring to the illustrious level of the 11th Hussars. You once treated me to your opinion of the derisive soubriquet given the 43rd. Your silence now will justify that derision, and your fellows will share your ignominy."

Rowan's jaw felt so stiff he could scarcely move it to ask, "Is that all, sir?"

"No, damn you, it is not!" roared his CO "You may

choose your path to ruin, but I will not have you taking an
entire regiment down with you. You have a week in which
to decide whether to hand in an additional report on your
mission, or apply for a transfer to another regiment."

"You know I cannot do that," he said with difficulty.

"Quite! Which is why you should consider very carefully
what you are doing, Captain DeMayne. I will endeavour to
make myself available at any time you wish during the next
few days. Meanwhile, I expect you to carry out your duties
in the usual manner . . . and that includes attendance at the
little soirée at this house later this evening. Be here, sir!"

Feeling ill by now, Rowan gave a small bow and spun
round on his heels, thankful to be leaving. But there was one
parting shot from his commanding officer.

"I noticed on morning parade today that you were still
wearing your sword on the right hip, despite my order to
conform to regulations. Change it!"

Halting only fractionally to say, "As there is no likelihood
of my ever using it, I suppose it will not matter," he walked
out and across the spacious hall to the door that resembled
an entrance to hell, with the fiery sunset lighting the cantonment outside. Once mounted he kept riding, on past the
hospital he had left only the previous day, then through the
gate where he had been discovered three weeks before that,
and on to the Plain of Khunobad. With open space before
him he spurred his mount into a faster canter, then finally
into a flat out charge, seeing only the distant Russian enemies in the Crimean hills, imagining the ranks behind him
thundering with sabers drawn to join battle, and shouting
silent encouragement to those under his command as steel
clashed against steel, sending sparks flying.

Only when it grew pitch-dark did he return, body aching
and throat parched. But that wild gallop had not banished
the vision of Lieutenant-Colonel Lord Paule and Major the
Honourable Montclare Verne DeMayne, both of the 11th
Hussars, campaigning yet again with the regiment that
should also have been his.

Entering his bungalow he was met by Gil, already in

evening regimentals, who informed him that he had best look lively if he did not wish to earn Daubnay's black looks.

"I'm off to join the Herriots," he explained. "We shall drive to our colonel's quarters together."

"Where is Wrexham?" asked Rowan heavily.

"Why?"

"Oh, for God's sake, man, I'm not seeking to attack the fellow again," he cried with heat. "You insult me, Gil."

His friend sighed. "He is gone to collect some music he left in the theatre. I understand Daubnay wishes him to sing this evening, that is all."

"*All?* Is there nothing that man cannot do to please Daubnay? No, I really cannot bring myself to stand correctly and attentively in a sweltering salon whilst that underbred play-actor blasts my eardrums with ballads."

"He has a very fine voice."

"Naturally," he sneered. "No doubt he is also a superlative performer with a whore."

Gil frowned. "You have already made an enemy of him by flying at him last night, and he is putting it around that you are gone out of your wits."

"So I shall if he remains in these lodgings. I cannot stop the regiment accepting tradesmen's sons, but I do not have to live cheek by jowl with them. If he does not go, I shall."

Gil shifted uneasily, one eye on the clock. "What kind of attitude is that from a man I thought I knew for the past six years? You are worth ten of him. I don't understand why you let him disturb you."

"Indeed?" he asked aggressively. "There is a great deal you do not understand, it seems to me. You have let Sophie make a toy dog of you, performing all manner of ridiculous capers to please her and caring nothing for what is happening around you. By God, Gil, you are as bland as every other man here."

Gil's face flushed dark with anger, and he turned away without another word to ride to the Herriots' residence on the far side of the cantonment. Rowan went into his own room, shouting to the bearer to bring brandy as he flung his shako with frustrated fury into the corner of the room. Everyone was so infernally complacent! Did they never look further than the cantonment boundaries? Tonight they would sit around sighing, singing and sychophanting, while the number of hours, weeks, years they had spent doing little else would not be given a moment's thought. He put his hands outspread against the wall and bowed his head between them as he thought of Daubnay's challenge. Free the regiment of reflected contempt, or resign his commission. He had a week in which to make the decision. Either way, it could be the end of him.

He arrived very late at Colonel Daubnay's bungalow, and so well-fortified with brandy that when a servant ushered him into a side salon his less than careful entry drew all glances in his direction. As it was apparent the guests were about to be entertained by a female seated at the pianoforte at the far end of the room, he turned with the intention of beating an immediate retreat. But the doors had been closed behind him, and the servant was standing impassively before them.

An incredible silence had fallen, and he turned to find the guests who were seated or standing ready for the entertainment studying him intently. For a moment or two he stood looking at the sea of faces, recalling that much the same thing had happened six years ago, except that his two brothers and grandfather had been amongst those condemning him then. Swallowing those memories he spotted a space next to an Artillery captain along the nearest wall, and edged his way to it during the continuing silence. Once there, he realized his host was glaring at him from his privileged position near the musical instrument. Rowan gave a slight bow of apology, then straightened up as his head began to swim. An excess of brandy was unwise when about to enter crowded rooms on a sultry night. But he knew it was not only the brandy. It was the seven days he had been given. They stood like a judge's sentence on him.

At that point, he became aware that he was gazing straight at the girl seated at the piano, and she was gazing back at him, hands poised over the keys ready to begin the performance he had delayed. He continued to gaze as the glitter of her vivid blue eyes pierced him like cold steel, sending a shock of excitement through him. It spread and intensified as she dropped her glance to the keyboard and began to play.

Rowan had never heard such sounds as she produced, and he forgot all else as he watched her pale, graceful hands fly over the keys in a scherzo, then almost caress them as she drew from them a melody so hauntingly moving he felt the initial pain of that piercing optical challenge turn like a blade in his breast. She was superb! She touched the desolation in his soul with her music, his yearning for perfection with her elegance and beauty. By the end of her performance he was fatally spellbound by something that had driven his demons back into the depths once more.

With his gaze still devouring every detail of her face and form, he said to his neighbour against the sound of enthusiastic applause, "Who is she, Stoddart, who *is* she?"

"Oh, I suppose you would not know," came the chilly response. "You have been *away*, have you not?"

"Her name," he insisted urgently.

"I say, DeMayne, are you all right?" asked the artilleryman with a mite more warmth. "You look deuced ill."

Rowan hardly heard as he grabbed the man's arm and began thrusting him toward a group beginning to gather around the pianist. "Present me to her," he demanded.

His unwilling captive protested strongly. "Now look here, this is a great deal too bad!"

"Present me, damn you!" snapped Rowan. "I cannot speak to her until you do."

So great was his determination, he had forced a way through to where the girl stood beside the piano stool, smilingly accepting compliments on her skill.

"Well, you know, it gives me such pleasure to play. I am only grateful that there are those willing to listen," she was saying in a clear light voice that set excitement rushing through Rowan once more.

But the sudden transfer of attention to a point just behind her made the girl turn, and he almost sighed at the perfection of a startlingly fair skin, a tumble of black curls and eyes that were as blue as the cornflowers on the acres of his family home in England. But they held a decidedly cool expression as they regarded him from head to foot, and her waiting silence seemed to be shared by those around her until his companion spoke.

"Forgive this unmannerly intrusion, Miss Moorfield," he began by way of apology, "but I have been enjoined by this gentleman to make him known to you."

"Have you, indeed, Captain Stoddart?" she commented in a tone as cool as her scrutiny. "If it is so imperative, then I suppose you had better do so . . . if he has really not already been presented."

"No, I have not," said Rowan ardently. "I could never have forgotten such an occasion."

"Then you are fortunate in your excellent memory, sir. Alas, I often find that among so many faces I often forget one."

Into the surrounding silence broke a giggle from a girl as pink and white as a marshmallow, and Stoddart hastily said, "Ma'am, it is my obligation to present the Honourable Rowan DeMayne, Captain of the 43rd Light Dragoons."

She offered her hand, and Rowan took it to his lips in a daze of confusion. Her manner was almost ungracious, yet everything else about her beckoned irresistibly.

"Miss Moorfield, I am honoured to kiss the hand that can turn music into poetry. I was entranced by your performance."

The hand was delicately withdrawn as her eyes flashed another subtle challenge. "It was apparent to us all that you were in a trancelike state, Captain DeMayne, but I had supposed it to have been induced by something *before* your arrival."

There was another giggle, followed by several others from the circle of onlookers, and his confusion increased. There was no doubt she was mocking him, but for what reason?

And why did the flaring interest in her eyes belie the coolness of her words?

"I apologize for my careless interruption to the start of your performance," he said as quietly as he could. "My only excuse is that I have just recently quit the hospital."

Her eyebrows rose. "You are a doctor, sir?"

He was affronted. "I am a dragoon, ma'am, as you must surely know."

"As to that, sir, I must remind you I have been in Khunobad but two months. You would not expect me to be *au fait* with every mundane detail of regimental life."

The situation was becoming impossible, surrounded as they were by a growing crowd of interested spectators, who hung on their every word. In order to rectify the bad impression his intoxicated entry had made on her, he must get her to one side where they could speak privately. Behind her glacial front he recognized a response that was far from cool, and it was imperative that he break the ice as soon as he could.

Too tense to manage a smile, he offered his arm, saying, "Allow me the privilege of escorting you to a chair, where I will fetch you something to drink and remedy those gaps in your knowledge, Miss Moorfield."

But he was left standing with his arm crooked as she turned away with a brilliant smile to greet a stocky red-haired man who had approached on the other side of the piano.

"Ah, Captain Wrexham, are you ready for me to accompany you?" She took the sheets of music he handed her and exclaimed, "How very delightful! You plan to include my favourite ballad, as promised."

Rowan was dumbfounded. He could not believe he had been so summarily dismissed. But she continued to chat animatedly with Kit Wrexham as if he were no longer there. Someone touched his arm and he lowered his gaze to find Sophie Herriot beside him, smiling.

"Poor Captain DeMayne! Perhaps you should not have

stood upwind of Miss Moorfield after rolling in the stables
prior to your arrival this evening."

During the next few days, the exciting diversion begun by
Rowan DeMayne's dramatic and controversial return, plus
his bizarre behaviour since, culminated in the realization
that he was violently and unconditionally ruled by a passion
for Lydia Moorfield. The spectacle of Khunobad's notorious
and invulnerable philanderer behaving like a lovesick school-
boy was one that completed the contempt of his fellows, and
gave the female residents acid satisfaction that narrowly
outweighed their natural pique at not being the cause of his
sexual downfall.

Lydia Moorfield was out of her depth in the totally unexpected situation. Used to being the bright star of the country set in England, she had travelled to India on the death
of one aunt, to join another—Clemence Dunwoodie, her
dead mother's youngest sister. Well-bred but impoverished,
Lydia had instantly realized her chances of getting a husband with wealth and position were first-class in a land
where females were few and Englishmen were lonely. Her
aunt, on first setting eyes on her charge, agreed wholeheartedly, but Lydia had no intention of jumping at the first offer.
With an abundance of bachelors at her feet, she would be
a fool to tie herself to one and deprive herself of the delicious
flattering adoration of an entire station, and the additional
delight of seeing men vie with each other for her attentions.
Knowing next to nothing of the military, she was dazzled by
the panache and colour surrounding everything they did.
Even more so did she enjoy the rivalry she instilled in the
officers in dashing uniforms, and played it to the full.

Having been regaled with tales of the infamous youngest
DeMayne in England, and throughout her journey across
India, she had most decided views on a man she had never
met. She had openly deplored the worship of those who had
filled the hospital with gifts he had declined to acknowledge,
and had made no secret of her intention to set him down
very thoroughly if the chance ever came her way. There was

no place in her life for men who regarded every female who crossed their paths as a sure subject for conquest. She intended to do the conquering, and was succeeding magnificently. The disgraced hero would not find her joining her feeble sisters. Quite the reverse.

But she had been unprepared for the shiver of attraction that had run through her when a young captain, plainly intoxicated, had stumbled through a doorway to draw all attention, and silence an entire roomful of people. His sweep of black hair, dark secretive eyes, and arrogant haunted face made Rowan DeMayne an irresistibly arresting figure. The additional insolence in arriving so late and in such a condition at a decorous soirée had made it impossible for Lydia not to feel the overwhelming individuality of the man about whom stories were legion.

Throughout her subsequent recital she had been conscious of his presence, aware of his scrutiny, and her fiery personality had responded with a virtuoso performance inspired by the determination to withstand temptation at all costs. Although his swift move to make himself known to her had taken her unawares, she had had enough command of herself to fulfil her boast to all those clustered around to watch the encounter. Astonishingly, it had appeared to be the fallen hero of the 43rd who had been captivated, rather than she. Khunobad society swore it to be a fact; Lydia viewed his behaviour with suspicion. Since the affair with Fanny Dennison six years ago, he had apparently done no more than amuse himself with as many women as possible, and she feared he was countering her deliberate indifference with tactics so subtle he imagined she would not see through them.

But, by the time it was clear, even to her, that his pursuit was desperately sincere, she was caught in the complication of her own making. To respond to his advances would make her the laughing stock of the station after her avowal to remain immune, yet she was human enough to delight in her unexpected conquest of such a notorious man and the subsequent ability to make him dance to any tune she wished.

Heady with feminine power she began to play an exquisite game, little realizing the other player was a man only one small step from mental and physical breakdown. The game consisted of beckoning him on enough to deepen his commitment, then gently snubbing him in the presence of as many others as possible. He was a helpless partner in the first rounds, and if a small voice within her told her she was being heartless, she smothered it with thoughts of all those he had treated in the same way. And she prayed the game would last a long time, because it was more exciting than anything she had ever done before.

Rowan was well aware of the malicious amusement his pursuit of Lydia Moorfield aroused during the following two months, yet was powerless to counter it. Not since Fanny Dennison had passion taken him so by storm. He was no longer a boy of twenty, and he was now deeply experienced with women, but his response was every bit as headstrong and public ridicule every bit as painful as it had been then. All the same, he was caught in a current of desire that swept him in any direction she wished, and had him adopting a pattern of respectability that made his fellows derisive and the fair sex astonished.

For Lydia's sake he strolled around the bandstand with women he had once dubbed 'ignorant old tabbies', and danced with the plainest, gawkiest girls. He even forced himself to sit through sessions of females singing, simulating enjoyment even though his eardrums protested at every note. But he was not so enchanted that he did not recognize very well what she was doing to him, and he endured the public sniggers and her precociousness because he suspected she was putting him to the test. He did not blame her for that; she must have heard his reputation as a libertine. If he wanted her he had to win her against all odds, and he took them all on, certain she was his only means of forgetting something he could never bring himself to tell another living soul.

Some good came from that anguished period, however. His sobriety, his impeccable social behaviour, his scrupulous attention to duty, his charming treatment of influential harridans, pedantic matrons and damsels so plain even the lowliest subalterns shunned them, plus the fact that he was now wearing his sword on the left hip, persuaded Maurice Daubnay to let his challenge ride for the present. Although he was a confirmed bachelor he was a great believer in the reforming influence of a good woman on a libertine. He, along with everyone else at Khunobad, watched the complex game with interest, sharing the smug feeling that Rowan DeMayne was getting just what he deserved.

Some of the smugness was driven away when news reached them of the attack foretold by the man suspected of treachery—and in the strength and direction his report had indicated—which, because it had been ignored, resulted in the outpost being overrun, the local commissioner being hideously murdered and the column of reinforcements now being sent to restore law and order in a district gone over to banditry.

Rowan DeMayne was exonerated, although the mystery surrounding his torture remained. It increased resentment in his fellow officers, doubled female admiration and had the men in the barrack-blocks cheering the commander they had never doubted. However, it occurred to none of them that a dangerous situation was being created by Lydia Moorfield's tormenting, although the signs that should have warned onlookers were there beneath the young officer's demeanour.

Before long, Rowan was quarrelling frequently with Gil and not speaking at all to Kit Wrexham, whom he could not like despite being asked by Lydia to try. Because of her he refused to change quarters, but the close proximity of the man who seemed his strongest rival for Lydia was an added pressure to his over-taxed self-control. The men of C Troop grew to fear the sound of his voice approaching, and even his horses suffered from his temper. The demanding routine of social and regimental inconsequentialities dictated by Colonel Daubnay grew more and more intolerable as news from the Crimea began arriving, reminding him even more forcibly of the events that had denied him the chance of being there with his brothers.

On the first Saturday in October the receipt of news that the Anglo-French force was being decimated wholesale by virulent cholera before it even confronted the Russians precipitated a drama Rowan had been expecting since his return from Multan.

At the height of the day, when he was resting on his *charpoy*, his own troop-sergeant galloped up to say one of their oldest troopers had had news of the death of his young brother in the Crimea and had run amok in the barrack-block with his sabre, screaming abuse at Colonel Daubnay and all those who had them prancing about like monkeys in fancy suits, while young lads were dying in the course of their honest duty.

Rowan went, just as he was in loose shirt and cotton trousers, but he failed to prevent the tragic outcome, despite his calm persuasion of an old soldier who had always been loyal and respectful. On the point of gaining possession of the weapon, he had to dodge back to avoid a slash which caught him on the side of the neck. Then, the man slit his own throat and fell to the ground pumping blood, which spread to colour Rowan's feet. As he stood looking down at the sight, the stifling atmosphere, the harsh light against the white-washed walls and the stench of impoverished humanity combined to symbolize his present desperation to a point where he saw his own body lying in that pool of spreading blood.

"Get a *dhoolie* here as soon as possible, Sergeant," he said in a hoarse voice. "I'll arrange the burial for sunset." Then he turned on his heel and strode out into the sunlight, his jaw tightly clamped and a film of sweat sheening his face.

Although it was not the custom for officers to be at the graveside of suicide victims, Rowan went, still feeling the man's death was vindication of what they all presently suffered, and the tragedy sat so heavily on him he went to fulfil his social obligations two hours later haunted by the presence of a metaphorical blade at his own throat.

The officers of the 43rd were acting hosts on the occasion of the forty-first anniversary of the regiment's inception. Even Maurice Daubnay realized that the unexciting history of the regiment did not warrant a grand dinner with the Officers' Mess silver and the colours draped proudly over portraits of past colonels. None of them had been distinguished enough to warrant it. Instead, the regimental orchestra gave a concert on the stage of the theatre, after which a lavish supper was served to the guests.

Lydia had agreed to Rowan's plea to partner her into supper, and he found her soft femininity and incredible beauty almost too painful to bear after the events of the day. Sitting beside her at the concert, he tried many times to tell her just that. But each time he leant toward her to speak softly and ardently into her ear, she raised her hand warningly to show that he was disturbing her enjoyment of the music. During the pauses between pieces she commented on the playing, the harmony, the skill of the soloists with such vivid expressive enthusiasm his desire to lose himself in her sexual solace grew to uncontainable proportions. He resolved to make his claim to her that evening, and further resolved that she would accept him. She must!

But his hopes for a tête-à-tête with her were dashed. As usual, she gathered a sizeable crowd around her at the end of the concert as the rows of chairs were cleared to the sides of the auditorium now softened with banks of flowers, and laden tables were carried in. At first, the conversation revolved around the contents of the concert they had just heard, then Lydia took Rowan unawares by broaching the subject of the suicide, something he was most unwilling to discuss, especially on such an occasion. It was scarcely to the 43rd's credit.

"How very terrible a thing to happen, Captain De-Mayne," she said sympathetically. "Was the poor man ill?"

"I am surprised that such news should have reached you, Miss Moorfield . . . and so soon," he retorted, knowing details of such cases were generally smothered.

"I do not live a hundred miles away, sir," was her teasing

reply. "And you, of all men, should know how fast gossip can travel." Then, as if to soften her jibe, she put her hand on his sleeve and her eyes glowed up into his. "I was very distressed to hear you were injured in the affair."

"It was nothing, I assure you." His heart was hammering at her touch, and that look that hinted she was almost his.

"Why should any man commit such a sin?" she asked sadly, continuing a subject he thought should be dropped.

"If it was a sin, ma'am, then it was an understandable one. You cannot be unaware of what is said about the 43rd."

She smiled wickedly. "A great deal is said about the 43rd, Captain DeMayne, and most of it concerns just one of its officers, does it not?"

It touched Rowan on the raw, and he said with some force, "Indeed, Miss Moorfield, you could not have been more perceptive. Since Colonel Daubnay arrived here last December he has done more to invoke frustration and rebellion than six long years of inactivity in this country."

His words caused a stir amongst those around them, and Gil said warningly, "I would advise you to guard your tongue, man. If you should be overheard in the wrong quarter!"

"The wrong quarter would be the *right* quarter, in this case," he continued recklessly, angered by his friend's words that seemed to add to the general attempt to rile him that evening. "I have tried telling him, to no avail, and this afternoon's tragedy is the result. We all suffer from the same malady, as you well know, Gil."

"But you are in a position to alleviate the malady, are you not, sir?" put in Lydia smoothly. "You are doing so now. The poor troopers can do nothing to lighten their misery, and I have to say that I am horrified at the conditions under which you expect them to live and obey you."

"They are the same as will be found in any regiment," he said swiftly, finding her accusation unacceptable.

"Even the 11th Hussars, sir?"

It was one of those softly teasing snubs she loved to deal him when in company. It aroused the usual ripple of amusement from their companions, but he was unable to ignore it that particular evening.

"Perhaps you should ask that of your friend who is the sister-in-law of my brother's wife, ma'am. She appears to know such intimate facts about Lord Cardigan's regiment, no one is quite certain how she comes by them . . . although there is only one obvious explanation."

Her cheeks grew very pink, and she said against the noise of chair legs scraping against the floor as tables were laid for supper, "Lord Cardigan's regiment is presently at war, Captain DeMayne. Do you not consider what you have just said to be scurrilous under the circumstances?"

"Oh come, pray do not let us be so gloomy," put in Sophie Herriot with a swift glance at Gil. "We are here to enjoy ourselves, not speak on such unattractive subjects."

Sensing that his hopes for the evening had now been irretrievably ruined, Rowan said bitterly, "Then let us by all means ignore it. We cannot have anything as uncomfortable as thoughts of a war in defence of our queen and country disturbing our endless round of pleasure."

Gil was furious. "I will not have such ill manners displayed against Miss Herriot. You will apologize!"

Rowan bowed stiffly. "I beg your pardon, ma'am. I had forgotten that the company in which I find myself would not appreciate my comments."

It was such a double-edged comment Gil looked all set to take the matter to serious length, until Lydia intervened.

"I think we must all excuse Captain DeMayne's lapse of good manners," she said, embracing the entire group with her smile. "Although we all thought him quite reformed, he *has* had a most trying day, and I am persuaded that he gave no thought to his own safety when seeking to ensure that of his trooper. I feel we must try to forgive him and believe that he did not mean any of the uncharitable things he has just said."

"Then that will be the first time, to my knowledge," put in a fresh voice, and Rowan looked up to find Kit Wrexham had joined the group. It brought a scowl to his face, which deepened when Lydia laughed gaily and said, "Shame on you, Captain Wrexham! Here we have all been trying to coax Captain DeMayne from his bad temper, and you undo all our good work."

Feeling the pressure of that metaphorical blade against his throat Rowan said, "My temper has been perfectly sweet all evening, and it will remain so if you will allow me to take you to supper now, Miss Moorfield. It appears they are ready to serve it."

She turned to him, her eyes widening apologetically. "Oh, I am so sorry, I have had no opportunity to tell you. We have been conversing on such serious subjects."

He tensed immediately. "Tell me what?"

"That I shall have to take supper with Captain Wrexham."

"*No!*" It burst from him with such force, even those who were not in their immediate group turned to look.

"I beg you not to shout at me in that manner, sir," Lydia chided coolly.

"I will not shout in any manner whatever, once you confess that you promised this evening to me," he countered with growing belligerence, careless of those joining the group in curiosity. The blade against his throat was now beginning to cut into his flesh too painfully. "I will not have that carrot-haired caroller stepping into my place with you."

Lydia was growing even more lovely with sparkling anger in her eyes, and she seemed just as careless of the numbers listening. "I was not aware that you had any 'place' with me, sir. Captain Wrexham and I have been asked by Colonel Daubnay to entertain with some songs at the end of supper, and we need to discuss our selection. I agree it was my intention to spend the supper interval with you, but I have been forced to change my plans."

With his heart thudding against his breast he said, "I suggest you speedily change them back, ma'am. I am losing patience with the game you are playing."

She drew herself up stiffly. "You are also losing all semblance of good manners. I deplore arrogance, and you have an excess of it."

"And you, Miss Moorfield, have an excess of coquetry." Heedless of the avid study of those around them, he took hold of her arm and pulled it through the crook of his own. "We shall go and have supper."

Her arm was swiftly withdrawn, and she cast him a furious glance that nevertheless held the knowledge of her power to hurt him.

"I am growing tired of your constant absurdity. You have quite ruined the evening for us all and surely embarrassed Captain Wrexham deeply. You have no claim on me *whatever*, as you must be well aware, sir!"

"*Lydia!*" he cried from the heart, seeing his only hope of survival vanishing. "You cannot mean that!" But she was starting to move off with Kit Wrexham, and he could endure no more. Striding forward he seized her wrist and jerked her round to face him, saying wildly, "No, I will not let you go with him!"

Vivid colour flooded her cheeks as she gazed pointedly at her imprisoned wrist, and her voice was trembling with passion as she said into the intense surrounding silence, "I am a *lady*, Captain DeMayne, not a courtesan to be fought over like a personal possession. Are you *still* unable to tell the difference—even after six years?"

There was an audible gasp from several directions, and he was once again the hot-headed young boy who had drawn a sword against his own brother in the Officers' Mess of the 11th Hussars and wounded him in defence of a lady, not knowing she was a mere courtesan favouring a great number of military men besides his two brothers and Lord Cardigan himself. He saw, once more, his loose-living brother become a hero in the face of such fraternal treachery, and heard quite clearly the voice of the egocentric Earl of Cardigan publicly stripping him of his right to remain in the family regiment.

Then his eyes focused on the same kind of contemptuous faces that surrounded him now, and finally on the face of the girl who had done what they had failed to do to him at Multan. Slowly he let go her wrist and looked at her for one long agonizing minute, before turning to push his way through the circle of onlookers.

When he reached his room he made for the table holding the decanter and glasses. But his hands were shaking so much he dropped the glass as he tried to pour brandy into it. Tugging open the high collar of his tunic he put the decanter to his mouth, then tipped his head back to gulp down as much as he could before it spilled on to the pale-blue fabric. Straightening, he stood swaying for a moment or two while his heartbeat thundered through his entire body. Then he pulled off the tunic and silk shirt beneath, before walking across to where his sword hung in its ornate scabbard from a hook beside his bed. He drew it out with his left hand and stared at the fine blade that glinted coldly in the light filtering through the window from flambeaux outside in the cantonment. This weapon had pierced his brother's shoulder six years ago. Now, it would finish what had been started then.

"No! For pity's sake, no!"

He spun round so fast the room rocked. When it settled he saw a dim misty figure near the doorway. Her satin gown gleamed in the moonlight that was streaming through a nearby window. Her face was as pale as the material.

"You looked so terrible, I was afraid," she whispered. "How could you contemplate such a thing?" Moving toward him she added, still in tones of deep shock, "Would you heap further disgrace on your family?"

He had thought her a ghost, but when she reached him she was real enough. The fear in her eyes was also real. Then, as he stood swaying and trying to collect his thoughts, she gave a gasp and involuntarily put out a hand to feather her fingers across the deep scars on his torso. That physical contact had him casting the sword aside to seek oblivion from her instead. He had no thought of time or place as he made her come alive beneath his lips, playing the final hand in her dangerous game. It was only when light from candles flooded the bedroom that he emerged from passion to find Gil, Kit Wrexham and four other officers staring at them with shocked expressions.

They were married before October was through. For once, Maurice Daubnay and Chatsworth Dunwoodie were in complete accord over the only course of action when an officer and a lady had been discovered in such damning circumstances . . . and the quicker the better. Rowan was overjoyed; Lydia was overwhelmed. News of the scandal raced through the cantonments, the province and every part of India where the British were to be found, gathering embellishment as it went.

In the quixotic way of human nature, the fact that the lovers had been discovered in *his* bedroom endowed the gallant Captain DeMayne with renewed charm and fascination. Had the scandalous meeting been in *her* bedroom, he would have been dubbed a seducing blackguard. Lydia Moorfield was condemned on every front as a scheming brazen hussy, not least by the aunt and uncle in whose home she had been welcomed so warmly. Shocked and horrified at her betrayal of their trust, they treated their niece with icy contempt until her wedding day, then made it clear they would wipe her from their family as if she had never existed. The female population spitefully reminded Lydia of her nose-in-the-air condemnation of those who admired an un-doubted hero, and her haughty declaration that she would never be so feeble-minded as to join them. Their greatest aggravation was that the girl had been so handsomely re-warded for her duplicity.

The DeMaynes spent a month in the hills following their wedding, but the honeymoon was not all bliss. Unable to forgive him for the shame and derision he had forced her to face, apart from putting an end to her enjoyable reign amongst the bachelors of Khunobad, Lydia gave Rowan a bad time for the first few days. But his reputation with women had not been lightly earned, and he triumphantly claimed his wife on the fourth night, after which she told herself that many a female at Khunobad was probably weeping nightly, in envy, and allowed herself to enjoy the adoration of her disreputable husband.

On their return she brightened further. Despite being disowned by his family Rowan was still a very wealthy man, who was able to rent an imposing bungalow situated along the track leading to the hospital and fill it with every luxury a wife could want. Her enjoyment of feminine power returned when she discovered he would buy her anything she fancied, do whatever she asked, dance on her string to any tune she played. He could also still be driven to jealousy over any man with whom she chose to flirt. All in all, the disaster could be turned to triumph very easily, she discovered.

Her reign resumed. Instead of the princess she was the queen. Rowan's public indulgence and devotion ensured that. He protected her from malice so totally it was not long before all but the most blue-blooded or toffee-nosed were accepting her. Rowan had been the subject of society disapproval too long to care what was said about him, but he challenged the residents to recognize his wife as the newest member of a noble family. None dared refuse a man known to be volatile in the extreme.

As a result, Lydia DeMayne very soon revelled in her new status which made her the cynosure among Khunobad's hostesses, while miraculously increasing the number of her male admirers. It was as well it did not occur to her that they saw her as a wanton spinster now become a wanton wife— a female species of particular interest to them. That they approached her with a modicum of caution was due to her husband's skill and quickness with the sword. It would be as well to let his ardour cool, as it surely would, before making a bid for her favours.

So, while Lydia luxuriated in flattery from all quarters, and a day-to-day life that was filled with nothing but pleasure, Rowan was almost drunk with happiness. His wife filled his mind with peace, she eased his sexual hunger, she soothed his troubled spirit with music, she enhanced his elegant home. Hardly realizing how totally she dominated his life, he could only marvel that marriage appeared to have made her even more beautiful. Small wonder his passion for her deepened and his jealousy of his fellows who still flocked around her grew even greater. Despite that, the combined pressures that had driven him to the brink of self-destruction eased to the extent of allowing him to contend with them as well as any man. Those blackest, most terrifying of memories retreated to the depths of his mind until he believed them forgotten.

But his contentment took a setback in the week leading to December, and he rode home after hearing the news with the stirrings of returning frustration darkening the afternoon.

Lydia was on the verandah talking to a girl in a brown dress when he handed over his horse and went to the front steps of the bungalow. She smiled a greeting and came across, leaving the girl holding a parcel.

"My dear, I was not expecting you so soon. But I must tell you that I have had the most splendid idea concerning those matching tables in the parlour. It seemed to me they would be of far more use if covered with floor-length cloths during the day that could be removed in the evening. I ordered the making of them and have the first here for my approval. Should you wish to see it?"

"My love, I rely entirely on your judgement," he said absently. "I'd be pleased if you would come inside for a moment." Taking her arm he began leading her into the parlour, and called to the sewing-girl, "Take all that away when you leave. My wife will send for you when it is convenient." He took off his shako as he went indoors, murmuring, "Why do you not employ Indians, like everyone else? Who is that white girl?"

Lydia looked up at him with a frown. "She is the widow of Sergeant Clarke of your own regiment. Do you tell me you do not recognize her?"

Full of his disturbing thoughts he said, "You are wrong, my dearest. Sergeant Clarke was never married. Besides, that girl is too young to be anyone's widow." Leading her to a chair, he said, "You are a great deal too good and too gullible. I have experience of these women, and you have not. They will spin any story that suits their purpose, take my word. But enough of that. I am come to tell you there is serious news from the Crimea." Sitting to face her, he sighed. "I have just been told my eldest brother is lost; Monty is wounded, but survives. He is one of but a few." The gravity of the news hit him again, and he found words difficult. "There has been a great battle at a place called Balaclava—last month while we were in the hills. The official bulletin is sparing in detail, but it is evident there was a bad error in tactics. The entire Light Brigade was sent to charge a full battery of Russian cannon. It is inconceivable that it could happen," he added, feeling the full enormity of such an order. "But that it did is indisputable."

For a moment, all his eyes could see was a mass of charging cavalrymen galloping headlong to certain death from great black cannon spitting shell and red-hot balls of lead. Only a madman could have issued such an order: only madmen could have carried it out.

"Rowan . . . my dear?"

The gentle prompt brought him back to the present, and he saw Lydia's beautiful face growing troubled. "I'm sorry . . . but it has taken us all aback, you know, for the report says the Light Brigade is virtually destroyed. Those few who survived the charge were either wounded or so shocked there is no question of their continuing to fight." He frowned. "It is a disaster so momentous there has never been the like of it before. Some regiments apparently have no more than a dozen men left. Each was already reduced by cholera, starvation and weather conditions . . . but *a dozen!*"

He sat silently contemplating wholesale slaughter of the finest cavalry regiments in the world, until Lydia said hesitantly, "Does it . . . does it mean the war is lost?"

He looked up slowly. "Not while there are even a dozen left. You should know better than to ask that." But he was well aware that his beautiful bride knew little of army matters, and even less of war. Brought up in a political family, her first real encounter with the military had been on coming to India. He supposed he should not feel disappointed that she did not feel the shocking import of what he had told her. Perhaps he should not have mentioned it at all. Females could not be expected to discuss a subject he had already thrashed out with his fellows in the Mess before coming home. But he had been so full of the weight of such news it had been more than he could do not to mention it to the girl he loved so deeply. Yet he realized he should have spared her the details of something so awesome. One thing he did spare her was his inexplicable feeling of having been cheated. The carnage must have been frightful, the spectacle hideous . . . yet in his heart he felt he should have been there in that charge with the 11th Hussars, and his two brothers.

"I am so very sorry about Lord Paule," said Lydia rising to come and sit on the arm of his chair.

He nodded. "Yes, Bel was a fine soldier."

"What of his wife and children?"

"They will be cared for by my grandfather, naturally."

She hesitated, then asked, "Have you written to inform him of your marriage?"

"I have not," he said grimly. "He wishes to hear no more from me, and I respect his wishes. But he will have learned of it without doubt."

She flushed and got to her feet, but he caught her hand quickly. "I'm sorry. That was thoughtless of me." He rose to take her in his arms and hold her close. "You know very well, my darling girl, that I thank God for your arrival in my room that night. It has cost you dear, but the cost to me would have been total if you had not come."

Her swift flash of temper vanished beneath his kisses but, even as she returned them, he wondered who would replace the lost Light Brigade when spring brought a resumption of hostilities.

The Khunobad November Ball, traditionally held on the twenty-seventh day of that month, was normally a grand affair, but the year of 1854 was to see the most exciting of

these annual events ever staged. That the old bunting used
year after year was discarded for new, more elegant trappings was due to Maurice Daubnay who, on a committee
representing the military element at Khunobad, fired his
fellow members with his own enthusiasm for social perfection. Native craftsmen were set to making elaborate latticed
bowers decorated with beads and silver ornamentation,
which were placed around the sides of the ballroom to create
an impression almost of the inside of a theatre. Parties
attending the ball could occupy their own box, but visit
others to stay chatting for a while before moving on. In view
of the deplorable imbalance of the sexes, Colonel Daubnay
also suggested the length of each dance should be reduced
to enable more frequent changing of partners. He also offered to supervise the choice of music.

The enthusiasm naturally extended to the females, outnumbered ten to one, who prevailed upon their husbands to
allow the dressmaker to sew a creation worthy of the event.
What defence did any spouse have against the assertion that
every other female was to have a new gown, and did he want
his own wife to look a dowd in last year's sad satin?

Lydia DeMayne was no exception, although she had no
need to employ sly tactics. Even if Rowan had not been the
wealthiest man on the station, he would have given her
anything she wanted. On this occasion it was a crinoline in
palest peach brocaded silk with broad flounces of pleated
gauze to add interest to the hem, and knots of silver ribbons
at the waist. The Indian tailor had sat cross-legged on the
verandah for a day and a half to make the gown and, when
Mary Clarke arrived at the bungalow with the second of the
tablecloths she had completed, Lydia had agreed to the girl's
request to be allowed to sit and watch the old man's skill
with such fine work for an hour or so. The young wealthy
bride felt compassion for a twice-widowed girl three years
younger than herself.

But, despite the eager anticipation for what promised to
be a glittering event, normal routine had to be observed. It
was Rowan's ill-luck to be Officer of the Day on the date of

the ball, which meant he would have to leave the dancing and festivity to make final rounds of the cantonment with the duty sergeant. Lydia was very disappointed, but he promised to be away for as little time as possible.

"I dare not absent myself for long when you are looking so ravishing," he told her ardently as they prepared to set out. "There is not a man in Khunobad who will not be dazzled by you tonight."

She cast him a teasing glance. "Will you be among that number?"

Pulling her against him he kissed her fiercely. "I was dazzled the first moment I saw you and have never recovered, as you are very well aware."

The first part of the evening set the seal of success on the whole occasion. Everyone declared the decor the height of elegance, the programme of dances refreshingly varied and the choice of music quite the best they had heard. The orchestras of the three regiments stationed at Khunobad alternated in half-hour sessions on the platform roped with scarlet silken cords. Maurice Daubnay exuded self-congratulatory smugness as he strolled around smiling at the guests and looking over the officers of his regiment with satisfaction. He had done a good job with them! His very own regiment—six hundred and sixty-four toy soldiers to do with as he pleased. He had made them into the most glittering impressive regiment in India during the year he had commanded them. The troopers were supremely fit and obeyed orders like perfectly-matched automatons; the officers were now more worthy of the term 'officers and gentlemen' than many in the more élite regiments. Even the Honourable Rowan DeMayne had been brought to heel after several disasters. It was better to forget the way in which his marriage had come about and concentrate on the extreme respectability of the couple now—a couple who perfectly represented all he strove for as commanding-officer of a cavalry regiment abroad. DeMayne was an undeniably handsome devil in the tight-fitting, silver-encrusted ball dress of the 43rd and, if one put aside the scandalous events of just one night, his wife looked the epitome of virtuous English beauty. Yes, all in all, Maurice Daubnay had a great deal of justification for his belief that he had created aesthetic perfection in his professional as well as his private life.

Rowan was on his best behaviour for Lydia's sake, and tried not to show his rioting resentment when Kit Wrexham took his wife on to the floor for a quadrille. Gil, also without a partner for that dance, castigated his friend.

"If you are going to resemble a storm cloud every time Lydia dances with any man but you, you had much better not attend these functions," he advised dryly. "There is nothing more deadly to a social event than a jealous husband."

Rowan cast him a smouldering glance. "When Sophie has become Mrs Crane, I will remind you of those words, Gil."

His friend looked mildly affronted. "I have every trust in Sophie."

"So do I in Lydia. It's Wrexham I need to watch. Any man who sings in a high voice is a sly devil, mark my words."

Gil laughed heartily. "I have never yet heard *you* break into song, old fellow. Are you to be trusted, I wonder?"

"I would not indulge in such a namby-pamby pastime," he scowled. "Especially would I not do it in front of an audience and expect their worship for it. I should like to see him face to face with an enemy. A ballad would not suffice then. His throat would be slit in the midst of a top C— something I have longed to do on many occasions." As Gil laughed again, Rowan stood up with a sigh. "I must go on rounds; Sergeant Meeker will be waiting outside for me. See to my wife, Gil. I rely on you to keep that warbling cloth merchant's son away from her side."

Catching Lydia's eye as she swung round in the third figure of the quadrille, he raised a hand to her then made his way to the exit where he had instructed the *syce* to bring his horse and sword. Regulations demanded that the Officer of the Day be armed, whatever his mode of dress.

He rode off beside the NCO, his thoughts back in the ballroom with Lydia. Of course he was a jealous husband. He was a man and knew Lydia's visit to his bedroom that night, even though six men had also gone for the same reason, had left her open to speculation on whether she would be persuaded to do the same again, in time. To his shame, he pondered it himself, when happiness seemed too great to be true. She was sweet and gracious, provocative enough to excite him constantly, and filled her rôle as his wife to perfection. But the marriage had been forced on her by his uncontrolled and compromising passion that night. Would she come to resent the bonds that tied her, when some possible new arrival fell beneath her spell and openly worshipped her, as he had? He was not so blind that he did not realize how much she enjoyed male admiration and the attention she earned as his seduced wife. Would she allow herself to be seduced, even metaphorically, by another in the future?

Full of such thoughts, he hardly spoke to the man who rode beside him until they had completed their rounds of the cantonment and arrived outside the Guard House prior to splitting up.

Without dismounting he said, "If anything comes in, Sergeant, I can be found at the ballroom until two A.M. Then I shall be at my bungalow." He began to turn his horse. "Don't disturb me unless it really can't wait until morning handover."

"Very good, sir."

But he was prevented from departing by a soldier who came from within the building with a sealed dispatch in his hand.

"Captain DeMayne, this came in a few minutes ago for Colonel Daubnay. I was going to send it with a galloper until I remembered the ball. Will you take it and decide whether it's urgent or can wait until morning?"

"Very well," he said. "Bring the book out and I'll sign for it."

But he never did.

* * *

Back in the ballroom the orchestra of the 43rd had just returned to the platform and embarked on a polka, a dance much enjoyed by the younger element who were inclined to become a little wild as the evening wore on. Colonel Daubnay, who thought the dance much too unruly, watched with distaste as some of his subalterns made great galloping dashes down the length of the room with their breathless but laughing partners. He began to frown. It did not befit his elegant officers to behave like schoolboys. He forgot that quite a few of them had been just that less than a year ago. The frown deepened and his lips pressed tighter together when one or two rowdy cornets, urged on by Bacchus, let out wild yodels as they entered the spirit of the dance. He was unreasonably annoyed that it should be his own officers who so lowered the tone of the evening he had planned so carefully. He could even see one of the elderly Misses Birkenshaw being propelled around the floor so energetically her turban had gone askew. Telling himself the expression on her face was a grimace, not a smile, he vowed to have young Fanshawe taught a lesson in decorum he would not easily forget on the morrow.

But, as his gaze travelled around the room with increasing sharpness, he saw something that made boisterous subalterns seem like angels in comparison. His mouth began to open and shut like a fish as his tight, silver-encrusted tunic threatened to constrict him to suffocation point. He could not accept what he saw. It was a disaster, outrageous . . . unpardonable!

Over the top of the swaying crinolines, scarlet jackets and pale-blue dragoon tunics, across the width of the chandelier-hung ballroom· with its beautiful arbors, past the rows of elegant, dignified onlookers, he saw the main doors open and one of his own officers enter . . . *on a horse!* He blinked, but the unbelievable image remained. There was the Officer of the Day, resplendent in ball dress, black shako and sword, with the sash of duty over his shoulder, riding a glossy chestnut clothed in the regimental shabraque straight into the midst of the guests at the November Ball. Maurice

Daubnay had never seen the equal of this in the whole of his military career.

Rowan DeMayne's arm was held aloft clutching a piece of paper. He was flushed and breathless, shouting something as he turned his head from side to side. But the music drowned his voice, and the dancers whirled on oblivious of his entry. The Colonel believed himself about to be struck down by apoplexy there and then, as the young captain set his excited horse prancing forward to the very centre of the ballroom.

The rider was attracting attention now, and those nearest him began to fall back and cease dancing. Then, as his words reached some of them, they all took up his cry. It was passed from couple to couple in a growing crescendo that eventually reached the ears of the bandmaster, who glanced round and nearly fell from the dais at the sight of erstwhile graceful couples clustered excitedly around a *horseman* in the centre of the dance-floor. He looked for guidance to his colonel, but the little dapper man was purple in the face and shaking from head to foot.

The cries were now growing louder. Officers were hugging each other—yes, actually embracing! The younger gentlemen were throwing back their heads and uttering piercing yells; captains were shaking hands and clapping each other on the back; ladies were being clasped in robust arms and swung round so that their petticoats showed in a flurry of whiteness. The bandmaster averted his eyes, but not before he had seen Mrs Dunwoodie's ribbon-threaded drawers as she was lifted high in the air by Captain Crane.

As nobody appeared to want music, he signalled his bandsmen to cut out the last reprise and rounded off the polka with a few nicely-balanced chords. His musician's soul would not allow him to tail off the music in miserable fashion, whatever the circumstances. The entire ballroom was now in an uproar. Since the music had ceased it was impossible not to hear the cry that echoed and re-echoed in waves of triumphant sound. *"The Crimea! The 43rd is for the Crimea!"*

The Crimea? The bandmaster threw his baton in the air and shouted to his musicians above the din, "Get off your backsides, you lucky bastards. We're going to war at last!"

Several violins would never be the same again, a small drum ended up as a collar around the neck of a blissfully-smiling corporal and music-stands went flying as dancing commenced on the platform. One piccolo-player slipped outside to break the news, but the entire cantonment was already in a ferment of activity. In the cavalry lines bottles were being tipped up, old soldiers were re-telling old lies, new recruits were burning with excitement at the thought of battle and Cossack swords. Those with an eye to finance slipped quietly down to the native bazaar to get a high price on goods that would soon fetch little.

In the ballroom, Rowan had, at last, ridden up to his commanding-officer, saluted smartly and presented the communiqué containing the order to proceed to war. The elderly man took the unsealed message in a daze, looking positively ill. But Rowan had no thought for the little man who would have to lead his toy regiment into battle. That it should have been his own turn for duty when the message arrived seemed prophetic, and the elation of sitting his charger in the centre of a cheering exultant crowd seemed to make him already a victor.

His dark gaze swept the room until he caught sight of a still figure in peach satin in the midst of a group of young officers. Her face was turned to him, and the expression on it intensified his joy until it was a pain in his breast. Pressing his knees against the smooth flanks of his mount he rode across to her through clusters of people, bent and seized her around the waist, then lifted her into the saddle before him. Then he cantered for the doors, knowing that room was too confining for what he felt. Tonight was made for madness!

Out in the chilly darkness the sounds of revelry could be heard emitting from the barrack-blocks of the 43rd, and he raced his horse toward their bungalow near the hospital, laughing exultantly as he clutched Lydia against him with the arm that would soon wield a sabre. He was still exultant

as he jumped from the saddle and pulled her into his arms
to carry her inside, much too engrossed to see a girl in a
brown dress standing beside the road, halted by their headlong approach.

Once indoors Rowan caught Lydia in a fierce embrace
and swung her from side to side as he told her, between
kisses, that this was the most marvellous night of his life. It
took a while before he realized she was unresponsive, and he
lifted his head to gaze breathlessly down into a face that
seemed strangely taut in the faint light of one candle kept
burning in their absence.

"Darling, what is wrong?" he asked in a voice husky from
shouting.

"Wrong?" she echoed flatly. "You do not know?"

"I . . . well, no. Do you not share our gladness?"

"*Gladness!* At going to war?"

"Of course gladness," he enthused, still high on the excitement of reading that despatch. "The regiment will have
the chance of showing its mettle at last, and gain battle
honours for its standards."

"But what is to become of me?" she cried.

He laughed exultantly, thinking he understood her bewil-
dering attitude. "You, my dearest tormentor, will come with
me, naturally."

"Come with you . . . to *war?*" Her voice had grown thin.
"Whatever are you saying?"

"You are now a military wife, Lydia. War is part of a
soldier's life."

"It is certainly not part of mine, Rowan. I cannot believe
you are serious. If that is what you expect of a partner, you
should have taken a trooper's widow into your bed that
night."

CHAPTER FIVE

The repercussions of that night of the November Ball were widespread. Colonel Daubnay attended morning parade in order to address the entire regiment. The gist of his message was that if the mere *prospect* of going to war created such undisciplined behaviour, drunkenness and rowdyism, he dreaded to think how his regiment would conduct itself when faced with the real thing. Because of it there would be extra drills every day, and morning parades would be in full dress uniform. In addition, he would be personally inspecting horses, accoutrements and quarters of each troop at unspecified times, and would expect to find no fault with any aspect of regimental life.

The officers had an additional separate reprimand for their disgraceful behaviour at the ball, and were asked how they expected to control their men when they could not control themselves. He vowed he had never witnessed such a spectacle in all his years as a cavalryman. News of it would go ahead to reach the ears of the remnants of the Light Brigade, who would then abandon all hope of a crack regiment coming to join them.

Rowan was put under immediate arrest pending court

martial, for making public the contents of a vital dispatch addressed to his colonel, and for introducing an excitable stallion into a ballroom and endangering the lives of all those present. The arrest was soon lifted when Colonel Daubnay realized the affair would not be settled before they were due to leave, and he could not afford to be short of a troop-commander, even one as troublesome as the youngest De-Mayne. Besides, it meant detailing another officer of equal rank to remain with the prisoner day and night just at a time when so much had to be done. In truth, Maurice Daubnay was acutely demoralized. His beautiful regiment of toy soldiers was about to be destroyed, and he was obliged to lead them to their destruction. His hopes were shattered; his ideals had flown. He had accepted command of the 43rd because of their bloodless history. Why, oh why, did their peaceful record of forty-one years' service have to be broken now?

The members of the regiment worked until they were ready to drop in order to prepare for war, Daubnay's extra drills and duties making life even more difficult for them. The regimental tailors were racing against time to provide clothing for a campaign in cooler climes, cobblers were turning out boots by the score, cutlers were sharpening swords and sabres to razor edges, native contractors were doing well in providing tents, collapsible washstands, trunks, folding beds and pack-animals to carry officers' personal possessions across India. The troopers would carry their own, as they invariably did.

Rowan's elation at the activity he had longed for was dimmed by the rift with his wife. He had been brought to realize the change in his circumstances very forcibly, and was still trying to come to terms with the fact that Lydia, having just recovered from the shock of her hasty marriage, could not reconcile herself with the idea of leaving the gracious life she had known to embark on something she did not believe any female should be asked to do. As if that were not enough, Rowan was shaken by the evidence that she would willingly be parted from him while he went to war, rather than go campaigning at his side. They had quarrelled bitterly that night, and had been prevented from making up by the presence, day and night, of Captain Fairlie, escort to the prisoner. By the time Daubnay changed his mind and withdrew the charges, the moment for spontaneous reconciliation had passed. Rowan was weighed down by duties and Lydia remained aloof as she was forced to accept that she must travel with the regiment. There was nowhere else for her to go.

Rowan rode up to the bungalow after the fourth morning of extra duties, grumbling to Gil over the senselessness of spit and polish when there was so much else to be done.

"Two of my horses are too highly-strung to undertake the journey, and God knows when I shall find the time to select replacements. I have to get a dealer up to the bungalow to give me a price for the furniture I bought only a month ago. It will be ridiculously low with everyone else selling in a hurry. All this on top of trying to purchase cloaks, thick boots, flannel shirts and enough fodder for all my horses. Lydia has her tailor sewing for her like the devil but, I tell you, Gil, you are damned lucky to have only yourself to think of at this time."

"You think so?" queried Gil gloomily, the prospect of leaving his fiancée in India with her family leavening his delight at the chance of military action.

Rowan gave him a swift glance. "Oh, marry the girl and take her with you! You know it's what you want."

"It wouldn't be fair on her. Battlefields are no place for females."

The comment so echoed his wife's views that Rowan said no more on the subject, and it did not help his mood to find Lydia in a mutinous state on reaching his rented home. She was sitting on a footstool surrounded by china and glassware which she was plainly putting out ready to be packed in the boxes he had paid to have made for the journey. At the moment she was tenderly arranging a tea set of particularly ugly design.

"Those boxes are to travel with us," he pointed out quietly.

"I know." She had not glanced up as he entered and kept her head lowered as she spoke.

"Did I not state quite plainly that we could take very few of our things with us? That tea set, in particular, should be left behind."

She looked up with colour in her cheeks, and he wondered, with fresh dismay, what had made her so angry.

"It was part of my dowry, as you should be well aware. A great-aunt bequeathed it to me."

Mention of a family that had turned its back on her as firmly as his had on him filled him with remorse. "I beg your pardon, my dear. I had forgotten," he said, still thinking the china very ugly. "You must take it, in that case. But one of those others will have to be left behind. I have six mules and two camels already. It really is out of the question to add any more."

Her eyes flashed. "How quickly gentlemen change when they have gained what they have set out to capture. A very short time ago you would have done anything I asked."

Trying to keep calm, he explained that the matter was out of his hands. "We have orders to keep baggage to the minimum and I have no choice but to obey them."

She stood up, her anger mounting. "I have not heard that you were so obedient in the past. Indeed, it seems you broke every rule in the book before I met you."

"This is different, Lydia," he protested. "We are going to war."

"How you glory in the fact!"

Ignoring that, he went on, "We shall be living in a tent, as I have tried to impress upon you."

"Ho, is it your intention that we shall eat with spoons from the cooking pot?" she cried.

"We may yet be eating with our fingers. Have you no idea at all what campaigning involves?"

"No, sir, I have not. No one has thought fit to tell me. You are forever clattering in and out with swords and pistols

—when you are not under arrest, that is—so that it is impossible to have a conversation with you. You forget that, until a few months ago, I knew nothing whatever of military life. I would never have *chosen* to share it, but a few moments of misguided impulsive compassion left me with no alternative, did they?"

Her words hurt him deeply, because they showed him as an ungrateful and insensitive brute. He moved toward her, accidentally treading on one of the plates as he did so.

"Darling, forgive me. I owe you my life; I will never forget that," he said huskily, taking hold of her waist. "These past few days have been hellish, and the nights have been worse. I have tossed and turned, longing for you. I love you beyond reason, you know that I do." Pulling her hard against him he kissed her with growing passion, covering her mouth and throat with his seeking lips until she protested faintly.

"Rowan, if the servants should see us!"

"To perdition with the servants," he murmured, caressing her temple with his mouth. "Say you are mine again, although I have been a selfish brute. I gave no thought to your natural dismay at embarking on something so sombre. But we shall be together, my dearest, and surely that is all that matters. I shall protect you to the best of my ability, and I swear you may take all you value even if it means disregarding orders. I want you as madly as ever. Say you are mine and end my misery."

She made no protest when he began fondling her bodice with unruly hands, but his heartbeat that had quickened at the signs of her surrender slowed again when she murmured against his tunic, "There is one item that need not bother you, Rowan. Captain Wrexham has offered to transport my pianoforte with his baggage. Being a bachelor, he has less to take than we have."

He held her away slightly, still halfway to passion. "Whatever do you mean?"

She gazed back round-eyed. "While you have been cross as a bear, I have been a dutiful wife. Rather than bother you with the question of transporting my pianoforte, I consulted the one man amongst the regiment who understands music as I do. He instantly offered one of his camels for the purpose."

"But . . . Lydia, a musical instrument?" he stammered, trying to control the rioting thoughts that mingled with his jealousy that she had been in touch with Wrexham behind his back. "You cannot take a piano to a battlefield!"

Her shoulders moved in an impatient shrug. "Mrs Constantine says all the ladies will remain well behind the lines in stout accommodation safe from gunfire, and that there will be long boring hours to fill during our husbands' absences. Besides which, there is that long tedious voyage to reach our destination. I really cannot spend months at sea without music. That would be asking too much of me."

His arms slowly dropped back to his sides as he broke the news. "We shall not be spending months at sea. Our orders came through this morning. We are first to march from here to Bombay, where we embark for the short voyage to Suez. We then go overland across the desert to Cairo, then on along the course of the Nile to Alexandria. There will be another flotilla awaiting us for the last stage through the Dardenelles to Balaclava."

Her gaze was shocked and unbelieving. "*Across the desert!* Do not tease me, Rowan, I beg you."

"They are desperate for reinforcements," he impressed upon her. "We have to take the shortest route."

"But are you seriously saying that a regiment of six hundred or more men, seven hundred and fifty horses, with all that equipment, is preparing to *walk* halfway across the world to a war? You are all mad!"

"No, Lydia," he said in despair at her ignorance of his profession. "We are all soldiers."

Mary Clarke had been lying awake on the night of the November Ball thinking of the peach gown she had watched being made for Lydia DeMayne, whom she regarded as a benefactress. From that first chance encounter outside the hospital there had developed a strange business association between the two young girls at opposite ends of the social scale. While there was no doubt Lydia DeMayne regarded Mary as a servant, she was always gracious in manner and Mary had no hesitation in taking advantage of it to build up her career as a seamstress.

It was with thoughts of the ballgown in her mind that Mary had been drawn from her pallet by the sounds of shouting and confusion further up the road that evening. Guessing it must be past midnight, alarm filled her. The tumult was so great there must be something desperate afoot. Had the cantonment been attacked? Was there a fire?

Coming from the store that constituted her quarters she had begun walking up the road toward the sound of the noise, when a galloping horse had approached the DeMayne bungalow. Unseen by the pair on the horse, Mary had witnessed an astonishing sight. Captain DeMayne, laughing wildly and apparently drunk, was in the saddle with his beautiful wife in his arms. He had jumped from the horse to carry her inside, where he had begun kissing her passionately as he swung her round and round. Mary had been able to see right into the room, and had felt no shame at watching and listening. She had paid a dear price for it. Not only had it confirmed Lydia DeMayne's selfishness, her own future had dropped like a stone into her lap.

Shaken and upset by what she had overheard, Mary had wandered on up the road to stand in the shadows near D Block, where the men were all in a state similar to Rowan DeMayne. They were drunk, but with excitement, not spirits. She guessed that would come later. The women she had grown up with had all been as silent as she, Mary had noted as she watched the riotous scene in the flickering light from the saucer-lamps at the corner of the building. They knew, as she did, that harder times were on the way for them. But they were still 'on the strength' of the regiment. The widow Clarke was no one's responsibility. When the 43rd marched out of Khunobad, she would be left behind, abandoned by a regiment that had been her family and home since her birth.

Too late now to realize she should have forsaken her aspirations to respectability and taken a third husband. Pride had governed her when Sam had died, and now she was reaping the bitter harvest. Having alienated herself from the group to which she truly belonged, she was left friendless and without status. There was no one to whom she could confide her fears or from whom she could gain even marginal comfort.

In the morning Harry Winters had confirmed the awful truth as he gently explained that she could not continue with her work.

"What Colonel Daubnay countenanced here is one thing, Mrs Clarke. But the regiment is going to war, which will be a costly enough undertaking as it is. You could not possibly be counted on the strength. Besides which, all the troopers' wives are being sent to England." He had looked down at her for a moment or two, before asking quietly, "What will you do, my dear?"

"What can I do?" she had returned frankly. "There's no man would take a wife when he's just off to war. So I can't get back to England. I suppose they wouldn't take me at one of the other hospitals here?"

"I think that's most unlikely. You have only been allowed in this one due to Colonel Daubnay's very strong sense of responsibility. I'm very, very sorry."

She had known he was sincere, but it had not helped her problem or her sense of panic as the days had passed. For once, her fertile mind refused to work, and she watched helplessly as the 43rd prepared for war in a distant country.

On the afternoon of the sixth day a servant came to summon her to the DeMayne bungalow. Mary went spiritlessly in the belief that she was required for last-minute mending jobs. Her heart would not be in the work, but the money she earned would stave off the inevitable as long as possible.

Ushered into the parlour Mary found Lydia DeMayne sitting surrounded by the most elaborate gowns and bonnets, looking decidedly stormy. Apparently, she still did not wish to accompany her dashing husband to the Crimea. *What a little fool she is,* thought Mary as she bobbed a curtsey. *It's a chance in a lifetime for any girl!* The Captain was nowhere in sight, she was glad to note, feeling tardy guilt at her deliberate spying on the quarrel that had ended with this furious girl smacking him around the face and flouncing from the room. In Mary's world, it was the men who hit the women, not the other way around, and she had been astonished by the scene.

"Mrs Clarke, we have had dealings in the past which have been satisfactory to us both, I believe," said the clear light voice that had been so coldly cutting on that other occasion. "Since I am desperately busy, I shall come straight to the point."

Mary blinked and brought her thoughts back from the memory of two dim figures by candlelight, who had given her her first insight into what went on inside these elegant beehive dwellings between people whose lives were a mystery to her.

"Yes, mum," she murmured, guessing all was still not honey and jam with the pair.

"You are naturally aware that the 43rd Light Dragoons are leaving for a war in Europe," said the girl in lavender silk, occupying a chair so beautiful Mary thought it a crime for anyone to sit on it. "I, along with other officers' wives, will be travelling with them."

There was a pause as if the speaker expected some kind of reaction, so Mary obliged with, "Oh, that'll be nice for you, mum."

Arched eyebrows rose momentarily in surprise, then settled again. "I have this morning heard details of the journey. It seems all Indian servants must be left behind in Bombay, and new ones employed at various stages of the journey. I do not care for the idea." There was another pause as the blue eyes looked Mary over. "Do you consider yourself capable enough for the post?"

"Post?" echoed Mary, wondering what a wooden pole

had to do with a conversation she was not following too well in her present state of mind.

"I know you have had no training as a lady's maid, but I would feel more comfortable with you than a succession of strange natives. I am prepared to teach you the rudiments which, presumably, will be all that are needed on this . . . journey," she finished with a throb in her voice. Continuing in a grave tone, she said, "Knowing the callousness of the military toward females, I suspect you are to be left to your own devices as no part of their responsibility. This would surely answer your problem nicely."

Suddenly short of breath and afraid she must have mistaken Mrs DeMayne's meaning, Mary gasped, "Are you asking me to go with you?"

The elegant head nodded. "All the way to the Crimea. To the *battlefields*, Mrs Clarke," she emphasized in warning tones. "There will be fighting, and all kind of unimaginable horrors. You must take that into account before you answer."

"Oh, *yes*, mum." Delight coloured her response.

There was an intent study of her face by those striking eyes, then, "I must further warn you that a great deal of the journey is to made *overland.*"

Almost laughing with excitement by now, Mary said, "Ma and me walked up here from Calcutta with the regiment. I were only small then, and some of the men give us rides on the wagons when the officers weren't looking. I expect I can do the same again."

"You . . . walked . . . from Calcutta!" The comment was made in a strangely wobbly voice.

But Mary was too carried away by excitement by then to take much notice. She was thinking of the incredible fortune that would bring freedom and adventure her way.

"Yes, mum. I was born into the regiment, you see, and Ma had to take me wherever the 43rd was sent. We had a bit of a skirmish on the way up here. C Troop was set on by bandits as they brought up the rear. There was a hullabaloo, but the Captain saw the bastards off, good and proper,"

she finished with enthusiasm, just as she saw from the corner
of her eye something pale-blue appear in the archway to her
left. Turning, she found the man of the house surveying the
scene with a frown.

"What, in the name of God, is going on?" demanded that
unforgettable voice. "What is *she* doing in here?"

Mary realized he meant her. She also realized he was
acting as if he had never set eyes on her before. It made her
curiously angry. She was in a decent dress, and she was very
clean. What was more, she was standing in the very middle
of his own parlour. He could not dismiss her as part of the
background now!

Lydia DeMayne rose, saying coolly, "I sent for Mrs
Clarke."

"Oh . . . for what reason?" He came wearily into the
room.

"She has been sewing for me these past two months. I did
tell you of it."

Her husband pulled off his round forage-cap and threw it
on to a nearby chair. "You should conduct such interviews
on the verandah, my dear. Or let the bearer deal with these
matters. He is used to it."

"I have asked her to accompany us to the Crimea as my
personal servant, Rowan. I believe she has just now agreed."

Mary was struck anew by the darkness of hair and eyes
that made this man so arresting to look at, as he said sharply,
"You have asked her to accompany us? You said nothing of
this proposal to me."

"My dear, you have been complaining of the multitude
of worries besetting you these days, and I did not wish to
trouble you with something which is my concern. Military
matters have to take precedence with your time; household
affairs must be my sole concern from now on." As he regarded her with a bemused expression, his wife said, "It is
my fervent wish to help you as much as possible, Rowan."

His lazy voice was caressingly soft as he murmured, "Very
well, my dear."

The girl turned back to Mary, still wearing the wide-eyed

innocent look with which she had regaled her husband. Mary marvelled at the way the Captain had changed his tune so quickly.

"Mrs Clarke, you will receive the same as I presently pay my native girl, with your food provided. I shall require you to wear suitable clothes, which I trust you can make for yourself from material I will give you. You may also purchase a pair of strong boots and a cloak for cooler climes." She began walking toward her husband, who was studying her hungrily. "Is there anything you wish to say to Mrs Clarke?"

He shook his head, smiling down at her as he took her hands in his large brown ones. "I am facing a *fait accompli*, am I not? All I would ask is that if I have to have her around me during the coming months, you attempt to teach her the Queen's English. And, for pity's sake, instruct her to address you as 'madam' not with some distasteful diminutive form of 'mother'."

Before she could stop herself Mary said hotly, "You can say all that to me, Captain DeMayne. I've got ears . . . and a tongue to answer with."

His head turned very slowly, and she received the full force of his aristocratic sleepy-eyed magnetism as he murmured with great amusement, "Have you, by God? Then use the ears to listen, and the tongue to copy what you hear. If you don't, I shall box the former and put vinegar on the latter until you do. I really cannot suffer 'Captain DeMine' all the way to the Crimea either. You will address me as 'Sir' . . . if you *insist* on addressing me directly." He turned back to his lovely wife, apparently forgetting Mary's presence.

But Lydia DeMayne concluded the interview graciously by saying, "You may go now, Mrs Clarke. I will inform you of the final arrangements in plenty of time."

"Yes, mum," said Mary without thinking, and hurried from the room with her mind in a whirl. But, as she walked down the road toward the hospital, a smile began to break across her face. An 'Honourable' had actually spoken to *her* —little Mary Tookey, who had become Mary Rafferty, then Mary Clarke! She was no longer part of the background. He had spoken to her; acknowledged that she existed. And she was going to go out through these cantonment gates with the regiment, and along those distant paths that had called to her so strongly for so long!

By the time she had reached the tree where she liked to sit, her smile had turned into unrestrained laughter. But, as she clutched the trunk and put the hand wearing the ring with the small blue stone to her cheek, it was wet with tears that mingled with the laughter.

"Oh, Sam," she whispered, "Sam, dear, I'm on my way, at last!"

The Advance Wing of the 43rd Light Dragoons departed from Khunobad in magnificent style and promptly to the minute. At six A.M. A, B, and C Troops formed up before the main guard house prior to moving off, and the entire garrison including the remainder of the regiment, who were to follow in two wings spaced several days apart, were there to see them off.

The infant dawn threw pale light across the rows of blue-coated horsemen, who wore the white covers over their shakoes, and who were fully-equipped for the long journey with bulging valises behind their saddles, rations for themselves and water-choggles filled to the brim. The sight filled Mary with sudden unexpected pride as she watched from amongst the assembled pack-animals and servants at the side of the lime-washed building. Each man sat so straight in the saddle, each held his horse easily in check with one hand on the reins, and each was elated with the prospect of becoming a real soldier at last. Mary was almost as glad of the fact as they were. She knew how their pride had suffered, and what good fellows they were beneath their roughness.

Her glance strayed to the man at the head of C Troop. Station gossip had it that Rowan DeMayne would move heaven and earth to prove himself a greater hero than either of his brothers at the Crimea, sacrificing duty to the regiment in order to do so. Mary did not believe that. She had seen him when he had been brought into the hospital that morning. Any man who could withstand such torture and still get himself back to his regiment needed no further proof of heroism, in her eyes. Yet she doubted his lovely young wife regarded him as more than a conquest.

The departure ceremony ended and troop commanders gave orders to form threes into the long formation in which they would take the road from Khunobad to the coast. But, before they could move off, someone in the crowd gave a call for three cheers for 'The Gingerbread Boys', and the quietness of that Indian dawn resounded with voices that told all those present the nickname would remain with the regiment, but the derision had changed to affection.

The regimental band struck up the popular march 'Cheer, boys, cheer!' and they rode out between cheering, waving crowds of Europeans and Indians with whom they had been associated since 1850. Not a single dragoon turned his head or broke ranks. The crowds followed on horses or in carriages as they moved toward the perimeter gate, so anxious was the desire to send the heroes on their way with good wishes and godspeed. Mary would never forget that morning. Frenzied camp followers, Indian sepoys, English officers of Indian regiments, even the comrades who would be following in a few days, all making a carnival occasion of the moment. Some of the carriages running alongside the blue-clad soldiers contained ladies with wistful faded faces who somehow saw the Crimea as 'nearly home', and personally faced the prospect of Khunobad heat and dust for another ten, twenty years. There were horsemen and women riding beside the dragoons, silently remembering a multitude of shared experiences—not all of them innocent— during their years of association, and having to return to routine in the old cantonment. There were anguished women running beside the regimental chestnut mounts as their husbands rode away from them, possibly never to return, and children trotting on skinny legs beside their mothers, crying for papa.

The band was still playing lustily as the long, long line of pack-animals surged forward at the rear of the troops, and

Mary took her first steps on the journey to experience and adventure beside the rumps of the DeMaynes' mules. Amidst the multitude of servants, she was the only European. But it did not worry her, and she was the only one not to be startled when some of the more boisterous officers remaining in Khunobad thundered past letting off their pistols in salute.

Throughout the whole riotous send-off, those departing kept in straight, perfectly disciplined lines until the limits of Khunobad station were reached. Then a shouted command from the head of the column set the two hundred-and-twenty-five officers and troopers all raising their voices in a combined 'hurrah'. Hitherto iron men now turned in their saddles to shake hands and clap old friends on the back, bent to kiss tear-stained, tangle-haired wives and waved large coloured handkerchiefs to sobbing children who had to stop at the gates. The crowds fell away, then turned back reluctantly to dull routine, leaving the column to be swallowed up in the vastness of Khunobad Plain.

When Mary walked through the last gate of that Indian station she could hardly see for the dust stirred up by the column ahead. It would be like that for most of the way, and she had provided herself with a gauze scarf from the native market to wrap around her head against the flying grit. Yet still her vision was blurred for a while. Behind her in Khunobad lay her mother and father, and two husbands. What lay ahead was an incredible journey across a world she had never seen and, at the end of it, bloody battlefields. What awaited her beyond that?

"Goodbye, Sam," she whispered to the only person she had ever loved. "I'll do my best not to let you down."

They took a long time to cross the plain, and the sun was well up before the first trees appeared ahead. Anticlimax had set in now the cantonment was no more than a distant pale blur. Mary plodded along in her new boots, drenched in perspiration and worrying about the duties she knew nothing of. Suppose she was no use as a maid. Would the DeMaynes abandon her by the side of the track and ride off without a care for her fate? *He* might, but she did not think his wife would, somehow. Whatever her faults, Mrs De-Mayne was not callous.

The baggage train was considerable. Mules, camels, even elephants comprising two thousand or more beasts carried tents, fodder, beds, clothing, rations, cooking-utensils, weapons and ammunition. In addition, there were the officers' spare chargers, and twenty extra troop-horses hastily bought in their unbroken state before they left. These were roped together and kept under control by a young cornet and two troopers who did not welcome the duty because the beasts were unpredictable. Mary had heard Rowan DeMayne had been given the task of breaking the horses in *en route*—a duty relished by no officer—firstly, because he was the best horseman in the regiment, and secondly, so it was rumoured, as a punishment from their colonel for riding into the ballroom. During the first morning he certainly kept an eye on them by riding back to check that there was no trouble.

All around her the Indian servants chatted animatedly together, and Mary realized she was liable to find the journey rather lonely. So she tried to pass the time by wondering what would happen when they reached Bombay. Surely they could not take all these animals on the ships. There would be no room for the men. Yet they must be intending to take the horses all the way to the Crimea. What use were dragoons without mounts . . . and she had heard there were none to spare at Balaclava?

Halfway through the morning the whole column rested for a while at a well, every person and animal drinking gratefully. Mary was feeling hot and weary already. Her feet were sore, so she took off her boots to ease them for a while, even though common sense told her it would only make putting them on again worse. She sat on the ground staring dolefully at her toes when a pair of dusty black boots appeared in her ken, and a voice said with amusement, "I've seen some lively blisters in my day, but those are really jumping, I'll wager."

She looked up quickly to find a trooper gazing down at her

sympathetically. "Not half as much as you will if you don't get back with the others quick," she warned him coolly. "C Troop, aren't you? Captain DeMayne's got a right tongue on him."

Completely unconcerned the man put one foot up on the low wall she was leaning against and bent forward confidentially on his raised knee. "He's just detailed me for the baggage-train. How'd you like a ride when we get going?"

The invitation put a different complexion on the situation, and Mary smiled at him. "So long as it won't mean trouble."

His return smile was very attractive and full of confidence. "Who for—you or me?"

"Either of us." She scrambled to her feet, brushing the dust from her skirt as she did so. "You're very quick off the mark, aren't you?"

"Not really." The smile broadened into a grin. "I've had my eye on you for a long time."

"Have you now," she retaliated tartly. "Well, you'd best take it off again smartish. I'm not a camp follower. I'm Mrs DeMayne's personal maid."

"I know that. I wouldn't offer a ride to a camp follower. They're not my style."

"And you're not mine. Let's get that straight, here and now."

"All right. But it's a long way from here to where we're going, and you might like someone to talk to now and again."

Taking time to consider that, she gave him a closer look. With his light brown hair and moustache and greenish eyes, he made a handsome figure against the backdrop of trees, and Mary sensed he was different from the other troopers. There was that about his appearance and manner of speaking that was even more impressive than Sam Clarke had seemed to her. He was not like the officers, of course, but he had a gentlemanly air about him that intrigued her. And he *was* rather nice.

"Can you read and write?" she asked.

He laughed and straightened up. "If I can, does it mean I'm acceptable?"

"Can you?"

"And a lot more," he said confidentially, picking up her boots. "I know a decent girl when I see one, for a start."

"You're too clever by half," she told him pertly. "What's a man like you doing in the ranks?"

"That's a long story. It'll take from here to Bombay to tell it."

The men were mounting again, and officers were going around chivvying the native drovers who controlled the pack-animals. Ahead Mary could see her mistress being helped into the saddle by her husband. She looked tired already, and Mary would be expected to help her at the end of the day's march. She looked up at the broad-shouldered trooper beside her.

"I'll listen to your story if it means a ride on one of the waggons. But I don't believe it'll take from here to Bombay to tell it."

He began walking off with her boots toward the baggage-train. "If it doesn't you can tell me one."

Hopping across rough stones with her bare feet she panted, "You're a funny kind of trooper."

He turned to give her a bold look. "And you're a funny kind of lady's maid. Doesn't that give us something in common?"

An hour later they reached a green area and began passing through a series of villages. The inhabitants turned out to wave as they passed through, and brown laughing children ran beside the horses, delighted by the shining, jingling accoutrements of these very grand-looking men in blue and silver on animals the like of which they had never seen in their village before. The more bashful women hung back in the doorways to watch the procession pass, their dark mysterious eyes intent on the memsahibs who rode in the midst of so many soldiers.

Mary was equally intent on watching them. From her perch on the edge of a rumbling, jolting waggon she was taking in every detail of the country she was leaving. She was sure she would never return to it and wanted to fix every sight and sound and smell in her memory. But occasionally her glance strayed to the trooper who rode on the right flank. Having had little to do with any troop save Jack Rafferty's, it still surprised her that such an attractive man had escaped her notice until now. But then, she had not been looking for one. Frowning at the way her thoughts were going she told herself it was useless to think of her future. There was a long time yet before they reached the Crimea, when most of the men riding ahead of her were destined to be killed. Much better wait until Mrs. DeMayne found a proper maid, then see what turned up.

They halted to make camp a short distance from a village where water could be obtained, and the whole area became a kaleidoscope of organized pandemonium. Each man had his designated duty and set about it with cheerful disregard for anyone or anything that tried to prevent him from doing so. The horses were picketed to long lines of pegs knocked into the ground with great gusto by men who were whistling or singing, forage was brought in by native grass-cutters, tents rose in lines of white pyramids, cooks unpacked the utensils of their trade and lit fires to get water boiling for tea before making a start on dinner for hungry travellers.

Mary picked her way through the military activity to where the officers' ladies were clustered beneath shady trees while their husbands attended to their first duties. But it appeared Lydia DeMayne was hardly charmed by any aspect of the busy scene. As Mary approached she was saying to her neighbour, "This really is too much! After making us endure six hours in the saddle, they might have the consideration to see to our comfort."

"They have many things to do, Mrs DeMayne," came the uncompromising reply. "This is your first march, is it not? I'm afraid you will find our husbands will have little time to spare for us."

"Indeed," was the tart retort. "Then I wonder at their insistence on our accompanying them."

Somewhat awkwardly Mary stood nearby waiting to be noticed. She had no idea what she ought to be doing. The Indian servants of the other ladies had vanished the moment the halt had been made, and were presumably occupied with vital tasks. Her blistered feet in the new boots were burning, and she longed to bathe her face and hands to remove the dust and dampness from them. But she dared not walk off to do so. There was always the fear of being dismissed by her employer if she did not satisfy him as a maid.

In the background the hammering, singing, neighing and banging of pots continued as the noonday sun blazed down on the surrounding countryside, and Mary was caught up in the joyousness of those men to whom each day's journey meant escape from their confining existence in Khunobad, without even their colonel—who was travelling with the Headquarters Wing so that he could wind up affairs before leaving—to mark their every movement. The second-in-command, Major Benedict, was a kindly man who sought peace and goodwill with his fellow men. His leadership of this advance section was very welcome.

So lost did Mary become in watching the activity all around her that she jumped when something rapped her sharply on the shoulder. Turning she found the Captain beside her with a dark expression on his dust-filmed face as he accosted her with his white leather gloves.

"Your duties are not to oversee the setting-up of camp, but to participate in the task," he told her in a voice that was husky from shouting. "Collins is erecting my tent at the head of those two lines there. Get across to him and do what you should have been doing the minute we halted."

She hurried off in the direction of his pointing finger, hoping the soldier-servant would throw some light on what she should have been doing the minute they halted. The batman was a simple-minded man who seemed to feel he was honoured by having Captain DeMayne to look after. He spoke gently to her of the sharing of duties as Mary helped him fasten guy-ropes and set out the interior of the tent. Theirs was the combined task of locating the DeMaynes' luggage at every overnight stop, erecting the tent and getting hot water for tea and their personal use. After that, Mary was to help her mistress with her dress and intimate needs. She must then launder and iron discarded garments, sponge and press Mrs. DeMayne's riding clothes, and fetch anything she might require when she retired for the night. In the mornings, the routine was straightforward, he told her. An hour and a half before marching, she must awaken her mistress with tea, help her prepare for the day, then pack all the possessions and clothes into the trunks when the main section of the column rode off. Collins would be in charge of preparing and serving meals. He would also see to all his officer's equipment and personal needs.

"Remember all that, gal, and we shall get on a treat," he told her solemnly. "But I want no reprimands from the Captain on account of *your* mistakes, mind."

It all sounded simple enough. How could she make any mistakes? But she did. Everything went well during the afternoon and evening of that first day and she was so occupied, the blisters on her feet had gone unnoticed. When she finally rolled herself in her cloak and blanket in the back of one of the waggons sleep came almost immediately. Morning brought a return of pandemonium in reverse as camp was struck. To avoid the worst of the heat they were to set off two hours before dawn, so it was still dark when Collins shook her awake. Sluggish and bewildered for the first few minutes she forced her protesting feet into the new boots and folded the blanket. It was eerie stumbling about the waking camp lit by infrequent flambeaux and the light of fires heating water. As she went with a canvas bucket to one of these she was momentarily reminded of those days in D Block, when women had squabbled noisily over the laundry and she had worn a soiled dress that had marked her a slut to those who now depended on her for their comforts. She had a decent one in grey cloth now, although she realized it looked decidedly crumpled in the light thrown by the flames. There was no time to do anything about it, however, because Collins was chivvying her to hurry with the water.

Taking the rope handle of a bucket in each hand she began walking the fifty yards toward the DeMayne tent. But a hand fell across her right one and a voice said, "My arms are stronger than yours. I'll take those."

It was the trooper from the afternoon before, his nice-looking face brown in the flickering flamelight. She felt instant suspicion. What was his game?

"I've carried buckets before," she told him sharply.

"I wasn't there to do it, that's why." He took the rope handles from her, and began striding across the camp site between the rows of tents that looked like pale pointed ghosts in the darkness. "Careful of the ropes," he warned. "You'll go sprawling if you don't."

"Haven't you got things of your own to do?" she challenged as she followed.

"I'll get them done, never fear."

"Very sure of yourself, aren't you?"

"That makes two of us." He put the buckets down outside the tent and turned to her. "That's why you didn't remain a trooper's woman."

"You know too much for your own good," she told him, bewildered by what he was saying. She sensed he was somehow more worldly even than Sam Clarke, yet there was none of Sam's kind fatherliness in his manner. He made her feel uncomfortable, even though she was curiously drawn to him. Especially when he smiled, as he did then.

"I can teach *you* all I know," he offered. "We're going to be travelling together for the next few months. If there's anything you want, come to Noah Ramslake."

"And what'll you get out of it?" she demanded.

"Your lively company on a journey that might prove to be my last."

With that poignant rejoinder he turned and walked off, leaving Mary to waken her mistress. She was relieved to see the other bed already vacated and guessed, by the absence of the folding wash-stand, that her employer was elsewhere preparing for the day. It was impossible not to hesitate for a few minutes, because Lydia DeMayne looked so lovely lying asleep with her dark hair spread across the pillow, and the lace at the throat of her nightgown frilling around the very white skin. Then Mary remembered she was supposed to collect tea first from Collins, and went outside again in search of him. He had it ready on a tray—a flower-patterned cup with matching saucer, and a plate containing buttered bread cut so thin she wondered that anyone would taste it.

But her mistress did not wish to wake up, and Mary abandoned calling her name to shake her gently by one shoulder. "It's morning, mum," she said bluntly. "At least, everyone's up and getting ready to go."

"But it's dark," came the protest.

"They always march early so's to miss the heat," she told her mistress matter-of-factly. "Where shall I put this?"

"On the small table . . . oh, bring it to the bed!" came the irritable reply. "I can hardly reach it there, can I?"

Doing as she was told Mary reflected that her youthful mistress was plainly expecting life to be as easy as possible on the march, and it would be as well to anticipate the fact if she wished to please.

"I'll bring in water for you to wash," she said, "although I see the Captain has took the cloth bowl on legs. I'll get Collins to fetch it back."

"Wait outside," came the sleepy rejoinder. "I'll call when I want you."

Collins brought the wash-stand, then continued cooking his officer's breakfast while Mary waited impatiently for a summons. Time was flying, and there were all the clothes to pack into the trunks which had to be loaded along with the furniture on to the mules tethered to a nearby tree.

"This water'll be cold before long," she grumbled softly to Collins. But he was engrossed in his own tasks and made no answer. "Them eggs smell good," she remarked wistfully. "Any chance of one?"

"Certainly not . . . but I might manage a bit of bread dipped in the grease," he said relenting. "And a mug o' tea."

She was just finishing her breakfast when a figure loomed out of the darkness and pushed up the flap of the tent to enter. It was impossible not to hear what followed, and Mary realized she had made her first mistake. She should have ignored her mistress's orders.

"Lydia, we march off in fifteen minutes!" came the ejaculation. "I had imagined you to be dressed and ready to ride. I see that girl brought you some tea. What is she doing outside kicking her heels instead of bringing water and generally waiting on you? I told you from the start that she was unsuitable."

"You had taken the wash-stand."

"I sent it back fully twenty minutes ago."

"Please don't raise your voice, Rowan. Is it your wish that the entire camp should hear how you speak to me? I notice none of the other officers shouting at their wives."

"They have no need. I'm sorry, Lydia, I did not mean to sound brutish. But the other ladies are already gathering outside."

"What paragons they must be," came the cutting response.

"Not paragons—just military wives on the march. I ask no more of you than to be just that."

"I have not yet heard you *ask*. You have stormed into my privacy to berate me on something with which I am completely unfamiliar, as you well know. I'll be glad if you will now leave so that I can rectify my deplorable failings compared with the other ladies of this regiment."

Next minute, the tent-flap was pushed up with some force, and Rowan DeMayne came out to say sharply, "Take some water in to your mistress, at once. Then start packing with all speed. I want this tent down and the mules loaded within fifteen minutes. In future," he added, glaring at Mary across the dying fire, "don't idle around here preventing Collins from doing his duty while your mistress is kept waiting. And I doubt she'll be best pleased to be attended by someone in clothes that look as if they have been slept in."

Despite her brave words to her husband, Lydia DeMayne seemed as fearful of his wrath as Mary while they embarked on a race against time. Haste made Mary's fingers clumsy, and her mistress finally pinned her own hair up into a severe coil that emphasized the paleness of her face, before fixing a plumed hat on the coiffeur. The errant wife then mounted and rode off beside her husband when 'Advance' was sounded. But Mary was left with a panic on her hands as the ponderous baggage-train began to move off while she was still folding clothes and packing them into the leather trunks.

It was her first lesson as a lady's maid, and she was to learn many more as the journey progressed. It was bound to take time, she knew. No one could learn a new job overnight. She must remember not to sleep in her dress again. Even so, Captain DeMayne had noticed her, which he never had before. That was surely a good sign. And so had Noah Ramslake, although in an entirely different way. He was riding with his troop again, and she missed him.

A week slowly passed. The first excitement over leaving Khunobad had faded as everyone realized the departure from one place was separated from arrival at the other by a very long time indeed. Routine took over. Mistakes were rectified so that the setting-up of camp became faster and easier as time went on. Aching muscles gave less trouble as they grew accustomed to the daily punishment, and life in a tented camp became not a great deal less uncomfortable than it had been in cantonments, with meals supplemented with fresh fruit and vegetables from villages they passed. In fact, the Advance Wing of the 43rd Light Dragoons voted life on the move a splendid innovation.

The officers' ladies had different views. What spelt freedom for the men meant great privation for the females who missed their homes, their luxuries, their elegant social life. Lydia DeMayne was no exception, despite the relaxation of playing her precious piano that was being carried across India on a camel with Kit Wrexham's items of heavy baggage. When the instrument was unlashed and placed on a carpet in the midst of trees or open lush meadows so that the graceful girl in satins and lace could play for those clustering round on folding-chairs or camp-stools, Mary was always on the periphery enjoying the spell cast by the music. But she often wondered what the Indian villagers made of such a strange spectacle. Would any of them believe this was a regiment going to war?

The musical outlet did little to help the growing moodiness of Mary's mistress, however, and it was clear to her that relations between the DeMaynes were growing more and more strained. She privately thought the Captain should give his wife a good shake now and again, and was astonished at the readiness with which he accepted her excuses and the gentleness with which he countered her petulence. She came to the conclusion that Rowan DeMayne was so dazzled by the beauty of the girl he had married so swiftly, he could not see beyond it. But, to someone who had known him during those days in the hospital, she wondered how long a man of his calibre would remain blinded by a lovely face and form.

Mary took to life on the march and thrived on food that was better than she had ever had in her life, and on the excitement of the sights she witnessed crossing the vast continent. She had longed for wider horizons and a chance to learn: this journey gave her both. Happier than she had ever been, even with Sam Clarke, she blossomed as her life became fuller and brighter than she could ever have imagined. She missed no detail of the splendid vistas when they passed through the hills, of the picturesque villages full of people with great dignity despite the squalor of their lives, or of jungles housing bright birds, monkeys, snakes and even the elusive tiger.

The officers went hunting, but never caught one, and whenever there was anything interesting in the vicinity of their overnight stop—a beauty-spot, caves, a temple—they mounted expeditions to relieve the monotony for their wives. Mary longed to go, but was never given the opportunity. Although her duties were very demanding, she would gladly have found the time to go exploring every aspect of this land she was leaving.

After the first fortnight she was acting the part of lady's maid with confidence, her employer's sharp criticisms spurring her on to perfect her ability. She watched the De-Maynes with continual fascination, and listened to the voice that made words sound like music. If his wife could produce magic with her fingers on a keyboard, he could do it with speech, in Mary's opinion. He certainly noticed her these days, but only because her way of speaking irritated him. She tried to learn from him, listened to what he said and the way he said it, then copied it when alone. Having gained his acknowledgement of her existence it strangely did not seem enough for her now. She wanted to earn his approval.

Noah Ramslake more than made up for her employer's lack of praise, and his company undeniably contributed toward her happy state during those early days on the march. He was an educated man, and they talked of everything under the sun during those days he rode with the baggage-train. When he had to ride with his troop, he usually made his way to where the DeMayne pack-animals were tethered which was where Mary settled for the night, and sat chatting with her as the camp-fires lowered to no more than crimson glows in the darkness between the regimented rows of tents. Mary could not analyze her feelings for him. She loved those long quiet talks as she waited for her mistress to retire, she missed him when he was with the troop, and something told her that when he eventually tried the old game with her she would not want to avoid it. But a faint feeling that he was too clever for her made her cautious. All the time her employment with the DeMaynes continued she was independent. Time enough to consider the demands of a man when there was no alternative.

For the first two weeks the weather had been easy for marching, but now they had travelled so far south-west it began to grow more humid and uncomfortable. Mary found walking more wearying, and perched on a waggon more often on those early morning marches. The humidity increased Lydia DeMayne's irritability and, inevitably, the sharpness of her husband's tongue. After an evening in which Mary had been so worked-up she had let slip too many errors in speech, Rowan DeMayne had told her to get out and stop bombarding his ears with a voice that was more offensive than the bray of a pack-mule. She had quit the tent furious with herself for giving him cause to treat her that way, and tried to make excuses by telling herself she was making too much of a bad temper brought on by her employer's long session that evening with the difficult and unenviable task of breaking the wild horses, which had brought a complaint of marital neglect from his wife the minute he had walked in hot and dusty to greet her.

Disconsolate, she took her plate of supper from Collins and went across to where she had stretched her blanket between two of the empty leather trunks for the night. She had worked very hard at improving herself. After that first night, she had never slept in her dress again; she washed and ironed her own things each day when she did those of her mistress, and her new-found skill in arranging hair had encouraged her to put her own brown tresses up in more attractive fashion. In addition, she really had tried to remember those phrases the Captain had corrected in forceful manner. But she supposed, somewhat gloomily, the ways of a lifetime would take a long time to change.

She had just finished her supper when Noah appeared out of the darkness to stand smiling down at her. "You look as stormy as the weather tonight," he commented with amusement. "Has 'Madam' been riding roughshod over you again?"

"If you're going to talk about Mrs DeMayne like that, Noah Ramslake, you can take yourself off smartish," she told him grumpily. "I won't have no one . . . *anyone*," she corrected quickly, ". . . speaking of her that way, and that's flat."

Her reprimand made him laugh softly as he squatted on his haunches before her. "So it's 'His Nibs' again, is it? The

Honourable Rowan DeMayne! He has no cause to look down on anyone. He joined the 43rd to get out of England. Did you know that? Tried to kill his own brother over some woman no better than a trollop, and was hounded out of the country by his own set."

Mary glared at him as she leant back against a trunk. "I don't believe a word of that. He wouldn't run away, not him."

"What about that last mission, then?" came the gentle probe. "He still hasn't told anyone what happened, has he? If it had been to his credit, he'd have been full of it. A man always wants to hide the things he's ashamed of."

Mary thought of that native ragged beggar covered in blood and filth who had been carried into the hospital that morning, and the terror that had ruled him during his delirium.

"Or things that horrify him so much he don't . . . *doesn't* . . . want to remember them."

Noah's teeth gleamed in the darkness as he smiled. "So he has more than high-flyers worshipping at his shrine."

"And what does that mean, Trooper Clever-boots?" she countered.

"Watch out, my girl, that's what it means. You've heard what happens when serving-girls make sheep's eyes at lords."

"That's it, you've got your marching orders," she snapped, insulted by his inference. "If you don't go, I shall."

He straightened up in leisurely fashion, the smile still on his face. "As you wish. Get well under cover tonight. There's a storm on its way judging by the sky over there beyond the hills."

Turning her back on him she studied the violent lightning flashes that continually lit the darkness to the west. But she ignored his soft taunt that thunderclaps were not confined to this section of the camp before walking off and leaving her still fuming at his words.

The storm broke half an hour later, bringing with it a total deluge without any warning. In a matter of minutes Mary was drenched to the skin as the wind flung rain in every direction, tugging at trees and tents with tremendous force. Thunder cracked like cannon-fire all around the encampment and lightning sizzled earthward to illuminate the battered area with eerie light. Gasping, Mary clutched her cloak around her as the ground turned to a mire before her eyes. The tethered mules were braying in fear and pulling at their restraining ropes. From all over the camp came faint shouts as soldiers battled to keep the guy-ropes of their tents from being snapped or turned out to run to the lines where the troop horses were picketed for the night. Soon, she heard bugles sound 'Stand to' through the uproar of the elements.

Huddling beneath her blanket, a sudden lightning flash showed Mary her employer leave his tent hastily pulling on his boots as he went, then start off in the direction of the place where the unbroken horses were kept in a makeshift corral. But he had not even passed the place where she sat before a new deeper thunder roar grew in the opposite direction, making her turn in alarm. Next minute, out of the darkness came a stampede of wild-eyed beasts mad with fright as they ran blindly to escape the cause of their fear. During another lightning flash Mary saw Rowan DeMayne start forward instinctively as if to attempt to halt the leader, but he was knocked violently aside as others swerved outward from their course, and she watched horrified as the white-shirted figure somersaulted through the air to fall heavily a few feet from her.

She was scrambling forward when a group of mounted troopers galloped past in pursuit of the runaway horses, sending mud over her in a great liquid mass. But the rain was so heavy it washed her clean and she battled against the wind to reach the body lying so still she feared he must be dead. There was certainly no sign of life as she reached him, but her instinct was to drag him clear of any others who might rush past without seeing him lying there. Although he was a big man the ground was now so slippery it was possible to pull him by the legs into the lee of the piled travelling trunks. Her second tug brought such a yell of pain

it made her nerves jump. Yet it told her he was very defi-
nitely still alive.

Knowing he was safely out of the path of possible horsemen, Mary left him lying in the downpour to run to the tent
for help. But Lydia DeMayne was huddled in the corner,
apparently paralyzed with fear. She heard none of Mary's
words, her eyes did not even register who was there before
her. But the hands that could produce spellbinding music
reached out to seize Mary's dress and hang on with such
fierceness she could not free herself.

"He's hurt," Mary yelled in her urgency. "He's out there
hurt. Come and help me bring him in. I can't lift him on
my own."

Teeth chattering, shaking violently, her mistress just
stared blankly as she clung to the dress as to a lifeline. Filled
with inexplicable fury Mary hammered at the restraining
hands with her clenched fists, wanting to hurt the other
woman.

"Don't you care about him?" she cried hotly.

Tearing her dress as she finally pulled away, she rushed
out into the night again to find help had come unbidden.
Noah was standing by the injured man, looking around into
the obscurity.

"Thank God you're here," she greeted, grabbing his arm.
"Them runaway horses knocked him for six. Give me a hand
to get him over there to his bed."

To Noah's credit he did as she said without question,
telling her as they bent to pick up the heavy body that the
horses had crashed through the wooden corral and careered
through the camp in fright.

"There are several tents down and some men hurt," he
grunted as they lifted a dead weight between them. "I saw
them come this way and worried about you."

"I'm all right," she told him, "but she's over there in a
right state that'll be no help whatever to him."

Even with Noah's help she found it hard going holding
his legs as they carried him across that storm-swept clearing.
But she had helped to carry drunken or sick troopers on

more than one occasion and battled on without losing her
hold on the drenched trousers. Pain made the victim yell
unrestrainedly once or twice, and Mary brought curses down
on his useless wife shivering in her corner. If she was like this
in a mere storm, what use would she be to him on a battlefield? He would want more than a pretty face and piano-
playing then.

Once inside the tent they ignored Lydia as they placed
the injured man on his bed. Noah lit the oil lamp to hold
up for an inspection of the situation, and Mary saw the cause
of the trouble immediately.

"Look at that right arm, Noah," she said breathlessly. "I
think it might be broke."

"Broken," muttered the patient. "I'm sure it is."

"Best get someone," Mary told her friend, staring at the
face on the pillow that had become so familiar to her now.

"I know a bit about things like this," said Noah putting
the lantern safely on the ground. "I'll never get anyone while
this storm's on, and we can't leave it like it is. It needs a
splint. You hold him still while I straighten it out first. Then
I'll find something to tie it to."

Putting her trust in his confidence, Mary took hold of the
shoulders in the soaked silk shirt, feeling the warmth of the
body beneath coming through. She was worried about his
paleness. The fall had been bad, and she was surprised he
was even alive, much less conscious. He squirmed as she held
him, and his eyes registered his brief agony as they fixed
themselves on her face during the assault on his twisted arm.

"I've got the . . . perfect excuse to . . . have my . . . sword
. . . on the left again," he grunted as Noah gently settled the
arm alongside his body. "That'll fix . . . Daubnay." Then he
passed out.

Letting out her breath in a deep sigh, Mary began to
cover him with blankets, saying as she did so, "Do you still
think a man like him would have anything to be ashamed
of, Noah?"

CHAPTER SIX

The lamp was burning low when Rowan opened his eyes to find a girl watching him with intent curiosity. She had a face that was deeply browned by the sun, grave yet full of liveliness, a mouth that showed determination and brown hair parted in the centre and arranged in braided coils behind each ear.

"Is your expression of stupefaction due the fact that your somewhat haphazard ministrations did not finish me off?" he asked quietly.

Thick eyelashes flickered nervously as she got to her feet. "If I knew what you was asking me, I could answer it, sir. I don't understand them long words."

"*Those* long words." He shifted his head slightly. "How is my wife?"

"Sleeping. I give . . . *gave* . . . her a powder. I doubt she'll be fit to ride—leastways not first thing."

He sighed. "I'll organize a *dhoolie*, or a seat on a waggon. My troop is to form the advance and rearguard today. You will remain with your mistress, since I cannot."

With thoughts of the day ahead he moved his shoulder experimentally, then grunted with pain. Sergeant Dobson, the medical orderly travelling with the Advance Wing, had pronounced the injury to be no more than a badly wrenched and bruised joint that would take a few days to settle down again. Telling Rowan it was sure to swell and prevent natural movement, he had also promised that the blow on the back of the head as he fell would be liable to cause dizziness for a short time. But it seemed to have caused more than that. His sleep had been beset by fleeting glimpses of horrors he had resolutely subdued two months before, and he had the distinct feeling he had volubly protested against their return. Had this girl been with him throughout the night hours?

"Have I been noisy?" he asked her.

"A bit . . . but there was no one to hear it but me," she said. "They're already on the move outside. Collins is making your tea."

Throwing back the blanket with his left hand he struggled to sit up. "Tell him to leave the tea to you. I need him here to help me dress. I hope, for his sake, he has my other trousers clean and pressed. These are in a disgusting state." He looked down with distaste at the only garment he was wearing.

"The storm took down Collins's tent," said the girl without any obvious relevance that he could see.

"That'll teach him and his fellows to pitch it more firmly in future," he growled, finding the throbbing in his shoulder growing worse. "Go and see to the tea. It's a simple enough task for you, although I don't doubt Collins will feel his sensitivities immeasurably bruised over it."

She went out, and he sat on the edge of his bed looking at Lydia. With something amounting almost to a feeling of guilt he knew overriding disappointment. For two weeks he had been making excuses for her; telling himself she had not been brought up to army life and could not be expected to cope with the journey as easily as those females who had. But there were other wives with the contingent who were no more experienced with campaigning, yet had settled to the routine after only a few days.

As he studied the creamy curve of the throat he had kissed

so ardently on many an occasion, he allowed that his wife was excessively feminine and artistic by nature, and to expect her to accept easily what he found stimulating and fulfilling was foolish. But he was forced to admit that he had not expected that she would demand constant attention when it was plain he had duties to attend to. Neither had he dreamed he would ever feel embarrassment over her behaviour. So total had been his pride in his wife, it had been a blow to discover she caused him some awkwardness in front of his men.

In the cantonment life followed an established social pattern. On the march—especially going to a war—it was vastly different. Camping made everything more intimate and on equal levels. Long boring marches were made bearable by camaraderie that was not necessary in barracks; the prospect of war filled men with the need for personal contacts and reassurances they did not desire in peacetime. The joy and personal sense of salvation Rowan had found in a girl who now possessed all his senses, he wanted to share, in some part, with those he led. As Troop Commander, he wished his wife to complement him and his authority at a time when the troopers had had to abandon their own wives and any other female company for an indefinite period. A good officer encouraged his wife to know the names of those under his command and show interest in their welfare. Together, they should ride the length of the moving column to encourage the men who were growing weary, and they should stroll around the perimeter of troop tents of an evening to show concern for their comfort and morale. Even the roughest, most reprobate trooper, could blush with pleasure when asked how he was feeling by a soft-spoken lady in elegant silks. An officer's wife could often do more for their spirits than her husband in times of unrest or danger.

As he studied her sleeping form Rowan ruefully admitted that he had taken for granted that love for him would be all Lydia needed to accept something she had never wanted to do from the start. Then his feeling of guilt deepened as he told himself that time would make no difference, because she had no intention of trying to accept it. It was a dilemma with no solution. The scandal surrounding their marriage had made it impossible for Lydia to go anywhere else, yet accompanying him to the Crimea promised more hazards than the battlefields awaiting them.

He ran a hand through his hair restlessly. Even loving her was difficult these days. Tents were notoriously un-private with camp-beds designed for one person only, and then provided he lay relatively still on it. Only once since leaving Khunobad had he managed to coax her on to a pile of rugs after the camp had settled for the night. But he had been left unsatisfied and bad-tempered by her lack of generosity at a time when desire had been heightened in him by her music earlier that evening. Knowing how wonderfully passionate she could be had only made his frustration greater. Yet, when she smiled at him in the centre of a crowd, or stood close laughing into his eyes, as she had done the previous afternoon whilst out viewing a waterfall, his heart turned over with excitement. But, in the early hours, with throbbing bruises to remind him of what he had to do that morning, he had to fight back worries of what lay ahead. India was a relatively benign country to cross compared with Egypt. How would Lydia cope with the desert?

With a flurry of grey skirts the girl was beside him again, holding a mug of tea and something that looked remarkably like a steaming wad of bread spread with a mess with an extremely vile smell.

"Where's Collins?" he demanded.

"Gone to sort out your clothes, sir."

"What is *that?*" He took the tea, looking suspiciously at what she held in her other hand. "I trust it is not your idea of a hearty breakfast."

To his surprise she burst into laughter, which he thought the most attractive sound she had yet uttered. "Lordy, no! It's to put on your shoulder."

"To *what?*"

"It's the best thing for something like that," she continued, surveying his bared torso with great interest. "It's swelling up fast. That blue'll change to purple, then black before it's done."

"You're a real Job's comforter."

"It comes of being used to troopers falling or being thrown, sir," she explained, apparently unaware of the meaning of the expression. "We always used to plonk one of these on quick, and it worked a treat."

"Did it, by God," he murmured, fighting a smile.

"It's best as hot as you can stand," she said pointedly. "This is getting cold while we are talking."

"Then put the abominable thing where you think best. I'll take your word on the medicinal qualities . . . but it had better work, my girl."

"It'll work," she promised with grave confidence. "Mind now, it'll take a while yet."

With that she slapped the steaming poultice on to his shoulder, and he let out a shocked yell as the concoction burnt his skin. Thankful that he had kept her talking as long as he had, he gave her a scowl between grunts of pain caused by the way she was expertly binding the thing into place with a length of cloth.

Her mouth twitched as she worked. "Don't worry, sir. They all yell when it first goes on. That shows it's hot enough to do a power of good."

"How very reassuring," was his dry comment.

Collins arrived with the uniform and hot water to wash and shave. The girl went without a word, taking the empty mug. Rowan felt incredibly giddy when he stood up, but fought it as he lathered his face in the dim light thrown by the lamp which, now that the storm was at an end, could be safely hung from the pole.

"I'll have to go after those horses, Collins," Rowan explained to his batman. "It might take several days to catch them all—that's if we're lucky. I'll ask Mr Anstruther to look after my wife until I rejoin the column. He'll also have to lead C Troop in my absence. It's damnable ill-luck that the storm should have struck at night." He shook his head to clear the giddiness, but it only worsened, so he stopped what he was doing in case he cut his own throat. "Collins, how do you get on with that girl?"

"Mrs Clarke, sir?"

"What do you know of her?"

The little man looked confused. "Know of her? I'm not sure what you mean, Captain DeMayne."

Holding his razor in the left hand as the lather began drying on his throat, he said irritably, "She seems to be on very familiar terms with the men—particularly Ramslake. Is she to be trusted?"

"As to that, sir, it wouldn't be up to me to say. She was born into the 43rd, sir, and married Rafferty of D Troop."

"Why is she known as Mrs Clarke?"

"Sergeant Clarke also left her a widow—oh, must be nine months ago now."

"Sergeant Clarke? He wasn't a married man."

"No, sir, but he took young Mrs Rafferty at the graveside, I heard. Then the poor creature was burying him four months later."

Rowan thought for a moment, then said softly to himself, "Good lord, how much happened when I was away!"

"After that, Mrs Clarke helped at the hospital. Captain Winters can probably tell you more when he comes up with us at Bombay."

Lost in thought Rowan made another attempt to remove the very dark stubble on his chin, peering into the mirror Collins held up to catch the best of the light. A very faint memory of a quaint creature who looked as if she had seen a ghost stirred in his mind. Could she have been at the hospital when he was there? Was this the same girl whom he had seen tending the troops on the day he had left with Gil?

Major Benedict decided to declare a rest day, after all. He had several reasons for the decision. It was essential to recapture the lost stallions, everyone had had little rest during that stormy night, and Mrs Benedict had disappeared again. The ageing wife of the second-in-command had been mentally disturbed since their young daughter had wandered into the horse-lines and been kicked to death by a regimental rogue stallion. Following on the loss of her twin sons from cholera two years before, it had been more than the poor woman could take. Never more than gently bewildered, she suffered from periodic wanderings, and from kleptomania. Major Benedict always knew where she put the things she stole and hostesses were confident silver cruets, spoons or knick-knacks would be returned to them the following day. When she vanished it was a little more worrying, because she slyly evaded the servant instructed to watch her. She had never come to any harm during her absences, but her worried husband realized she was in a strange area now, and he would not know where to look this time.

Rowan was relieved at the news that the column was to stay put for a day. It would make his unwelcome task easier, knowing they would be one day's less journey ahead when he had recaptured what he could of the lost horses. He was also relieved he would not have to send Lydia off that day. Knowing it was useless to set out himself until dawn, he lay back on the bed after hearing of the reprieve. But he could not sleep. The pain in his shoulder gnawed at his nerves, and he could not shake off that feeling of disappointment in Lydia. It was ridiculous. He loved her with his life, he would defend her against any man, or any number. Her beauty and vivacity set him afire. How could he find her wanting? Yet, undeniably, he did.

When he eventually dragged himself up from the bed to eat ham and eggs brought by Collins for his breakfast, Rowan discovered the stiffness he expected to feel in his right shoulder and arm was relatively minimal considering the force with which he had been thrown on to it. The girl Clarke was right, perhaps. She would be useful on this journey.

Dressed ready to set out he gently awoke Lydia to explain the facts to her. She seemed full of fears, clinging to his sound arm and gazing up at him with apprehensive eyes.

"Rowan, you are in no fit state to go anywhere," she

begged. "Major Benedict must see that. You should rest for a few days, then travel on in a *dhoolie*. You have been badly hurt, I can see by the strain on your face. It is inhuman to send you out like that . . . and those horses will be miles away by now. It is imbecilic to go out after them."

"Darling, those animals are my responsibility," he said, with patience despite the advancing morning. "Daubnay put me in charge of training them as troop-horses."

"He did not expect you to be with them night and day. Besides, he is not here to order you to recover them."

He took her hands from his arm. "I have to recover them —at least, as many of them as I can. They were costly beasts and are our only spare mounts for when we arrive at the Crimea."

She looked down at his hands while they held hers. "We may never arrive at this rate. I wonder there is anything left of the camp."

"It was only a storm," he said as gently as he could. "The men know how to peg their tents well down, and how to cope with all kinds of weather. It is always like that on the march or campaigning."

Her beautiful pale face turned upward again. "What do you know of campaigning? Rowan you speak so . . . so *joyfully* of something you have not yet experienced."

He frowned. "If I do, it must be because I am a warrior at heart."

"Well, it has always been apparent that you are not a peaceful man . . . and I saw last night that you were excited by the storm. Yes, Rowan, *excited,*" she insisted accusingly.

He sighed. "You are wrong, love. I was merely spurred into action by it."

"You certainly gave no thought to me," came her damning pronouncement. "You quit my presence muttering something about horses, and did not give a second look at the one who should have been your first concern when there was danger."

"But you were perfectly safe," he said in bewilderment.

"Was I? How could you be so confident of that?" She

drew away from him and left her bed to stand a few feet away. He thought she had never looked more beautiful. In the long nightgown with her dark hair curling down over her shoulders she was too enticing to leave for several days. He cursed that storm . . . and those horses.

"Rowan, when I was a small child I was caught in a storm when walking in the grounds of my home with my governess. She ran with me to the shelter of a tree." Her hands began to twist within each other as she spoke of something that plainly caused her great distress. "Lightning struck that tree and she fell at my feet with her face twisted and burned. Since that day, I have been terrified of storms. I cannot stop or control it, and when you left me alone last night I felt totally abandoned by you."

He stepped forward quickly and drew her into his arms to bury his face in her hair that always smelled of rose petals. Guilt and remorse filled him. "My darling, I did not know. How could I have known? Why did you not tell me when I so obviously meant to go out?"

"Would you have stopped to listen?"

The gentle accusing question had to be answered honestly to himself. The feeling of guilt increased as he knew he must set out immediately on his search for the missing animals. There was no time to explain, to show his continuing love.

"We have had so little time together, and so much has happened to keep us from knowing all we should about each other," he murmured before putting her away from him reluctantly. "When I get back I shall enquire so deeply into your past there'll be nothing I do not know about you."

"When you get back?" she echoed faintly. "You do not still intend to go?"

"Lydia, I *must*. I thought you understood that." When she refused to say anything, he went on crisply, "Mr Anstruther will look after you in my absence, and it might be as well to have that girl of yours close by all the time. She appears to have vast experience of military life."

"Which I have not. You persistently disregard that fact, Rowan."

"I hoped you would attempt to learn." It was out before he knew.

Flushing she said, "Who is to teach me? You are always off on some duty or other, when you are not with those wild horses, attempting to school them. Now they have run off, and I am to be left while you chase fruitlessly around the country in search of them." Putting her hand up she threaded her fingers through his hair to pull his head down for her teasing kiss that played with his mouth, while her slender body arched against his. "Stay with me, my dearest, and teach me all you wish me to know."

The whispered invitation was all he had longed for over the past days, and his body was already responding to his desire as he put her away from him with a faint groan.

"Never have I cursed duty more. Wait three or four days and I will teach you what it is to be in paradise."

She stepped back from him, colour heightened and eyes full of disturbing glitter. "All that has ever mattered to you is the chance to prove yourself a bigger hero than your brothers, and recover the approval of those who shunned you. Go to your duty with your precious regiment."

It took his party three days to find and make captive fifteen of the horses. It was a period of exhaustive riding during daytime heat, and sleeping in the open during the hours of darkness. There was danger involved in cornering and roping the beasts who had tasted freedom and fought against the restraining lassoes. Then came two days of hard riding to overtake those who had forged ahead, with none of the advantages of cooked meals and relaxing company at the end of them. Even so, Rowan would have found physical and professional satisfaction in something that demanded a great deal from a man, despite his wrenched shoulder, if it had not been for his black thoughts during that period.

Lydia had suggested his only interest in life was the regiment as an instrument to banish the slur on his name. Was she right? Did he care more for that than for the girl he had compromised so badly she had been left with no alternative but to marry him? No, or he would never be filled with such driving unhappiness over a situation he had been forced to leave unresolved. But the means of winning her over was elusive. That damned tent was impossible. He could tumble a wench within its confines with no difficulty, but a girl of high birth was a different proposition. Lydia would not thrill to conquest of the earthier variety, he knew.

They rode back to camp on the fifth day and he had to curb the longing to seek out his wife in the tent at the head of C Troop lines. But the lesson of losing the horses had been well learned, and he first made certain they were well tethered in a corral formed by loaded waggons. That done, he mounted again and trotted round the perimeter of the camp, filled with ridiculous nervousness at the coming reunion.

The nervousness vanished as he came upon a convivial scene outside his own tent. Kit Wrexham was sitting in relaxed ease beside Lydia, who was dressed in crimson silk shot with scarlet as flames from the camp-fire put changing lights upon the skirt. True, Gil was also in the group, with Tom Anstruther making a fourth, but the red-haired man was laughing into Lydia's eyes in a way that suggested some kind of sway over her.

Rowan's head began to pound with impotent fury, and in that moment the deeply-buried horrors within him stirred dangerously. Staring at that scene it subtly changed before his eyes until there before him was a dark-haired woman clothed in blood, and a group of laughing men around a fire challenging him to make an impossible choice.

A cry of involuntary protest burst from him, and he spurred his horse into a headlong charge at that unacceptable scene before he was aware of what he was doing. Only when he was no more than a few yards from them did reality show him the shocked staring faces of men he knew well— white men! Instinct took over. Dragging on the reins he crouched low across his mount's neck for the mad jump. Tired though it was, the stallion—the same that had crossed the nullahs with him so many months before—again met the challenge. Horse and rider sailed over the stunned group with mere feet to spare, and came to a halt, both breathing hard, just short of the trees where a girl sat beside the pack-mules in company with a trooper.

Confused and shaken Rowan dropped from the saddle and stood for a moment with his face against the neck of the beast in strange brotherhood with a spirit he knew was as wild as his own, trying to orientate himself. Next minute, someone had taken the animal in charge, and he looked up to see a man from his own command.

"I'll see to Cavalier, Captain DeMayne," said the confident educated voice.

He turned away abandoning the horse, and blinked as he stared toward his tent. Lydia was standing in a shimmering gown of dark red, looking at him with all he could ever want to see written in her expression. The grouped chairs were empty. He began walking toward her like a man in a daze, pulling his forage-cap from his head as he did so. Her fingers threaded through those on his left hand to draw him into the tent. Once inside, she was immediately against him, gripping his thick black hair to pull his head down to hers.

"That was madness . . . you could have *killed* us all," she said against his mouth.

She was trembling with excitement, and her tone denied any hint of fear. There was a sense of triumph in her whole demeanour as he stood before her hot, dishevelled, covered in dust, aching in every limb, and still trying to shake off that moment of *déjà-vu*. But, when a discreet cough outside preceded Collins's voice saying, "Shall I bring water and fresh clothes, sir?" he murmured thickly, "Later. I'll shout when I want you."

Things resumed their normal course just before three A.M. as the Advance Wing and its cumbersome baggage-train prepared to set off again. But Gil had a cryptic comment to make on the event of the previous evening, wandering up as Rowan checked his saddlebag and water-choggle prior to mounting to lead the advance guard that morning.

"I thought you knew your colleagues better than that, old fellow," he commented remarkably mildly after greeting Rowan with a 'Good morning'.

"Better than what?" He was busy and therefore somewhat abstracted.

"Without you here for protection, I regret the other ladies angled their well-bred backs away from your wife, to a certain extent. It's a lot of damned feminine nonsense, but young Tom Anstruther had felt inadequate to rectify the situation. He enlisted the help of the two remaining troop-commanders—both of whom do not have a lady with them, you will mark."

Rowan turned at that, some of what Gil had said sinking in at last. "I'm hellish busy, Gil. What is it you are trying to tell me?"

"Dammit, Rowan, you know what a parcel of females are like when they get a bee in their bonnets."

"I should have thought they had more to do now they are accompanying their husbands to war."

"Yes . . . well, the fact don't seem to have registered with 'em yet."

"Wait till we reach the desert, then it will," he promised grimly.

Gil fidgeted about adjusting his shako, shifting his sword-belt, and generally looking so uncomfortable, Rowan relented. "My friend, you had best speak your mind clearly, or I shall be out on the road before you have found the necessary courage."

Taken unawares, Gil coloured slightly. "You know too well what I am about this morning," he blustered. "When a man is away his friends naturally look to his wife in every respect. There was no call for such damned bad behaviour, you know. It . . . well, it casts a slur on our honour."

Rowan burst out laughing. "Oh, Gil, you dear old fellow, one of your most engaging facets is your impeccable *uprightness*. Did I once say I suspected you of dallying with Lydia in my absence?"

"You *said* nothing," came the hearty reply. "You damned near killed us all instead."

He sobered slightly. "That was not what it seemed, Gil. But I would never mistrust you. If you ever once betray a tenor voice, however, I shall call you out to settle it with sabres."

"Now come, Rowan, young Wrexham was no more . . ."

Laughing again Rowan prepared to mount. With his foot in the stirrup he looked back to say, "If you protest much more, Gil, I *shall* start to suspect you." With that he swung into the saddle and moved off through the criss-cross of men, horses, waggons, camels, mules, elephants and native servants to where his leading subaltern was trying to calm his highly-strung stallion that was anxious to be on the move.

"Hey, Tom, you'd best heed my advice and get rid of that individualist before we leave India," he called heartily. "At the first cannon-roar he will take you off in any direction he wishes. If it is to the rear you will be branded a coward; if to the front you'll be dubbed a fool—a *dead* fool, without doubt."

The youngster grinned with cheerful disregard of the warning. "I'll have him sweet and docile by the time we arrive, I swear."

"Never. It is a fruitless hope!"

"Do you care to wager on it?"

Rowan grinned back, full of happiness and well-being. "I'll give you a hundred to one if you achieve it."

The boy's grin faded a little. A hundred pounds was a lot of money to an impecunious junior lieutenant. But he accepted the odds in a spurt of bravado. "Done! I shall use my winnings to purchase a fleece-lined coat. My cousin writes that the troops are wearing all manner of strange items by way of uniform at Balaclava. So long as it keeps them warm and dry, anything is apparently acceptable."

Rowan pulled a face. "Until the pretty 43rd arrives to show them how a regiment should look. I cannot see Daubnay allowing you a fleece-lined coat, lad."

Anstruther slapped his now steady horse on the neck, and said slyly, "Nor you a weapon that is worn on the right, sir."

He laughed boisterously. "If it comes to another confrontation I shall wear two—one for show and one for fighting, for I cannot draw and wield a sabre with my right hand, however hard I try."

They signalled to Major Benedict, who had found his wife in a cave with another officer's valuable silver ornaments, and then slowly moved out to head the column on the next section of the march leading to a range of hills that constituted the worst terrain they had yet had to encounter. They planned to encamp for the night at the approaches to the hills.

After almost three weeks of nomadic life it seemed as normal as any other, and the small advance party rode with leisurely confidence through the dark early hours. Rowan was happy in the knowledge that Lydia was riding with Gil at the head of A Troop that day. Yet, even as he remembered the wonderful reckless urgency of the previous night in her arms, a small voice told him he must attempt to remedy the cause of the other ladies' shunning of his lovely wife. Lydia still shut the regiment out of her life: she must be persuaded to think of herself as a member of it or she would be unhappy forever.

An hour after dawn they came to a narrow river running from the hills beside the track they were following, and Rowan made the decision to halt for the usual short break. Not only was it good to douse one's head in the river to banish somnolence, it was a spot that gave a fantastic vista of the morning hills. Not normally of an aesthetic turn of mind, Rowan nevertheless stood with water running down his face from his wet hair, surveying the distant beauty with appreciation born of happiness and physical well-being. *Anything* would look marvellous this morning.

It seemed almost an insult to natural grandeur when he noticed three horsemen approaching from the hills. But his feeling of initial irritation changed to one of curiosity when he saw it was a British officer flanked by two native cavalry-

men plainly coming to meet them. He knew there was a
military station some miles to the west of the road they were
taking. Could they have been sent from there to intercept
them?

The officer smiled a greeting as he approached. "Ah, glad
I caught up with you when you were halted. I've been on
the road since midnight, and I'm damned tired and thirsty."
The way he swung from the saddle betrayed his weariness,
and he came up to Rowan saying, "Lieutenant Grassmore
of Hooper's Horse. Mind if I duck my head in the river
before giving you the news?"

"I'm DeMayne. Help yourself," invited Rowan waving a
hand at the river. He was still curious rather than alarmed.
The man would hardly be as casual as this if he carried vital
papers.

A moment or so later Lieutenant Grassmore stood beside
Rowan and Tom Anstruther, water running over his face
and throat as it did theirs. He was smiling blissfully at the
refreshment of it.

"Hellish hot, even this early," he commented. "I envy
you going to the Crimea."

"From what I've heard you've had plenty of action of your
own with the local insurgents."

The man grinned. "Not quite the same as you've had,
Captain DeMayne. Been hoping to meet up with you. Even
down here we've heard of your exploits."

"Oh, really? So what brings you to meet us?" asked
Rowan coolly, wandering across to a mount on the other side
of the road away from where the troopers were sprawled on
the riverbank. The other two followed him.

"I have an item of news which came down to our cantonment through the usual means. We were asked to intercept
you along this road. Enquiries at the village at the foot of
the hills told me you were still back here. Frightfully glad
you'd progressed this far, old fellow. Saved me another day's
journey."

"It must have been urgent news," prompted Rowan.

The round youthful face darkened by the sun broke into

a faint smile. "Not really. Nothing you can do about it. The Rear Wing of your regiment has been delayed a week at Khunobad. Seems no sooner had your Headquarters detachment marched out with due pomp and bombast than the local chieftain surrendered to duress from his bastard half-brother and mounted an attack on the station while it was considerably undermanned."

"By God . . . Khairat Singh!" exclaimed Rowan furiously. "I *knew* he was a treacherous devil! Was the cantonment overrun?"

"Not entirely. But it was serious enough to force the military to call everyone into the cantonment perimeter for several days. The 43rd lost a few men, but a deuce more rifles," came the calm information. "That's what they're usually after. They'll use 'em in the next attack against the men they stole 'em from."

"There won't be another attack, in my estimation," murmured Rowan. "The ingoing regiment will have arrived, and it is more than likely *they* will see the truth of the situation there."

He was back in thought in Khunobad, seeing the rich palace and the man who had made such a trusting friend of Maurice Daubnay. He could only reflect on the irony of military action occurring only when the bulk of the 43rd had left the garrison. Was ill luck still following the regiment? Would they all arrive in the Crimea to find the war over?

When the rest of the column caught up with them at the restingplace, Rowan and his small detachment had to prepare to depart again almost immediately. All talk was of the news from Khunobad, of course, and Gil as one of those who had left loved ones back at the station was very concerned about the safety of the residents. Rowan took his friend across to Lieutenant Grassmore for details, had a quick word with Lydia to ensure that she was all right, then had to set off.

"When we reach camp I shall be all yours to command," he said warmly, "and I shall not have to form the advance guard again for several days."

"You are never all mine to command, Rowan," she pointed out quietly. "You belong to the regiment."

"So do you, my love. You'll see that as we go along."

With that, he kissed her and mounted ready to depart. But he was deep in thoughts of the developments at Khunobad which drove away the problem of having to discuss with Lydia the duties of a Troop Commander's wife. He rode for a while occupied with the evidence of Khairat Singh's duplicity, and it was some time before he was drawn from introspection by the youngster swaying in the saddle beside him.

"Those are fearful groans you are making, Tom. What is amiss?"

"I think I'm about to be most frightfully ill," came the faint reply. "Oh, damnation, it's too late!"

Rowan watched him drop from the saddle and lurch to the side of the track. "Let that be a lesson to you, lad," he called out unsympathetically. "I'm always cautioning you on your passion for mangoes. Catch us up when you have emptied your stomach."

It was a longer than expected ride to the area chosen for the camp, just beyond the village and a mile or two from the hills. So the morning was well advanced by the time Rowan's party arrived to survey the place and decide where best to site the camp. The two officers had spoken little to each other since Tom had rejoined them, although the troopers had been full of talk of the attack on Khunobad, voicing their envy of the lads bringing up the rear who had already been blooded against an enemy.

Seeing what he thought was a good flat area circled by trees, and giving views in every direction for piquets, Rowan turned to his subaltern.

"Tom, get those horses . . . oh, dear God," he breathed as the youngster pitched from the saddle and began vomiting into the earth while his body strained and arched convulsively as he lay.

Acting quickly he dropped to the ground and began dragging Tom across to a clump of trees. Then, as he wrapped

the boy around with blankets from both saddlebags, he
called to his NCO whom he trusted was not yet suspicious.

"Corporal Chase, picket your horses and start marking
out the lines. The column will be riding in shortly, and I
don't want any confusion like we had at the waterfall. Make
it snappy now!"

"Yes, sir," said the Corporal gazing across with interest.

"Mr Anstruther has eaten too many overripe mangoes, I
fear." He forced a smile. "No doubt we shall also have some
of the men sorry for themselves."

"Yes, sir. Can't stand them myself. Too squashy by half."

Fortunately he walked off to supervise the marking of
lines, and Rowan forced another smile for Tom's sake.
"There you are, lad. Too squashy by half, according to
Corporal Chase."

But the victim was retching, doubled-up and moaning
with pain, far too ill to appreciate light banter. Doing what
he could to ensure the boy was concealed from the troopers
by ferns, Rowan looked back along the track they had travelled and saw the dust from the approaching column.

"Carry on, Corporal," he called across the clearing in a
hearty voice. "I see them on the horizon. I intend going to
meet my wife. Should you encounter any difficulties fire your
carbine, and I'll return."

At the end of a six-hour ride his horse was tired, but it
gamely recrossed the few miles at a fair speed. Rowan met
up with Gil leading his troop at the head of the column.

"Where is Lydia?" he asked sharply, instantly worried.

"Back with Wrexham. Now, Rowan, don't fly into a
mood," Gil added with a swift attempt at pacification.
"Young Denison is also there with Mrs Benedict." Then he
saw what must be written on Rowan's face. "Why have you
come back? Is there trouble ahead?"

He fell in beside Gill momentarily. "Just checking on the
state of the men, that's all."

Gil raised his eyebrows. "Not one hundred per cent, I
think. Must have been those damned mangoes from the

village yesterday. I don't mind admitting *I* feel devilish queasy—and you look as sick as a spade."

Rowan fought a battle with himself, then told Gil the truth, in a low voice. "We have cholera riding with us. Anstruther is finished, and there'll be no hiding it by to-night."

Gil stared at him. "There's no doubt?"

"None!"

A wry expression twisted Gil's mouth. "Thanks for your honesty. I'll cheer my men in. I don't want them dropping here."

"That's why I rode out to meet you. I'll work my way down the column and have a word with all the officers."

He swung his horse round and headed back along the straggling column, filled with anxiety that forced him to give Lydia no more than a cursory salute as he passed. He would sooner send men out to face ten times their number than lose them to a filthy loathsome disease and watch their death-throes. For the same reason, the other officers swore to persuade any man who was feeling sick the cause was overripe fruit eaten the previous evening. So dread was the disease of India, men mentally dug their own graves the minute the first symptoms struck. But there was no way of preventing the truth from eventually becoming obvious, and they could only hope the men would not realize it until camp was safely set.

It was later than usual before Rowan, as Duty Officer, could get to his tent for a meal prepared by Collins. Lydia was sitting in a wrapper with her hair hanging loose. She did not berate him for his lateness, and they were both silent as Collins served cold meat and some preserved vegetables with wine. Only when the servant left the tent did Lydia look across at her husband and say, "Mrs Clarke has told me what ails the men."

"I see." He was taken aback, unsure whether or not to be angry with the girl who seemed to know as much about the regiment as he for telling Lydia something he had hoped to withold from her as long as possible. "I trust she has not been putting it out amongst the men."

"I think not. She says they have seen it too often to believe for long that the cause is bad fruit." She watched him tackle his meal but left her own untouched on her plate. "How is Mr Anstruther?"

He looked up across the table. "He is gone. He wished to be a hero in battle, but he rode in here a dying man and I did not know of it. That is courage enough for anyone, I think."

After a moment or two of shocked silence, she put her face in her hands as her shoulders began to heave. Depressed and worried he found her tears unacceptable. This was only the beginning. There would be many such deaths before the attack subsided.

"I cannot believe it," she said through her weeping. "A mere few hours ago he was laughing as you set off . . . and only yesterday he was telling me of his sisters in England of whom he is so fond."

"Then they are the ones to weep for him, Lydia. All they will know of it is when a communication reaches them some two months hence. If you feel compassion, you will write and tell them of your sympathy at his passing."

She lifted a wet face to stare at him. "But I hardly knew him."

He sighed. "Then why the extravagant tears? I am asking you, as the wife of his Troop Commander to pen a few lines of commiseration to Tom's family in England. I shall send my condolences with his effects, but think what comfort a letter from a female would be to a grieving mother and sisters who will scarcely believe his young life ended so cruelly."

"I see you manage to enjoy a hearty meal, as if he were of no account."

He gave her a long look. "Any man's death is of great account, but those of us who are not victims will help no one by going into a decline. The worst aspect of cholera is the fear and despair it engenders. We have to help the men believe they will survive it, or we shall have no regiment left to take to the Crimea."

She got to her feet, rocking the table with her swift movement. "Is that all you ever think of? Is *that* why you are aiming to keep your men alive—so that they can be killed in battle instead?"

He also got to his feet. "Yes, perhaps it is, Lydia. If they have to die they would rather it was in honourable fashion."

"Honourable fashion!" she cried contemptuously. "Death is death, Rowan, and they do not all share your passion to become a public hero. I suggest you ask them if they would prefer to be shot to pieces."

"Why don't you ask them?" he asked quietly. "You might find out something about the regiment you have joined." He dropped his napkin on to the table and prepared to go out again. "If you cannot bring yourself to speak to the men on the subject, I suggest you approach Gil. He has been ill since arrival and is only still on his feet through sheer effort of will. Southerland-Stewart is preparing to take command."

"Oh no!" she exclaimed on the verge of fresh tears. "Rowan, can nothing be done?"

"Yes . . . those who are fit can abandon the indulgence of self-pity and attempt to raise morale." He clapped his forage-cap on to his head and pushed up the tent-flap. "Eat your food, Lydia. I cannot have my wife fainting from hunger when others are dying all around me."

His throat was tight with anger and disappointment as he made his way to Gil's tent. What had happened to the joyous understanding they had shared last night? Did it extend no further than the bed?

Gil was not in his tent, and Rowan was informed by the worried batman that Captain Crane had taken himself off into the bushes with a brandy flask. It was there Rowan found him, shaking and beaded with sweat, dragging himself determinedly back and forth until the next spasm shook him and he was forced to dive into the bushes.

"Gil," he greeted heartily. "No one expects you to stay on your feet when everyone else is taking a well-earned rest."

"Then why aren't you?"

"I am Duty Officer."

"This is the . . . only way . . . to defeat it," his friend groaned, straightening up from another retching attack. "I must keep upright. It's impossible for a man to die if he is standing up."

Intensely worried at the stage Gil had reached, Rowan forced a light laugh. "There's logic there, I have to admit. Here, lean on me while you recover a little."

So they walked back and forth together, Rowan practically carrying Gil along at times, while the sick man talked himself into remaining alive.

"I'm damned if I'll die in this disgusting fashion, to be put under a mound by the side of the road, while you go off to honour and glory at Balaclava," he panted in real agony from the pain clawing at his stomach. "I'll not give Daubnay the satisfaction of keeping one of his precious toy regiment from facing bullets that might spoil his . . . pretty uniform." The last two words were wrenched from him as he dropped to the ground, despite Rowan's supporting arm. He lay there staring up helplessly, teeth chattering and life emptying from him in the most debilitating manner. "I can't get up again," he moaned. "God help me, I haven't the strength left. But I will not die here, Rowan. I *will* not."

"Of course you will not," he echoed with determination. "I'll fetch a *dhoolie*. You'll have to ride this out more gently, old fellow."

He hurried off to the medical tent, but the situation there was critical. Sergeant Dobson himself was in the final stages of the killer disease, and there were rows of men waiting for the harassed orderlies who knew they could do nothing to help. The very sight of comrades dying before their eyes made others give up the ghost, Rowan knew, so he went to see Major Benedict about the possibility of separating the sufferers. The second-in-command was already putting the plan into operation and had sent a galloper back to intercept Headquarters Wing three days' march behind them on the same road.

Returning to where he had left Gil, Rowan spotted one of his troopers walking past and called sharply to him. "Ramslake, I have a job for you."

The man turned and came over immediately. "Yes, sir?"

"Are you feeling fit?"

"Yes, sir, perfectly."

"Good. You helped Mrs Clarke when I had that fall, didn't you?"

"That's right."

Rowan smiled. "I haven't thanked you for that. You're a strong stout fellow. Help me to carry Captain Crane to his tent. I do not intend to take him to lie in a line of puking men until an orderly finds time to dose him. This way."

Gil was on all fours, which was as far as he had managed to get toward standing up, but the spasms were coming more frequently, showing that he was nearing the crisis of the illness. Rowan was deeply worried at the sight of him. They carried him to his tent and dropped him on the bed, but Gil's determination was being undermined by the onset of delirium. If he were left alone he was liable to slip quietly away without anyone knowing. Yet, as Duty Officer, Rowan was unable to stay by his friend at the most vital time. He stood looking down at Gil, indecisive for a few moments. Then he dismissed Ramslake, asking him to fetch Mrs Clarke immediately. After the trooper had gone, Rowan wondered if he had done the right thing in bringing a servant-girl to look after a sick officer. But there was no alternative. It was useless to ask Lydia, and the girl had apparently helped at the hospital. Anything was better than letting Gil die for the want of someone to talk him into holding on to his life. Besides, a servant could be given orders; a wife could not.

The girl appeared in her neat grey dress, looking decidedly apprehensive as she looked up at him through shadowed eyes. But she spoke up before he could say anything.

"Madam told me you were angry with me. But she was upset, and it's my experience that not knowing and imagining things for yourself is worse than being told the truth, however bad it is. I didn't spread it around, sir. The men know cholera well enough to recognize it when they see it."

"Yes, I see," he murmured, struck by her calm practicality in the face of panic.

"I only done what I thought best."

"*Did,*" he said absently, thinking she could not be more than eighteen. "You appear to have the right philosophy, Mrs Clarke. Would you be willing to stay here with Captain Crane and talk him out of dying?"

It was plain she was surprised, but no more than he at finding he had made a request rather than issue an order.

"Yes, sir. If you think I can."

He found himself smiling down at her resolute brown face. "Keep up a non-stop prattle, and your abominations of speech will do the trick, I swear. He will have to hold on in order to correct them." He turned to go. "I'll return whenever I can to see how he goes on."

"Captain DeMayne, what about your wife?"

He halted in the entrance to look back at her. She seemed to have filled the canvas cone with confidence already. "She can manage without your services for a while, I should imagine." He smiled again. "You can't be expected to do everything."

By sunset there were eleven blanket-wrapped figures ready for burial, and the spirits of those in camp were pressed under the weight of fear. Gil was holding his own, but another subaltern had succumbed along with Tom Anstruther. It looked to be a virulent germ this time, and Rowan went about his routine as Duty Officer with a heart as heavy as any man's beneath his outward confidence. The 43rd had been dogged with ill-luck throughout its existence. Was it to be entirely decimated before facing a foe on equal terms?

With such thoughts for company he was walking back in the firelit dusk for one more look at Gil when his steps slowed in disbelief. From the direction of his own tent came the sound of lively singing to a musical accompaniment.

There was only one such instrument with the Advance Wing; there was only one person who could play in a way that made music cascade from the keyboard. Heart thudding he stepped quickly toward the head of C Troop lines, feeling a sense of bizarre enchantment in an evening hung with the smells of India, quiet with a sense of fear, purple-dark between the evenly-spaced glow of fires, peopled by men in agony, yet riven by the culture of another, far-off world.

He thought it a moment he would never forget, however long he had left to live, as he broke into the clearing to see Lydia, in her most elaborate dress of yellow satin and wearing the emeralds he had given her as a wedding present, playing as if she were seated in the most elegant salon. Candles in the sconces illuminated her perfect creamy skin and heightened the blue brilliance of her eyes. Rowan felt a lump forming in his throat as he surveyed the troopers gathered around, the flames of the fires bathing their plain blunt features with yellow light, singing lustily such popular songs as 'Master Robin's courtship', 'Threading through the buttercups', and 'Greensleeves'.

The place, the time, the situation were so very different yet, as he watched Lydia put new life into fearful dispirited men, Rowan felt the same breathless yearning as on the night he had stumbled intoxicated into a salon and encountered a pair of flashing sapphire-blue eyes. It remained with him as he forgot all else but the girl who possessed his senses, until it grew to such proportions he thought he would burst with the yearning.

When she finished, acknowledged the applause and cheers of her audience as she got to her feet, Rowan went forward quickly, knowing this wonderful girl was his alone. He took her hands, saying with difficulty because he was so moved, "I was so wrong—so very wrong. You are truly a lady of the regiment."

She smiled dazzlingly at him, then half-turned to draw forward a figure from the shadows. "Captain Wrexham persuaded me it would be beneficial for morale, and lent me his music. Was it not a splendid idea of his?"

"Yes . . . indeed," said Rowan hollowly.

The Advance Wing moved off, as usual, at three A.M. the next morning. The ranks were greatly depleted and the sick contingent at the rear was swollen to alarming proportions. A small detachment was left behind to bury those about to die. The *dhoolies* were all filled, so other patients had to be jostled and bumped in the hackeries, or stretchers slung between mules. All the ladies in the party now rode with the sick, doing what they could to keep up the spirits of those who grew progressively worse.

At dawn, Corporal Chase died. Four more succumbed shortly afterwards, and a digging party was detached to see them buried deeply enough to prevent native raiders from disinterring them to steal their clothes. When two more died an hour later, Major Benedict decided to carry the bodies to the next camp for burial, or he would be leaving so many digging parties along the road his column would be split into indefensible groups.

Gil, placed into one of the coveted *dhoolies* by a determined Rowan, was holding on with great tenacity, even managing to chat to Lydia as she rode alongside him as soon as it was light enough to see clearly. But it was to Mary Clarke that he gave his heartfelt thanks, despite the embarrassment she showed at being so singled out by an officer in front of the troopers.

By the sixth day, during which time they had straggled through the hills on roads both rough and stony, crossed streams and negotiated upward and downward slopes, there were no fresh victims. Those who had the disease were holding on to their lives by thin, but unbreakable threads. The epidemic had been short-lived because they had been on the move, but they had lost two officers, their Sergeant-Orderly, two corporals, eighteen troopers and twenty-two camp followers. Most distressing of all was the loss of young Mrs Southerland-Steward, wife of Gil's leading lieutenant.

With her two young children she had been travelling with her husband as far as Alexandria, where she had intended embarking for England to spend the duration of the war with her parents in Essex. Her husband was extremely distressed, and the children were taken in tow by another officer's wife with a son of four, also intending to leave the regiment at Alexandria. The widower was left with the prospect of selling his furniture and his wife's possessions on reaching Bombay.

Mrs Southerland-Stewart's funeral was conducted separately, and the remaining officers' wives picked wild flowers from the hillside to place on her grave. This death—the last in a long series—broke the spirits they had bravely maintained over the past few days, and mad Mrs Benedict vanished again. A search party discovered her wandering aimlessly with the dead woman's silver-framed mirror, gazing at herself in it and singing a lullaby popular with her own lost children.

But it was not only amongst the ladies of the officers that despair had set in. Knowing they were destined to be paid off in Bombay in any case, quite a few of the Indian servants had left the column, slipping away into the night in the belief that the cholera was travelling with the British troopers.

So Mary found herself part of a much smaller group with the baggage as they drew nearer to Bombay, and she enjoyed Noah's company even more during the long weary treks each day. But she was nevertheless taken by surprise when her employer walked across from his tent one afternoon as she was resting during the worst heat of the day, for he usually sent for her, if wanted. Scrambling to her feet she could not help thinking, yet again, what a fine-looking man he was, and what a grave mistake he had made in marrying a woman who would do nothing to stabilize his career—or him, for that matter!

"Yes, sir, does Madam need something?" she asked as he stood looking her over assessingly, arms folded and leaning nonchalantly against a tree trunk.

"No." He continued his scrutiny. "I think I have never adequately expressed my appreciation for your ministrations to Captain Crane. I would not normally expect my domestics to undertake such responsibilities . . . but we are not presently experiencing normal conditions, are we?"

She had no idea what he was saying, but guessed it was something to do with the time she had sat with his sick friend.

"Sam was taken with cholera. I couldn't save *him,*" she reflected sadly.

"Sam?"

"Sam Clarke."

"Ah . . . yes. Collins told me all about that."

"All about what?" she asked suspiciously, not liking the idea of being discussed behind her back.

"I was absent from Khunobad at the time," he explained mildly.

"Oh yes, so you was."

"*Were.*"

"Were."

"Collins also said you had helped in the hospital."

"I didn't want a third husband, that's why."

He was quiet for so long she began to feel uncomfortable beneath his speculative gaze. "Sam was good to me. I wasn't going back to a barrack-block after that," she said defensively. "And Colonel Daubnay has got a proper sense of honour," she added for good measure, thinking it would impress him and put an end to his questioning.

But it produced a chuckle and fervent agreement. "That he has . . . but what do *you* know of it, girl?"

Since Mary had never fully understood the meaning of Harry Winters' words that day, she evaded an answer. "Is there something you want me to do, sir?"

Still leaning casually against the tree, he sobered. "Were you helping at the hospital when I was there?"

She nodded. "When they brought you in I thought you was . . . *were* . . . dead. Later on, it almost seemed you wanted to be."

He changed the subject abruptly. "How old are you?"

Growing increasingly bewildered by an interview that seemed to have no purpose other than prying into her affairs, and uncertain what he was really up to, she said airily, "I don't know."

"Nonsense," was his crisp reply. "You've been married and widowed twice. That must make you at least thirty-four."

"*What?*" she cried in protest. "That I'm not! I was eighteen last New Year's Day."

"Then why did you not say so?" came the smooth challenge.

She glared at him. "Is it that important?"

"To you, obviously." His sleepy eyes studied her face for a moment or two. "How old were you, in God's name, when you first took a husband?"

Her refusal to answer brought a corresponding silence from him, and there was an expression in his dark gaze that she could not fathom, yet which strangely warmed her. Then he nodded briefly.

"Quite right. It's none of my affair."

"I didn't say that," she told him hastily.

A faint smile touched his mouth. "I know . . . and you would doubtless have phrased it more bluntly, if you had. But here's something that *is* my affair. My wife feels she would like you closer to her, from now on. So I have decided to purchase a mount for you in the next village."

"A mount?" she repeated in stupefaction.

"A horse. Something to *ride*," he clarified in teasing tones.

"Me ride! That's daft," was her immediate response.

His sleepy eyes narrowed. "I shall decide what is 'daft' and what is not, Mrs Clarke."

"Well, this is," she declared roundly. "I've never rid a horse in my life."

"Oh, for God's sake," he expostulated in soft tones. "I've never *ridden*. Surely you've heard me say that enough times to remember it."

She gave him a straight look. "I can't remember everything you say."

"Neither do you heed it, my girl, that much is obvious." He shifted to a more comfortable position against the tree. "So it seems you have never ridden a horse in all your short mysterious life with a cavalry regiment. Well, well, how excessively unique you turn out to be!"

She sensed he was laughing at her, so she retaliated. "Have you ever stuck a needle in a boil . . . or washed twenty pairs of cotton drawers?"

"By George, no," he chuckled. "Neither have I any wish to."

"That's the same to me as riding a horse is to you."

He held up his hands in a gesture of surrender. "Your point is made, girl. Now can we call pax?"

She looked at him suspiciously. "Is that a horse?"

Fighting to control his mirth, he spluttered, "No, my dear, it is not. But it looks as though I have a rider to break in besides a cluster of wild horses."

She was dreadfully alarmed at that. "I can't get on one of those mad creatures!"

His smile was deeply attractive, and just for her as he said, "Don't you mean 'one of *them* mad creatures'?"

The teasing sentence was made in the most silken tone that lovely voice could produce, and Mary knew, with a sudden lurch inside her, that the most incredible thing had happened. This man, this officer, this person who was the son of a lord, had stopped treating her like a servant and more like a person in her own right.

CHAPTER SEVEN

A, B, and C Troops of the 43rd Light Dragoons arrived at the spot a day's march from Bombay where they were to await the rest of the regiment, at the beginning of February 1855 after more than eight weeks on the road. The horrors of cholera had been pushed to the back of everyone's mind, together with the sadness over those who had been lost. Soon, there would be the voyage with bracing sea air and relaxation on decks; a welcome break in the marching routine. There would be a farewell to India, the continent that had taken more members of the regiment than they cared to remember.

Seven years of upholding the power of Crown and Empire. Seven years of sun, sickness and stench. Seven years away from the green homeland and beloved families. Seven years that could nevertheless not be dismissed from their minds by the departure from these shores. Harsh and unrelenting though it might be, India was in their blood for good or bad, and a small part of them all would be left behind when they sailed. Friendships had been forged, strange customs had been learned, understanding had been broadened; there had been dazzling sumptuous spectacle, luscious women, stunning vistas, unforgettable plants and animals, princes and paupers—mostly paupers. Some would depart leaving all they held dear under the soil of this continent; others would leave a great deal richer in pocket and experience.

There was one member of that company encamped outside Bombay who had been changed almost beyond recognition during those seven years in India. Arriving as an eleven-year-old child of the regiment tramping through the dust behind the drum, Mary Clarke was about to depart as a mature, twice-widowed lady's maid, who rode behind her aristocratic mistress and slept in her own small tent a stone's throw from that of her employers. With that burning desire to learn forever flaming in her, she had almost perfected the art of arranging even the most complicated coiffeur, was a faultless laundress of delicate garments which she could also repair with almost invisible stitches, and could read her mistress's mood infallibly. She inspired confidence; she gave service with respectful but un-servile dignity. She corrected her slovenly speech with furious devotion to detail, listening to *what* was said in addition to *how* it was said. But, as she often had to tell herself, Rome was not built in a day, and the ways of eighteen years could not be banished in two months.

The horse-riding was almost a catastrophe until she persuaded her tutor he had much better let her do it *her* way and ride astride. Since he was adamant that he would not let his wife's maid don a pair of dragoon trousers for the purpose, Mary compromised by turning the skirt of one of her grey dresses into a pair of voluminous wide-bottomed trousers that allowed her to ride astride but still appear decorous. Her appearance had caused some mirth amongst the troopers at first, but one look from the commander of C Troop was enough to iron the laughter lines from their faces. For Mary, it was a giant step in her bid for 'respectability'—one of which she had never dreamed. Not only was it an exciting luxury to ride with the column, as if a member

of the regiment, but the riding lessons had forged a relationship with Rowan DeMayne she could scarcely credit.

Now that he had broken that seemingly unbreakable social barrier, he revealed to Mary a personality that was the
key to so many doors that had been closed where he was
concerned. Unused to men of his type, Mary nevertheless
knew male prides and weaknesses well enough to recognize
the unhappiness that was covered by immersion in some
other outlet. It did not take a great brain to deduce the cause
of his unhappiness, and she was to wonder many times at
the incredible weakness of otherwise strong men when it
came to a pretty face.

In her rôle as servant she saw behind the public façade
adopted by her employers. Their marriage was proving a
disaster, and she was not in the least surprised. Whilst Lydia
DeMayne had been a gracious sweet-tempered person
amidst the luxury and attention of her life in Khunobad, she
had now become carping and petulant, driving her husband
to the depths of frustration at a time when he had more than
enough on his mind. Mary thought anyone could have seen
that her mistress's basic selfishness would make her totally
unsuitable as a soldier's wife. Whatever had possessed
Rowan DeMayne . . . There, Mary always broke off in her
musings, for she, more than anyone save Harry Winters,
knew exactly what had possessed him. When Lydia Moorfield had come on the scene, the man Mary had watched
over in the regimental hospital had been seeking escape
from something that had threatened his sanity. Because of
that he had tied himself for life to a girl who would surely
drive him back to that same desperate state before long.

If Lydia DeMayne chased the smiles from her husband's
face, Mary saw them in abundance during those half-hours
every day when, relaxed in shirt-sleeves and breeches, he
taught her the rudiments of riding. He seemed an entirely
different man—perhaps the one he had been before that
other scandal over a woman six years ago. During those
lessons he seemed very much at ease in her company, to the
extent of discussing regimental problems with her and ask-

ing her solutions to them. At times, she suspected he was teasing her, but he always listened with interest, dubbing her his 'oracle'. Unaware of the meaning of the word, she had asked Noah. It had made her ridiculously pleased. But, although during those happy times, she found chatting to him a natural and stimulating occupation, she sensed there was a difference once the riding-lesson ended and they both returned to normal routine.

Even so, those days leading up to arrival outside Bombay produced a happiness inside Mary that made her dizzy with fulfilment. They were incredible, educational, exotic days when it seemed anything could and did happen. And the closer she grew to the man who had been the source of inspiration to her, the broader grew her appreciation of the world around her. For Mary there would be no looking back when they set sail from India. Out there beyond the sea lay a whole lifetime of discovery for a girl who had once believed the world no more than a washtub and twenty pairs of cotton drawers a day.

But widening horizons also meant the accompanying yearnings. Education bred dissatisfaction. In Mary's case it was personal dissatisfaction. Her world was now rosy enough, heaven knew, but she felt inadequate for it. Her personal appearance had improved beyond recognition, and she was trying very hard with her deplorable speech. But it was pointless knowing how to say words if a person could think of no words worth saying. She wanted knowledge that would give her the power of easy conversation . . . like Rowan DeMayne! How many times he made remarks in teasing tones that eluded her because she did not know the meaning of words she had never heard before. Sam Clarke would have explained them, taught her their meaning. Captain the Honourable Rowan DeMayne expected his listeners to know!

There was a partial answer to her problem. Noah Ramslake. Her enthusiasm overcame caution where the good-looking trooper was concerned. She therefore unhesitatingly agreed to go with him to visit a nearby beauty-spot after he

had asked her employer for permission to take her one afternoon. With a choggle full of water Noah arrived to collect
her exactly when he had promised, and they set off side by
side, Mary aware that they were being watched by those
dark sleepy eyes that missed nothing.

They said little as the animals picked their way towards
the tree-lined track leading to a lakeside temple, and they
passed others of their party returning from a visit. But once
they reached the dappled shade of the track, Noah turned
to smile at her.

"I never thought the Captain would agree."

"Didn't you?" she said in surprise. "He's a very reasonable
man."

"Reasonable?" he echoed with a laugh. "I've heard some
epithets used about him, but never that one."

She rode for some moments thinking about the word
'epithet' and making a guess at what it meant. Then she said
hesitantly, "Noah, you know such a lot. Where did you learn
it all?"

"Well, my dear, I went to school, if that's what you mean.
And I'm a few years older than you. Living is learning, you
know."

She turned quickly in the saddle. "There you are . . . you
see? That's what I call a clever remark. What is it that makes
a person think of things like that to say?"

He grinned. "Brains."

His teasing made her cross. "Everyone's got brains. It's
how you use them that makes you different."

"Different from whom?"

Colour crept into her cheeks so unexpectedly she could
think of nothing to say immediately. But persistence came
to the fore. "You've never told me about yourself . . . about
school and things like that."

"Neither have you, Mary."

Her shoulders rose briefly. "Me? There isn't anything to
tell. I'm a child of the regiment. That speaks for itself. But
you're different. I know troopers like the back of my hand,
and you're not like the rest." She cocked her head sideways

as she looked at him earnestly. "What's a man like you doing
in the army anyway? And why aren't you a sergeant or
suchlike?"

He rode on as if deep in thought, so that there was just
the soft fall of hooves in the dust and the slumberous heat
of the afternoon all around them that was filled with the
singing of insects. Then Noah said reflectively, "I was too
good to be a sergeant, and not quite good enough to be an
officer. So they solved the dilemma by making me a
trooper."

She thought about that and tried to make some sense
from it. Then she asked, "Are you content to be a trooper?"

He glanced across, his attractive face shadowed by overhanging trees. "Were you content to be a trooper's
woman?"

Sensing that he was almost as complex as the man she
served, Mary tried a fresh attack. "Have you got a family in
England?"

His mouth twisted. "Oh yes, indeed I have. Every honest
upright citizen should have a family."

Thinking of the one she had never really had she asked,
"Are there any brothers and sisters?"

"Two sisters, five brothers . . . at the last count."

"Lordy, that must have been a houseful!" she exclaimed,
trying to picture it and seeing only a vision of a barrack-block
with rows of beds and a communal urine-tub in the centre.
She had no idea what an English house looked like. "Is that
why you took the shilling?"

Her companion appeared to be far away as he said, "In
a way. It made life easier for them."

Well into her stride, Mary continued her questioning.
"Do you get letters from them?"

"They never know where I'll be," was the vague answer.

But Mary was full of her own thoughts. "I've never had
a letter. But, then, I've never writ . . . written . . . one,
either."

"If you want one so badly, I'll write you one," he said
softly.

"Well, that'd be really daft!" she exclaimed. "Letters are for when you're away somewhere. What could you put in it that I wouldn't see very well for myself?"

"That I've grown very fond of you, Mary Clarke."

It took her completely by surprise, and yet she had sensed there was a purpose behind the friendship. In her experience, men began by making saucy remarks, followed by cruder ones which were, in turn, followed by fumbling hands on breasts or buttocks. This was something new, and it made her more wary than the usual approach. A good poke in the chest, or even a knee in the groin dealt with the other situation. Was he telling her he wanted to tumble her? If so, she had to be careful with her answer in case it suggested that she agreed. She had never thought much of the business when married to Jack Rafferty, and certainly had no intention of warming any man's bed now . . . or any wish to.

Inspiration came in time. "All right, then, put it in a letter to me."

He looked at her assessingly. "You're getting very quick, my girl. But I suppose you've got an astute tutor."

"I don't know what that means," she said truthfully.

"Captain the Honourable Rowan DeMayne, that's what it means, Mary."

Instantly defensive, she said, "What about him?"

"You spend too much time in his company."

"I work for him."

"No, you work for his wife." He pursed his lips as he studied her face. "Getting to know him quite well, aren't you?"

She turned back to gaze at the track ahead. "I don't think he even knows himself well. Ah, there's the lake, at last. I thought I catched . . . *caught* . . . sight of it just now through *those* trees."

There were others at the lake and inspecting the temple, so their conversation was limited to remarks on all they saw as they handed their mounts to natives jostling for the coins they demanded for the service, then strolled around the side of the water toward the temple. Noah offered her his arm,

and she pushed her hand through the crook of it as she had
seen her mistress do when walking with the officers.

The little gesture made her feel very grand and she was
suddenly swept with yearnings once more. Walking like a
lady did not make her one. Ladies did not wear cambric
dresses that were really full trousers. She had been a fool to
insist on riding astride instead of sideways, in a long elegant
skirt. Riding astride was not 'respectable' and that was what
she wanted to be more than anything.

As they strolled slowly together Mary tried to remember
all she had observed of her mistress, then realized it could
not be applied to herself. During exertion even ladies per-
spired in the heat of India. But they had sweet-smelling
lotions to pat on to their pale skins. Mary's brown flesh was
beaded with it now, and all she could ever do to stay fresh
was constantly wash herself. (Funny how the thought had
never occurred to Mary Rafferty!) And Lydia DeMayne
always cast up glances at her escort from beneath beautiful
feather-trimmed bonnets. Mary had never worn a bonnet in
her life, and she always looked a person straight in the eye
in forthright manner. But the illusion of respectability was
too pleasant to spoil as she strolled with Noah. She knew he
was a handsome enough escort for any girl, and thought it
strange that he had said he was too good to be a sergeant
and not good enough to be an officer. It was one of those
sort of things people said that she did not really understand.
Rowan DeMayne would know what it meant, of course.

The temple was not much different from the others they
had seen along the route, and they sat on a stone wall to eat
some fruit Noah bought from a woman squatting beside the
lake. It was then he saw the tower on a low mound a short
distance further on, and suggested they investigate.

Sensing that he might have another motive for leaving
the sightseers behind, Mary said doubtfully. "I don't suppose there's anything there. It's a look-out, isn't it?"

"I should imagine so . . . which means there must be a
good view of the surrounding area." Noah stood up and
smiled at her persuasively. "I thought you were avid for

knowledge, Mary Clarke. Think what you could go back and tell your mistress—or master—if you see something surprising."

Refreshed by the fruit, she found herself smiling back at him. It was difficult not to when he was being so charming. "All right. But I must put these sticky fingers into the water first, or I'll have flies all over me."

They took the climb in easy stages, Noah helping with a hand beneath her elbow when the surface was uneven, chatting as they went in comfortable friendship.

"We'll climb to the top and look out over the view," said Noah. "It might be possible to see the tallest buildings in Bombay. That would be almost as good as being there."

She glanced up at him as they neared the tower. "You sound anxious to move on."

"Oh yes," he nodded. "I can't wait to get on that ship and away. I've no love for India."

Remembering snatches of conversation between her employers, she then asked, "Are you like the rest—can't wait to reach the Crimea?"

"Not quite . . . but I'd like to keep on the move. Ah, here we are! There's a door over there to the right."

At that point Mary realized there was a dreadful smell hanging in the air, and she hesitated. "It's a bit lonely and it seems a funny sort of place."

"Abandoned, I expect."

"It smells horrible up here," she pointed out, still hanging back.

"All these places do. Come on, let's investigate the view now we've climbed all the way up here." Taking her hand he walked up to the door in the cylindrical stone building and pushed it open.

Mary only got one foot inside before she pulled up in total horror. There on a grating in the hollow centre of the tower lay a partly-decomposed body, the flesh hanging from the bones and clothed in ants. Filling the space was the aura of death to make anything she had yet seen in her life pale to insignificance. Rooted to the spot by the initial shock, it wore off to send Mary spinning round on her heels and running, hand to mouth, out into the sunshine and the living again.

She ran blindly, so filled with fear of the gruesome sight she did not notice the stones or shifting ground during her headlong flight. Brought to a halt by losing her balance, she fell down just as Noah caught up with her. Going on to his knees beside her he drew her up in his arms until she was sitting against him.

"Mary . . . Mary, my dear, it's gone now," he said urgently.

With a gasp she turned against him, and his arms closed protectively around her as he murmured more reassurances.

"I'm sorry . . . deeply sorry. I would never have taken you up there if I had realized what it was."

"What is it?" she asked against his sleeve, still feeling the chill of decaying death around her.

"It must be a *dakhma.* I've heard about such places where Parsees leave their dead, but I've never seen one. I'm so sorry. Please forgive me."

His distress broke through Mary's temporary panic, and she pulled slightly away from him looking up into his troubled face. "It's just that it was so unexpected, that's all. It wasn't your fault, I know that."

"But I took you up there—almost dragged you inside. Will you ever forgive me?"

He seemed so very upset she felt impelled to put his mind at rest. " 'Course I will, silly."

Then, as they still sat there in a close embrace, it seemed the most natural thing to do when Noah dipped his head to kiss her gently on the lips, for her to kiss him back. When he kissed her again the pressure was harder, and his hold much tighter. After the shock she had received it was strangely comforting, even welcome.

When the kiss ended and he raised his head to look down into her eyes, she said softly, "You're real daft, Noah Ramslake."

"No, I'm not," he said against her temple, "I told you I knew a decent girl when I saw one. I'm not going to let you go now I've found you."

They had been in the vicinity of Bombay a week, still waiting for the Rear Wing to arrive when dismaying news reached them from the Crimea. The defeated, dying Anglo-French force at Balaclava had, in November, been hit by the worst storm ever recorded in the memory of man. The hurricane that had accompanied it had blown away tents, supplies, furniture, equipment and everything vital to plain human survival. Horses had been snatched up and carried for miles in the teeth of the gale; an entire flock of sheep had disappeared overnight. The hospital marquees had gone right away leaving patients lying in a sea of mud and exposed to the full fury of the storm. The last remaining trees needed so urgently for fuel had been uprooted and tossed away like matchsticks, and every waggon had been smashed to pieces. When the exhausted men had crept from beneath sodden cloaks the following morning, they had been greeted by a terrible sight that sealed their fate. The tiny harbour had been filled with split hulls, broken masts, torn rigging and sea that was covered with floating clothing, rotting food-stuffs and useless medicines. Every supply-ship had been sunk, taking down with them the supplies for the bitter Crimean winter. The brave army that had endured so much was now dying of frostbite, exposure and lack of any medical aid. It was also starving.

Coming two months after the event, the news was particularly devastating to those on their way to the battlefields. What was the situation there now? Was there an army left to reinforce? What, in God's name, awaited them at the end of their journey? The visions of honour and glory began to blur; the hot red blood of the impatient warriors chilled with uncertainty. This did not sound like war: it was wholesale inexorable destruction in every conceivable manner that did not give a man a fighting chance.

But, if the men of the 43rd were shaken by the news,

Maurice Daubnay was shattered by it. Travelling with Headquarters Wing he had now met up with the first three troops of his regiment and was already depressed at the state of their uniforms, the casualness of their bearing and the number of gaps in the ranks due to cholera. He could not bear to think what would become of his beautiful soldiers when they reached the Crimea. Tales of men and horses freezing to death as they stood on piquet duty, descriptions of soldiers clad in ragged Turkish coats, sheepskins, old horse-blankets, with sacking wrapped around their frostbitten feet, and reports of troops eating the raw carcases of horses the minute they dropped dead, all appalled the Colonel. As his ideals and dreams broke apart, his temper worsened. Woe betide the man who caught his eagle glance for even the slightest reason.

Rowan was in deep trouble on two counts. He had lost the regiment five valuable horses, and he was wearing his sword on the wrong hip again. The resulting interview was devastating. He emerged from Colonel Daubnay's tent with his sword where he could no longer effectively use it, and with a bill for five horses to pay. As a very wealthy man he could produce the money. The alternative that had been suggested was a court martial for which he would have to remain behind in Bombay when the ship sailed.

He stormed across to where a group of his fellows lounged beneath the shade of trees, discussing the exhaustive subject of the war they feared would be over before they could reach it.

"Well?" asked Peter Knight, Captain of E Troop.

Rowan threw down his forage-cap in disgust. "I'm damned if I'll be placed in arrest again and languish here while you all take ship. I have to pay for those damned animals."

"Great heaven!" exclaimed Gil. "He surely does not hold you responsible for that storm."

"No, but he says I should have ensured the stockade was strong enough to contain them whatever happened." He sank down on to a wooden box and drew the back of his hand across his beaded forehead. "For once, the confounded man is right."

"I could not afford to replace five horses," reflected Gil.

"Nor I," murmured several others.

"Neither, I imagine, would you take kindly to being ordered to wear your sword in a position that will render you impotent in battle," fumed Rowan. "He blames my left-handedness on lax upbringing, then further blunders by making me carry a weapon where I cannot use it. That man is a worse enemy than the Russians."

Gil laughed. "Oh come, that is a little too hard. I suggest we all go and cool off with a glass of iced porter in my tent."

Even the porter could not lift Rowan's depression. He was hot, incensed by Daubnay's stupidity over the sword, and at his wit's end over Lydia. India would soon be left behind, and the desert lay ahead of them. Travelling would be even more uncomfortable then, and water would have to be rationed. Naturally, he still hoped she would eventually adapt to campaigning but, although their daily routine was now performed by her with complete familiarity, she made no attempt to disguise the fact that she loathed it and blamed him for subjecting her to it. In truth, he would now be prepared to consider separation from her while he was away at war, except that there was nowhere he could send her. The style of their marriage and the swift call to the Crimea had left him with no time to arrange his affairs. He owned no property in England to which he could send a wife, and no family willing to see her settled in the land of her birth. She had no friends who would now acknowledge her. It was a problem all the more worrying because it was essential he solve it by the time he reached their destination. If he should fall in the coming battle, there must be provision made for his widow, yet he shelved the question because it was something that must obviously be discussed with Lydia, and the moment for that never seemed to come.

There was something else besetting him these days—something he would not allow to formulate into clear thought because it was so unthinkable. However, he was forced to face it when he walked despondently into his own tent an hour later and surprised a lone figure there. She jumped nervously at his forceful entry, and her eyes were wide with guilt as they stared back at him. They also reflected the feeling he refused to acknowledge, which further disturbed him.

"What are you doing with my silver brushes," he asked sharply, to cover his relief at finding her rather than his wife there.

"I wasn't trying to steal them," came her defensive answer.

"Did I suggest you were?" He dropped his cap on the nearest bed. "Where is Mrs DeMayne?"

The girl put the brushes down on the chest he used for his personal possessions, saying, "Gone riding with Major and Mrs Benedict, and Captain Fairlie . . . to the temple, I think. I told Madam about it, but advised her not to go right to the top. There's a *dhakma* there."

"Indeed? What do you know of *dhakmas?*"

She turned fully to face him at that, and he was struck by how calm and peaceful she seemed in that growing dusk. "They're places where Parsees leave their dead instead of burying them. As the bodies disintre . . . disrinti . . ."

"Disintegrate."

"Disintegrate," she repeated carefully, "they are carried away by the water underneath that leads to a river."

"Doesn't the thought of disintegrating bodies horrify you?"

She shook her head. "Not the *thought* . . . but the one I seen . . ."

"*Saw.*"

"The one I *saw* the other day upset me with the suddenness. I wasn't expecting it, you see . . . and lordy, it had a powerful smell."

He began to chuckle, the weariness of the afternoon already leaving him. "I well believe it."

He stood looking at her for so long she asked, "Is there something I can get you?"

He had to shake himself from his wild thoughts. "Do you have a name aside from 'Mrs Clarke'?"

"Yes, of course."

"Well, what is it?"

"Mary"

It suited her. Plain, lacking in frills, uncompromising, it well matched her appearance and personality. It was restful, like she was. Mary Clarke—an honest English name given to hundreds of her class, no doubt. There was no noble family attached to that name, no long line of illustrious ancestors to live up to, no obligations to honour. How fortunate she was!

"What is your philosophy on life, Mary?" he heard himself ask.

"You'll have to explain that. It's another of your clever questions."

He smiled. "There's nothing clever about it. Never let long words confuse you. It simply means, what is your opinion of the world and those in it?"

She looked back suspiciously. "You aren't making fun of me?"

"No," he assured her softly. "You should know me well enough now to recognize when I am."

Still she stood there uncertainly, and he thought again what a peaceful kind of person she was. He could not remember a time when she had lost control of herself during the eight-week journey that had seen several crises. There, confined together beneath the white canvas cone growing dim in the light of closing day, he realized that, but for accident of birth, she would make the perfect companion on a military campaign.

"Well, I've not seen much of the world," she said at last, "but it seems full of interesting things. Some are really lovely . . . and some are plain awful. But they all seem to be there for a purpose, don't they?"

"Yes, they do," he agreed with a nod, watching the calm face full of an intelligence no one had tried to exploit.

"As for people." She smiled. "Much the same can be said for them, I s'pose."

He smiled back. "Excellent observation . . . except that you neglect to comment on those who fail to serve the purpose for which they are created. What of the man born to paint, who somehow finds himself selling shoes instead?"

"That's plain daft," was her instant decision. "If he can do something wonderful, he should do it. Anyone can sell shoes."

"You think a man should follow his true destiny, come what may?"

She nodded abruptly.

"What are you going to do with life, Mary?" he asked, oblivious now to the sounds outside that tent, and somehow seeking the answer to his problems from this uncomplicated girl.

She coloured slightly. "I don't know. Make the most of it, if I can. I can't paint, and I can't see that I'll ever sell shoes, so I'll have to wait and see what turns up, won't I? Things don't turn out like you expect, so it's best to take each day as it comes."

Amazingly she had given him his answer, he felt, and before he knew it he was telling her so. "How right I was to dub you my oracle. I shall come to you whenever I want simplification of my problems."

"Now I know you're having me on," she told him frankly. "You've got any number of people to talk to about them."

"Have I?" he asked somewhat bleakly, moving toward her.

"You can add me to them, if it's any help," she said gently.

There was a short period during which they just looked at each other without words then, when she seemed about to turn and go, he asked, "What were you doing with my brushes, by the way?"

"Just looking at them." She smiled back at him, and it was

grave and sweet at the same time. "Are they really silver?"

"Yes, naturally."

"What's that picture on them?"

He had reached her and caught himself putting an arm about her shoulders to turn her back to face the chest containing the brushes. "That 'picture' is the Drumlea coat of arms."

"What on earth's that?" She angled her glance frankly upward as his arm dropped back to his side.

Then he perched on the box to face her, and their eyes were almost on a level as he told her, "I am the youngest grandson of the Earl of Drumlea, therefore I am permitted to use the family heraldry on anything I own."

"I still don't understand."

Folding his arms, his brow wrinkled as he thought of the best way to explain to her something quite beyond her present comprehension. "In very ancient times England was ruled by just a few families with enormous wealth and great power—so much so they even had their own private armies. When they joined in battle there had to be a method of distinguishing which men were on each side, so their lords devised a 'picture', if you like, to represent the family. Anyone seeing this design knew immediately whom it symbolized, and either rallied to it or ran like the devil away from it," he finished with a grin. "These designs became known as 'coats of arms' in consequence."

She looked deeply impressed. "Lordy, did your grandfather rule England before Queen Victoria?"

He was so highly amused by her he tipped back his head and laughed heartily, but the laughter faded when he caught sight of Lydia standing at the tent entrance, ravishingly lovely in a riding-dress of coral broadcloth, looking at the scene with amazement.

He got to his feet immediately. "My dear, I'm persuaded the other visitors this afternoon went to see you rather than the temple. Did you have a pleasant ride?"

"Yes, very pleasant," came her cool response, and she moved away as he approached.

Thinking quickly he said, "Mrs Clarke was just telling me that she warned you of the *dhakma.* " But when he turned to her he found the girl had vanished.

"You appear to be on very good terms with my maid," Lydia commented, removing the provocative plumed hat from the severe arrangement of her glossy hair.

"I cannot ignore the wench," he murmured. "And you are very civil to Collins."

She turned, and her eyes were devastatingly blue in the glow cast by the setting sun on canvas. "Exactly, I am *civil* to your man. I do not sit in here laughing with him in your absence."

"How many times have you castigated me over my ignorance of the terrible existence endured by the women of the regiment?" he countered smoothly.

"I did not suggest that you should invite them to share ours."

Aware that they were on dangerous ground, and finding his temper rising quickly, he said, "You invited her to accompany us, my dear, not I."

"You bought her a horse."

"A hill pony, that is all."

"You did not have to devote half an hour every afternoon to teaching her to ride it. That trooper who has his eye on her could have done so equally well."

"He has other duties to do."

"So have you!"

The heaviness of his frustrating day returned in full measure, with the reminder that the most difficult part of the journey had yet to come. Underlying all that was a need that had been heightened by his encounter with a girl who appeared to offer him all he sought in this one and could not find. Even relief from that need had to be carefully bought these days, and he began paying out the compliments that were the price for something Lydia should have given him freely. Taking it by force would not be worth the reckoning.

"Darling, we are both suffering from the same malady— you know we are—and seeking relief in quite the wrong way.

All I do is for your sake, because I love you. Can you deny that? I tried to teach the girl manners, a little knowledge and a better way of speaking so that she could be a worthy servant for my wife. As for the riding, you asked me to provide a means whereby she could be at your beck and call during the march, and she would be of little use if she were continually falling off or being carried away by a beast she could not handle." He reached for her, desire now too strong to deny. "I am mad for you, Lydia. Have I ever made any secret of the fact—even to the entire regiment? No one else doubts it, and I must ensure that you never do, my adorable tease."

Beneath his uncontrolled kisses she succumbed with a great sigh. Highly skilled in the art of disrobing a woman with the maximum erotic pleasure for them both, he had Lydia trembling, and as desperate as he by the time she lay naked on the rug he had flung on the ground. As he took her he forgot all else but the perfection of her pale body, the magnificence of her beauty, the driving need to forget horror in possession of something untouched and aesthetically calming. Giving full reign to his frustrated passion, gentleness was replaced by the fire of almost brutal strength, until the girl beneath him gasped, "Ah, Rowan DeMayne, I sometimes think you have the devil himself in you."

At seven A.M. the Advance Wing of the 43rd Light Dragoons lined up with regimental precision ready to embark for the port of Suez, and each man's face stoically hid from Colonel Daubnay the consternation he had felt on discovering that their vessels were waiting some distance from the shore. The Colonel and his officers had yesterday vociferously expressed their objections to their counterparts who had arranged the transport, but it had all been to no avail. They had been dubbed 'hysterical effeminate popinjays' by men whom they, in turn, classed as 'ignorant desk-thumpers'. A right royal argument had ensued. But nothing could be done to change the situation.

The cavalry officers had no option but to ferry their men and horses in native boats out to the larger vessels. Their imaginations baulked at the prospect of coaxing their highly-strung chestnut stallions into small open boats but, true to military tradition, went ahead with authoritative commands to their NCO's that suggested there was nothing out of the ordinary in the task. The NCO's passed the orders to rank and file in similar manner. In truth, no dragoon worth his salt had any intention of betraying by the slightest degree that he had no idea how to accomplish embarkation.

The first part of each man's task, that of unsaddling and packing his corn-sack, was normal routine. But when the horses, starting from the left began to be led to the first small boat, it was clear there was trouble ahead. The sight of a heaving surface surrounded by brown, litter-strewn water, was too much for the temperamental pampered animals, who rolled their eyes and began kicking and biting anything within reach as they fought against being led on to such a contraption.

There was an immediate tragedy. Taken unawares by a savage bite on the hand as he attempted to drag his horse forward, the leading trooper let go the neck-rope, leaving the beast free to race back into those following up. It charged straight at another trooper, knocking him into the sea, before dashing through the immaculate ranks, squealing and lashing out with its hooves. In the resultant confusion no one gave a thought as to whether or not the soldier could swim, and it was some time before faint cries and the sound of splashing were heard above the din. The widowed Lieutenant Southerland-Stewart roared orders and two of his men dived in. But the poor victim was drowned before they could reach him.

The incident created such an element of shock it stilled all further activity until Gil strode up to the loading-point and treated those in the vicinity to a masterly expression of his views on their competence, before coldly ordering his NCO's to get the horses loaded without delay. With more caution and less military precision despite the watchful eye of their commanding officer, the troopers finally found the way to success was to work as gangs rather than individuals, and the first boat tardily departed from the shore with its strange load of blue-coated men and panic-stricken mounts.

There were more difficulties awaiting them when they drew alongside the old sailing ship that was to be their home for almost a month, for the horses had to be hauled aboard one by one by means of a sling around the belly. The operation might have been comparatively simple for a steady dock but, in a wooden shell that was pitching and tossing, it took four sturdy troopers to fasten each beast securely. The men, who were devoted to their animals despite their temperamental natures, all felt a pang at the sight of the poor creatures dangling helplessly in midair as they were winched up very slowly, then lowered into the lower deck that had been converted into floating stables through a padded hatchway specially prepared to prevent possible injury. The ship's seamen waiting to receive them had no fond feelings for the horses for, no sooner were they released from the sling, than they began to rear and plunge with dangerous thrusting legs. Several broke loose and started fighting, until they were finally separated and forced into one of the stalls that had been constructed between decks.

Half an hour after commencement of embarkation no spectator would have recognized the men as the smart cavalry who had formed up on the dock beneath the eye of their fussy commanding officer. Totally undermined by the impossible confusion and incompetence of his beautiful dragoons, Colonel Daubnay had removed himself from the offending sight to lie on his bed with a damp towel around his head, unable to face the thought of what impression the 43rd had given to the inquisitive crowds flocking the dockside area. With the departure of their colonel, proceedings improved. Marine work had to be tackled differently, the soldiers discovered, and soon stripped to the waist, winding their shirts turban-wise around their heads as extra protection from the sun and bending their backs with a will. Although the embarkation went easier once they were free of their restricting uniforms, the troopers were to regret the removal of their shirts when sunburn plagued them for much of the voyage.

Slowly, the numbers on the pier grew less and those aboard increased. But the operation did not go at all smoothly. On more than one occasion a horse jumped from the small boats and swam back to the shore, where it proceeded to run amok, resisting capture for as long as it could. One native craft unfit to hold its cargo sank fifty yards out, forcing men and animals to get back to land as best they could. All did, save for one foolish terrified horse who swam further and further away from those trying to help it and was drowned. A large number of troopers received kicks or bites during the loading, and many were seasick—to the callous amusement of the sailors—during the short but extremely rough journey from shore to ship.

Rowan not only had C Troop to supervise, but the additional and more dangerous task of embarking the spare horses, who were even more wildly resistant to any notion of sea travel. He had seen Lydia safely installed in their small cabin, with Mary to help her, at first light, and by the time he finally climbed aboard the ship himself he was sweating, filthy, exhausted and husky from shouting. He had also been bitten on the arm by one of the half-broken mounts.

"The damn thing took the titbit I offered, then sank its teeth into me for dessert," he panted to Gil, who came up to ask how he had come about the rip in his pale-blue sleeve. "By God, my men look more like a prison chain gang than Her Majesty's Dragoons. If old Daubnay saw them now he'd have a seizure. I've never known anything like this, Gil."

His friend scowled. "*Embarking horses* is the official term for it, but it's hellish dangerous work I defy any man to accomplish easily. I lost Jackson in the first five minutes. Poor fellow drowned a few yards from the shore, because not one person realized he might not be able to swim. I have now taken the names of all those unable to perform this simple exercise, so that I can arrange for other men to keep watch on each of them. With two voyages ahead of us it's a precaution that must be taken. I advise you to do the same. But it was too late to save Jackson, and I must now go ashore again to arrange for his burial and so on."

"And I must address myself to the task of settling my wife," he told his friend.

"Then I would not go as you are, old fellow. Lydia was not looking in the best of spirits when I passed her just a moment ago. She was complaining to a naval officer that she could smell horses even in her cabin. The sight of you covered in corn husks and animal lather is not likely to cheer her up, if you want my opinion."

"I do not," snapped Rowan. "I'd be pleased if you'd keep your damned opinions to yourself."

"Just as you wish," came the reply in tones of subdued humour. "But I trust your present black mood will stretch to obliging me by seeing my horses safely installed with your own."

He sighed and ran a hand across the sweat gathering on his brow. "Yes, surely. I'm sorry, Gil. Women are the very devil. You are a great deal better off as you are, if you want *my* opinion."

Gil grinned as he prepared to disembark once more. "You may keep your damned opinions also. I'll see you anon."

Rowan could not take Gil's advice to clean himself up before seeing Lydia, for the only place he could do it was in the cabin she already occupied. So he walked through the narrow gangways just as he was, and it did not alleviate the tribulations of his morning to hear his wife giving petulant orders to Mary as he arrived at the door.

"I cannot see how we are possibly able to live in this confined space, Mrs Clarke. The tent was bad enough, but here we are already falling over each other. And the Captain has not yet unpacked his things. We shall have to have another cabin as a dressing room."

"That is not possible, my dear," Rowan told her, ducking his head to enter the tiny place strewn with crinolines, petticoats and bonnets, isolating his wife and maid in the centre of it. "We are lucky to have one of the larger ones which Captain Maidstone set aside for married officers. The vessel is crowded, Lydia. There are no spare cabins, and the subalterns are sharing one smaller than this between three."

She turned to face him. "They are men, Rowan, and I have to say are apparently enjoying every possible discomfort like boys on a juvenile adventure. Even captains forget everything in the face of their enthusiasm, I vow," she added as she looked him over from head to foot.

He leaned on an arm outstretched against the doorjamb. "Have you really not witnessed what has been going on for the past four hours? A trooper has been drowned, and so have two valuable horses. Half the men are seasick, and the other half are suffering injuries inflicted by attacks from crazed animals. This is not a juvenile adventure. It is a regiment going to *war.*"

She flushed angrily. "Then I doubt it will ever arrive, for there will be no regiment left. Even should there be one or two survivors of this incredible ordeal they will be unfit to fight anybody. The whole concept is madness. I had used to think the military a necessary and organized establishment. Now I see it is run by lunatics."

Rowan looked at Mary and said shortly, "You may go, Mrs Clarke."

"But Madam wishes me to . . ."

"Do as you are told, damn you!" he cried, unable to cope with his feelings for her on top of all else. "Ramslake is aboard this ship. Seek him out and get him to find you a secluded corner on deck. I'll send for you later."

The girl pushed her way through the foaming sea of petticoats and went out, walking beneath his outstretched arm to do so. He felt better once she had gone.

"I wish you would not speak in such terms when we are not alone," he told Lydia.

"She is a servant, that is all. You used once to ignore her."

He straightened up and went inside, kicking the door shut behind him. "Servants gossip. I have no wish for the men to hear that we have quarrelled."

"I am not quarrelling with you, Rowan," she protested, eyebrows raised in innocence. "It is you who are in a danger. Going to war does not seem to suit your temperament a jot."

"Neither does it suit yours, I must point out," he responded testily. "I have had the most trying morning. My troop is split between two vessels making my command very awkward; the young subaltern who transferred to us yesterday to replace Tom Anstruther is not yet familiar with the men, and certainly knows no more about embarking horses than we do. I naturally do not expect you to assist in any of this, but it is surely not too much to ask you to manage with a little inconvenience as you settle into your cabin."

She appeared to calm down somewhat and said no more as she bent to take her brushes and lotions from a portmanteau beside her. Since their passionate interlude things had been slightly better between them, although it still only needed the suggestion that he was not entirely devoted to her welfare to put her in a wilful mood. Knowing it would be wise to keep her happy during the voyage before the hardships of the desert crossing were made apparent to her, he said in softer tone, "As senior captain Gil is commanding officer of the contingent on this ship and has been given a small cabin on his own. I am sure he would not refuse my request to share it, if it would make things easier for you."

Her face was glowing when she looked up. "Rowan . . . *dearest* . . . how very sweet and thoughtful of you. If you did not smell so much of the stables I would reward you here and now."

He prepared to leave. "No, my dear, you would not. If I wanted solace from you, I would take it, smelling of the stables or not. I think you now know that. It so happens I have pressing duties to do. However, although I shall be sharing Gil's cabin, I shall be with you often enough to take my 'reward' many times over."

He had reckoned without Captain Maidstone, who was a notorious ladies' man and rejoiced in the presence of three cavalry wives on his vessel. The ladies, sick of eight weeks

or more of camp life, could hardly be blamed for falling
victim to the breezy flattery of a man who offered them
comforts and attention they had not had since leaving
Khunobad. In short, they all willingly left their husbands to
their onerous duties at sea, and thoroughly enjoyed every
minute of that voyage beneath the lazily flapping sails and
hypnotic sunshine.

The Advance Wing set sail at four in the afternoon in two
ancient sailing vessels that were towed by steamers in order
to accomplish the voyage in the shortest possible time. The
first contained A Troop and half of C Troop; the second
carried the rest of Rowan's split command with B Troop,
under the charge of Major Benedict. Practically the entire
European population had gathered on the shore to see 'The
Gingerbread Boys' sail off to war, and the sound of their
cheers was not entirely drowned by the rousing tunes played
by an infantry band that had turned out to pay tribute to
a regiment about to face its first blooding in battle. As they
slipped away from Bombay, the crews of the ships anchored
in the harbour crowded their decks to shout acclamations,
and there was hardly a tough blue-coated dragoon who did
not feel moisture in his eyes and a constriction in his throat
as he realized the 43rd was receiving cheers rather than jeers
for the first time in its history. They were heroes already!

By nightfall they were well away and steering toward the
Straits of Bab el Mandeb, and those who were still on deck
could see the small bright speck on top of Bombay light-
house—their last link with India. The officers and three
ladies dined with the captain that evening. Randolph Maidstone was a proudly-built man with turquoise eyes, who had
a breezy gallantry that stood out against the disciplined
manners of the military men, and he upset them right away
by establishing himself as the person of greatest importance
during the voyage.

"Well, gentlemen, I shall not interfere with your routine
unless I must," he told them heartily. "But a ship is not like
a horse, you know. I cannot pull on a simple strip of leather
to make it go where I wish, as you can. Being at the end of

the towrope takes a lot of skill, and I shall have to demand that you 'jump-to' and obey any orders I may give. You are at sea now, sirs. A man cannot simply say 'Gee-up' or 'Whoa' to a great sailing vessel!" His gusty laugh incensed them even more, and their pride was further bruised when the ladies joined in the merriment. After the fair creatures had retired, the military officers made an excuse to curtail the evening, and went on their rounds expressing an opinion of naval officers and seafaring men in general that should have made the timbers in their vicinity smoulder and blacken.

But it did not end there. Captain Maidstone had an awning rigged on deck in a sheltered spot where the ladies could sit in comfort, and often joined them there for a cup of tea, or to answer their endless questions. Rowan grew more and more furious at Lydia's apparent avid interest in anything to do with seafaring, since she had betrayed no inclination to hear details of the difficulties of soldiering on board ship with several hundred horses. The other two married officers faced the same problem, but they did have the solace of sharing their cabins—something Rowan had rashly sacrificed.

As the days passed Rowan saw, with something of a shock, that Lydia was playing her old game with him. The sea air, the flattery of Randolph Maidstone and the semblance of civilized living after weeks of weary marching made her beauty and charm flourish as before, and he often heard her gay laughter floating down from the upper deck as he inspected the horses on the sweltering stable level. She was dangling her beauty on a string before him again, and attempting to humiliate him into adoration by flirting with the naval officer, knowing he could do nothing to rectify the situation while they were all in such cramped proximity without making an exhibition of himself.

Things came to a head after ten days at sea, when his lusty personality could stand no more. Excited by her overwhelming beauty, despite all else, he accompanied her to her cabin that evening after dinner, and closed the door firmly behind him.

"Perhaps you would be good enough to send for Mrs Clarke, Rowan," she said lightly. "I am a little tired tonight, and the sea appears to be rising somewhat alarmingly."

"You have no need of Mrs Clarke, my dear," he told her with suave finality. "I can assist you to undress. I can also deal with the rats that are sure to be flushed out by this approaching bad weather."

"Rats?" she echoed.

"The ship is overrun with them. They congregate in vast numbers below decks—but then you have been so busy studying nautical lore that you have had no time to interest yourself in *my* routine aboard this vessel. You may start in the morning."

She looked at him with nervous uncertainty. "Rowan, I do not understand. I have no wish to go down to those terrible stables."

"And I have no wish for my wife to hang on another man's every word."

A smile played around her mouth. "You are jealous!"

"I admit it . . . but I have had enough of your game, Lydia. Starting tomorrow you will learn all there is to know about the work of a cavalry regiment—including a visit to 'those terrible stables'. The intense interest you have shown in seafaring will now be extended to soldiering. Have I made myself clear?"

"Perfectly," she agreed faintly.

"And starting from now you will learn all there is to know about husbands who are jealous. If you choose to play the coquette I shall treat you as such—and my former libertine ways ensured that I had a great deal of practice."

That night solved the present problem, but it did nothing to stabilize a marriage that had been built on a quagmire.

The troopers' routine was soon set. They awoke around five A.M. and were not slow in going to the galley for a mug of good strong tea to compensate them for a night spent on a hard deck with only a blanket between them and the boards. Their designated quarters below decks had been abandoned after the first night, due to the rats, cockroaches and other pestilent creatures that swarmed over them the moment lights went out at eleven. Each and every man preferred to sleep in the open, however hard and chilly the main decks might prove.

At six the stable trumpet was blown—a ceremony the sailors found constantly fascinating—and the horses were groomed in the best way their masters could manage in the narrow stalls between decks. Since there was no room for the animals to lie down they were each put in slings during calm weather, this precaution easing the strain on their legs, which swelled painfully from continuous standing. The troopers could not help feeling sorry for the beasts who looked so undignified swaying in their canvas cradles. But they knew it was the only humane thing to do.

The men had breakfast at seven-thirty, then relaxed until eleven when it was time to clean out the stalls. This was the time the ship's crew hated most, for even a fresh sea breeze could not dispel the stench of horse-manure steaming in the heat below decks. They all agreed the dragoons might look fine and dandy when sitting in their saddles, but they had to get down to some real pesky work at times. Cavalrymen might have been nurtured on the aroma of the stable, but the nautical men preferred the smells of tar, oiled rope and salty air. The horses were fed again at one P.M. before the men had their own dinner, and evening stables was sounded at five, when the horses were groomed and watered for the night.

As the days passed the first wariness between the two services was overcome, soldiers and sailors learning to appreciate the hardships and pleasures of each other's profession. The sailors were, to a man, amazed that a cavalryman always put his horse before himself. No dragoon ever got fed or rested before his mount. That these hefty pretty-coated men accepted it without question was quite beyond the comprehension of the seafarers. In turn, the soldiers learned to admire the skill needed to handle a ship that was being towed by another, when every veer of the wind or rise in the seas could put both ships in peril of snapping the cable or overrunning.

Evenings soon became a joint social gathering where yarns were exchanged with appalling disregard for truthfulness, and the men sang and danced to music on a concertina or penny-whistle. The soldiers gradually found their sea legs and began to forget the terrible news they had received from the Crimea. All was peaceful and calm as they left Aden to pass through the Red Sea, the only upsetting thing being that the water was the same colour as any other and not bright scarlet, as many had thought.

But one person was disappointed by nothing during those days at sea. Apart from the first few days afloat when she had felt decidedly queasy, Mary was fascinated with all she saw and experienced. Noah had found her a cool shady place away from the men where she slept, did her washing and mending and watched the daily bustle of the ship's routine. She was a unique passenger—neither soldier nor wife—because the other officers' wives had dismissed their servants at Bombay and planned to take on fresh ones at Suez. It might have been difficult for Mary if it had not been for Noah, who must have given the general impression that she was his intended, because no one pestered her. He also contrived to roll himself in his blanket not far from her corner each night, which gave her the confidence to sleep.

She found herself enjoying his company more and more, and looked forward to the times he came to her little corner on deck to chat to her while she worked. They talked of everything under the sun, and she responded eagerly—except when the subject was her employers. What she thought of the state of affairs between the DeMaynes she kept to herself, as she did her disappointment that the Captain had dropped his friendly approach to grow extremely brusque and businesslike with her since that day he had explained about the coat of arms. She had no idea what she had done to earn his displeasure, but did not allow introspection on the subject to spoil her enjoyment of the extensive adventure her life had become. Besides, she had Noah.

They were sitting together one afternoon when they spotted a shoal of flying fish, and Mary laughed with delight. "Look, Noah, they could be little silver birds coming up from the sea, they shine in the sunlight so."

"If they were silver, there'd not be many left," he commented teasingly. "Every sailor for miles around would be netting them."

She turned to him. "Is silver *very* valuable?"

He nodded. "It's a wealthy man who can afford to buy it."

"Captain DeMayne has silver brushes with his coat of arms on the backs. He's also got cups he calls goblets, a cruet, candlesticks and cutlery all made of silver. There are other things all over the place that I reckon are the same. As he's an 'Honourable' he must be rich. But is there anything else about silver apart from just looking nice? I mean, is it just to show people you have a lot of money?"

His smile was even more attractive these days, since the sun and sea breezes had tanned his face so deeply, and his greenish eyes contrasted sharply with his skin.

"You're a funny little thing, Mary Clarke, and no mistake," he said softly. "Silver is a very enduring material, so articles made from it can be passed down to sons and grandsons. It's a symbol of family pride and greatness in many cases. It usually goes to the eldest son, along with the family jewels for his wife to wear. The aristocracy likes to keep valuable things where they belong," he added with a trace of bitterness which eluded Mary because she was on a different thought pattern.

"Is it only the eldest sons who get the things?"

"Traditionally, yes. But sometimes family quarrels result in certain things being willed to another son who is more favoured. Why the interest?"

"Captain DeMayne is the youngest grandson, so that would explain why Mrs DeMayne hasn't any jewellery and he had to buy her some in Bombay."

"Oh, really? What was that, then?"

"A pearl. I don't know much about it except that I saw it in its box just after he give . . . *gave* . . . it to her. She seemed very pleased, so I suppose it must be valuable. All I know is that it is the most beautiful thing to hang around your neck I've ever seen."

"Describe it."

She looked up from her stitching, the breeze playing with tendrils of her hair so that she had to push them back with her free hand. "Describe it? Oh dear, well, it was bigger than my thumbnail . . . and surrounded by dark blue stones."

"Sapphires," came the pronouncement. "Good ones, by the sound of things. What colour is the pearl?"

She looked at him in surprise. "Can you get different colours? This is white-ish. But it's so shiny you can see the blue of the other stones in it."

Noah whistled. "Your mistress is a very fortunate lady."

Reflecting that Lydia DeMayne had taken her good fortune very lightly, Mary simply said, "How is it you know so much about valuable things?"

"I once worked with them. My father is a jeweller."

She took in that surprising information, then asked the old question again. "Why *did* you take the shilling, Noah?"

He looked away from her intense glance, way out over the sparkling sea where the flying fish were still accompanying them. "I wanted adventure, love. England was too small for me."

Tentatively she put out a hand to rest lightly on his, and he looked back at her quickly. "Don't you sometimes miss your family?" she asked sympathetically. "You never speak about them. Does it upset you to think about them?"

He closed his other hand over hers. "You could become my family, Mary. We could get married. The ship's captain is empowered to conduct the ceremony, you know."

It took her unawares and she did not know what to say to him. He was very, very nice, and she regarded him as her close friend—another Sam. And yet she knew there was another element here that had not been present with the sergeant she had loved as a father. Reluctant though she was to admit it she liked being kissed by Noah, liked having him near to ward off the other men, liked the gentlemanly way he treated her. Why could it not remain just as it was?

"You know what'll happen when we reach the Crimea, don't you?" he went on. "There'll be French maids easily available, and you'll be dismissed to fend for yourself. What'll you do then—or haven't you thought of that yet?"

The answer was not something she wished to think about, but she knew what he predicted was more than likely to be the truth. Her mistress was growing irritable and more difficult to please. Mary had no illusions that what had started as a benevolent gesture to solve a problem in Khunobad would soon end when the journey did.

"Think about it, my dear," said Noah gently. "But don't take too long about it. I may not be as rough as the men you've been used to, but I have their same desires. And these nights beneath the stars knowing you are only a few yards away are growing more difficult to stand."

She was beset by the problem for the rest of that day, and the petulant mood of her mistress as she helped her to dress for dinner highlighted all Noah had said. But she had come so far in her search for life she was loath to make such a decision. If and when the DeMaynes dismissed her, there was always the chance of being taken as a maid by someone else. But she knew from what she had overheard that the wives of officers already at the Crimea had gone to Constantinople and found numbers of maids from France, who had been shipped out for the purpose of serving ladies of the French and English officers involved in the war. Even so, Mary wanted to keep her freedom, for a while at least. If she married Noah and he was killed in the coming battles, she would be a widow again with all the accompanying problems. But, most weighty of all the arguments against marriage, was that marrying Noah, gentlemanly and charming though he was, would make her a trooper's woman once more, and she would be back where she started.

Because her spirits had been lowered by serious thought

on a subject that had so many ifs and buts, she felt strangely lonely that evening when the soldiers and seamen gathered for their usual singsong on the deck. Seeing Noah amongst them she left her solitary corner where she usually dreamed the evening away with background music to add to the romance of sea and stars, and went to sit beside him on the outer edge of the circle. He gave her a glad warm smile and slipped an arm about her waist as they listened.

Gradually Mary relaxed and forgot her cares. It was a very atmospheric occasion with the indigo night lit by a dazzle of stars, and the lanterns on the poles casting swaying light over the suntanned men in uniforms so casually worn Colonel Daubnay would have been horrified over every undone button and pushed-up sleeve; and others, bearded and completely at home on the scrubbed decks. Their combined voices raised in song were strong and confident, breathing the heart of their true homeland, and Mary, who knew little of England, was filled with something she was too unsophisticated to recognize as nostalgia. Leaning against Noah she let her head rest on his shoulder as she surrendered to the evocative call of the moment.

Then, a seaman playing a concertina began a tune Mary knew and loved. It was an Irish jig that Jack Rafferty had danced to on many an occasion, and to which he had taught her to dance. It was infectious and irresistible. Her feet began to tap and she turned enthusiastically to her companion.

"Can you do a jig, Noah?"

He laughed. "That I can't. My dancing would make an Irishman weep." Studying her face he urged, "Get up and do it, girl. The boys would love it."

"Oh no, I couldn't do it on my own," she protested, longing to release her wayward spirits.

On the instant Noah called out to a man further round the ring. "Paddy, here's a girl wanting to do a jig and can't for want of a partner."

It all happened quickly then, and Mary found herself swung to her feet by the man called Paddy, who was in A

Troop. A great cheer went up, and a great deal of clapping accompanied the reprise of the jig tune. The dance began decorously at first, but was so popular with those watching that the musician began again, increasing the beat of the music as he went. Mary grew more and more elated. She was free, she was beholden to no man, she was on a ship traversing the world. There was nothing she could not see or do! Her feet flashed through the intricate steps Jack had taught her, and she had to pull her skirt up so that it would not impede her. The clapping of the spectators added to the frenzy of the dance; the shouts and cheers rang in her ears like notes of the music. She felt so happy she threw back her head and laughed as she twirled about the deck, her partner becoming nobody yet anybody she wished.

But the music began to slow, then peter out altogether. The clapping stopped; there were no more cheerful shouts of encouragement. It grew remarkably quiet. Breathless, bosom heaving, Mary came to a standstill, still holding her skirt free of her feet. Then she saw the reason for the change in the atmosphere up there on deck. Standing in the shadows in full mess dress that he had been obliged to wear for dinner, was Rowan DeMayne looking at her with an expression she could not begin to fathom.

With a faint feeling of apprehension, for some unknown reason, Mary dropped her skirt as if the material burnt her fingers, and began to walk across the deck through the parted ranks, conscious that her hair had fallen from its pins due to the frenzy of her dance. Nearing him she saw those dark sleepy eyes were blazing with something that was as intimidating as the pin-dropping silence around them. Had she neglected some vital duty?

Swallowing nervously she asked, "Is there something wrong, sir?"

It seemed an age before he replied, then it was in a devastating undertone heard only by her. "I will not tolerate your making a disgusting public exhibition of yourself! You hoodwinked me into believing you wanted to learn, to climb from that pit of ignorance and squalor into which you were born. But it is damnably obvious you will never be more than a trooper's woman!"

With that he turned and strode off into the darkness, leaving her feeling as she had when Jack Rafferty had covered her with bruises . . . except that the bruises just inflicted were internal and infinitely more painful.

CHAPTER EIGHT

The Advance Wing was conducted to a camp barely two miles from the town of Suez; Headquarters and Rear Wings joining them on landing several days later. After the sea breezes and lengthy voyage the desert proved unpopular the moment the regiment set foot in it. The days were as blisteringly hot as the worst India could produce, with nights colder than they had experienced for years. The barren landscape seemed even more formidable after the comradeship of the voyage with its lovely changing colours of a sea they had not seen for seven years. The officers were allowed into Suez itself, but none paid a second visit, there being nothing there of interest to them. The rank and file longed to see the town, but were confined to the camp.

But even the most disgruntled trooper could not complain of the arrangements that had been made for them by advance officers of the Honourable East India Company's commissariat to ensure adequate supplies of water, rations, forage, and Egyptian porters to facilitate the long overland march to Alexandria. Drinking water would have to be brought by camel from the Nile every day—a matter of ninety miles from Suez, but less as they advanced toward

Cairo, their first main stop. All along the designated route water troughs had been constructed, along with regular supply depots to serve the total of three cavalry regiments that were making their way to the Crimea.

But this third stage of their journey meant a changeover from Indian to Egyptian porters, who were sullen and resentful, with no wish or ability to communicate with their military masters, and whose camels were miserable highly-odorous beasts. The troopers could see the reason for their attitude, because they had been torn away from their fields and families by order of the Pasha and press ganged into service with all three of the regiments passing through, without reward or payment. Since the British troops were going to fight on behalf of the Turks, and the Ottoman Empire, it was to the Pasha's advantage to afford them every assistance, but he did so at the expense of his own people.

But understanding the Egyptian porters' attitude did not mean the soldiers accepted it. Trooper Collins told Rowan quite frankly that he felt the sullen devils had no reason to spit at soldiers who offered them a cheery word, or a bit of music by way of friendship. He forebore to comment on his own officer's lack of response to a cheery word these days, but Captain DeMayne's partial return to the black moods he had suffered just prior to his marriage had been noticed by C Troop and the other officers, particularly Maurice Daubnay. The Colonel made a note of it, along with the general reluctance for the coming lonely desert march, and vowed to hold a review or similar entertainment on reaching Cairo in order to revive morale. Since he had no alternative but to march his regiment to war, he was determined they would arrive looking as they had on leaving Khunobad.

But it took great resolution to continue making such plans, especially when the horses were hit by an outbreak of glanders which took fifteen of them in a very short time. The Colonel was fighting his own growing depression as the distance to their destination lessened. Already his immaculate mechanical soldiers looked more like an unruly dishevelled rabble, and the necessity of travelling in three separate wings robbed him of the ability to maintain discipline of the highest standard. Whilst at Suez he took the opportunity of giving his officers a blistering opinion of the deterioration of the Advance and Rear Wings, but even he was shrewd enough to see that their present mood was such that criticism was the last thing they wanted.

The ebullience of the regiment's departure had been dulled by deaths and deprivation. The march across India had been on territory and amongst people to which they were accustomed; the voyage had been something of a rest period out of their control in the hands of seafaring men. They were still only halfway to their destination, and no one relished three weeks crossing this unknown land, whose peoples were as wild as any encountered in India and whose ways were as mysterious and unpredictable as the desert itself. One only had to stand on the perimeter of the camp and gaze into the distance to feel one's blood run cold with a strange presentiment of fate. Once out there, it seemed unlikely that an entire regiment could avoid being swallowed up and never seen again. It did nothing to boost the men's confidence that the porters and camel-drivers seemed likely to vanish into the darkness one night leaving them stranded out there.

With the Advance Wing due to move off at two A.M. on the first leg of the march to Cairo, spirits dropped even further. With a need to cover twenty-two miles each day in order to arrive four days later, it promised to be gruelling in nights that were bitterly cold to men who had spent seven years in India. On the march the standard routine was ten minutes at the trot, ten at the walk, then ten leading the horses. This meant lack of really energetic movement to warm the travellers. But, worst of all, was that the regiment's lack of experience in desert, where men crossed the trackless area by study of the stars, resulted in the need of a guide loaned by the Egyptian government to walk at the head of the column with a lantern on a pole. Without him, they would certainly become lost and perish in the dunes. That an entire regiment of men, plus seven hundred or more valuable horses, camp followers and pack-animals should put their lives into the hands of that one solitary lantern-bearer by following his bobbing light, seemed nothing short of ludicrous. The man was no general, yet he would be leading a regiment that was part of an army second to none in the world.

At the end of that first night's march each member was tired and dispirited. Six hours in the saddle, half of which had been taken at walking pace, had seemed endless. A hot breakfast raised their spirits a little, but it was interrupted by the horses breaking loose from their lines because the piqueting-pegs would not hold in the shallow sandy soil. Once the beasts found themselves free they galloped about kicking and squealing at anyone who attempted to catch them and, no sooner had the first group been rounded up, than another lot pulled free and set off in a fair imitation of a stampede through the hungry soldiers eating breakfast. The second rush of horses veered off in the direction of the area where the spare mounts were tethered, and charged through them to loosen the ropes, before heading off across the dunes in high glee, augmented by their wilder brothers.

Rowan, as officer in charge of these animals, was alerted when almost at his tent for a much-needed breakfast, and had to head off to supervise a chase after the animals. He cursed and swore to those around him, causing an exchange of looks between men who had noticed the marked decline in his equanimity since arrival in Suez. For once they resented his authority. It was all very well for him to rant and fling oaths in every direction; they would like to see him try to piquet horses in loose shifting sand and see what kind of job he made of it.

In one respect they were fortunate, for the horses were brought to a halt by the difficulty of making a passage through the sand dunes, but it still took close on an hour to return them all to camp, for the wily creatures led their would-be captors a dance before they decided to surrender. Rowan's parting shot to men who were every bit as hot and weary, consisted of the advice to secure their mounts firmly or he would have all of *them* sitting at the end of ropes until they thought of a way to do it. He then departed for C Troop lines sweating, parched and considerably aggrieved.

Lydia looked up at his entry and took in his dishevelled state. They had all been looking less than immaculate lately, but he now resembled a phantom with uniform covered in fine sand that also lay in a film across his face. It fell from his shako like powder as he took it off and flung it on to the bed.

"Your breakfast is quite spoiled," she said to him in weary tones. "Whatever have you been doing all this time?" When he made no answer, she went on, "I saw Gil and Captain Wrexham eating at least an hour ago. Why do you always seem to have more duties than anyone else?"

Unfastening the heavy blue jacket that added further to the discomfort of the swiftly-rising temperature, he said shortly, "Because I was foolish enough to express my feelings by riding a horse into a ballroom—something Daubnay will never forgive."

She sighed and dabbed at her forehead with a cologne-scented handkerchief. "You knew the character of the man before you did it. You have only yourself to blame . . . and I am made to suffer as a result."

"I'm sorry. But I cannot guard against the circumstance of horses being ineffectively piqueted. I have been chasing them all over the desert this past hour."

"Why do you not leave such things to the troopers? It is so *undignified.*"

"So is much of what we have done these last three months, Lydia, but if an officer is seen to shirk anything that spoils his dignity he will be of little use to his men in battle."

"For pity's sake," she cried, "is that all you ever consider —war and battle?"

"Yes, naturally," he returned in raised tones. "It is for that we are making this confounded journey."

Her lovely eyes closed and she put her hand to her forehead again. "Please don't shout, Rowan. My head is aching enough as it is. This heat is quite insupportable, and Mrs

Clarke had to shake everything free of the most appalling variety of insects before I could change my clothes. The ridiculous amount of water Collins was given for my bath was such a dreadful colour I almost refused to let it touch my skin. Not that it refreshed me one jot, and I am certain it contained some damaging element, for I am now suffering from the most unpleasant irritation that is likely to grow worse with every day we spend in this abominable desert."

Feeling himself tighten with anger, he flung his jacket down with more force than was necessary. "Lydia, that water was brought by a relay of camels from the Nile, which is ninety miles from here. An advance party of men has worked miracles to provide water and provisions at a chain of stations across a sea of sand, so that we and the following regiments could traverse it. I think it a wonderful achievement . . . and so should you."

The deep-blue eyes opened to their full width. "I think the whole concept smacks of lunacy."

"So you have said before," he snapped. "You have never made a secret of your opinion of how the army treats women who marry into the ranks of a regiment—or the men themselves, for that matter. Now you are witnessing the reason for it. If they were kept in cushioned luxury they would be useless on a journey such as this and break down in horror on a battlefield. Harsh we might be; lunatic we are not, Lydia. You have the British Army to thank for your national freedom and prosperity. Let us have an end to your constant complaints and a little more support for those you joined by your marriage to one of their officers."

Sitting up abruptly his wife spoke with frost in her voice. "How you have changed, Rowan. In Khunobad you were almost unbearably romantic. It was plain to everyone that I was the centre of your life, and you browbeat them with your arrogant superiority to accept our marriage on normal terms. Nothing was too good for me; there was no luxury you did not provide in your public reverence of someone you considered sensitive and well-bred. You protected me with fierce dedication and charmed me into returning your affection.

"But, from the moment that order arrived, I was supplanted by your ambition. You have thought nothing of dragging me half across the world in the most appalling conditions. You abandon me for the greater part of the day while you chase after runaway horses or tramp around asking if those burly brutes are comfortable. If that is not enough, you are posting piquets, practising swordplay or writing reports. At the conclusion of all that, and when you have time, I am expected to please you on a pile of rugs thrown upon the ground. I think those few complaints I make are warranted." The frost turned to ice as she concluded, "That melodramatic pretence at suicide was merely a ploy to ensnare the one female you could not win by your usual means. You have used me in the most inhuman way."

He sank on to the box containing his possessions and gazed at her in despair. "You are wrong, quite wrong. I loved you deeply, or I would never have allowed you to humiliate me the way you did. But *you* have changed, Lydia, have you never considered that? In Khunobad you were radiant, grateful and affectionate; you played the part of a military officer's wife to perfection. I was so very proud of you. What we are doing now is the more serious requirement of my profession, and you have made no attempt whatever to adapt to it. I have given you time; made allowances. All that has happened is that you have grown more and more aloof from me. For love of you I would have done anything—even taken my own life. I am now forced to believe you have never loved me."

Her expression was as cold as her voice when she said, "Have I ever said that I did?"

He had to be cruelly honest. "Not in so many words, but I . . ."

"This marriage was forced upon me," she interjected. "As I said just now, you can be unbearably romantic, and I am but human. However, I do not care to vie with six hundred and sixty men for your devotion. Especially do I not care for it whilst suffering extreme hardship and constant neglect."

The tent flap opened and Collins came in with a fresh plate of breakfast.

"Get out, I am having a conversation with my wife," Rowan flung at him.

"But, sir, it's your . . ."

"*Get out!*"

The batman vanished again, and Lydia said, "Everyone is the victim of your black temper these days."

Exhausted after the long march, thirsty, yearning to wash the grime from his body, he looked at the lovely girl he had turned to in order to banish something he could not accept, even now. That demon seemed to be hovering near him lately, and in something approaching desperation he said, "Help me, Lydia. Give me your support and understanding. Give me your wholehearted devotion."

She lay back again with her handkerchief to her forehead, and sighed. "No, really, Rowan! It grows increasingly obvious to me that you have had no experience of *ladies*. Your reputation was built on your success with courtesans like Fanny Dennison, and with a long line of lightskirts with skins of varying colours. Half an hour on a pile of rugs will not earn my support and devotion, I assure you. It will require a return to the man you were at Khunobad to do that."

The second night's march was accomplished in the same manner. On reaching the camp site the horses were tethered by the only possible means—that of filling corn sacks with sand and anchoring the beasts to them. The spirits of those in the column remained low. No one enjoyed the long night marches chilled to the bone, followed by even longer days of blistering sunshine with no trees to provide shade, and the atmosphere beneath canvas suffocating. Tempers grew short, idle hands and brains thought only of mischief, and the poisonous insects abounding were killed in the most savage manner possible to relieve pent-up feelings.

Rowan's mood was as dark as anyone's as he swayed in his

saddle, or tramped the loose sandy ground leading his charger and watching Lydia flirting with Lieutenant Cleaver, her latest conquest. How could he have made the same terrible mistake twice in his life? For Fanny Dennison, whom he had believed to be a virtuous lady, he had sacrificed his right to serve in the DeMayne regiment and alienated his family. For Lydia Moorfield he had almost sacrificed his life. Neither woman was what he had imagined her to be. He had been no more than a boy when he had adored Fanny. At almost twenty-eight he should be so much wiser, and it made the revelation even more humiliating. Lydia's beauty and vivacity had blinded him.

Yet he was no longer blind to his feelings for that girl who was a child of the regiment; a trooper's widow. During those long hours shuffling along behind the guide with the lantern, Rowan allowed the astonishing facts to surface. In company with Mary Clarke this journey could have been the triumphal progress it had started out to be. He was shaken by the conviction; almost horrified by the feelings aroused in him by a girl who had been born and reared amongst some of the roughest breed imaginable. She displayed all those qualities he had found wanting in a wife who had once set his blood alight with longing. Mary had courage and common sense; a feeling for adventure. She had honesty, humility, and a fierce pride for the regiment. She had skin almost as dark as a native, hands that were stubby and lacking in grace, a way of speaking that fell on his ears almost as painfully as females singing and a hint of independence that suggested a man would have to work hard to earn her respect.

Yet he could not dismiss her from his mind; could not help the illusion that she was his because she was dependent on him on this journey. When he had caught her dancing a jig, with her skirts held high and her head flung back in abandonment, he had been filled with jealousy at the sight of a circle of men watching and enjoying her.

Since the day Lydia had caught them laughing together in the tent, he had been very careful to avoid a repetition of such intimacy. In fact, he hardly spoke to the girl these days. But his respect and admiration for her was growing stronger daily as he watched her cope with those hardships his wife deplored, and he began to wonder if his wildness was inborn rather than the result of that affair seven years ago.

Once on that subject, his thoughts progressed to the other problem he had tried to ignore. Every step he took, every hoof put forward by his horse, was taking him nearer to the Crimea, where he would have to face his brother Monty and the other surviving officers of the 11th Hussars, including the damning Lord Cardigan. At a time of war, would they put aside personal enmities or cold shoulder him to a man when he arrived? Would he be subjected to further social humiliation in front of his regiment?

Small wonder those desert nights racked him with doubts, fears and passions until he felt much as he had on leaving hospital nine months before. And that darkest of all his demons began stirring in the deep recesses to which he had driven it on claiming Lydia. He had not conquered evil by confronting it with the power of virtue after all.

The drowsy daytime hours at that second camp brought the chance of a little excitement when the outlying piquets were approached by a man in flowing robes who purported to be a messenger bringing a request to the colonel of the illustrious regiment presently traversing his homeland. His master was an Arab chieftain passing incognito through the area after secret talks with his neighbouring rulers, and he asked permission to visit the camp that evening to pay his compliments to the army of the great Queen Victoria.

Not wishing to disillusion their guest, Marcus Benedict assumed the rank of colonel for the evening, trying his best to view it as Colonel Daubnay would, and knowing the facts would be certain to come out when the three wings met up in Cairo. So a lavish reception for the Arab and his staff was planned, with the officers of A, B, and C Troops under compulsory invitation to attend the Officers' Mess tent that evening. Mess staff were harried and hounded, and reserve supplies raided in order to provide a cold collation suitable for the occasion. Individual officers were obliged to surrender bottles of valuable wine brought all the way from Khunobad or Bombay, cigars and jars of favourite preserves, besides having to unpack their full dress uniforms for batmen to sponge and press. The tables were laid with spotless cloths and, because the mess silver was with Headquarters Wing, the members of the Advance Wing had to lend personal tableware. Although none would dream of saying so, each officer was thankful Mrs Benedict would not be present amongst such temptation. The ladies planned to dine together in Major Benedict's tent, and the Major himself secretly arranged for a guard to be posted outside. He had heard tales of Arab chieftains that told him such a move would be advisable.

Rowan was pleased with the diversion. It gave him a legitimate excuse to avoid another silent meal with Lydia, and it would be good to eat with his fellows again, as he had when a bachelor. But he recoiled on entering because the profusion of candles in the loaned candlesticks made the interior of the tent thick with smoke, and appallingly hot when dressed in the heavy, tight, silver-encrusted uniform. But they all voted the decor and transformation of the dreary tent a great triumph for their popular second-in-command.

As they stood around waiting, Rowan noted that young Lieutenant Cleaver looked totally lovelorn, and sympathy overrode jealousy. He knew too well how the poor devil felt. Kit Wrexham evoked no such sympathy. He was so full of his own importance he would never be lorn over anything in Rowan's opinion. All he hoped was that some fool did not suggest the ginger-haired warbler should sing for their guests.

When the chieftain arrived Major Benedict greeted him with a bow that was neither too obsequious nor too condescending, and the welcoming speech seemed to delight the visitor. He responded with a flourish as he explained that he was returning to Cairo from a private visit, and felt impelled to pay homage to a regiment that was known through the length and breadth of the land, and whose officers were legends of courage and honour. He would, of course, arrange

a reception worthy of such warriors when they arrived in the
city, he told them, and very much hoped the Colonel and
his estimable gentleman would accept his humble hospital-
ity.

The officers thought the whole situation highly entertaining, and offered seats at their table to the half-dozen hench-
men, who must have been personal bodyguards judging by
their physiques and the great jewelled daggers at their
waists. The chieftain took a great interest in them all, asking
about their antecedents and whether any had personal acquaintance with Queen Victoria. Some of his questions
brought on serious attacks of mirth from the most junior
officers, which had to be disguised behind spasms of feigned
coughing, or smothered with gulps of wine. The visitor also
showed fanatical interest in their uniforms, their weapons
and the legendary chestnut horses they rode. For the latter,
Marcus Benedict—promoted to colonel from necessity—
arranged to show them over the horse-lines at the conclusion
of the meal.

The sight of the magnificent matched stallions so excited
the guests, the officers of the 43rd quickly realized what the
visit was really all about. It needed only a broad hint that
the chieftain had brought a gift with him for the colonel,
to force Major Benedict to offer one of the horses in return.
It was one of those occasions when a quick decision was
necessary and any hesitation would be fatal. The 43rd was,
after all, crossing territory occupied by various chieftains
with their own private armies. It would be dangerous to give
an unintentional insult, or denigrate the regiment's power
and importance by showing lack of generosity. But when the
Major selected one, his officers hid their smiles. It was one
of the half-broken spare mounts known as an incorrigible
rogue. The regiment would be better off without it.

They all walked back to stand around one of the camp-
fires while two of the bodyguards walked off into the darkness to fetch the chieftain's gifts to the pseudo-colonel. As
Rowan stood there, however, something about the flickering
firelight and dark-skinned men in robes laughing together

took him back to that other place near Multan. Suddenly, his stomach began to churn and the scars on his torso became open burning wounds again. Fighting the bile in his throat and the cold sweat breaking on his skin, Rowan hung between then and now, both seeming equally unreal and frightening. He knew what was going to happen next; knew and was forbidden to prevent it. The scene began to swing about before his eyes until all he could see were dark laughing faces and the leaping flames of the fire.

Then it was there before him, happening as he had known it would. First, they brought forward the great curving knife with a blade that gleamed orange from the flame-light, and agony overwhelmed him until his brain was ready to burst with it. Next minute, two great brutes dragged the girl forward, and she was already running with blood. One anguished look at her and he could stand no more.

"No-o! *No!*" he screamed at them as he drew his sword and ran at them right through the fire with it raised above his head.

But he was caught and held by too many hands, then dragged to the ground with such force his head thudded back on to something hard. Everything turned black.

When he came to he was lying on a bed in a tent. There was a man with him, still in the elaborate dress uniform. Rowan frowned, trying to think.

"Feeling better?" asked Marcus Benedict.

"What happened?" He sat up gingerly and swung his feet to the ground.

"We almost had another war on our hands."

"*Oh, God!*"

"I averted it by telling him you were the regiment's most heroic officer, who had been tortured by our enemies and had been ill, as a result. He went away full of admiration for your courage."

Rowan was beginning to feel very sick and could not seem to stop shaking. There was nothing he could say; he had only a hazy impression of what had happened.

"Thank your lucky stars Daubnay wasn't here," said the

other man. "I've sworn the others to silence, and I think you can depend on them. But, if the chieftain really does organize a reception for us in Cairo, he might let the secret out. You had best be prepared."

Looking up at the senior man all he could say was, "Yes . . . thank you."

"Look, Rowan, don't you think it is time you spoke about that mission to Multan to someone? I take it this business tonight has something to do with it."

He made no answer. If only he could lie down and go to sleep!

"My dear fellow, you must see what impression has been gained by your behaviour tonight. Whilst no one doubts your courage, your fellows are going into battle beside you and need to have confidence that they will be ably supported on all sides. And your own subalterns were there, you know. It is essential that they should respect your leadership."

"I won't fail them." He looked up sharply at the other's silence. "Do you doubt me?"

"Not under normal circumstances. But you are a man who has faced abnormal circumstances . . . on more than one occasion. After this evening, don't you doubt yourself?"

"I . . . I am not entirely certain what happened."

Marcus Benedict sat down facing him. "Two of the body-guards had just brought in a jewelled dagger and two slave girls as a present for me, when you rushed at them with sword drawn, murder written all over your face. If it had not been for the prompt actions of Gil, Kit, Edward and Duncan there is no doubt they would have been badly cut up."

He put his head in his hands, appalled. It could not possibly be kept from Daubnay, and would really be the end for him this time.

"I had to refuse the slave girls, of course," said the Major lightly, to give him time to absorb the truth. "At the risk of offending the man I had to explain that we were on our way to war and regimental rules precluded the presence of unmarried females in our company. I just prayed none of our wives would appear and see them." He waited a moment or two, then said, "Rowan, I do urge you to confess to someone before you destroy yourself."

He could not tell this man, of course. He could not tell anyone. But he could not return to his tent to face Lydia. He could not face his friend Gil. There was nobody he could go to, so he walked out into the darkness of the desert, taking with him the only possible companion.

Mary had just spent two of the most fascinating nights of her life, and had still not recovered from them. The hill pony she had ridden had been sold at Bombay, it not being considered worth the expense of sea-transport, besides being unsuitable for the desert. She now travelled in a wicker basket that was one of a pair on a camel, relinquishing it only when the troopers rested their horses by leading them, and Mrs DeMayne rode in the basket in her place. Although the whole experience was mystic, enthralling, unbelievable, those periods spent in walking were the highlights that set her heart racing with something she did not understand.

Resting on a straw mat within her tiny tent she thought about it once more. Darkness, a chill that nipped the nostrils and made the great spread of stars appear brilliant, silence broken only by the squeak of leather, the grunt of animals, low voices that seemed afraid to shatter the peace and the swish of thousands of feet on sand commanded night in the desert. The swaying motion of the camel had resembled that of the vessel she had recently left, and she had been filled with wonder at the sensation because Noah had told her camels were called 'ships of the desert' and she could now understand why. Everything was so different, so intriguing, so satisfying to her soul. Once, she had been a slut living amidst dirt and squalor. Who would have dreamed that same girl would be crossing the world, treading a desert, riding a camel toward yet another strange, fascinating place —a place where men were killing each other for the sake of one person living in a great secret palace; the Russians for their Tsar, the British for their Queen. Noah had also told her that astonishing fact.

Pushing back her hair with a hand that felt cool in the
late evening chill Mary felt the surge of excitement in her
again. In two more days they would arrive in Cairo, where
Noah said there were wonderful things called pyramids that
reached way up into the sky, that had been built before
England had been civilized. And there was another monstrous half-person/half-animal built of stone that looked out
across the desert for miles. It was called a 'Svinks', but was
not spelt that way, to her surprise. Noah had promised to
take her to see them, because Colonel Daubnay had decided
to halt for three days at Cairo before setting out on the long
twelve-day march to Alexandria.

She was impatient to see them, but that evening had
provided yet another experience to widen her knowledge. It
had soon got around the camp that a chieftain was coming
to visit the officers, and Mary had been determined to see
the man arrive. Together with Noah she had wandered
around the perimeter in time to see the party ride in, robes
flowing out behind them, armed with great knives and leading two girls on a camel. The girls, one dressed in a bright
red robe and the other in blue, were possibly a present, Noah
had said. But Mary would not believe that anyone would
give *people* as presents, and he had laughed telling her there
was a great deal in this world she would find unbelievable
if she knew the half.

But her pleasure and excitement over her full and interesting life was nevertheless clouded. Since the evening she
had danced the jig, her happiness and confidence had been
shaky. She could not forget the way Rowan DeMayne had
looked at her, or the tone of his voice when he had said she
would never be more than a trooper's woman. Deeply hurt,
she had found her employment disagreeable since then.
Afraid to say anything in case she said it wrong, she went
about her chores in silence, and avoided being present when
he was with his wife. The pleasure she had found in his
company was a thing of the past, and he seemed just as
anxious to avoid her. In addition, her mistress was snappy
and fault-finding—so much so, Mary wondered how much

longer the situation could continue without a major storm blowing up in the DeMayne tent, with dramatic results.

Her thoughts then moved to the problem of her own future. Noah was still trying to persuade her to marry him on reaching Cairo. Maybe that was what she would be driven to do, yet something inside her protested strongly against such a step. It was irrational, because she was fonder of Noah than she had been of anyone save Sam, and he was like no ordinary trooper. But her strange uncertainty over him was part of a general confusion of feelings and ideas lately; a restlessness that pervaded even the daily adventure of crossing the world. Why, when she had everything she had once wanted, did she feel bereft?

Suddenly, her nerves jumped as the flap of the small tent was pushed up, and someone almost fell in. He stood there swaying, covered in sand, his open shirt revealing the scars on his body. In his eyes was that same look that had been there in the hospital. Heart thudding at the intrusion she scrambled to her feet, feeling at a disadvantage in just bodice and petticoat.

"Is there something wrong, sir?" she asked, realizing they were the same words she had used many times before.

"Yes . . . very, very wrong," he replied in slurred tones. "I was hellish lonely out there."

Thinking he was ill she stepped toward him in concern. Then she smelt the unmistakable whiff of brandy, and knew the truth. He was as drunk as a trooper. Still shaken by the shock of his violent entry, she set about doing what she had done on numerous occasions in the past. Taking his arm, she said, "Come along, my laddo, time you were in bed."

But she was not dealing with a trooper this time. They were invariably noisy, abusive or amorous, but biddable when drunk. This man was quietly, desperately inebriated, and certainly in no mood to be told what to do.

Standing his ground he said, "It's hellish lonely there, as well."

For a moment Mary was worried. The situation was potentially dangerous. She was alone and half-dressed; he was liable to behave unpredictably. A call for assistance would focus unwelcome attention on something it was essential to keep private, for all their sakes.

With that in mind, she said as sternly as she could, "Captain DeMayne, you really ought to leave."

His dark despairing gaze burned down into hers, as he swayed unsteadily a few feet away. "I can't. There isn't anywhere else to go."

In an instant, those stark words told her what she had been unwilling to own to herself all these weeks. They told her the reason for her restlessness, her reluctance to tie herself to Noah, her inner yearning despite the fullness of her present life. Shaken to the core that she had ignored the truth for so long she felt, more than ever, that every second that passed increased the danger of this nocturnal meeting —danger of a forbidden kind.

"I think I should call Collins," she said with an effort. "He'll help you."

"No one can help me," came the hollow mumbled reply. "I thought she would drive it away, but it's . . . it's still there. It comes . . . dear God, it comes when I least expect it." There was fear as well as despair in his intent gaze then. "It's like . . . it's like being the only one left alive in the land of the . . . of the dead." He staggered and almost fell, but grabbed at her for support as he added bleakly, "Or like being dead in the land of the living."

Inwardly seared by an emotion that defied all sense and social barriers, Mary was too overcome to do more than provide a prop beneath his fierce grip as she revelled in the knowledge that some instinct had led him to come to *her* when all seemed black.

"There's no one to turn to," he continued in that voice that smote her with its desolate tone even when slurred by intoxication. "No one to understand. And it's . . . it's so hellish *lonely* I can't . . . I can't . . ."

But the sentence was never finished. Despite his hold on her arms, his knees suddenly buckled and he fell heavily at her feet in a stupor. It was only a moment before she sank down beside his prostrate body, still trembling from the shock of what had happened in so short a time. With an effort she managed to roll him over on to his back, then very tenderly brushed the fine grains of sand from a face she now knew in its every mood.

"You poor dear," she whispered. "You're not alone. I could help you . . . but I'm the only one who will never be allowed to."

Cairo provided an outlet for the restless spirits of the soldiers come from the desert. Three days' halt were planned before the second stage to Alexandria was begun, and there was enough in the city to provide pleasant diversion for all tastes. This was the first real sample of civilized living the men had had for some years. There were hotels and cafés to frequent, a visit to the pyramids for the serious-minded, mosques and other Eastern marvels of construction to see and note in a letter home; and hundreds of little shops to tempt fingers to loosen purse-strings.

For once, the regiment was accommodated in barracks three miles out on the edge of the desert—new buildings that had been erected for the Pasha's troops and now most hospitably put at the disposal of the British as they passed through. The men rejoiced at not having to set up camp, but their chins soon dropped when they saw the state of their new quarters. They might have a pleasing and impressive outside appearance, but the Egyptian idea of cleanliness did not extend very far, and prospects of an immediate excursion into the city faded beneath the necessity of making the rooms habitable.

By evening, no one would have recognized the place and permission was given to all those not on duty to take advantage of a little free time. The rank and file descended on the city in fine fettle and, being cavalrymen, elected to go everywhere by donkey rather than be seen walking. It was not to be expected that such celebrated horsemen would travel at the speed of the donkey-boy, and the good people of Cairo were astonished to see lanky dragoons galloping headlong through the narrow streets astride beasts goaded into such speed by the spurs of the riders. Luckily for them, most of the officers had disappeared into Shepherd's Hotel, or various dignitaries' homes for dinner, so there was no need for a curb to their exuberance, and many a cavalry charge was rehearsed that night.

They soon found it was useless to stroll behind any of the voluptuous veiled women who passed through the streets, as most of them had bodyguards who appeared from nowhere when the occasion demanded. But there were many discreet premises where a soldier could spend his accumulated pay on discovering what lay behind the veil . . . and a lot more besides.

The quarters allotted to the officers were quite pleasant, even though they smelt of disinfecting powder battling with the inevitable essence of the East. Mary had a tiny annexe to herself at the end of the corridor, and noted wryly that there was a huge rusty bolt on the door to keep out nocturnal visitors. It was unlikely there would be any. Noah was some distance away on the other side of the barracks, and Rowan had been scrupulously sober and attentive to his wife since that fatal episode.

She had fetched Collins to help her that night, and the little batman knew enough of the DeMayne marriage to agree to Mary's suggestion that they should pretend the Captain had gone down with a sharp attack of fever and get a *dhoolie* organized for him to travel in. The deception appeared to have worked, and the 'patient' had looked sufficiently haggard when sober to bear out the suggestion of illness. Carefully avoiding his presence, Mary had nevertheless come face to face with him in the doorway of his present quarters. Standing aside to let her pass he had transmitted a brief startling glance that had contained so many messages that she had not yet unravelled. Better, perhaps, that she never did.

But she had unravelled her own feelings enough to realize she could not continue with the new situation that had been brought about by that dramatic encounter. When she thought of Rowan there was no confusion with what she had felt for dear Sam, nor was there any comparison with her feelings for Noah. But were infinitely pale beside the vibrant glow of that mixture of tenderness, pride, longing and fierce passion she experienced at every sight of him now. Worst of all, she knew she could not let it die now it had been born.

All through that first night in Cairo she tossed and turned, not knowing what to do. Unless the unexpected happened, the DeMayne marriage looked set to deteriorate further and, as it crumbled, Rowan was returning to the state he had been in in Khunobad hospital. With only war ahead of him, Mary feared the man she loved would end by destroying himself. That Lydia was not prepared to lift a finger to help him—did not even see the need to do so— was a situation Mary felt she could no longer endure. If Rowan turned to her a second time in an unconscious search for help, the outcome might add further scandal to a reputation already blackened. For both their sakes, their association must end.

After fruitless searching of her tired brain for solutions, only one possible path emerged. She would have to marry Noah, here in Cairo. He had been urging her to, but he did not know the regiment as well as she. While officers' ladies could travel with them to war, the wives of the soldiers had been shipped home from India. If she married Noah now, once they reached Alexandria, she would be put aboard a ship for England along with the officers' wives taking children, the sick and the unfit for battle. It would mean a homeland she did not know, and nowhere to live. But she felt able to search for employment as a servant now, and had learnt enough to have confidence in coping with yet another change of lifestyle. If Noah survived to return from the Crimea she would face the squalor of a barrack-block again; if he fell in battle . . . but that was best left until it happened. The urgency lay in severing her tie with the DeMaynes before it was too late.

Putting all painful thoughts aside, Mary set off the next morning on her greatest adventure so far. Noah was taking

her to see the pyramids and the thing that was called a
Svinks and was spelled Sphinx. To make it even more of an
occasion he took her first to the bazaar to buy her very first
bonnet. Due to the very fierce heat in Cairo it was fatal for
English visitors to go hatless on the trip, and Noah swore he
had been waiting for the opportunity to give his sweetheart
a present. Letting the possessive description pass unchal-
lenged, Mary allowed the pleasure of choosing her present
literally go to her head, and selected a pale-blue chip bonnet
that was trimmed with a tiny cockade of yellow and black
feathers. It was as close to the regimental colours as she
could find.

"Since I can't wear a shako," she told Noah gaily, "I'll
have my own headdress to show I belong to the 43rd."

"But you don't," Noah pointed out. "They disowned you
when Sam Clarke died."

"I was born into the regiment," she replied, wondering
if she should tell him she intended becoming a trooper's wife
again at this stage. "No one can really disown their child."

"Yes, they can."

He sounded so strange and faraway Mary put her hand
on his sleeve. "Noah, what is it?"

He turned to give her a bitter smile. "Nothing. Come on,
let's get into one of those carriages before they all fill up."

On reaching the sight of what Noah told her was one of
the seven wonders of the world, Mary was silenced by what
she saw. As they left the carriage to wander around with the
other visitors, she told herself it was a day of her life she
would never forget. But she had no notion then just what
the day would contain.

Walking with her hand tucked through Noah's crooked
arm she gazed in fascination at all they saw, and listened to
the guide without being able to absorb the amount of figures
he quoted regarding the building of such monstrous monu-
ments. For Mary, the past came alive. She could see in her
mind's eye the myriad white-robed figures toiling up and
down with stones, while the pointed shapes rose higher and

higher. Statistics went over her head; it was the human element that caught her imagination.

But the day was speeding past, and she had something to settle—something very vital. It was settled for her, however, when they sat in the shade to drink lemonade that had been kept on ice, and Noah smiled at her, asking if she was enjoying herself.

"Need you ask?" she replied, smiling back. "What more could a girl want than a bonnet and a trip to the pyramids?"

"A husband to look after her," he retorted with surprising urgency. "Mary, I've given you time to think things over, and you'll agree I've been very patient. We could be married in Cairo this evening. I could arrange it without any trouble, I promise you. What do you say?"

"Yes," she said simply.

He stared at her in disbelief. "Say that again!"

"Yes, I'll marry you, Noah. This evening, if you like."

Happiness and relief broke across his face and he seized her hands, spilling the lemonade she was holding. But it was only a minor incident at a momentous time, and they both ignored the wet patch spreading across her grey skirt as he kissed her beneath the shady brim of her new bonnet and told her he was the luckiest man in the world.

"I'll be honest with you and admit I made up to you that first day in the hope of having some light relief on the march. But I didn't know, Mary dear, that you would creep into my heart the way you have," he said. "I'm going to give you all the things you've ever wanted, I promise."

"That'll be a tall order," she warned with a smile that contained an element of sadness. "I knew what you were up to, Noah Ramslake, when you first came up to look at the blisters on my feet. But I do truly believe you will be a good husband, or I'd never agree to it." Then she knew she could not go on letting him believe something that could not happen, even if it meant he withdrew his offer. "You don't know this regiment as well as I do, love. There's something you haven't thought of. The minute we get married I shall be taken on the strength . . . and that means I'll be sent to

England from Alexandria. They won't let a trooper's wife go to the Crimea."

He took the glass of lemonade from her hand and gripped it tightly, lowering his voice for fear of being overheard by the crisscross of visitors passing against the gigantic background pyramid.

"There's something *you* haven't thought of. They'd never give me permission to marry on the way to war, so you'd not be taken on the strength. And we're not going to the Crimea."

Totally bewildered and feeling the heat sapping her strength, all she could say was, "Whatever are you talking about?"

"I've never had any intention of going to the Crimea."

"*What?*"

"Mary, listen to me," he urged, squeezing her hand even tighter. "You do promise to marry me, don't you?"

"Yes . . . I said I would, didn't I?" She did not really know what either of them were saying now. The great stone constructions rising out of the sand seemed to have put an air of unreality over everything, and the morning had turned into a shimmery-hazy time that suggested she was dreaming.

"Then you must put your trust in me," Noah said emphatically. "Because I am putting mine in you now by telling you something you have always wanted to know—why I joined the army."

As she looked at his good-looking brown face, Mary sensed she was about to find out what he had meant by saying he was too good to be a sergeant and not quite good enough to be an officer.

"Go on, Noah."

Strangely, her prompt made him hesitate. Then he began telling a story that was familiar to her. "I come from a good family. Not aristocracy, but high-class tradespeople with a solid reputation for honesty, morality and sobriety. As soon as I was old enough, I joined my father in the family business and started at the bottom, as he insisted, by serving in the showroom. I was passionately interested in gems, but my passion was soon exceeded by another." He frowned as he thought back on those times. "She came in with an elderly man who said he was her father, and plainly was not. I was bewitched by her, and her experience in such things told her she had made another conquest. But that's a long story we need not go into. I can hardly believe now that I behaved as I did, but she could persuade me to do anything for her . . . and that included buying her things I couldn't afford." He swallowed. "I began by taking the odd shilling out of the till, then I was promoted to the cash-desk and began taking much larger sums."

She was shocked. "From your own father?"

"That's why it didn't seem like stealing. It would all be mine eventually," he explained simply. "I always believed I would put it back, in any case."

"But you never did?"

His frank gaze appealed to her. "How could I? She kept demanding more, so I took more in order to keep her from straying to someone else. But she did when Father discovered what I was doing and turned me out of the house with orders never to go back. He stood the loss rather than let scandal touch the family, and I have never seen any of them since that day. I have no idea what he told them, what reason he gave for my leaving so suddenly."

Appalled at what he was saying Mary nevertheless marvelled at another otherwise strong man being reduced by a pretty woman. What was there about the male character that could produce great strength of personality, yet equally great weakness when it came to females?

"They have no idea where you are, then?"

"They have no wish to know," he said bitterly. "A man only has to break the rules once for family and society to condemn him as a blackguard."

It sounded like the echo of another story that haunted her. "So you joined the regiment."

"Oh no," he replied, surprising her. "I joined a theatrical company to be near her lodgings, and watched in mounting jealousy as her new elderly lover showered her with gifts in return for nights up in her room. Then, one morning when he walked down her steps, I shot him."

It so shocked her she stared at him speechlessly. He gazed back with the frown on his forehead deepening. "I can scarcely believe I did it now, but I was young and full of a passion that took no account of reality. Mary, I don't know if my identity was ever discovered. I was picked from the gutter by a recruiting sergeant and thankfully enlisted in a regiment sailing next day for India. I think seven years in stinking barrack-blocks in company with ill-bred, uneducated ruffians is enough to pay for the life of a lecherous old man already nine-tenths to the grave, don't you?"

What could she reply? Stunned by his revelation she could think only of another infatuated boy who had drawn his sword against his brother in a moment of passion over a female. How could she understand or condemn when she had had no experience of such emotions? What she felt for Rowan now was strong and overwhelming, but her instinct was to run away from it, not kill Lydia DeMayne.

"Say something, Mary."

Noah's voice brought her back to focus on his anxious face again. "Why didn't you tell me this before?"

"I've only told you now so that you'll understand why we're going."

Still as if in a trance wrought by the surrounding echo of past violent centuries, she asked, "Going where?"

"Leaving the regiment."

"Leaving the regiment?" she repeated faintly. "Whatever are you talking about?"

Gripping her hands with renewed urgency he said, "I've paid for what I did with sadistic bullying by NCO's, and a standard of living similar to that of men in prison. I'd been trapped in India for seven interminable years, so when orders came to go to the Crimea I rejoiced more wildly than any man. It spelled freedom at last. Let them all be heroes if they wish, but I've no intention of setting foot on any battlefield. I have no Queen and Country now, therefore no obligation to fight for them. We'll get married this evening, then slip into hiding until they march out the day after tomorrow. With a full water bottle and a few pieces of bread we could even stay here for a day or two, mingling with the visitors. I knew from the start that Cairo was the ideal place to leave. They've ships at Alexandria that can't be kept waiting."

"It's not *leaving,*" she cried, "it's desertion. You must know what they'll do to you if you're caught."

"We won't be. They're going to war and can't delay for anything."

"There are two other regiments passing through; there are authorities here in Cairo," she told him in insistent tones. "Of course they'll catch you."

"We'll move on the minute they're clear of Cairo."

She gave a long deep sigh designed to steady the thudding of her heart, and pulled her hands from his. "I won't do it, Noah."

He stared at her for a long minute, then seized her arm to draw her along the rough path where processions of people were passing back and forth.

"Mary, don't let me down now. I've put all my trust in you. I've made the plans with a great deal of thought and I swear they'll work. There's a good life to be had out here. I know all about gems, and a man can make a fortune in a country like this. We'll have a fine house with marble floors, and a courtyard full of flowering trees. I'll make you into a lady, which is what you've always wanted, isn't it?"

"No one can be *made* into a lady," she said, totally out of her depth. "You're either born one, or not."

"I'll make you rich, then."

"You'd always be running away. What kind of life is that?"

He turned her to face him. "Better than living like a mindless brute in a hot stinking building, or dashing off to be cut to pieces for a cause that isn't worth the sacrifice." He shook her impatiently. "Mary, I need you for the sweeter side of life . . . but I'll go on my own if I have to. I'm not leaving with the regiment."

"I must."

"Why?" he cried. "What has the 43rd ever done for you?"

Turning away from his gaze she said, "It has been my home and family for eighteen years. I couldn't leave it on those terms." Her decision irrevocably made, she turned back to him in appeal. "Noah, don't do it! I'll give you the sweeter side, even if we can't get married, so long as you stay. Sam taught me a saying that two wrongs don't make a right, and running away a second time is only going to make life worse for you."

"It couldn't be worse. You've lived with troopers; you know what it's like." He sighed heavily. "You could have compensated for those seven years. Together, we could have gone from strength to strength. Alone, you don't stand a chance in life. You're not a child of the regiment; you're its slave, Mary."

She shook her head sadly. "You are the one who will never be free."

He stood there indecisive, and she could see the faint desperation in his eyes. "What am I going to do now? I've given away my plans, and you'll tell your employer what I intend to do."

"You should know me better than that," she told him quietly. "I believe everyone should live the way they want . . . but, don't do it, Noah."

"I have to," he insisted. "Can't you see? Ever since that order to war came, I've lived for this chance of freedom, I can't let it pass by. I *can't.*" He studied her closely. "Do you mean it when you say you won't betray me?"

"You're the one who's been telling lies all this time, not me," was her response to that.

That evening the officers of the regiment, and the ladies with them, were invited to dinner at one of the Viceroy's residences along the banks of the Nile. Carriages were arranged to take them from the barracks to a steamer provided for the short voyage. It being a formal occasion, dress uniforms were to be worn, and the ladies brought out their finest dresses and cobwebby Kashmir shawls. Lydia called Mary earlier than usual to help her to dress. She was visibly excited by the thought of this taste of civilized luxury after two-and-a-half months on the move. It meant her temper was sweeter than it had been for some time, and Mary needed only to answer briefly the flow of happy chatter from her mistress.

She was beset by thoughts of Noah, who was planning to leave under cover of darkness that night. He had brought her back and said goodbye outside her small room a few doors from that of her employers, ignoring her last whispered plea not to do something that could only turn into tragedy. Sadness sat heavily on her now as she realized that she had been disillusioned for the second time in her life— the first being the treatment of her former friends when she had married Sam Clarke. It struck her that education taught people how to be evasive and deceitful; it showed them how to hide the things that they were and the things they thought. She was doing it herself, at that moment, by waiting on a woman she would give anything to replace; hiding her love for a man dazzled to the extent of weakness by his wife's beauty. Perhaps she had been better off as an ignorant trooper's woman.

Her nerves jumped and she dropped the curl she was pinning into place when Rowan stepped quickly into the room through a curtained arch. He looked so very impressive and proud in the flattering uniform that she felt colour creep into her cheeks. It was not due to admiration, but guilt. One of his own troopers was going to desert the regiment during his absence tonight, and she knew but would not tell him. He had enough to contend with, heaven knew, but she could not betray Noah to anyone, even the man she loved. Would he understand that? Would he approve of loyalty in this instance?

"You look so lovely I am almost afraid to take you there," he said to his wife in tones of forced flattery. "I am not sure I can hold off so many prospective rivals."

She turned a dazzling smile on to him, apparently oblivious to the nuances of his voice. "What use have I for rivals, my dear, when you look so excessively handsome?" She angled her slender body toward Mary. "Fetch my pearl pendant. Captain DeMayne will fasten it for me while you finish my hair."

Mary walked across to get the blue velvet box, convinced Rowan could see right into her mind and read the knowledge she possessed. It took some resolution to return and stand right beside him. Did knowing about it and saying nothing make her as guilty as Noah?

The velvet box was empty. It was so unexpected no one said anything for a moment or two. Then Lydia said hollowly, "It's not there."

"That's all too obvious," said Rowan crisply. "Are you certain you put it away?"

"Of course I'm certain. At least, I gave it to Mrs Clarke to place in the box after the concert at Suez."

The dark heavy-lidded eyes swivelled to look at Mary. "Was that the last occasion my wife wore the pendant?"

"Yes, sir. I put it away myself, then gave Madam the box before I left."

"Rowan, what could have happened to it?" cried Lydia.

"There must be a simple explanation," was his reassuring verdict. "I put the box with the silver and took it all to be locked up with the rest of the valuables under guard for the journey. Are you sure it hasn't fallen here on the floor? I only collected our things two hours ago from Marcus Benedict."

At those words, the pair exchanged significant glances. Then Rowan said, "Surely not! She usually only takes silver."

"There is always a first time. Check with him, Rowan. I couldn't bear to lose it. The piece is magnificent . . . and I am denied any of the Drumlea jewellery."

He went out swiftly, and Mary made a thorough search of the room while he was gone. But it appeared Mrs Benedict had not taken it. Her husband would stake his life on it, he told Rowan. By that time Lydia was thoroughly upset, and time was passing too quickly.

"We have to leave, I'm afraid. The carriages have already arrived," Rowan said with emphasis. "The pendant cannot possibly be lost. I took it to the guards at Suez, and collected it only a short time ago. It has been in this room ever since."

"I was resting on the bed. I did not have my eye on it the whole time," Lydia said testily.

"But Mrs Clarke was here."

"I went to see the pyramids," Mary reminded him quietly. "Madam gave me permission. I didn't get back until this afternoon."

"But before I collected our valuables, surely?"

"Yes . . . but Madam said she wouldn't need me until four. I've been in my room."

"With the door open?"

It was like a cross-examination, and her guilt over Noah made her stammer her reply. "Y-yes . . . I mean, it was for a while."

"Did you see anyone pass through this corridor?"

"I wasn't really looking."

"No . . . of course." He sighed. "Well, it cannot possibly be lost."

Lydia stood up. "It has been stolen by one of those murderous-looking Egyptians for certain."

Picking up her shawl Rowan said, "No, they are not allowed in here. Guards are posted to prevent it. Only members of the regiment come into this part of the barracks."

"Then it has been taken by one of the troopers."

"Out of the question," he said curtly. "You should know the men better than that. In any case, they would not know where it was kept." Arranging the shawl over her shoulders, he added, "I have every confidence Mrs Clarke will have found the pearl by the time we return. It is a great pity you cannot wear it as you hoped, but it has doubtless fallen somewhere out of sight and there is no time to look for it." Turning to Mary he said with the briskness he adopted toward her lately, "Would you please search once more? It cannot have gone far."

Mary was glad when they had gone. It was too much of a strain to have Rowan raining questions on her when she had a guilty secret locked within her regarding one of those men he defended so immediately. Although she searched every inch of the rooms allocated to the DeMaynes, shook out every one of her mistress's gowns and petticoats, looked inside shoes, slippers and boots, turned out drawers and cupboards, there was no sign of the missing pendant. After an hour of concentrated searching she was hot and tired and her spirits at very low ebb. The day that had begun so well had turned into a nightmare; her proposed change of fortunes had collapsed.

Looking at the DeMaynes' little travelling-clock she realized it was past nine. Evening stables were well over, and Noah would be on his way. Where would he go; what would he live on? He could only take so much food and water with him, and his pay would not stretch far when had to provide everything for himself. How did he propose setting up as a gem merchant with no money for such a venture?

Her heart raced with sudden apprehension as thoughts piled into her brain one after the other. Noah had been a thief before, and could be again if desperate enough. A very valuable pearl and sapphire pendant was missing: Noah knew all about jewellery, including the details of that pendant. Mary had told him.

Getting to her feet in agitation she pushed back her tumbling hair in a distracted gesture. No, he surely could not have taken it! Yet he had stood in the corridor outside her room during that vital time, and she had been so upset at his farewell she had gone inside without waiting to see him walk away.

Only members of the regiment come into this part of the barracks. In any case, they would not know where it was kept.

Mary put her hands over her face. In her foolish trusting manner she had prattled a description of the pearl and sapphires, the long gold chain, the elegant blue velvet box containing it that was always kept with the DeMayne silver. All this while she had sat with Noah on the deck watching the flying fish. His interest in it had flattered her sense of importance; the pendant's existence had somehow boosted her own feelings of respectability by being entrusted with such a thing.

"Oh, lordy," she breathed in stricken tones. "What have I done?"

But she was not a person to wither beneath self-condemnation, and she ran from the room knowing there was only one thing to do.

CHAPTER NINE

Rowan found that evening something of a test. In addition to Lydia's tendency to flirt with Kit Wrexham and young Robin Cleaver in a social atmosphere that well suited her personality, he discovered one of the other guests was the chieftain he had attacked like a madman three nights before. For much of the evening he managed to avoid a confrontation, but knew it was inevitable before the event was over.

Surprisingly, Maurice Daubnay had approved Major Benedict's actions in the desert as necessary to uphold the honour of the regiment. It was fortunate that the Arab accepted the explanation given him by the real colonel, and regretted there was insufficient time in which to entertain the noble gentlemen of the 43rd in return. Finally face to face with Rowan he had nodded politely and asked if the blessing of good health was on him again, whereupon Rowan assured him that it was. Colonel Daubnay appeared to read nothing significant in the exchange, so he had to believe that nothing had been said by those who had witnessed his wild behaviour that night. But if they said nothing, it was certainly there in their eyes these days. Even Gil seemed wary of him. He was not surprised. He was wary of himself.

One more night, then they would set out on the most arduous section of the entire journey—almost two weeks across some of the worst cavalry terrain imaginable, each march having to be made in daylight because of the high risk of becoming lost during the hours of darkness. At the end of that mammoth journey lay Alexandria, on the sparkling Mediterranean, just a short journey from those suffering, broken regiments they were to join.

The news awaiting them at Cairo had been of further losses and suffering due to the severe winter, with such appalling numbers of sick and wounded they were even dying as they lay exposed to the weather on the beaches outside the overflowing hospital at Scutari. There was word of a harridan called Florence Nightingale arriving there with a following of female nurses, but no one supposed they would be anything other than a nuisance, with demands for comforts and attention because they were women.

But, despite the gloomy news, the members of the 43rd told themselves it would be April in two days' time, and spring would have come to the Crimea by the time they arrived. In addition, Cornet Wilde had heard from his sister in England that pleasure cruises to Balaclava were being organized, and parties of sightseers were already packing for embarkation. The Wildes were intending to be amongst the number and were looking forward to seeing their youngest member in little less than a month's time. These conflicting pictures persuaded the would-be heroes that the war was likely to last long enough for them to share in the action, and also that it would not be as bad as they had been led to believe.

Neither picture brought much comfort to Rowan. If the battlefields were to be turned into pleasure-grounds for pic-nic-parties it was more than likely the area would be full of people he knew who would undoubtedly cut him; if Bala-clava was as grim as the other stories suggested would he be again able to earn the confidence of his fellows in battle?

Either way, the Crimea looked set to make or break him.

There was a more immediate problem on his hands when they got back to their barrack-quarters, for there was no sign of Mary. Enquiries of Collins gave no clue to where she might be, for he said he had not seen her since they left for the steamer. So, through means of an interpreter, Rowan questioned the native girls who had been employed by the other wives for this part of their journey. That was a waste of time, for all they did was giggle and lower their eyes as if he were importuning them for nocturnal companionship.

Already in an uneasy mood he found alarm growing in his breast. What could have happened to her? This was a savage country where people vanished frequently enough for it to be commonplace, and he had no illusions about the probable fate of a young white girl. He also had no illusions about his dependence on her happiness. Although he remembered very little about the incident, he had a vague picture of a sweet young girl in her underwear who had seemed to be the only other person in his tortured world. There was no doubt it had been Mary who had organized a *dhoolie* and spread the story of a swift attack of fever, and the knowledge had been there between them, unspoken yet undeniable, since. Sensing danger he had tried to put it out of his mind, in vain. If she was not there to turn to when the demon returned —as it surely would—he would be finally lost.

Lydia was pacing the room when he re-entered it, and looked up hopefully. Seeing he was alone she cried, "You have not found her? How very distressing. I lived in hope that there was a simple explanation of her absence. But, much as I dislike the thought, it has to be faced. It is particularly unpleasant, because she had always appeared to be so reliable, and I had believed her gratitude for all I had done for her to be genuine."

Completely immersed in thoughts of Mary being sold into bondage of an unthinkable nature, he looked at his wife blankly.

"Gratitude?"

"My dear, have you forgotten I employed her as a sewing-woman in Khunobad, besides saving her from heartless abandonment by the regiment when I employed her to travel with us? I was even foolish enough to *trust* her," she added in throbbing tones. "Of late, she had improved herself to such a degree I was prepared to keep her on until we reached England. But she has reverted to kind, after all, and repaid me with treachery. I am quite shattered."

Still away on thoughts of his own Rowan said, "I am not following what you say, Lydia. Treachery? What can you mean?"

She stepped up to him, her face paler than usual. "She has stolen the pendant and run off."

Anger rushed through him. "Impossible! She would never do that."

"But she has! The evidence is indisputable. The jewel is missing, and so is she."

"No, I will not believe that," he countered fiercely. "She is a woman of the regiment and would not dream of robbing one of its officers."

Speculation sprang up in her glance. "You have always condemned the women of the regiment as sly creatures. What is there about this particular one that persuades you she is of sterling worth?"

"Those same qualities that persuaded you to become her benefactress, no doubt. Like you, I trusted her . . . and I still do. There is some simple explanation. There must be."

At dawn the truth was discovered. One of Rowan's personal chargers had gone from the stables, and Noah Ramslake and his horse were missing. No one had seen Mary Clarke, and all Rowan had to go on was a report from an outlying desert piquet that he had seen a cloaked figure heading along the road to Giza, and had taken it to be Captain DeMayne on Drummer Boy. That had been the previous evening.

Lydia did not have to put it into words for him, but she did. "Only a fool would refuse to see the truth now. They have absconded together with my pendant."

He was stunned by the indisputable facts. Ramslake had

always been something of a mystery man whom he could not promote because he did not have the necessary toughness to make the men obey him. But he had always seemed trustworthy, and he had been courting Mary. The biggest shock, however, was this further evidence of his fatal misjudgment where women were concerned. It hit him like a body blow. He would have staked his life on Mary's loyalty and utter honesty.

"They will pay for what they have done, by God, they will," he swore, the anger of betrayal making his voice harsh.

There was something against her mouth; wonderful trickling moisture in her aching throat. Her head was being supported by a strong arm. Thank God she was no longer alone. With an effort she opened her eyes. All she could see was a dark outline against the blinding circle of the sun, but her heart leapt when that unmistakable voice said, "Come on, drink! Now more!"

It seemed incredible, impossible, but as her eyes grew used to the brightness she saw the pale-blue jacket with captain's insignia on the sleeves, the white-covered shako and the tall dark-red stallion standing behind him. Wherever else she looked there was sand.

"How did you find me?" she murmured after drinking again.

"Pure chance. Four of us are out searching a wide area." He lowered her again and drank from the choggle, still on one knee beside her. Corking it again he demanded, "Where is Ramslake?"

"I don't know."

"So he abandoned you. Did you quarrel?"

She stared up in bewilderment, the peak of his shako casting enough shadow over his face for her to see it clearly now. The satanic quality of his features had never been so apparent. It was almost frightening.

"Come on, answer me," he rasped. "There is little point in being evasive. I have men after him. It will be easier for us all, in the long run, to give me his direction."

"I don't know it." She was still trying to recall everything that had happened, and was confused beneath his attack.

"So you are playing your part to the final scene," he said contemptuously. "Do you realize it will be prison in Cairo for you, and a damned sight more for your lover when he is caught? I suggest you save what anguish you can by telling me the truth, at this point . . . if you are capable of such a thing."

The full hostility of his manner got through to her then, and she struggled to sit up. He made no attempt to help her, just continued his sharp questioning.

"Where is my horse, Drummer Boy?"

Hand to her temple as a wave of giddiness hit her, she murmured again, "I don't know."

Next minute, he had seized her hair forcing her head back so that she had to look him in the eyes. They were jet-black with fury. "It would cause me no pang to ride away and leave you here. Unless, of course, you still have the pearl on you. I warn you to start answering my questions. The alternative is a search of your person for the jewel, and rather more forcible persuasion until I get the truth from you."

"*Please,*" she cried, putting her hand up to his. "You're hurting me. I haven't got the pearl. How can you think I have?"

He released her roughly and stood up to survey her with disgust. "Still lying! I should have known it was second nature to your kind. You don't warrant my concern. Ramslake is in the service of the Queen and must be apprehended. But you are of no account whatever."

"*No,*" she cried, in fierce protest as she looked up at him. "No, you can't say that now. You once galloped past and covered me with mud. I understood why, then. But I challenge you to ride away now as if I don't exist."

"You are in no position to challenge me to do *anything,*" he flung at her. "Your fate is entirely in my hands."

"It has been since we left Khunobad," she flung back. "You could have abandoned me anywhere along the route. But you didn't, did you?"

"What a fool I was."

Scrambling to her feet, still unable to accept the evidence of his behaviour, she asked, "You don't really believe I took the pendant to give to Noah, do you?"

"Didn't you?"

It was an unbelievable blow. "I thought you trusted me," she said in a low voice.

"I trust damning evidence. It is usually more reliable than personal feelings." Then, as she continued to gaze at him, he demanded harshly, "Do you expect me to accept that you did *not* plan to go off together?"

Facing him frankly as the sun bore down relentlessly on that isolated stretch of desert, she said, "It was what he asked me to do. But I found I couldn't leave the regiment."

"Why? It has done very little for you."

"That's what he said."

"Damn what he said!" Rowan snapped. "*Why* couldn't you leave?"

"It's all I've ever known."

For some reason it did not seem to be the answer he wanted, and he renewed his attack as she stood before him, burning with the heat of growing day, covered with sand and aching all over. Yet none of it seemed as terrible as his condemnation. She still could not believe it after all that had been forged between them over the past four months.

"For someone who claims she could not leave, the theft of a valuable pearl pendant and a very fast horse on which to make a nocturnal get-away needs some explanation, wouldn't you agree? For God's sake, girl, do you take me for a gullible idiot?"

She shaded her eyes with her hand because the sun was right behind his head and she was staring into it. The glare highlighted the passion on his face. She was glad. It matched her own.

"Noah told me at the pyramids that he was going to desert. That was after he had asked me to marry him," she told him simply. "But I refused to go with him on those terms, and I tried to talk him out of it. But he had made up his mind and nothing I said changed it. I gave him my promise not to betray him." She moved slightly so that she was not so blinded by the sun, and confessed, "I felt awful when you came into the room last night, but I couldn't break my promise . . . not even for you."

"Choice of loyalties?" he asked cuttingly. "What about the regiment to which you owe so much?"

"I also owed Noah a lot," she cried. "He had been very kind to me."

"So much so you had agreed to marry him."

"Yes."

"The evidence against you is mounting with every word, and I am growing tired of listening. As a defence, it is ludicrous."

"You asked for an explanation, and this is it," she countered fiercely, the pain of his lack of trust hurting more and more. "I'm not clever, like you. I can't put things so that they confuse and bewilder people, like you can quite often. But I can tell the plain truth . . . and if you can't even stand and listen to it, you'd better ride off and leave me, like you said."

But that was a challenge he was no longer prepared to take up apparently, and her bold attack appeared to impress him more than her defence had. Wiping the sweat from his brow with the back of his hand in an unconscious gesture, he prompted in a quieter tone, "Go on . . . you owed him something in return for his kindness."

Uncertain of his new attitude she continued hesitantly. "It was only after you had left for dinner that I began thinking about Noah's plans for the future, and then I guessed he must have taken the pendant. I didn't want to believe it, but it did make sense. I felt to blame, because I had told him all about it—even where it was kept in the blue velvet box."

With a spurt of renewed anger he said, "Don't you have any sense at all?"

She looked back with unflinching dignity. "I trusted him . . . the same as you once trusted me."

"Didn't I just query the reliability of personal feelings against damning evidence?" He shifted his booted feet that were gradually sinking into the sand. "So you are saying Ramslake has the pendant?"

She nodded. "I think so. That's why I took your horse to go after him. I wanted to persuade him to give it back."

"And?"

"I never caught up with him. The horse was more than I could manage. It threw me and ran off."

"Little fool! It was madness. You ride like a pedlar on a lame donkey," was his blunt comment. "Which way did Drummer Boy head?"

She pushed back her sand-filled hair with her hand, and sighed. "I don't remember much after I fell. I hit my head, and the horse had disappeared by the time I got up again. I began walking, but it was dark and I couldn't see where I was going. The sand started getting deeper and, after a bit, I knew it was silly going on. I tried to sleep, but the cold kept me awake. When dawn came I realized I was miles away from anywhere. It was hard trying to walk in the sand, but I kept going as long as I could. Then it grew too hot, and every dune looked the same. I sat down and must have gone to sleep." She paused seeing her folly so clearly now. "I'm sorry, truly I am . . . about everything."

He looked at her for some moments as if trying to decide how much of her story he believed, then he nodded at his horse. "We'll have to ride together, which will slow us up. But you won't fall off this time."

With that he took the white cover from his shako and placed it on Mary's head, with the flap hanging down to protect her neck. Then he lifted her into the saddle where she sat astride, her skirt rising to reveal the white cotton drawers tied at her ankle. Climbing up behind her Rowan set the animal forward, saying that he would have to rest it frequently in such heat and terrain until they regained the road.

Mary sat rigidly upright at first, reaction setting in with a vengeance. She realized the justification he had for his attitude. Would she have believed ill of him on such evidence? Maybe, but only because her love for him was such a precious forbidden thing that was doomed to fail. Then, surely could he possibly . . .? The necessity of his arms around her, and the swaying motion of the horse made it inevitable that she should lean back against him as they rode, and she contemplated the wistful absurdity of one possible explanation of his anger on finding her. Isolated in the middle of the desert, as they were, anything took on the realms of possibility.

The sun was pushing out unbearable heat now to make the blood pound in her head despite the protective cover, burn her hands, and assault her eyes with blinding light. For as far as she could see in any direction there was wave after wave of pale sand with no relief whatever. How could she have wandered so far? What act of providence had decreed that Rowan should find her?

They made only slow progress and, after a period, he drew rein and said they must rest the horse if it was to carry two riders. Dismounting, he lifted her down beside him and uncorked the choggle to hand to her. She drank gratefully before handing it back to him. He took it in silence and quenched his thirst, before taking off his shako and pouring a little water into it for the beast. It was no more than enough to dampen its mouth and tongue, but it would keep it going for a while. Throughout all this Mary was watching Rowan's face, to no avail. She could not read his expression, could not guess his thoughts. But she could clearly recall the occasion three nights before when he had stood inside her tent declaring his intolerable loneliness. He had come to her then. Was that why he had come after her now?

He glanced across with sleepy-eyed inscrutability still. "Ready?"

She nodded and set off beside him as he coaxed the horse forward, trudging through deep sand that was burning hot now. But he set a punishing pace, which he covered with long-legged strides. Was he doing it deliberately, she wondered. Tightening her mouth she struggled along in his wake, determined to meet his challenge, as silent as he. But her determination exceeded her strength, and she was finally compelled to break that silence.

"All right, you've got some of your own back," she panted coming to a halt.

He looked round in surprise, as if he had forgotten about her presence. "What?"

"I can't keep up with you," she confessed. "I've tried, but it can't be done in a long skirt."

He looked her over for a moment or two, then said, "You are such a lightweight it won't matter if you ride. I'll walk for a longer period."

"That's not necessary," she told him at once. "I know we have to rest the horse. I can walk if you'll just go slower."

"Or you could discard the dress and petticoat to make walking easier." A faint smile suddenly appeared on his face. "With my reputation, think what would be said when you rode into Cairo in that state of undress."

A rush of incredible gladness filled her. It was all right! He believed in her; he trusted her! Slowly she took the few laborious steps to reach him and looked up into his sand-sheened face. "You'd have done better on your own. Why didn't you leave me and ride off?"

He knew very well what she was asking, but was too complex a person to answer in straight manner. "You are so determined not to desert the regiment, I could not very well let it desert you, could I?" was his taunting response. "Now, let's get this straight. You might have put yourself into this predicament, Mary Clarke, but you will kindly allow me to get you out of it without causing any more trouble than you need." Putting his hands on her shoulders he turned her resolutely to the horse. "Up into the saddle with you."

But that turning movement showed them something that drove every other thought from their heads. On the horizon was a dark swirling mass advancing toward them fast, and in its van came a hot buffeting wind that stung their faces with flying grit as a prelude to disaster.

"Oh lordy," breathed Mary in horror.

"Sandstorm," came the terse confirmation. "There's no time to lose. Take off your petticoat and tear it in two. We shall need to cover our heads."

As she hastily did as he said, she saw him strip to the waist then tie his shirt as a blindfold over the horse's eyes before replacing his jacket. Unstrapping the dark-blue cloak from the back of the saddle he threw it to her before unstrapping the saddle itself and fastening it to the reins as an anchoring weight. With her eye on the approaching wall of sand Mary waited for further instructions with complete confidence in him.

He turned and spoke frankly. "This might last half an hour, or half a day. It will be extremely frightening and dangerous. Do you understand?"

She nodded. "What must we do?"

"My horses have been trained to lie while I fire over them. We shall shelter behind him as long as I can hold him. You will hold on to me. Don't loose your hold, whatever you do. We must cover our heads, so we shall be unable to see each other . . . and the essential for survival is to avoid being buried. If you feel sand piling on to your back you must struggle free of it."

By this time the advance edge of the tornado was reaching them, and he calmed the horse before getting it down on to its side. Then he pushed Mary flat, dropping down beside her to add his weight to the saddle that was to act as anchor for the beast. They wrapped the petticoat lengths around their heads, then she linked her arms through his, and he threw one leg over her to add extra anchorage. Only just in time, for the storm was upon them. They then began a battle to ensure survival for themselves and a horse that was their only means of returning.

It was like waking to peaceful reality after a night beset by fearful bludgeoning nightmares that caused her to fight desperately to hold them off. The silence was almost frightening; the heat was incredible. Her whole body felt battered and bruised. She could scarcely breathe. Her arms hurt as if they had been loosened from their sockets, and had been clamped around her companion so long she thought they would never unbend. But, slowly and painfully, she drew her left arm away to pull the covering from her face.

Sand. There was nothing else in sight. Then the mound before her eyes shifted, and the grains ran down to reveal chestnut hair. It shifted some more and a great head swung up. Mary breathed in relief. The horse Charade was alive and still with them. Rolling over with an effort Mary looked at the sand-covered man beside her, who was just pulling the cover from his face. Their glances met, and she knew her own must echo the gladness in his as they realized they were still together. That was all that mattered to her.

"Is it over?" she rasped.

For answer he pulled his arm from beneath her body and reached for the choggle. "Drink slowly," he said huskily. "There's not much and we can't afford to spill any."

She did exactly as he said, then he drank sparingly before looking around to assess the situation. Mary struggled to sit up beside him, and was awed by what she saw.

"My God, the whole landscape has been altered," he said softly. "Somewhere out there I have three men searching for you and Ramslake. This could have swallowed them up without trace."

She knew he was right. The dune that faced them was now twice the height it had been; the dip they were in was now a plateau surrounded on all sides by veritable mountains of sand. They could see no further than fifty yards in any direction. It did not require experience of the desert to tell them they were in dire straits. There was not much water, and what there was would have to be shared between them with none for the horse. The sun had reached its zenith, and there was absolutely no shade to be had.

Rowan got to his feet and coaxed Charade up beside him, untying his shirt from the animal's head before glancing down at Mary. "I'll go and take a look from the top of the dune. You sit there and rest."

It took great effort to climb the dune. Mary watched his

struggle as he slipped back almost as fast as he advanced, but he finally stood at the top, shading his eyes with his hand, a tall impressive figure outlined against the brassy sky. After what seemed a very long time he took off the pale-blue jacket and spread it on the sand before slithering back to her, raising small avalanches as he descended. The scars across his upper body looked particularly bizarre in that wild place, and she had to drag her gaze from them as he reached her and began to don his shirt once more.

"Well . . . what did you see?"

He glanced down at her from fastening the buttons. "Sand."

"Nothing else?"

"Oh yes, I saw the pyramids in three different directions, two caravans of camels, a great gilded palace and the roof-tops of Cairo. Mirages," he finished briefly.

"What?" she asked, not understanding.

He squatted beside her, and there was gentleness in his eyes and tone as he said, "Pictures of the imagination, Mary Clarke. When sun shimmers on dry land it is possible to see anything one wishes. Now, I'll tell you what we are going to do. I arranged a signal with my troopers—four shots to be fired at intervals if we wished the others to come to us. I am going to fire those four shots, and I have left my jacket up there to show we are nearby. After the signal I shall erect some kind of shelter for us so that we can conserve our energy until the sun goes down. We'll move then, and once the moon rises it will be as good as daylight."

She did not ask what would happen if there were no moon. She knew he was doing all he could under the circumstances, and determined to help him by staying calm and confident. All the same, her nerves jumped when he fired the pistol into that incredible haunting silence, and the sound of that signal put the first real sensation of time running out into her breast. But it did not stop her from thinking. When he stuck the saddle on end into the sand and looked around for another prop, she suggested piling their four boots into each other. In no time they had the

cloak spread on the sand with the yellow lining upward, and
her grey dress draped over the upturned saddle and boots to
provide shade for the upper part of their bodies as they lay
side by side beneath it. She settled there in her bodice and
drawers, but Rowan took time to relieve Charade of the
bridle and bit before dropping down beside her.

With his head close to hers he murmured, as he gazed up
at the grey cambric shelter, "So, you end up in undressed
state after all."

She gazed up at it too. "It has nothing to do with your
reputation."

"They'll never believe it, I assure you."

They lay in silence until she said, "I am responsible for
this."

"No. Ramslake is."

"But you wouldn't have come in person if I hadn't taken
Drummer Boy."

"Yes, I would. Ramslake is in my troop, and he has stolen
an army horse. It has nothing to do with my personal property."

She turned her head to look at his profile. "I think that's
a lie."

"Think what you like, but don't speak," he said, still
gazing upward. "Talking will only make your throat dryer.
Try to sleep."

She took his advice and they lay side by side beneath their
rude shelter as the sun beat down. She drifted between
sleeping and waking, tormented as much by her thoughts as
the burning heat, and longing to maintain verbal contact
with him even though she knew it would be foolhardy.
What his thoughts were she could only guess, and his eyes
were guarded on the occasions he put the choggle to her
mouth and allowed her a brief drink. At only one of those
times did she break the silence he had practically enforced.

"Why aren't you drinking?"

"I can go for a while yet."

"Don't be daft. You're as thirsty as me."

"I don't need as much."

"Rubbish! You've been doing more—going up and down the dune. Have some."

"Conserve your voice!"

"It's some silly rule about giving it to females first, isn't it? What'll be the use of that if you die of thirst? I'll be here all alone."

He waited a moment before saying, "Neither of us is going to die of thirst."

"You will, if you don't start acting sensible."

"Sensibly," he corrected quietly.

She turned so that their eyes were only inches apart, and pleaded with him. "Look, I'm not a lady. I've roughed it with the troopers, so I can stand more than they can."

He answered without hesitation. "Being a lady has nothing to do with one's way of life; it is how one behaves. I've known highborn females who don't hold a candle to a courtesan."

It was his last word on the subject, and she turned away again. When she came out of her thoughts on his reputation with women he appeared to be asleep. She let her head roll sideways and slept too.

As soon as the sun lowered enough Rowan decided they must move. But it was quite clear from the outset that they would not travel far in an area now covered in mountainous dunes with deep dips between but, setting a rough course by the dying sun, Rowan climbed up behind Mary in the saddle and set Charade forward. The fact that there had been no response to their four shots meant either that the other three were no longer searching or that they were all lost. Mary was not clever, but she was sharp, and it did not take much to realize the only advantage of moving was to keep at bay the creeping chill of oncoming night.

After a period during which Charade had gallantly struggled hock-deep up and down shifting slopes, Rowan dismounted to lead the animal for a while. Brooking no argument he made Mary put on his jacket and cloak, since she would be sitting still whilst he was walking to keep warm. They set off again, with Rowan walking and encouraging the

animal forward while he stumbled and groped his way alongside. Knowing in her heart that only an act of providence
would save them, Mary nevertheless said nothing to the man
fighting to keep going. She knew he needed to do something, knew his personality was such that he would fight the
inevitable to the last breath. But when he stumbled yet
again and sprawled headlong to bring Charade to a thankful
halt, Mary scrambled from the saddle to drop beside him.

"We can't go on," she said gently, sparing his pride by
adding, "That poor horse is in need of a rest, and so am I."

He pushed himself into a sitting position and said with a
nod, "All right. We'll sit here for a while."

Settling close beside him she wrapped the cloak around
them both, and he circled her with his left arm. It was then
Mary discovered he was shivering in the thin shirt, so she
snuggled even closer. They were on the crest of a dune
where it was possible to see the silver waves of the moon-
washed sea of desert all around them. The night was immense and theirs alone; the stars were high and clear in a
black sky that looked as cold as the deepest, darkest lake. Yet
Mary found a curious inexplicable enchantment about facing her destiny with this man who had changed her life so
drastically. Socially so impossibly far apart, emotionally separated by his marriage, divided by educational barriers of
immense proportions, these few square feet of silver sand in
a desert that was seen by nothing other than covering darkness were the only place where they could simply be a man
and a woman who needed each other. Nothing else was
important; no other person existed. Mary knew their time
was running out and wanted this moment to equal the rest
of the life she would never live.

"We're going to die, aren't we?" she said, startling him
with the sound of her voice in the stillness.

"Of course not."

"Don't lie to me. I don't mind knowing."

"I'm not lying," he lied.

She said no more for a moment, just rested against him
revelling in the freedom of being allowed to accept his arms

around her. Then she told him, "When I've thought about dying—and I have many times—I never thought it would be this way. My father was killed by a mad horse in the lines at Khunobad; my mother died from native grog. Jack Rafferty dropped from his horse with heatstroke, and my dear Sam had the cholera. I've never known anyone to die of old age, so I always guessed I'd be the same. Well, it looks that I was right about that. But I don't mind dying, after all, yet I always thought I would."

His arm tightened around her, and he rested his cheek against the top of her head. "You're not going to die, Mary. I won't let you."

"Shall I tell you why I don't mind?" she went on. "It's because I've done more than most girls have ever done. Me —little Mary Tookey, child of the regiment. I've seen the ocean and the desert; I've learnt to ride a horse and I've travelled in a basket on a camel. Did you know they were called 'ships of the desert'? Noah told me. I've seen big cities and strange countryside. I've learnt to read big words and pronounce them properly—you taught me that, as well as the riding and all about coats of arms. I've seen the pyramids, which is one of the seven wonders of the world, and the Sphinx, although I think it's spelt funny. I've watched horses being loaded on to a great sailing ship, and seen those beautiful flying fish that look like silver birds. Don't you think that's enough for anyone?"

His response was startling. He pulled her round to face him with a roughness born of a sense of the sands of time running through that narrow channel separating life from what lay beyond.

"What right have you to feel that life has given you enough?" he demanded. "My God, you have had nothing —nothing at all! You're a child, an innocent when it comes to the complexities of existence. What do you know of the twists and turns of the human mind, the pressures of honour and duty, the price one has to pay for conflicting passions?" He shook her shoulders as if to emphasize his words. "Do you really think that all there is to life is learning to read and seeing flying fish?"

"Of course not," she said equally fiercely. "But it's a bloody lot when you've been used to nothing."

He gazed down into her face, his eyes silvered by moonlight, and his fingers dug into her shoulders as he said softly, "Damn you, Mary Clarke, I'll get you back to Cairo, I swear it!"

In that moment she did not want to go back. She would lose him forever. Yet she loved him for his vow. Because of that love she put up her hands to touch his lips, and said, "Why do you always fight so hard to do what you know can't be done?"

He caught her hand in his. "You mustn't believe that."

But she had to go on now. "Why do you always feel you have to do more than anyone else? You're just a man, like they are."

"What damned new philosophy is this?" he demanded huskily, so close now his breath fanned her cheek.

"Why are you always so dissatisfied with yourself? Why do you risk torture again and again just to prove you have courage?" Then, only because she could now speak to him in such a way, "And whatever happened to you at Multan that you thought you could forget only by marrying a beautiful, selfish girl who isn't what you want at all? Everyone makes mistakes, Rowan. Why won't you let yourself make any?"

She thought him silenced by her battery of questions, until he said wonderingly, "My greatest mistake was in not leaving you at Khunobad. You've hardly given me a minute's peace of mind since we left."

His kiss showed her she was the child, the innocent he had dubbed her, for she knew nothing of his kind of ravishment. Yet she responded instinctively to gentleness in passion, hands that possessed without pain, the urgency of a body that worked to take her along step by step in willing bondage toward a mysterious beckoning surrender.

Perhaps it was the unreality of their total solitude beneath the stars, perhaps it was his renowned art of conquest, perhaps it was that she truly loved this man, or perhaps they both realized it could never happen again. Possibly it was a combination of all these that made their eventual sustained union inevitable, unanimous and unbelievably wonderful. Mary found tears of joy on her cheeks as Rowan lay spent across her. How right he had been to question her claim to have been given more than enough. Until a short while ago she had had nothing at all.

The sun was straight up in the heavens, and Rowan could no longer think coherently. Their water had run out; Mary was in a coma. He knew death was all but a few hours away, but he was not happy to die as she was. There were so many things he would now leave undone, so much he would never be able to put right now.

He turned his head weakly beneath the shade cast by his cloak and looked at Mary. She was certainly not beautiful. Her face was deeply darkened by the sun and possessed no purity of features. Yet it was moulded by experience and an innocent wisdom of human frailties. It was never covered with artful smiles or provocative teasing. Her eyes never held promises that would not be kept, or invitations a man dared not accept. Her lashes lay darkly against the tanned skin, hiding eyes that were an unremarkable greenish-brown, and her mouth was too straight and unyielding for feminine allure. He would never be driven to draw his sword across his own throat because of her, yet he knew he would die in her stead if it would save her now.

Drifting into a kind of nightmare composed of burning heat, thirst and hunger, he knew the next time he closed his eyes he would never open them again. It had been like that once before—delirium, pain, desperation. But he had been all alone then, ruled by a will to return that had been stronger than any affliction. For an instant, it seemed to be that other time again and he felt the agony of the cuts on his torso as he fought to hold on to his senses.

Fingers suddenly brushed his, and he looked across to find

Mary gazing at him, very lucid and plainly understanding his thoughts. It was then he knew he must confess before it was too late. This girl who had seen his return on that terrible occasion must know why he had done it. Know, and understand.

"There was a girl—a brown girl. Very beautiful," he rasped with a great effort. "I had been to Multan, and there were vital secrets I had to take back if a great number of our soldiers were not to be caught in an ambush. I was on my way back to Khunobad when I was overtaken by a group of men from an obscure tribe with reasons for particular hatred of the British. They invited me to travel with them, and I had to accept. Their dialect is difficult for a white man to pronounce and . . . and I must have aroused their suspicions." He lay for a moment fighting the dryness of his throat, yet knowing he must tell her everything before he was silenced forever. "Whilst I was asleep, they seized me and bound me hand and foot. They charged me with being an English infidel. When . . . when I denied it, they vowed to extract the truth."

He was back again in that wild place, with white-robed men laughing around a fire with leaping flames. When he struggled to continue, it was a croaking confession to the Almighty as well as the dying girl beside him . . . a confession to purge his guilt-ridden soul. The agony was on his skin again, and he remembered writhing to try to escape it; the ruthless hands that held him down.

"I knew I dare not cry out in case I used my native tongue. I resisted all they did," he managed in something bordering on appeal for understanding. "I swear I did not break. I *swear* it."

Fingers gripped his own, and he rolled his head slowly to look at her, panting in the unbearable heat that seemed to take even the breath from their nostrils as they fought for it.

"They stopped when one man said he knew a certain way of deciding if I was truly what I claimed to be. Englishmen, he said, revered women more than their own lives."

It was almost impossible now to form the words, and they

came out in jerky indistinct fashion from a throat that burnt as painfully as his skin.

"They brought a girl. A thief and adulteress, they said. I . . . I was to witness her punishment." He tried to swallow, but his throat was now so swollen he nearly choked. "They began by . . . by cutting off both . . . her hands, so that she would never steal again. Then they . . . then they heated the knife they had used on me in the . . . in the fire . . . and began ensuring she would never . . . commit adultery again. They forced me . . . to watch it. But they were watching me. Watching and waiting for me to . . . cry out in her defence . . . or break under the ordeal. I did neither." He closed his eyes in anguish at the memory. "I let her suffer without saying one word . . . and I . . . dear God, I *laughed* with them as . . . as they did it. I have not been able to forget the way she looked at me as . . . as she died."

The scene faded as he opened his eyes to find a different girl there. She was weeping, the tears making tracks through the fine sand that sheened her face.

"I *had* to do it so that I could return," he insisted hoarsely. "I had to do it to save many Englishmen's lives. They believed my false identity and sent me on my way with deepest apologies for my wounds." He lay back weakly, gazing up at the brassy sky through the tears he had not been able to shed until then. "By letting that poor creature suffer, I also saved my own life. I have lived with that guilt locked inside me, but . . . but I swear I will not die with it. I have confessed. Now I am free."

The girl tried to say something to him. Although her mouth moved no sound came from it. She was still weeping, and her tears seemed to purge the guilt from him as they lay gazing at each other with the revelation of true devotion that had come too late. Their entwined fingers said all they could not put into words as the grip tightened, knowing they would both slip away without the other being aware of the fact.

They lay like that for a long time until her eyes slowly closed. The rise and fall of her chest was very slight, and he knew deep sadness as he realized she was near the end. Struggling on to his side he cradled her head in his arm and prepared to watch over her, determined not to slip away himself until his spirit was alone in this vastness. He roamed through many ages and experiences as time became immaterial and he saw how he had wasted the years he had been given. With this girl at his side he could have been all he had wanted to be.

Just when the shadow fell across his feet he was not wholly aware, and when hands lifted him it was part of the unreality. Brown-faced men in white flowing robes were so much a continuation of his thoughts, when cool water was poured on to his face he gasped as if being burnt. Through his swollen throbbing throat a trickle of moisture ran. Then again, and again. The blinding brightness had dimmed a little. After a while it vanished altogether, and it grew very cold. He was tightly bound and there were leaping flames. He writhed and cried out in English, knowing that by saving her he would condemn himself and many of his countrymen to death. But he could endure her agony no longer. She was grateful to him and bent over him to give him water and a little food. Her hands were gentle on him, and her dusky skin was miraculously unblemished. He had saved her, spared her any injury. He could rest easily now.

When daylight returned he was lying in a tent with Eastern hangings wherever he looked. The rugs that had covered him during the coldness of night had been cast aside. Watching him was a man he remembered, but did not know.

"Good, good, you are returned from the journey toward death," said the man. "Only a strong body and a determined will could have been responsible. Your colonel truly named you a most courageous man. You have suffered much, I think." His dark gaze moved to the scars across Rowan's chest. "The evidence is there for all to see, and it is even more of an honour to have been the instrument of continuing life."

Memory began to return. "*You* found us?"

A broad smile lit the face. "I found your horse wandering. Such a beautiful creature could not be mistaken for any other, I knew. My men searched the area for the rider we knew must be nearby."

"Mary!" cried Rowan in sudden fear, and struggled to sit up.

"The handmaid lives," came the reply accompanying a nod to his right. "She has not a strong body, but a very determined will, sir."

Rowan looked across to see Mary lying asleep no more than a few feet from him, dressed in a loose robe.

"The desert shows a man many truths," the accented voice continued. "But it takes more than wisdom to accept them, it is said."

On setting out from Cairo, the 43rd Light Dragoons, now in one long column, made its way through cultivated areas irrigated by numerous canals and smaller waterways, which made the progress of over seven hundred horses plus the equivalent number of pack-animals difficult and slow. Between cultivated areas lay expanses of deep sand, and many times the column elongated for miles when the horses were forced into single-file on narrow tracks between water, or across the dunes that had them sinking in up to their bellies. Obliged to remain within easy distance of water, the route was tortured. But it had been decided that some baggage and non-essential supplies should go up to Alexandria by boat, which prevented the worst delays.

The troopers enjoyed every new sight and sound with an added fervency since their trek across the desert. They noted details of the cultivated fields, the people working them and the villages where they lived, so they could write home about them. Only when they crossed the stretches of desert did they fall to chatting and ignored their surroundings.

But the villages of flat-roofed mud houses, with few if any windows, tapering palm trees, and the inevitable pigeon-houses, whitewashed and decorated with ochre patterns, held their rapt attention, as did the oxen working irrigation contraptions of rows of revolving buckets out in the fields. At first the villagers hid away when they saw the column approaching, for it was the habit of the Egyptian soldiery to descend and take everything they wanted before riding off. But they soon realized these foreign soldiers were better-behaved, and came out to swamp the men of the 43rd with produce for sale. They profited extremely well from the move, because fresh eggs and milk, and an abundance of poultry were welcomed by men who had been marching almost continuously for three months and were now coping with a particularly arduous section made in daylight all the way, with the accompanying heat.

But there was the lighter side to provide entertainment and relief from the hard routine. One day, another Arab chieftain rode into their camp to challenge any one of the British cavalrymen to race against him, because he claimed his horse was unbeatable. Rowan DeMayne was immediately chosen to accept the challenge, and Colonel Daubnay then had the ticklish problem of deciding whether to uphold the honour of the regiment, or avoid offending a leading citizen of their host country. Being the man he was, the dilemma did not last long, and Rowan was ordered to 'out-ride the pompous devil' with as much panache as he could muster. The Arab gave his horse its head right from the start, dashing away from Rowan in flamboyant style. But the beast was winded well before the finishing post, and Rowan's prime stallion Cavalier romped past with as much panache as any cavalry colonel could desire.

As the Arab rode off with his chin on his knees, the dragoons found an admirable way of celebrating the win when several men slipped accidentally down the steep sides of the canal whilst watering horses. Soon, men were being flung into the water willy-nilly, and a great deal of aquatic horseplay took place. Needless to say, the victorious jockey was one of the first to go in.

The outcome of the desert rescue had made Rowan De-Mayne a fresh hero to men impatient for action. Everyone conveniently forgot the Arab who had found and brought the pair into Cairo, and concentrated on the officer who had kept himself and a young girl of the regiment alive during a sandstorm of epic proportions—which had swallowed up one of the search party and driven the others to take refuge in a ruin—then preserved their lives for a further two days with the minimum means of survival.

Delayed by the storm the 43rd had marched off complete save the trooper lost in the desert, and Noah Ramslake. Information had been given to the authorities in Cairo, who had passed on details of the dragoon and his chestnut horse to all the chieftains in the environs of that city. There the matter had to be left.

Lydia DeMayne had been considerably sobered by the drama. For three days and nights she had faced the prospect of widowhood. The thought had been terrifying, and brought home to her her degree of dependence on Rowan. It also brought home the truth of some of his words because, during that anxious period, the officers of the 43rd together with the wives whom she had kept at bay with her attitude, all rallied round to reassure and help her. She was part of the regiment whether she welcomed the fact or not.

Rowan's absence—perhaps forever—had shown her a strength of feeling that surprised her. When he had left her in India to go after the runaway horses she had been extremely peeved, and sought to punish him by encouraging the attentions of Kit Wrexham and her other admirers. His dramatic equestrian leap over them on his return had thrilled her with its implications of the hold she had over him still. This time, he had gone more to catch the girl and recover the jewel that had been a token of his love, than to apprehend the deserting Ramslake. He could have sent one of his subalterns, or even the troop-sergeant to do that. It had been for her sake that he had gone. If he died . . . ?

During that anxious period she recalled so many things about him that she had taken lightly, and had even resorted to tears when she thought of his constant devotion that might have ended in some lone place where he would never be found. The tears had increased when she considered what would become of her as his widow. Even if he returned from the desert, he could fall on the battlefield to which he was hurrying so eagerly. Life without him had suddenly seemed intolerable.

It was a semi-repentent wife who thankfully welcomed him back to her side, and she readily accepted the truth about her little maid's foolhardy attempt to recover the pendant alone. In truth, she was glad to have Mary back, for three days of looking after herself had been uncomfortable and inconvenient, and she told the girl it had been at her own instigation that Captain DeMayne had gone in person to search for her. Blooming in the reflected limelight of her husband's gallant action, and enjoying the new rôle of devoted wife, Lydia persuaded onlookers that the shaky De-Mayne marriage had steadied.

Gil, who knew Rowan better than most, was not convinced. His friend had him extremely puzzled. With his beautiful, precocious wife publicly displaying her affection for him, he was suddenly flinging himself into regimental duties to an astonishing degree, meticulously observing routine demands that were often dispensed with on the march, and training the spare horses during rest periods with such dedication they were all perfectly ready to replace the existing troop-horses. What was behind his behaviour?

One person who was delighted with his dedication to duty was Maurice Daubnay, who kept at bay the knowledge that they were growing ever nearer the Crimea by thinking of the race run against the chieftain which had shown the stuff of which the 43rd was made. In addition, he made plans for the grand ball that was to be held in Alexandria for the regiment. The men would need to look to their uniforms during the days prior to their arrival and smarten themselves up generally. Military precision and smartness had grown slack due to the splitting of the regiment for most of the journey. Now was an opportunity to remedy it. So the Colonel occupied himself very enjoyably putting to rights all he felt marred the perfection of his soldiers, and heard nothing of their curses behind his back as he moved on.

*　*　*

Noah Ramslake was brought into camp on their fifth day out from Cairo by the Arab who had lost the horse race. It was obvious from his smooth story that he had not personally apprehended the missing trooper, and the men of the 43rd guessed he had used his status to bully those responsible into handing over their prisoner so that he could claim the reward whilst also gaining a little revenge for his bruised pride. The regiment's honour was discredited by a deserter when on the way to war.

Due to the unusual circumstances—they were equidistant from Cairo and Alexandria, they were on the march and they were *en route* to a war—a Regimental Court Martial was convened to try the prisoner they did not want on their hands. It was a unique case. Deferment for trial in Alexandria would have tied up all the witnesses there for weeks, thus lessening the strength of a regiment on the way to war, and Colonel Daubnay also felt strongly that he wished the matter speedily judged and speedily settled before arriving amongst Alexandria society. The case would do the regiment's reputation irreparable harm at a time when he hoped to impress everyone with its qualities.

With Major Benedict presiding, and Gil and Kit Wrexham on the panel, the prisoner was tried and found guilty of desertion whilst under orders for war, theft of an army horse—the attempt to sell which had led to his apprehension—and theft of a valuable pendant belonging to his troop commander which had been found on him when apprehended. He was given the stiffest punishment possible, to be carried out when camp was set the following day.

The time chosen was sunset, and the scene was one that onlookers would not easily forget. In a clearing beside a high-walled canal, with a distant range of blood-red sand dunes and a crescent of swaying palms that protected a village, the members of the 43rd, in immaculate uniforms, formed three sides of a square facing inward. The officers sat on their horses in front of them, like statuettes glittering with reddish-silver embellishments, as they stared at

Trooper Ramslake, who was stripped to the waist and tied by both wrists to a large metal triangle. The small group around him consisting of the Troop Sergeant, two troopers as escorts, and Surgeon Captain Winters, all had their eyes on the Farrier Sergeant who held the whip.

Behind the regimental ranks clustered the porters, camp followers, and people from the nearby village, all excited by this brutal foreign ritual of torturing a man while the entire regiment watched his agony, unmoved and dressed in their fancy trappings of justice. Amongst them stood a grave-faced girl in the grey costume of a servant, and she was anything but unmoved.

In Mary's throat was a lump that made swallowing painful, and in her heart was an ache that was increasing by the minute. Bound and helpless out there was a man she had been prepared to marry. Whatever Noah had done, in the past he had been very kind and loving to her. He had given her rides on carts when she had been condemned to walking with the baggage. How long ago those days now seemed! Noah had taught her so much, given her cheery companionship, and protected her on the boat from the lustier of the men. He had bought her her first bonnet. He had even wanted her to share the good life he was certain would be his. Did that all cancel out the fact that he had betrayed her confidence and friendship by stealing something for which she was more than likely to be blamed? Rowan had set out after her believing in her guilt. Noah could not have foreseen the outcome of his actions.

Mary had seen men flogged before, but had never been so personally involved with the victim. The reason for her final decision to be present when the sun went down on that seventh day of April 1855 was a strong one, but it still took all her resolution to stay when the drums began to roll and an ominous silence followed. Then, into that silence, a bird began to sing its heart out in praise of the day just ending.

The sweet beautiful sound was almost Mary's undoing but, cutting across those liquid notes, came the harsh words of command that preceded the sound of a whip cutting human flesh. Mary jumped as if she had received the shock of it on her own back, and put her hand to her mouth as a sadistically ecstatic 'Aah' rose from the Egyptians surrounding her. The men of the 43rd stood immobile and expressionless as the Farrier Sergeant began counting the lashes he inflicted, one by one.

Twenty-seven, twenty-eight. The whip was making a different sound now as it repeatedly landed on bloody pulp that had been smooth white skin. Even the Egyptians were quiet now. Mary felt so close to fainting she reached out to grip a nearby box for support. Yet she knew she must somehow stay throughout the entire ordeal if she was ever to begin to understand what Rowan had suffered on that night near Multan, when he had been forced to watch another's agony.

She was haunted by what he had told her, continuously troubled by that nightmare picture of a hideous scene that was fixed in her mind. It was enough to break any man's mind, without the agony of his own tortured body. Now she understood all that had happened at the hospital, why he could not speak of it even to clear his name of treachery. Now she understood why he had become so obsessed with a girl whose perfect physical beauty had driven away the vision of another girl torn and bleeding. Lydia had provided only temporary escape because she took from him instead of giving. Yet his heavy burden of guilt was unnecessary. No gesture from him would have saved the girl, as he must be aware. His captors would have regarded her as merely the means of forcing him to betray himself, and killed her anyway.

After those days in the desert when he had gone without water to give to her, and shivered in night temperatures so that she should be warm, Mary knew he would never save his own life by letting another be sacrificed—especially that of a woman—and now also understood why he had told Dunwoodie he would never work for him again. Danger to himself he had been prepared to face time and again, but not what he had endured at Multan. He was a soldier and, as such, preferred to face his foe openly and on equal terms.

Forty-one, forty-two. The victim of the lash was in such anguish he hung by his wrists from that triangle. His back was running with blood that looked all the more obscene in the red light of sunset. Her stomach churned with revulsion as she saw a man she had kissed, laughed with and given warm friendship to during a period of four months. No, she could not watch any more. But, on the point of running from the terrible sound of whipping, she remembered why she had deliberately gone there. Only by understanding this kind of mental suffering could she ever help Rowan to recover from it.

Yet, as her gaze strayed to where he sat at the head of C Troop, she realized with a shock that he would never allow her to do so. He was gazing straight back at her with the unacceptable truth shadowing his face. What he had told her had been a dying confession to someone who had reached him across life's barriers to tumble them one by one. By surviving, that confession had forged a bond that could not ever be socially or emotionally acknowledged. He saw himself a prisoner of his own words, with her as his jailer, and plainly found such bondage intolerable.

They were still gazing at each other when the flogging ceased, and Harry Winters ordered the victim to be carried off.

In her new restless uncertainty of mood and attitude toward herself and her possible future, Mary found inactivity in a basket slung beside a camel irksome. So she spent the last four days of the march toward Alexandria mostly on foot. Rowan noted the fact and warned her, in curiously impersonal tones adopted before the troopers, that she would tire herself too much. She continued the practice, and he said no more on the subject. Although she gained no companionship from the Egyptian serving-girls, it was clear her desert adventure had made her the subject of renewed regimental interest. As such, the troopers chatted to her freely as they walked their horses during the unmounted periods, clustered around her when they halted for the customary halt for water, and even offered to share those little extras they bought in the villages through which they passed.

She had lived with such men all her life, yet it now seemed difficult to respond in her usual easy manner—even to those of D Troop whose washing she had done ever since she could remember. Strangely, it was to C Troop she felt she now belonged—if she belonged anywhere, these days— but the fact that she had been taken in passion by their commander and held the only key to the secrets of his soul put a restraint on her. Her trust had been shattered by Noah; her emotions had been shattered by a man now forced to ignore them. Small wonder Mary Clarke seemed unusually subdued to the regiment she had refused to leave in company with Noah.

It was in this new quiet mood that she eventually came face to face with him when they bivouacked on the last night before Alexandria. It was an inevitable confrontation, yet she had done her best to avoid it. Hurrying to Collins to get her dinner, Mary almost crashed into the man making his painful way from the horse-lines. He put out a hand to steady her. She swallowed in distress as they stood, glances locked, for some moments. There were many similarities between the man she loved, and this one she might have loved. Passion for a heartless woman had put them on down-hill paths; both their bodies were marked with lifelong scars —one through courage, the other through dishonour. Yet both punishments had been the result of a strange legacy of guilt from their youth.

"Hallo, Noah," she offered, at last, distressed by his broken stance, the evidence of pain on his attractive features.

"You look different," was his surprising comment. "Have they been unkind to you?"

She knew who he meant. "No. Just the opposite."

Awkwardness fell between them, yet neither was able to leave the conversation unfinished. Around them the sunset was creating its customary orange glow that threw up the silhouette of palms in black relief, and the rattle of pots and pans as dinner was prepared, the splashing as water was

drawn from the nearby river, the laughter and curses of
soldiers settling after a tiring day all added a poignant background to the subject they knew had to be broached.

More than usually touched by the exotic atmosphere
around her, Mary found herself asking sadly, "Why did you
do it, Noah?"

"You know why I did it," he responded heatedly. "Nothing has changed, Mary. You surely understand. That . . . that
bestiality was my greatest vindication. They don't do things
like that to even the worst criminal in prisons. I have paid
—*more* than paid—for what I did seven years ago. I'll take
no more of this life. It's fit for no one but mindless brutes."

Aghast she cried, "Noah, you can't. They'll kill you next
time."

He gave her a straight look, and she saw no criminal but
a man driven off course by another's selfishness. "I'll face
worse at Balaclava This way, I get an even chance."

Into her mind came Rowan's question: What of the man
born to paint, who finds himself selling shoes instead? This
man, who was too good to be a trooper, yet not quite good
enough to be an officer knew the truth of the answer to that.
Should he be condemned for what he was saying? Knowing
full well his fellows would now be shunning him, the NCO's
giving him the worst duties, the officers—including Rowan,
especially Rowan—treating him as vermin, Mary found her
sympathies gathering.

"I didn't betray you that night, Noah. Why did you
betray me? I told you about that pendant in good faith."

He stepped toward her and took one of her hands in his.
The movement made his sleeves rise, revealing the raw
burns around his wrists where he had twisted in agony on
that triangle.

"I didn't plan that, I swear," he said with such swift
passion she believed him. "I was upset and worried, because
I'd told you what I was going to do in the belief that you
would come with me. I wasn't absolutely certain you
wouldn't still try to stop me by telling *him*—DeMayne.
When you said goodbye so finally and went inside, it was a

blow." He swallowed and gripped her hand. "I really thought a lot of you, Mary. I still do."

"Go on about the pendant," she prompted, conscious of several passing troopers watching them suspiciously.

"I . . . I walked along that corridor feeling angry. Their door was ajar, and there was the box on a table across the room—blue velvet, as you'd said. No one was about, and it seemed as if providence had meant me to have it. It was an impulse; there was no time to think about it." He looked hard at her as if trying to divine her feelings. Then, when she said nothing, went on. "Did she really accuse you of stealing it? Some of the men are saying she did."

Mary sighed. "It doesn't matter now what anyone thought."

"But you didn't—surely you didn't believe I would have deliberately implicated you." He gripped her hands so tightly the raw places on his wrists began to glisten with fresh beads of blood. "Mary, there's still time to change your mind. What lies ahead for a girl in your situation? Drudgery and eventual abandonment. Battlefields. Privation, misery and suffering. Come with me this time. It'll be all right. We'll just go. I won't take a thing—not even the uniform."

She pulled away from him, certain all surrounding eyes were on them, all ears listening to his dangerous words. "It's madness, Noah," she told him with low-voiced urgency. "Don't tell me any more. I don't want to hear it. You know why I wouldn't go with you before. It's the same now."

His arms fell to his sides, and he tried to straighten up. "It's a better form of madness than there is here. Can I still trust you, Mary?"

"Of course," she told him sadly.

A faint smile touched the good-looking face marred by bitterness. "I think it's more than loyalty to a regiment that keeps you tied to its heels, my dear."

He turned and shuffled away through the crisscross of a regiment preparing to bivouac on a sandy stretch bordering a village on the banks of the Nile. Mary stood there in that foreign sunset with its alien smells and atmospheres, feeling a wistful unreality. He was probably right in his estimation of what lay ahead for her. Perhaps she would do better to go with him. Yet she knew she would not. *Could* not.

The 43rd Light Dragoons entered Alexandria on April 11th after an exceptionally long march. Ships that were to take them to Balaclava were in port and the first were due to sail on the morrow. Although the men were fatigued, there was an air of re-born excitement on reaching the end of their long tramp across Egypt, with the war now only a week's voyage away. At long last they were almost there.

Alexandria seemed impressively elegant as they clattered through the suburbs and into the main part of that Mediterranean town, with its solid colonial buildings, date palms bordering the wide streets to provide flickering shade, and the numbers of windmills wherever one looked in the surrounding hills. In such a cosmopolitan area, where streets were full of camels and carts driven by people in exotic national dress, a long column of men in blue-and-silver uniforms, mounted on chestnut stallions, caused little stir. Indeed, with their faces burned brown by the constant sun, and the shako-covers with flapping neckpieces giving them a foreign touch, they could have been a pasha's private desert army coming in from an outlying fort.

The barracks that had been allotted to them diminished some of their pleasure, for the buildings were without windows and swarming with lice and other vermin. And there were no stables. The horses had to be tied up in the barrack-yard as best as could be managed and, as night fell, the men began emerging from the suffocating flea-ridden rooms to sleep with their animals.

The officers, apart from the few on duty, were quartered at one of the fine hotels along the Mediterranean shore, but were destined to get little sleep in the soft welcoming beds. A ball in their honour had been arranged at the British Consulate, and all Alexandria society had been invited. Tired and weary from the desert they might be, but no one was excused attendance by Colonel Daubnay, who saw the event as one last opportunity to parade his beautiful dragoons before they became muddy and bloody on the battlefields to which they were rushing with such eagerness.

Rowan dressed for the occasion with even less enthusiasm than his brother officers, who would sooner have had a long luxurious sleep to prepare for embarkation on the morrow. If it turned out to be anything like the shambles at Bombay they would need to be well-rested. Having endured all they had over the past four-and-a-half months and arrived on the threshold of war, a ball struck them as a rather bizarre interruption to their routine.

Rowan's reluctance to attend an event welcomed by his luxury-loving wife was augmented by his sensation of loss, of being ruled by forces that once again threatened to lead him along thorny paths. Those days and nights in the desert haunted him to the extent that he often found his mind returning there involuntarily, and the long dark hours giving birth to the wish that he had never returned. In believing that he would not, he had cast aside sanity to acknowledge a love for a girl of the regiment and taken her as his own. Because of it, he had told her something intended to cleanse his soul in death. Now he felt he had placed it in her hands, and it would never be entirely his again.

To escape the sensation of shackles he had thrown himself into the masculine military routine that tired him physically. But his mind never seemed to sleep as it told him time and time again that he had found a woman who could satisfy every aspect of his wild nature, but he was irrevocably tied to another who had turned out to be no more than a beautiful shell. Unable any longer to respond to one, and forbidden to respond to the other, he longed to reach their destination where he could forget them both in pursuit of his profession in its most dangerous guise. Somewhere on the fields of the Crimea he must come to terms with life. If he fell it would not matter—except that memories of the desert would be with him as he did. Meanwhile, he had to continue in close proximity with them both and pretend nothing had changed.

He was supremely conscious of that silent figure in grey
when he went to collect Lydia from her room that evening.
But his wife soon commanded his attention by saying, with
a brilliant smile, "How very handsome and distinguished
you look. I'declare you will have every female in Alexandria
setting her cap at the hero of the 43rd."

His return smile threatened to crack the stiffness of his
jaw. "I am sure they will have more intelligent things to
occupy them on such a significant night."

But she was not to be cheated of wifely devotion. "Your
modesty almost exceeds your gallantry, my dear." She
turned to the girl across the room. "There is no need to
await our return, Mrs Clarke. I shall not need you tonight."

The inference of her words put the seal on Rowan's
mood, and he said curtly, "I think we should go. The reception is at nine, and Daubnay has made it clear he will arrive
sharp on the hour."

"Madam's cloak, sir," said a quiet voice as Mary came to
him with the garment.

He wanted to shout at her not to be so servile, not to call
him 'sir', not to accept her lowly state as Lydia's maid. But
he took the velvet cape to put around his wife's shoulders,
feeling those shackles tighten. Then he led Lydia almost
roughly to the wide curving staircase, filled with anger he
could not possibly vent. To be compelled to attend a ball was
asking too much of him.

In the carriage Lydia kept up a flow of bright chatter until
he had to put an end to it. "I have a small item of unhappy
news for you, I fear. Word has come round to all the officers
that baggage on this voyage is limited to military equipment
and essential camp furniture. Your pianoforte will have to
be left here with the rest to be sold after our departure."

He had expected a rage, even tears. But all she did was
draw away slightly to look up at him in the shadowy interior.

"How very unromantic you are this evening, Rowan. A
new instrument can always be purchased . . . but how am
I to win back a straying husband?"

"What do you mean by that?" he asked with instant suspicion.

"Only, my dear, that I have taken extreme care with my appearance tonight so that I shall be of the greatest credit to you, and you do not appear to see me. Where are you, Rowan?"

He sighed faintly. "Forgive me. It must be the thought of the voyage and all that has to be done tomorrow."

He was feeling even more *distrait* by the time they entered the Consulate and handed their cloaks to waiting servants. The whole place was swarming with bejewelled people creating unbelievable noise and laughter as they trod up the stairs to be announced. Rowan seemed to be alternating between the scene before him and another of a vast silent expanse of desert, when he had lain beside a girl to speak of something that should have remained locked inside him. Which scene was real; which man the true one? His body was here in the social sphere he had known all his life, yet his spirit still wandered beneath those desert stars.

"Good evening . . . How do you do? . . . Honoured to make your acquaintance." They were inexorably swallowed up into that excited elegant crowd, and Rowan was lavished with praise and adulation. All he could think of, however, was that tomorrow they would embark for the war. Eight days hence they would be facing shot and shell . . . and Major the Honourable Montclare Verne DeMayne. How would the so-called hero of the 43rd deal with *that?*

"Ah, DeMayne, allow me to make some introductions," said the voice of Colonel Daubnay at his elbow, and he turned still full of thoughts of his brother.

Maurice Daubnay was wreathed in smiles as he made the presentation of his prize officer in the social and gallantry stakes.

"Captain the Honourable Rowan DeMayne, and Mrs DeMayne—Sir Pomfret and Lady Teale."

The gross, balding Sir Pomfret flushed purple as he glared at Rowan in disbelief, and seemed bereft of speech. But Lady Teale smiled a greeting which Lydia returned warmly.

Beside her Rowan felt as if the ground had suddenly collapsed beneath his feet, leaving him to contemplate a fatal
fall. Marriage to the elderly statesman had not impaired
Fanny Dennison's beauty one jot. With her golden hair
drawn back into a corona of curls around her shapely head,
her superb body clothed in blood-red silk and her violet eyes
laughing up at him, it was as if eight years had melted away
in an instant.

Automatically taking to his lips the hand he had smothered with kisses on so many occasions, he saw his past mistress as yet another threat, especially when she murmured,
"We shall be seeing a lot of each other, I suspect. My
husband and I are booked on the first ship to Balaclava that
sails in the wake of the 43rd. Sir Pomfret wishes to review
conditions there, and assess the cut of the men on whom
England's honour rests."

CHAPTER TEN

Embarkation for the final phase of that mammoth journey proved to be a great deal easier than it had been in Bombay, and the entire regiment sighed with relief. At Alexandria the steamers were able to berth alongside the jetty, and it was simply a case of each trooper taking his mount by the headrope and running it up the gangplank. However, the chestnut stallions being what they were, this was not accomplished without a great deal of squealing, biting and kicking as a sign that they did not take kindly to having to enter another of the abominable floating stables. But the soldiers now had their measure, and the animals were very soon standing in orderly fashion in the newly-constructed stalls they would have to occupy for the seven or eight days it would take to reach Balaclava. In fact, the process of loading the Advance Wing on two steamers was accomplished so smoothly, there was a period of several hours to wait before the ships sailed.

Mary stood on deck gazing at the shore with a heavy heart. The country she was leaving had taught her so many things, the most memorable of all being the foolishness of human nature. Noah had believed he could escape his past weaknesses by simply running away from them again, Rowan now saw with undazzled eyes that he had tied himself forever to a supremely unsuitable wife, Lydia DeMayne was feverishly seeking a revival of the adoration she had treated with such selfish arrogance when it had been lavished on her. But Mary, herself, had been the most foolish of all.

Eighteen months ago she had been a slut in a barrack-block, who had wanted no more than a bed, two dresses, books to read, and *freedom*. Now she knew she would never be free. Life had been simple as a trooper's woman; ambition and education brought complications. Every step forward induced yearnings to take the next one. But the goal was never reached, because it grew more and more elaborate along the way.

She looked at the bonnet in her hands and sighed. Noah had vanished again. This time he had taken nothing with him. The authorities had been told to look out for him— he would undoubtedly be shot, if apprehended—and the 43rd counted themselves well rid of him as they struck him off the strength of the regiment. But Mary could not wipe out memories of him so easily, and recalled his kindness and laughter with a great deal of sadness.

A pretty face had been the cause of his downfall. For love of a heartless girl he had thieved, shot a man, lied and cheated, and finally taken fifty lashes of a whip on his back to scar him for life. How would he live now in this alien country? By his wits? And how would he die . . . a military firing-squad or starvation in an Egyptian slum? Mary burned with anger at the thought of that girl still in England, skipping her selfish path having forgotten the young jeweller she had fancied for a while.

Deep affection, or destructive love had not touched Mary's life until recently. At the end of a barrack-block, survival had been the paramount concern. There had been a rough kind of loyalty and comradeship in times of adversity, but emotion had been a luxury they could not afford. Love, as Mary now knew it, would have been termed 'bloody

284

daft'. The physical expression of animal desires, and an essential dependence on a husband for survival were the basis of married relationships. It had been simple and clear-cut, free of the painful refinements of longing, jealousy and deceit.

Another young woman somewhere in England had driven Rowan to social alienation and family betrayal, which had led him to take on impossible burdens that had, in turn, thrown him into the arms of another precocious female. Now, he was further burdened by what he saw as a lifelong shackle to a third.

Perhaps it was. Their glances could never meet in innocence these days; when they were forced to speak to each other their voices were too carefully controlled. Only Lydia's inherent self-absorption could have kept her from noticing and associating the facts with Rowan's marital coolness. That he had neglected Lydia's bed was clearly apparent, and Mary could not deny her gladness at the fact. But she had been reared in the most down-to-earth schools and knew a man's needs were basic and unaffected by depths of feeling. Rowan would avail himself of his wife when the drive became too great, and Mary would have to accept it.

She had thought long and hard about the best thing to do before boarding the ship. Knowing Rowan would never bring himself to dismiss her to fend for herself in a dangerous place like Alexandria, the decision was hers alone. There was a possibility of returning to England with those wives and children leaving the regiment here. But England seemed as foreign and full of pitfalls to a girl who remembered nothing of it and knew no soul within its shores. It also meant leaving a regiment that was parents and family to her. She had been unable to desert it in company with Noah; she could not do it now alone. Neither could she desert the man she loved on the eve of war. If he fell in battle, she wanted to know and be there at the end with him. If he came through victorious, she wanted to see his eventual triumph. Beyond that she would not look. For once, she had no wish to see what lay over the horizon.

The steamers left Alexandria on time, and all those aboard took up shipboard life as if they had not marched across a desert for nearly three weeks since leaving the last vessel. This time, Mary had no Noah to find her a safe corner at night. During the days there was no friend to come and chat while she did her work; no one to teach her about the world and its wonders. One of the other officers' wives had employed a girl at Alexandria on the recommendation of her former mistress *en route* to India, but the girl was sullen, unfriendly and very seasick, so Mary soon gave up the attempt to be companionable.

Rowan had forcibly insisted that Lydia should have the cabin to herself with space for all her clothes, as she had had on the other voyage, and he seldom appeared there during the first four days. But the cabin had a narrow annexe at the entrance and this provided Mary with a place to sleep, which solved her problem of seclusion and satisfied Lydia's wish to have her on hand night and day.

So they steamed slowly across the vivid Mediterranean, past the very beautiful Greek islands into the Aegean. Then they headed for the narrow Dardanelles that would take them into the Black Sea, which everyone on board was now convinced would be no more black than the Red Sea had been scarlet. And as each day passed, the atmosphere changed. Although they were still five days' distant, ears began to strain for the sound of gunfire, eyes searched for puffs of smoke on the horizon. They were on the doorstep of war now. After six thousand miles, over a thousand of them on foot, battle was about to become a reality. All their training, their superb horses and the sharpened glittering weapons were to be used in earnest for the first time. The men of the 43rd grew quieter, more alert, more thoughtful.

The officers were no exception. There was a sharper authority in their manner as they carried out their duties, and the times between were spent in groups on deck discussing the situation they were likely to find facing them on arrival. At night, they tended to linger after dinner in deep conversation that concerned the side of their profession they had never yet been able to exploit. Small wonder those few wives still travelling with the regiment felt neglected and forgotten.

The close proximity of war occupied Rowan's thoughts almost exclusively during those days of steady steaming across deep blue seas. Utterly weary of emotional demands, he threw himself into totally masculine company as an antidote. Rediscovering the pleasure of male comradeship, conversation and interests, he discussed horses, weapons, tactics and other professional matters as avidly as any man anxious now to set foot on the battlefields about which they had heard so much. Each one of them longed to see the notorious valley where the Light Brigade had ridden to its death, and each wondered again and again what he would find the true situation to be after four-and-a-half months of speculation.

The end of winter would have brought about a resumption of hostilities between the Russians occupying the great fortress of Sebastopol, and the Anglo-French troops who had been holding it under siege through pestilence, attack and extremes of weather since the autumn. It would have to be taken before another winter smote the peninsular . . . and the 43rd would be there to help effect the victory. Surely the regiment would soon embroider their virgin colours with the name Sebastopol—the first of many future battle honours!

But, although Rowan spent most of his time contemplating the warlike aspect of his profession, he still had marital obligations he could not shirk, no matter how weary of them he might be . . . as he was reminded on their fifth night at sea when he escorted Lydia to her cabin, bade her goodnight, and prepared to leave.

Putting her hand on his arm as he turned away, she said, "You surely do not have to return to those with whom you have spent every waking minute already. Am I no longer entitled to your company?"

"I have been with you throughout dinner," he pointed

out, marvelling that he could look at that perfect face and body feeling nothing more than abstract appreciation.

"So have half-a-dozen others," she replied spiritedly. "But you are my husband."

"That circumstance seemed not to matter to you on our other voyage, as I recall. Is it that you do not find Captain Fosse the nautical cavalier that Captain Maidstone must have been to monopolize so much of your time?"

She chose to ignore that. "Rowan, what is come over you lately? I seem not to know you any more. Why have you begun behaving as a stranger to the wife who has accompanied you faithfully on this terrible journey, and means to remain beside you even at the battlefield?"

"Oh? Why then did young Cleaver hear from Mrs Cox that you had every intention of settling yourself comfortably in Constantinople as soon as it could be arranged?"

"But, Rowan, it is what most of the officers' wives have done throughout the war," she protested instantly. "You surely would not wish me to live in a primitive wooden hut within reach of shot and shell?"

"Of course I would not," he assured her truthfully. "I was merely trying to clarify your statement that you intended to stay by my side on reaching the battlefields."

Plainly at a loss as to how to counter that, she drew near him in the tiny cabin and looked up with an appeal that once would almost have melted his bones.

"I am at your side now, and I told Mrs Clarke I should not need her tonight. We are quite alone."

He put his hands on her shoulders and turned her slowly away from him. "Then allow me to unhook your gown for you." As he performed a task he had done for more women than he could remember, he thought once more of the trick of fate that decreed that Fanny Dennison should follow him to the Crimea. He might have undressed a great number of females in the past but, at the moment, he wished them all to the devil.

"There," he murmured as he unfastened the last hook, "I

am confident you can manage the rest for yourself. I will wish you good night."

Lydia spun round clutching her bodice, her eyes wide with disbelief. "You do not mean to go! I have just *invited* you to remain. You know very well that I have."

"I am honoured . . . but I decline."

Looking as if he had struck her, she cried, "I am your *wife*. I am entitled to your devotion."

He frowned at words that exacerbated his present disillusionment with emotional bonds. "As my wife you are entitled to my protection, my name and fortune, and my responsibility for your welfare. But you are not *entitled* to my devotion, Lydia. You have to earn that."

She faced him with that glittering blue gaze he had encountered on that first evening at Khunobad. "Did I not— from the very first moment? You have told me on so many occasions how helpless you were from the start."

He shook his head, remembering those days in the desert that had shown him the truth he had tried not to face. "That was worship. Blind adoration of an ideal. I see now that true devotion is vastly different. Sighs and kisses are not enough, Lydia. There must also be loyalty, understanding and selflessness."

Her colour rose as she took in the implication of his words. Then she attacked in full fury, a selfish woman who was being severely flouted. "How dare you say such things to me! I sacrificed my honour, my reputation, my entire future to come to you that night. *I saved your life* . . . and I have paid as dearly as a woman can for doing so. How dare you suggest I lack understanding and selflessness!"

He sighed heavily, knowing it must be said. "Saving my life that night was only settlement of a debt. It was you who drove me to consider sacrificing it—you and your game of cat and mouse with my helpless infatuation. It was your awareness of guilt that sent you after me—not understanding and selflessness. I owe you nothing. However, I will continue to give you my protection, and take responsibility for your welfare for as long as I am able. Do not expect my affection along with it. I believe it died somewhere along the route we have taken from Khunobad."

He left her standing and returned to the others, where he drank heavily and spoke to Gil of dark things like coming death in battle.

The advance edge of the bad weather hit the steamer in the very early hours of the morning, when seas rose rapidly and the cyclone-force wind sent heavy rain to mingle with the saltwater that bombarded the decks. The captain of the ship was not unduly worried. He had ridden out many a storm during his career and knew he had a good ship. What he failed to take into consideration was the fact that the adaptation of the vessel to take two hundred men and the same number of horses had altered its stability—and horses were a shifting unpredictable cargo. It did not occur to him to inform Major Benedict of the oncoming storm, therefore— a precaution that might have prevented the worst of the disaster.

Rowan and Gil were jerked awake almost simultaneously by the violent juddering of the ship as it was hit by a wall of water, and both reached for their trousers to pull on over nightshirts. Next minute, Gil was flung backward on to his bunk and Rowan sent crashing into the bulkhead as the vessel slewed round and dropped into a well left by a giant wave. A grim look between them was enough without words. There would be total pandemonium below decks where the stables were situated.

They instinctively made for the door, and lurched with difficulty through the passageway to reach the steps that would take them below. They were halfway there when the trumpet sounding 'Stand by your horses' told them Major Benedict had acted quickly. The repetitive call echoed bizarrely in the confined space between decks as Rowan and his friend jumped the last three steps to the stables where the stench of manure and sweating horses made the hot stifling atmosphere almost unbearable. Next minute, men were pouring down into the din and panic in response to the trumpet-call, but with only the dim light from the few lanterns there it was not easy to assess or help the situation.

One or two of the more alert troopers had gone to their horses before the general call, but they were too few to be of much help to those beasts that had been thrown off their feet and slipped down between the wooden walls of the stalls, where they were being kicked and trampled by their brethren. In the narrow spaces it was impossible to get them back on their feet again, so all efforts were concentrated on calming those who were plunging at every lurch of the ship and fighting to free themselves of the restricting head-ropes.

Rowan halted for a moment appalled at the noise and confusion. Waves were thundering like cannon shot against the ship's sides, the timbers were groaning beneath the onslaught, men were shouting in order to be heard, the animals were lashing with their hooves at the stalls surrounding them and splintering them with great cracks of tearing wood as they squealed and snorted in fear. In the confined space it was deafening and ominous, especially when the deck was heaving so badly it was difficult for the men to keep their feet or stay in one place for long.

In the dim, shifting light it was impossible to see just what was happening in any one place, but Rowan fought his way to where the horses of his split troop were stabled, alongside fifteen of the spare mounts he had trained during the journey. It was a terrible situation. The horses' coats being dark, in the depths of the stalls where the light did not penetrate, it was only possible to tell when a horse had slipped by the vociferous screams from the victim and those around the unfortunate beast.

The NCO's were roaring imprecations at the troopers, but they were doing their best in dangerous circumstances. The petrified horses were killers now. Rowan had already seen two men in great pain being dragged from the stalls by their fellows, one with an obvious broken leg. Others could hardly be blamed for fighting shy of entering between those narrow walls where a huge stallion was crazy with fright.

Passing on after showing his NCO's he was there should

they need him, Rowan grabbed the arm of the lovesick Lieutenant Cleaver and signalled that the boy should help with the remounts, who were as wild as the rest. It was certainly a case of taking one's life in one's hands, and Rowan forgot about his subaltern in the impossible business of trying to calm the beasts in a storm that seemed to be intensifying further. As he struggled to re-tie loose head-ropes, wedge splintered wood back into place and separate a pair whose forelegs had interlocked beneath the stalls, he was thrown violently so many times he felt winded and bruised, besides being in pain from a bad bite on the left hand that was now covered in blood.

Leaving that area to claw his way up the deck to where his personal chargers were stabled next to Gil's, Rowan felt a tremendous sense of helplessness. What they were attempting to do was impossible; what was happening was utterly tragic. They had come so far, endured so much. Fate was very cruel.

He had just reached Cavalier when a new source of terror arose as farriers began shooting horses that had broken their backs or gone mad to the point of being a danger to others. The sound of shots in that dark, closely-confined area was particularly distressing to the men, and the final straw for the horses. Then he saw that his favourite and most coura-geous stallion was finished. Thrown off balance, the poor creature had fallen and slipped on its own manure half beneath the stall housing Charade, who was foaming at the mouth and rearing dangerously. Those killer hooves had staved in the side of Cavalier, who was shrieking in agony with every further onslaught of those crashing feet.

Torn between the need to go for a farrier or stay to risk injury himself while calming Charade, Rowan was just curs-ing last night's brandy that had dulled his wits when he spotted young Cleaver staggering around with blood pour-ing from his head. Lurching toward him, Rowan had just pulled him clear of the lashing back legs of one of the remounts when a particularly huge wave must have hit the side of the ship and the pair of them were thrown right across the gap to land amongst the horses of A Troop, where the widowed Lieutenant Southerland-Stewart was fighting desperately with an animal that had seized his arm and would not let go.

Dazed by a blow on the head, filthy with manure and horse urine that made the deck impossibly slippery, Rowan struggled on to all fours beside the stamping legs of the horse that held the officer by the arm, and feverishly began dragging Robin Cleaver to safety. The boy appeared to have passed out. His face looked particularly ghastly in the light of flickering lamps, with blood smeared across the greater part of it. Grabbing a passing trooper Rowan yelled at him to get the injured subaltern to the room where orderlies were taking charge of the human victims of that slaughter.

Hardly conscious of what he was doing now Rowan somehow managed to find a farrier and take him up to put a shot in Cavalier. The death of a valued servant and friend all seemed part of the general tragedy. It went on and on. The frequency of shots increased, and more and more men were led away in pain or so seasick they were only adding to the chaos. Those remaining were exhausted and realizing it was a hopeless situation. The storm would continue until it abated and would take its toll whatever they did. The cost would then have to be counted.

Yet, even as that unspoken decision was reached, the most dangerous situation possible occurred. Careless carpentering resulted in a set of stalls collapsing one after the other like playing cards, and two of the animals simultaneously pulled free of their tethering. Momentarily unaware that they were now free agents, they were sliding from side to side trying to keep upright. But once they realized the fact, they would certainly run amok and cause infinite danger to men and horses.

Seeing the situation at the same time, Rowan and Gil struggled forward calling to those beside them to fetch spare ropes, and approaching one on either side of the nearest animal. By use of optical messages they closed in on the unsuspecting horse, ready for its slightest move. Just as they were alongside the ship lurched and Gil was thrown off balance. But Rowan grabbed at the head-rope that was still attached to the piece of wood torn from the wall, and pulled the beast's head round with a savage jerk so that lassoes could be thrown by those following behind them.

The creature was safely held, but the concentration of movement beside it had the other horse rolling its eyes and dancing backward before the same could be done to secure it, too. Finding there were no longer any restraints on its movements its aim was to get as far from terror as possible, and it turned to face the open corridor between the stalls.

"Gil . . . watch out!" yelled Rowan, but the warning was useless. Just getting to his feet after his fall, Gil was right in the path of the horse about to charge, and too bewildered to see his danger. So, as the horse made its initial lunge, Rowan threw himself in front of it to knock Gil to the ground again a split second before certain injury and possible death. But the flying legs of the runaway caught Rowan, deflecting him into its continuing path, and he instinctively protected his head with his hands as he rolled over and over, believing he would be crushed any moment. But there was a deafening report followed by a great crash as the horse pitched forward on to the deck, and lay dead a few feet away. Hands helped Rowan to his feet, and he stood panting and giddy facing Kit Wrexham, who was just lowering his pistol. The red-haired man was regarding him with a calm expression, seemingly unruffled and remarkably tidy in the midst of that chaos.

Rowan pushed back the hair from his own forehead and nodded to the man he had never liked. "My thanks, Wrexham."

"My pleasure, DeMayne."

Mary was having a difficult time trying to control her mistress's fear and her own seasickness. She was herself extremely frightened and believed the vessel about to founder with all souls. The urgent trumpet-calls, the sounds of running men, the cries of poor horses trapped between decks, all added to the thunder of waves to give an impression of impending disaster. The ship was still afloat, but she wondered how much longer it would remain so in such conditions.

The powder she had just given Lydia had quietened her considerably. It had been a physical battle to keep the girl in the cabin. Storms made Rowan's wife demented, and her one aim had been to go to him. Mary had had to resort to violent restraint to prevent Lydia from running headlong through the ship and creating worse problems. But the hysterical girl had fought tooth and nail, and Mary felt quite spent after being thrown heavily several times when the ship had plunged during their struggles.

Lydia now lay on the bunk staring at the ceiling with eyes that held the remnants of wildness, but she seemed to have finally accepted Mary's word that she was safer where she was than with her husband who was fighting a dangerous battle amidst maddened horses.

"We shall all perish," came the toneless voice from the bunk, as Mary moved toward the tiny washroom. She still felt miserably queasy and in an uncomfortable, untidy state.

"No, we shan't," she argued firmly, despite her own fears. "Storms at sea are commonplace, and the men on this ship know exactly what to do. I trust them to bring us safely through."

"I had no wish to come on this journey," Lydia rambled on as if Mary had not spoken. "From the moment we set out he has not cared for me. I suspected it, but now he has put it into words. I was the one he could not win—that was all it was. Now he has abandoned me at the time of greatest danger. He does not care for me."

Although it was clear the girl was speaking her thoughts in abstracted self-absorption, Mary continued to answer in soothing tones as she stood in the small washroom feeling no compunction in splashing herself with her mistress's cologne, before setting about wringing out small towels in scented water to lay on the brow of the invalid.

"The Captain *hasn't* abandoned you. You know he would

never do that," she murmured over her shoulder, worried to
death herself over his safety down in that hell between
decks. "At times like this his first duty is to the regiment.
It's the same with all the men. Our duty is to carry on as
best we can, and be ready with hot water, fresh clothes and
a meal when they get back. They might be very brave and
tough on the outside, but they all need a bit of fussing now
and then."

Having just finished speaking, a particularly violent lurch
sent her headlong over the shelf containing jug and bowl,
then threw her backward just as swiftly, so that the bowl
containing water and wet towels landed on top of her. Letting out an involuntary cry as her head cracked against the
wooden bulkhead, she lay where she was for a few moments
fighting for breath as the cold water soaked through her
bodice to her skin. Then, as she struggled to sit up in that
cramped space, there was a tremendous resounding crash
above her head that shook the deck. Was it a mast broken?
If so, their plight was desperate indeed. Her fear grew. What
chance would those below have if they foundered? The sea
would rush in relentlessly, drowning them even as they
struggled to the companionway. They would have no time
to reach the lifeboats if, indeed, they could be launched in
this tempest. Had Rowan returned from the horror near
Multan, survived their ordeal in the desert, only to die in the
jaws of the ocean when he was so near to the hope of glory
on the battlefield that he sought? Fighting down her tears
of protest, she told herself she would not leave the ship, if
he could not. There was no life for her, if he was lost.

Getting painfully to her feet on a deck that was now wet
and slippery in addition to being unsteady, she was about to
pick up the wet towels when some sixth sense told her
something was wrong. With rising alarm she stepped out
into the cabin, half-prepared for what she would see. The
cabin door was swinging open; the bunk was empty.

She stood for no more than a few seconds telling herself
she should have been prepared, should never have left the
girl's side even though she had seemed quiet. Then she set

off along the narrow way between cabins, her heart thudding with an accelerated beat as she grew nearer the ladder leading to the lower decks. The noise of shouting, neighing and occasional pistol-shots was even louder, and she turned a corner to witness her first sight of the results of the drama playing out below.

Bleeding men were being manhandled up the companionway that soldiers found difficult to negotiate with the ease of the seafarers. Alternately swearing and praying, the orderlies did their best to subject their human burdens to as little pain as possible, but they stumbled and fell frequently due to their inability to steady themselves with their hands. Others were retching convulsively, having emptied their stomachs below yet feeling so ill by now, they could not stop heaving.

Mary was appalled but not unnerved by the sight. All that was in her mind was to stop Lydia DeMayne from going below. Surely she could not have passed the orderlies and done so already. The answer was provided by sight of a figure in a long white nightgown at the end of the passageway, where there was another flight down.

"Oh, lordy, it's too late," she breathed. "I'll never reach her in time."

All the same, she began to run, pushing past the trail of troopers wending their way to the makeshift medical post, bruising her arms as she was thrown against the sides, and stumbling in the sudden forward plunges. Lydia had vanished from sight by the time Mary reached the top of the companionway, and involuntarily recoiled. From that dim well came the stench and heat that had made so many of the men seasick; down there were the sounds of crazed horses, frightened desperate men and instant death from hoof or pistol. Lydia must have been temporarily crazed to go down there.

Seeing a tangle of men appear at the foot of the difficult stairway, Mary set off down it before they could start their climb with another victim. They spotted her and began shouting abuse. But they stopped suddenly, and appeared to be transfixed by something on their level. Mary guessed what it was, and her stomach heaved with the combined smells and with apprehension over what was happening out of her sight.

Dropping the last few feet when her handhold was lost on rails now slippery with blood, she landed in a heap on the deck. It was from this position that she witnessed, in the fitful light from swaying lanterns, the frightful situation that had developed. The half-demented Lydia was wandering through the mêlée searching for the man she believed should have been at her side, and everyone was too busy to notice the strange figure. Those at the foot of the companionway, who had were shouting warnings that were swallowed up in the deafening noise made worse in that confined space.

On the point of scrambling to her feet in pursuit of her mistress, Mary saw through the dimness to where Rowan was trying to calm a horse of A Troop that had broken free. At that same moment he spotted Lydia and momentarily froze with disbelief. Then Mary saw his mouth moving as he shouted, but who could hear just one voice in that din? Lydia must have recognized him, however, for she started forward in his direction, oblivious of the nearby subaltern who, with tears on his cheeks, had his pistol to the head of a fallen beast. The sound of the shot made Mary jump, but on Lydia the deafening crack had a fatal effect.

Rooted now to the spot she began screaming, head turning from side to side in hysteria, the sounds of her panic lost to all but those beside her. A trooper seized her, but she turned into an Amazon as she clawed and kicked her way free of him. Rowan started toward her, letting go the bridle of the horse he had been calming. The animal, deprived of its comforter, rolled its eyes in panic and started after him. On her feet by this time, Mary ran forward seeing the danger Rowan could not.

She had forgotten he was an instinctive horseman. That instinct now caused him to look over his shoulder even when his attention was drawn by the dramatic presence of his wife in nightgown and shawl. Lydia, seeing his backward glance and plainly believing he was about to turn away, darted forward to fasten her arms round his neck in a hold he could not immediately loosen, and the pair struggled for a moment or two while he fought free. Mary came to a halt, realizing the new danger. Any threatening forward move now could stampede the horse so close to the couple. All those in their vicinity realized this and stayed where they were, isolating them and the stallion in a small open area between stalls.

The danger seemed to be passing when another wall of water hit the side of the ship with a thunderous roar that set Lydia clutching wildly at her husband again, just as he lost his footing on the slippery deck. They went down together, Lydia's shawl flying up to flap in the face of the chestnut horse. It was the last straw. Throwing back its great head, it reared up in fright; a huge rampant beast with pawing hooves.

Paralyzed with foresight Mary had her hand to her mouth as the hooves crashed to the deck once more. Rowan, seeing the danger, frantically spread-eagled himself across his wife's prone body to protect her. It was no more than an instinctive split-second movement, and it did not save her. In continuing wild panic, Lydia turned her head into the path of those great hooves and they caught her right temple as they plunged down.

A trooper leapt at the horse and struggled to control it; men rushed to the still figures on the deck. Mary found herself shaking uncontrollably as they dragged Rowan up and supported him while others picked up the inert figure in a nightgown now stained by the mess on the deck. Lydia hung limply, arms dangling and head thrown back unnaturally. There was the dark gathering of blood on the right side of her face. The soldier holding her stared at Rowan, who seemed about to fold up as he stared back. Then he pulled free of those holding his arms and stepped forward to take the body of his wife, like a man in another world.

Mary had grown fearfully cold and her teeth were chattering as she watched him cross toward the nearby companionway, staggering each time the ship rolled. She moved toward him in instinctive comfort, but it was as if he did not see her there as he prepared to climb up out of that semblance of hell, carrying the dead girl over one shoulder.

Apart from Lydia DeMayne, two troopers were dead, six severely injured, thirteen badly cut and twenty-six horses had been destroyed by morning. The carcasses of the animals were winched overboard; the funerals were timed for sunset. It was time for the 43rd Light Dragoons to forget the glory and count the cost of their journey to war.

Mary felt completely disoriented; had no idea what to do or where to go. Shock slowly passed leaving her to face the fact that Lydia's death had brought a drastic change in her own circumstances. In four more days they would be at the Crimea. What would she do then?

When the deck was finally clear she found a quiet corner where she could sit gazing out at the sea speeding past with flecks of white foam edging the dark-blue rolling surface. Her mind teemed with memories of the past four-and-a-half months, starting with Lydia calling her up to the bungalow near the hospital to ask if she would go with the regiment to the Crimea, and passing through all the stages of the journey and her own growing education until this moment. Now, she wondered whether she had given the best answer that day at Khunobad. Those far horizons she had yearned to explore had brought her far more than she had bargained for. The afternoon wore away as she weighed the good against the bad, but had reached no final conclusion at the end of it.

The ship's company turned out with the regiment for the solemn occasion of burials at sea when the sun was low in the west. Mary stood at the side wearing the bonnet Noah had bought her, her grey dress and a black shawl, even though it was stiflingly hot. She had never before witnessed such a ceremony and thought the three flag-covered bodies lying on the deck an emotive sight in the rosy light of sunset. But if she was affected by it, Rowan was plainly even more so. He looked haggard and almost inhuman as he stood at the head of the furthest body, and her heart went out to him as she wondered how much more a man could take. Would this journey have also destroyed him before it ended?

The ceremony was simple, and extremely moving when the bodies slid over the side to drop with a splash into the ocean, leaving only the flag covering the board, with no headstone or mark to show the last resting place.

Then it was the last of the three. Mary felt her throat constrict as she thought of that young, dazzlingly beautiful girl who had sailed out to India only a year before to find a husband and a future. If Rowan had not returned from Multan when he had, she might now be happily still in India enjoying endless flirtations, doted upon by an elderly wealthy husband who demanded no more than an ornamental hostess to grace his solitary home. Officer's lady or trooper's woman, they were all of the same weak flesh.

The ship's captain spoke the final words of the service, and the plank was tipped once more as the sun began to sink below the rim of the sea. Mary's throat constricted further. Lydia DeMayne had departed the world with no more than a splash to mark her going. But, even as she realized too late that some gesture, some symbol of that lost life should have marked the spot, Rowan stepped forward to the side and flung something out into the vastness. The deep red light of the sun caught the gold of the chain and the sparkle of the sapphires before the pendant vanished beneath the waves after the girl who had worn it.

It was too much. Mary turned away and hurried to the spot right up in the bows where she had often stood in moments of solitude. The wind dried the tears on her cheeks as she shed them, and it was a long time before she could move away in any kind of composure. It was completely dark by then.

Halfway along the upper deck the full implications of her predicament hit her, and she hesitated in the act of going down to the cabin. Could she still claim that annexe as sleeping-quarters now she no longer had duties to perform?

What was she to do about food? Could she still expect
Collins to provide her with her supper? The only way to
solve the problem was to look it in the face, so she resolutely
continued on her way. There was no response to her knock,
so she went in, expecting it to be empty.

It was a shock to discover she was wrong. By the light of
just one lamp she made out the figure sitting hunched and
motionless beside the bunk, staring into space. He looked so
desolate she sighed with compassion and went to sink down
beside him as she looked up into a beloved face grown old
and yellowed in the lantern-light.

Putting her hands over his she said gently, "It's the way
of life. Some are taken young, and there's nothing any of us
can do about it." There was no response, even though his
eyes seemed to be staring straight into hers. She continued
to hold his hands as she went on. "When it's quick like that
it's always more of a shock. Sam went in a matter of hours."
Remembering that sad time, she drew even nearer him. "I
know what you're feeling."

"Do you?" he asked, his voice sounding as if it came from
the dead. "Do you know how it feels to destroy someone?"

"Oh no . . . no," she cried in real distress, "you mustn't
think that way. If anyone was to blame it was me—but she
was determined to get to you. I did my best with her, and
that's all anyone can do in a crisis. You didn't destroy her,
you tried desperately to save her. I saw you."

He appeared to hear none of her words. "I killed her just
as surely as I killed that girl in Multan."

Overcome with pity, she put up her hands to cup his face
as she spoke urgently and deliberately. "Listen to me,
Rowan. You're speaking wild, d'you hear? You didn't kill
either of them. If you don't accept that you'll end up destroying yourself."

As he put his head back away from her hold, she knew he
was well aware of her presence and what she was saying. "I
did that some years ago. They were all right. Everything I
have done since *has* been designed to win back my honour,
and I inflicted immeasurable suffering on others for that

cause. In the end, I have failed. There is no honour in watching the butchery of another. There is no honour in the death of someone I ill-used and betrayed." He stood up slowly, sending her back on her heels and breaking all contact. "There is no honour in desire for a servant-girl, a child of the regiment. Go back where you belong, Mary Clarke. Forget all I have ever said and done to you. The touch of the devil is on me, and I want no more lives on my hands. Go back where you belong. You'll be safe from me there."

When he turned away and went to stand gazing from the port-hole she knew, without further words from him, that he had shut her resolutely from his life.

Everyone crowded on to the decks as the steamer edged into the harbour of Balaclava, the place that had been no more than a name to them since setting out. Their excited chatter faded, and died altogether as they took in the scene. Mary, standing isolated in the bows, felt herself grow cold despite the considerable warmth of the mid-April day as she looked on war for the first time. They had travelled from Khunobad in full colour. Now life had turned mud-brown.

The entire beach around the harbour was littered with debris; planks, masts and tangled rigging was all there was left of the ships that had been pounded apart during the hurricane of the previous November. But that was nothing to the sight of human arms and legs that had been amputated and thrown into the sea to be taken out on the tide, but which had tangled with other stagnant flotsam in the harbour to slowly rot and putrefy as grim evidence of past battles.

Taking her horrified gaze from the water Mary saw that every jetty was congested with carts and waggons being loaded with sacks, boxes and crates of provisions; sections of wooden huts ready to be erected; packages of medical supplies, barrels of grain for men and animals; and great nets containing round-shot and shells for the continuing bombardment of Sebastopol. Most of this was being transported to a railhead where trucks were being filled for the journey to nearby hills on a track running up into the distance.

To counterbalance all the ingoing activity came a downhill stream of ambulance-waggons, with even more sick and wounded in baskets tied to oxen, bullocks, mules and camels. The poor victims looked pale, ragged and filthy, bound with blood-stained cloths and so emaciated it was a marvel they were still alive. These men were bound for the infamous hospital at Scutari, where it was rumoured their only hope of survival was to refuse to enter its doors.

Mary was very shaken by all she saw. War had become a reality, and the gloss, the golden aura of courage, national pride and noble sacrifice was ridiculed by the tragedy in that harbour. She had heard that Colonel Daubnay had despaired at having to send his beautiful regiment to war, and Mary could now understand why. Did the men of the 43rd really long to become like these broken pathetic creatures with faces that betrayed their lost hopes and ideals? 'The Gingerbread Boys' might finally embroider battle honours on their virgin standards, but how many of them would be there to see them fluttering proudly in the breeze?

The gangplanks were let down, and the hollow clatter of hooves from below signalled the fact that the regiment was on the move. Only then did Mary realize the fair sprinkling of bearded wild-looking men in shaggy fur coats gathering near the jetty were not foreign cut-throats, but British cavalrymen on horses that would normally have long ago gone to the knacker's yard. Their distinctive shakoes and *czapkas* that identified them for what they really were began to blur as Mary thought of the 43rd who, despite the hardships and tragedies of their long journey, looked so fine and splendid against the battle-decimated men awaiting them.

The picture blurred even more when A Troop began leading the magnificent chestnut stallions off the ship, and a cheer went up from those ashore. Mary then knew the answer to her question as to whether the 43rd really wished to become like their comrades. *This* had been the reason behind the past months of journeying, *this* had been driving them all on, filling them with impatience, ruling their thoughts. For this moment they had travelled six thousand miles across two continents and two oceans. They had been needed by their brothers-in-arms, and had come to their aid. Their arrival had put new heart into those ashore, their smart turnout and prime horseflesh revived the pride of those who had suffered every kind of defeat since setting foot on this land.

Mary watched the whole of the Advance Wing gradually assemble on the jetty and form up in immaculate ranks. A pale sun broke through to glitter the silver embellishments on the pale-blue jackets and sheen the reddish coats of the horses, transforming the new arrivals into even more of a phantom sight against that terrible heart-rending backdrop of Balaclava, and when the three troops rode off toward the sinister hills overlooking Sebastopol, Mary felt their regimental pride as if she had been amongst them. The 43rd was her regiment, those troopers were her friends, and riding at the head of C Troop was the man she loved. Small wonder she shared their moment of acclaim by the survivors of the Crimea, that wiped from the board all their past indignities and insults.

"*Clarke,* what do you think you are doing idling up here?" came a sharp voice behind her. "My baggage has to be carried ashore and there is a great deal of it. Get to your work, girl! Mr Cox will be sending a waggon for us as soon as one can be arranged, and he will be considerably vexed if we are not ready."

Mary moved away from the ship's side in resignation. She knew it might have been a very different story for her now if the wife of Lieutenant Cox had not offered her work as her personal maid on the day following Lydia's death. But the woman called her Clarke, spoke to her as if she had no wits, and treated her like a barrack-block woman. Had she travelled six thousand miles across the world to end up as she had started?

Picking up several hatboxes, Mary began transferring her mistress's baggage ashore and, despite her sadness and fears, nevertheless experienced a thrill when she first put foot on the soil of the Crimea. What lay in store for her here?

CHAPTER ELEVEN

The cavalry was encamped on a hill two miles above Balaclava near a village called Kadikoi, where they were in a good position to defend the vital harbour from any attempt by the Russians to recapture it. The 43rd was given a site slightly above the existing disorderly straggle of tents, shacks and lean-tos that were gradually being replaced by a fresh supply of sturdier tents and huts that would have saved countless lives if they had been sent when asked for during that terrible winter. The new arrivals were considerably shaken when they saw the conditions prevailing, and the state of men and beasts existing in that legendary place.

The 43rd caused a sensation, and quickly became the subjects for sightseeing parties who rode up to watch the rest of the regiment arrive and set up camp in their Indian-style tents in orderly rows. But, if they were curiosities to those already there, the men who had fought the battles and the winter on that peninsular were just as much curiosities to them. There was a toughness about their manner and speech, a casualness about their dress, an air of hard-learned experience about their behaviour that spoke volumes to those as yet untouched by battle.

As the regiment settled into its new home, which promised to be fairly permanent, the members looked with amazement around the hinterland of the Russian seaport that stretched as far as they could see in a series of undulating hills and long valleys that were green and dotted now with spring flowers. Every part of it was covered with the camps of English and French regiments holding the tiny sea-fortress under siege to landward. Outside the walled town of Sebastopol the Russians had erected huge earthworks on retreating from the invading Allies last year, and had survived their siege throughout winter without any sign of surrender. Reinforcements had managed to break through the cordon of weakened cavalry to reach the town, and this coming summer would surely see a bitter battle to finish the war by capturing the besieged stronghold.

But the most amazing circumstances to the newcomers was the fact that the regimental hospitals, and the road down to the hospital-ships were filled with casualties. There had been no real battles since the autumn, yet men were dying in thousands from old wounds turned gangrenous, starvation throughout the winter, fever, frostbite and total exhaustion. Many others had gone mad, committed suicide, or been shot for attempted desertion. A few had been too weak to withstand the shock of the severe floggings for drunkenness on duty, and were buried along with their comrades on the slopes around Balaclava.

It seemed amazing to those who now saw the Crimea in its April beauty and knew nothing of the horrors the others would never forget. To the men who had been on the march for so long, these pleasant green hills seemed delightful. In fact, they would have been hard put to realize there was a war in progress at all if it had not been for the sound of constant bombardment from the trenches of the front lines near Sebastopol . . . and for the shock of their first war casualty.

Two days after the arrival of the Rear Wing that made the regiment complete, Colonel Daubnay had reviewed his toy soldiers in full glittering dress, while the regimental band

had played rousing marches, the sound of which had drawn
huge crowds to watch a spectacle they had not seen for over
a year. Puffed with pride, Maurice Daubnay had ridden off
afterward with another cavalry colonel, who took him on an
informative tour of the outer defences. A waggon had
brought his body back to the 43rd's camp two hours later,
shot through the head by a Russian sniper as he had inspected the forward positions he would need to pinpoint.

The officers and men of the 43rd were dumbfounded;
could not believe it had happened. Major Benedict took
command of the regiment within a week of its arrival at the
seat of the war, and 'The Gingerbread Boys' buried the man
who had never wanted to take them to war, knowing he had
died being spared something that would have given him
aesthetic pain. It could not truthfully be said that any member of the regiment deeply mourned the passing of their
commanding officer, but his death served to dispel the feeling that the surrounding hillsides were serene and idyllic
after the harsh terrains they had travelled. War was flitting
there unseen.

Seven years in India did, however, instil delight in the
43rd when steamers arrived bearing loads of sightseers from
England, and pretty girls in the most delicate crinolines
were to be seen everywhere picking their dainty way around
old battlegrounds, and even venturing amongst the big guns
in forward positions overlooking Sebastopol. These visitors
lived aboard the steamers, but there were a number of intrepid wives of officers and soldiers who lived in tents or huts
with their regiments and looked upon the frivolous invasion
with grief and disparagement.

But regimental life had to be maintained, and the 43rd,
together with the two regiments that had followed them
from India, were thrown unstintingly into duties that had
been shouldered by the decimated, sickly, exhausted survivors of the Light Brigade throughout the winter, who now
took a well-deserved rest. With such a vast area to protect,
a great many outlying piquets, reconnaissance patrols and
skirmishing parties were required, and the men of the 43rd

had to learn the terrain and positions of all adversaries very quickly. They also had to familiarize themselves with the profuse varieties of uniforms worn by their allies—French, Turks, and Sardinians—so they would not be mistaken for Russians and shot at.

During those first days Rowan was fully occupied with duties and organization for their new rôles. He and Gil had come to an excellent arrangement whereby they shared his double tent for living quarters, and put their beds in Gil's smaller one, giving them much more room than either had had before. The death of Maurice Daubnay and Major Benedict's elevation to lieutenant colonel had sent them both one step up the promotion ladder. Gil was now a major, leaving Rowan as the new senior captain of the regiment. The loss of their commanding officer had also left them both with a feeling of inexorable fate. Daubnay had never wanted to go to war; neither had Lydia. Both had had their wish. Was a person's life so designed that it was dangerous to go against destiny? Subconsciously, the two friends felt a sense of surrendering to the inevitable in the coming days.

At the first possible opportunity Rowan took his horse Charade and rode across to that valley where the Light Brigade had galloped to its death. On a hot afternoon just before dusk he walked that renowned vale leading the horse and trying to imagine the sounds of cannon, cries of men upholding their country's honour, thundering hooves, and the stirring sound of the bugle sounding the Charge. Here, his brother Bel had fallen, and Monty had been wounded. Here, the regiment he was denied had met immortality. He walked slowly over grass thick with larkspur and forget-me-nots that grew in a riot of shot and shell that lay there still, even pushing their way through skulls and partial skeletons scattered in that evocative place running between hills that rose all around as if to preserve memories forever. He heard nothing of the birds singing so joyfully above him, did not notice the hares that ran at his approach—life continuing amidst death.

For an hour or so he wandered alone in that place desperately trying to feel the drama, the courage, the sacrifice of the day in October when the area had been full of the clamour of battle. But it eluded him. All he could hear was a voice asking: *Why do you always feel you have to do more than anyone else?*

He sat for a while, his isolation unable to keep at bay the thoughts that occupation and companionship held off. He had packed up all Lydia's clothes, possessions and dowry items, leaving the trunks at the jetty to be shipped back to Chatsworth Dunwoodie and his pious wife in Khunobad, asking them to sell them for the best possible price and give the money to the women of the regiment that replaced the 43rd—something of which their niece would have approved. He had added words to the effect that although they had turned their insufferably hypocritical backs on her in her life, he trusted they would be more charitable to her in death. He had kept nothing to remind himself of her. His wedding present of emeralds had been sent home to his banker in the same box as the silverware. A widowed man sharing quarters with a bachelor had no need of fancy trimmings so necessary to females.

Gil had been a godsend. Readily agreeing to take up their old relationship, it had been possible for Rowan to continue that tragic voyage and establish a new way of life in calm unemotional manner. In point of fact, he found that former masculine bond a great relief after the past six months, and realized how much he had changed in order to please Lydia. He was probably one of the very few men who actually resented the female sightseers. The vision of crinolined figures beneath frilly sunshades was one he wished to blot completely from his mind.

It was that very vision that drove him to mount and ride from the valley of death soon afterward, for yet another group of voyeurs escorted by officers who had seen or experienced the Charge appeared at the mouth of the vale to break the peace with giggles and exclamations of exaggerated admiration.

It was a breathless evening as he neared camp again, with

stars already appearing in a sky still dusk-blue, and the distant sea was silvery-mauve except where lights in the harbours of Balaclava and Sebastopol put shimmery gilding on the water. The bombardment had stopped for the day and the distant sound of Russian bugles within the fortress gave Rowan a sense of brotherhood with the foe he had crossed the world to face. Those poor beleaguered devils had their own troubles, no doubt.

The tent was empty when he went in and pulled off cap and jacket. There was an appetising smell coming from the fire where Collins was cooking dinner nearby, and the brandy stood ready on a tray with glasses. He sank into one of the canvas chairs, put his booted feet up on the travelling chest, and poured himself a stiff drink, lost in those thoughts better kept suppressed.

Suddenly, a figure appeared outside the tent, bent its head to enter, and straightened up slowly once inside. Rowan's feet dropped from the chest and he got up warily, glass in hand, as he finally recognized his brother. Eight years had passed since their last bitter meeting, and this direct approach took him completely unawares.

"Crimean manners have grown casual, you will find," said Monty easily. "We no longer ask permission to enter a man's tent. My apologies if it is inconvenient."

Rowan was shocked by his appearance. The thickset figure had been honed down to little more than whippet wiriness, the fleshy face was taut, and dark eyes normally full of humour now contained that inexplicable haunted quality to be found in the eyes of most old campaigners. Monty looked an old man at thirty-seven.

"Do you still drink brandy?" Rowan asked to cover his mixed feelings of shock, wariness and old wounds re-opening.

"Does a man ever stop a habit of that nature, even when circumstances force abstinence? I'll be glad of a draught the size of yours."

While Rowan poured a generous measure, Monty settled

uninvited in the other chair and stretched his legs in the shabby crimson overalls of the 11th Hussars.

"Saw you ride off to the valley earlier. Searching for Bel's grave, were you? You won't find one. He was scattered across the turf with half-a-dozen of his comrades. Happened to more men than I care to think of." He reached forward to take the glass. "Many thanks."

Rowan was too tense to sit. The confrontation had come too soon, too unexpectedly, and was too unpredictable. He stood where he was and tossed the brandy quickly down his throat in order to pour himself another.

Monty sipped with great appreciation for a moment or two, then glanced up to say, "It's been a long time, Rowan."

"Yes."

"My condolences on the recent death of your bride. Word of your marriage had reached me only a few days before that tragic news. It seemed more than tragic in consequence."

"Did it?" he asked heavily. "I can't think why. For the past eight years we have lived as strangers—worse than strangers, in fact. I find it difficult to believe you care any more for me and my affairs than I do for you and yours. I have learned to live very well without my family."

"There's not much of it left," came the quiet comment. "Bel's son was taken by typhoid at Christmas and our grandfather has finally gone to his Maker. I received the notification this morning."

"Is that why you came? You should have saved yourself the duty. The old man and I ceased to be related on September 4th 1847. His death does not concern me."

"A man can never deny his blood kin."

"He did . . . and so did you."

Monty stared at him with a frown. "My God, you still feel it after all these years?"

"Feel it?" cried Rowan. "I would have arranged to be absent had I known you were going to call on me."

"Then I am glad I gave no advance notice of my intentions."

His brother seemed no more than slightly disconcerted, which shook Rowan more than ever. "Well, you have delivered your message and said all that is deemed fitting by convention on the subject of my recent loss. Now you may leave with my blessing."

Monty leant back in his chair and shook his head. "No, Rowan, you will have to throw me out, and I think even your astonishing bitterness will not allow you to do that."

Lowering his glass to the folding table, Rowan said, "This beats all, by God, it does! Have you really forgotten Bel's taunts, the way his friends seized and held me there to listen to his public stripping of my character, your own failure to prevent all he and those same men chose to do to add to my humiliation and spread the story so that society buzzed with it? Have you truly managed to put from your mind Cardigan's withering dismissal from the regiment in the presence of all its assembled officers, or our grandfather's brief unhesitating move to erase my name from any connection with our noble ancestors? *Astonishing bitterness?* I have lived with the consequences of that affair ever since. It has ruled my life, dictated my actions, coloured my every word and movement. There is not one moment of the past eight years that has not been affected by an event you appear to regard with hazy impatience. *Astonishing bitterness?* You do not know what you are saying, man."

Monty stared at him, perplexed. "You were a hot-headed boy under the influence of an immature passion for a woman who played on your exaggerated sense of gallantry whilst she was distributing her favours throughout the regiment. You made the fact public, and had to be taught a lesson."

"Oh yes, a lesson that denied me my birthright, blackened my name and fed the gossips in every salon in India from the moment I landed there."

"But it was *eight years ago*," pointed out his brother in mild reprimand. "There have been a hundred scandals since then to drive it from the public mind—scandals of far more serious nature."

It was Rowan's turn to be perplexed. "Are you suggesting it was nothing; that it has been forgotten?"

"Superseded, shall we say?"

"But . . . the regiment. All those men who shunned me!"

Monty took another pull at his brandy. "Most of them are dead—killed in the Charge. Others have transferred or sold out. I'll wager there is no officer in the 11th you would know now. Only Cardigan would doubtless turn his back were he not in England. It was he who made such a thing of it at the time, and his eccentricities are now become so excessive he is seldom taken seriously by anyone. Any one of my brother officers would be eager to shake you by the hand, Rowan. Your reputation for courage is known throughout the British Army. The hero of the 43rd is regarded with honour."

It was too much for him to take in; too much at variance with what he had believed for so long. Sitting down slowly he heard that voice saying once more: *Why do you always feel you have to do more than anyone else?*

"The British Army did not want to know me once," he reminded the other man. "Even the only regiment that would have me made no secret of the fact that it was almost an act of charity. The whole of Anglo-India has never let me forget it."

"Phoo," exclaimed Monty in a dismissive expression. "It is universally known that Anglo-Indians are a parcel of gossiping tabbies who are a decade behind the times in a backwater of the Empire. If you had only retired to the country for a year, I'll wager there was not a regiment you could not have entered freely." A faint smile broke through at that. "But you were wild in those days, and suffering badly from an excess of lust you mistook for love. Nothing would satisfy you than to make the lady in question some gesture that would reveal your true worth. So you signed up with a paltry ragbag of men in order to go to the ends of the earth and prove yourself."

"The 43rd is no ragbag of men," he said sharply. "It is a very fine regiment."

"Mmm," mused Monty. "You defend it, despite its treatment of you?"

"Its treatment of me was nowhere near as shabby as that of my brothers."

"A point, Rowan. You always were a mean swordsman." He held out his glass. "May I beg another *soupçon* of that excellent brandy?" While Rowan poured it he leant back in his chair watching him. "We were all a great deal younger then, and full of self-importance. We had the ridiculous airs of inexperience, and thought ourselves very fine fellows with even finer distinctions of honour and integrity." He accepted the glass and raised it in salute before drinking. "As a child, you were spoiled and uncurbed by our mother after Father was killed in China. It was due to her that you had such an idealistic attitude toward the fair sex, and always expected your own way. Everyone would agree that Fanny Dennison played an exquisite and cruel game with your fatal faults. Even so, you should never have drawn a sword against your own brother. It was distasteful enough without choosing an officers' mess as the venue. In private, it would have probably done little more than alienate Bel for some years; in public it was unforgivable and broke every code we guarded so carefully. Your family had no option but to cast you off."

Rowan sighed heavily. "Is this all necessary? I am more than fully cognisant with every fact."

Monty nodded. "I suppose I am conducting a defence. At least, I think I am. The scene I'm describing seems more like a drama I once saw in a theatre. Did we really all take part in it?"

Once again Rowan felt astonishment that what had dogged him so vividly for eight years seemed almost forgotten by his brother, who had played a leading part in it.

"If you have doubts, ask any of my brother officers," said Rowan with resignation. "They will acquaint you with every detail."

Monty let out his breath thoughtfully. "The Crimea will soon change that, Rowan. We all came out here full of

316

notions of patriotism and glory. But this has been conducted like no other campaign I have experienced. Men have been reduced to less than animals, we have been betrayed and ill-used by our commanders who are now blaming each other and disgracefully excusing themselves from responsibility for blunders that caused wholesale slaughter. We have been unforgivably ignored by the Government, who sent us needlessly to war ill-equipped, lacking supplies and with deplorably few facilities for sick and wounded." Growing heated, he went on, "The Light Brigade was sent to commit suicide through a communiqué everyone now denies writing—over six hundred men and horses sent to certain slaughter by an anonymous officer who is too ashamed to confess, and probably does not now know why he scribbled those few words onto a piece of paper. It is infamous, Rowan. *Infamous.*"

"You were wounded, I believe," he said, caught up by his brother's words.

Monty nodded. "A swordthrust in the thigh. It was indescribably, that mêlée. The charge was so unethical, so against all military wisdom, the Russians were rendered inactive by disbelief until we were almost at their guns. Although only a handful of our men survived, our enemies regard it as our victory. Our apparent willingness to sacrifice ourselves against such overwhelming odds as heavy cannon has put the fear of God into Russian regiments, who dread having to face us in battle. Fortunately for them, winter enforced a postponement. But it was not our friend. I have seen things I would not have believed possible—depravity, bestiality, madness, strong men crawling on all fours whimpering like babes. I have seen animals reduced to walking skeletons, frozen to death as they stood on piquet, or cannibalized whilst still breathing." He tossed back the rest of the brandy, then gave Rowan a straight look. "A lovesick boy pricking his brother's arm with the point of his sword in defence of a whore no longer seems important, or real . . . or worth a family feud. This war has made a mockery of the arrogant fools we were. Our brother's life ended in a second; my own hung in the balance. And from what we have all heard, you

have diced with death on a number of occasions." He held
out his hand, saying, "I no longer have the stomach for finer
feelings that are affronted by nothing at all, have you?"

Rowan stared at the hand that renewed brotherhood,
finding it difficult to accept that the insuperable barriers of
eight years had fallen without a sound. Then he reached out
and gripped it gladly, finding himself strangely moved. They
both had another drink and fell to discussing the present
state of the war. It was not for some while that Rowan
recalled what his brother had said earlier, and asked, "If the
old man has gone, and Bel's boy too, are you now the Earl?"

"No. Bel had another boy just before he left for the war
last year. He will take the title. I've applied to go home and
sort out affairs for the family."

"You're taking leave?"

Monty shook his head. "I'm selling out."

"Leaving the army for good?" cried Rowan in disbelief.

"Don't make it sound like treachery," said his brother
heavily. "This family has more than served its country,
wouldn't you agree? Five generations of soldiers, only two
members of which have not died on a battlefield somewhere.
You seem certain to go the same way." He frowned. "I have
had enough, Rowan. These months have shown me something I hadn't the courage to face before."

"What is that?"

"That we were never given any choice. From the moment
we were born our names were put forward for the regiment.
We were educated to be soldiers, fed military facts almost
exclusively, forced to believe that anything other than emu-
lating our illustrious ancestors would make us weaklings, and
we were burdened with the obligation of becoming heroes."
He smiled faintly. "It was even worse for you, I suppose. Bel
and I were already distinguishing ourselves when you
reached maturity."

How well he remembered his brothers being held up as
examples as he stood before the grandfather he had always
feared as a boy.

"You have the decorations to prove it," he said quietly.

"Ah, medals," put in Monty disparagingly. "Medals are given to men who happen to be in the right place at the right time, that is all. I have seen more courage on this peninsular by men who will never be decorated for it. It takes all forms, and one does not have to be in the illustrious 11th to possess it, I assure you Rowan. For me, courage is to now stand up and say I have had enough of soldiering. I shall not bring my sons up to be inevitable warriors, neither shall I force Bel's boy into a cocked hat and tunic as soon as he can walk. What I have seen here has given me the courage to defy my family name and retire from the lists with a clear conscience. As I said earlier, we once had the ridiculous airs of inexperience and fine distinctions of honour and integrity that made us behave like arrogant fools. All I want now is to live my life out in peace, and allow others to do the same. I will be ruled by my own conscience from now on."

Completely taken aback by all this, Rowan said, "Will they allow you to sell out at this precise time, when every man possible is needed?"

"Every *infantry* man possible is needed," corrected his brother. "The only thing left to do in this pointless war is to storm the fortress at Sebastopol, and that will be done by foot regiments with scaling-ladders. Men on horses will be needed for nothing more than patrols and messengers for the rest of the army. The cavalry has done all it can here." He shook his head. "If your ragbag regiment has come looking to cover itself with glory, it has arrived too late, I fear."

The Coxes had set up their tent on a level area with a spectacular view of the sea to the west of Balaclava, and from where they could also see practically everything that went on in the camp of the 43rd. Mary had discovered her new employers were inveterate gossips, whose prying into the actions and conversations of others provided them with hours of delightful speculation. She had also discovered the difference between them and people of real quality like the DeMaynes. Lieutenant Cox was the youngest son of a minor official of the railways; his wife was sharp-faced, sharp-voiced, and lacking any form of graciousness. They addressed her imperiously as 'Clarke', conversed and behaved in her presence as if she were not there, and expected her to do far more than she had for Lydia and Rowan.

Lieutenant Cox's batman was a coarse bovine man on too-friendly terms with his officer, who had a raw sense of humour and a great appetite for women. The pair often exchanged ribald jokes outside the tent, their conversation easily audible by the woman inside. Flossie Cox seemed unaffected by it, and Mary had heard worse in a barrack-block. But she could not help constant comparison. Rowan was an acknowledged libertine, and doubtless joined in purely masculine lewdness. But he always behaved like a gentleman in mixed company, and his relationship with Collins and other troopers was liberal without ever crossing the line between officer and subordinate.

As for Lydia, the stamp of an undoubted lady had been upon her even during hysteria. Only now did Mary realize how fortunate she had been in her employ, for Lydia had always called her *Mrs* Clarke, and even at her most fault-finding had not treated her as she was now being treated. Her relationship with Rowan had been unique, of course; impossible to compare with any other. Because of it she watched him during those first weeks with compassion weighing heavily on her. He looked so lifeless and weary. But she avoided the temptation to pass by the tents he shared with his friend, feeling he was best left without reminders for the present.

Her employers' habit of gossiping did have the advantage of keeping her in touch with him, however, for the Coxes found the widowed captain a source of constant interest. One day whilst putting clean laundry away she overheard; "That high-flying brother of his confronted him in his own tent yesterday. Simms was passing and said he heard the sound of raised voices within. Didn't suit our hero to be put in his place by big brother, it seems. And judging from the number of bottles outside the tent come morning, the Honourable Montclare has a thirst the equal of DeMayne's.

The whole family is tarred with the same brush. McGregor was talking to some of the 11th and heard some hot tales of the other one killed in the Charge. Randy as they come, the three of them. Turkish, French, Sardinian, even a Russian woman who came into the camp for food, they said. The lusty Lord Paule took his pleasure of them, then passed them on to his brother."

Flossie Cox giggled. "Pity you haven't a young brother to pass me on to."

The Lieutenant reached across to put his hand down her bodice, and growled, "Are you saying I don't satisfy you, jade?"

"Charlie, you're hurting me," came the delighted squeal.

At that point Mary hurriedly left, and found the sound of grunts and squeaks issuing from the tent strangely nauseating, especially when she remembered that night in the desert with Rowan. Their union had been so beautiful in its quietness and dedication, its passionate tenderness. For all his supposed lechery Rowan would never behave like Charles Cox, she was certain. It was not the first occasion on which they had indulged in marital romping as if she were not there, once having reached the stage of lifted petticoats and unbuttoned trousers so quickly Mary had been taken by surprise.

Lieutenant Cox also made a habit of being present when his wife washed and dressed—something Rowan had never done—and Mary found it distasteful when he made coarse comments on his wife's figure and slapped her buttocks whenever she passed back and forth.

With people such as they, the information Mary overheard was embroidered with fancies and coloured by exaggeration. She was therefore extremely dismayed one day to hear her employer say, "Here's great diversion, Floss. Brideswell has it on excellent authority that the newly-arrived Lady Teale is none other than Fanny Dennison, the courtesan who duped our hero into defending her honour while she was entertaining the entire 11th behind his back. We shall see some sport now, damme if we don't. With one

DeMayne ripe for consolation, and the other looking for two bare legs on his sheepskin coat before he returns to his virtuous lady and baby sons, we could have another swordfight to review."

"But he would surely not do it a second time, Charlie."

"He has never drawn arms against this one, my pet. It was the eldest he winged. They were all three savouring the lady's favours."

"Yes, but he's now aware of the colour of her petticoat. Why would he fight his brother for a wanton?"

"Because his tastes have run wild since then. There was not a lightskirt in Khunobad he did not entertain, at some time or another. And that wife of his might have put on airs, but she went to his bed to snare him . . . and who is to say she did not do the same thing with Wrexham and young Cleaver without being caught at it on those occasions? A born harlot does not change with marriage—as I know to my constant pleasure."

Charles Cox launched himself at his wife at that point and rolled with her over the floor until they reached Mary's booted feet, where she was trapped in the corner by his sudden attack. Looking up, he grinned as he jerked his head toward the tent-flap.

"Get out! Go for a walk for an hour. No, better make it two!"

Mary was trembling with anger as she stepped over them and made a rapid escape. Even at the end of a barrack-block public displays of lust were unknown. The pair always went elsewhere for their pleasure—or resignation, which it usually had been in her own case. How dared they roll about the ground like a pair of mating animals, then expect their so-called inferiors to respect them? How dared they talk of the DeMaynes as they had? How dared they condemn people who were worth a hundred of their sort?

Walking past the washing she had hung on the line rigged by her to catch the breeze, she decided to do as she had been told. It was safe enough to walk about, and she had never been up on the heights where it was possible to look down into the town of Sebastapol. Perhaps up there she would be able to dispel some of her feelings of unhappiness and resentment.

As she walked past Oates, the batman, he called, "Off on yer own, dearie? Let me come wiv yer and show yer a surprise or two."

Ignoring him she continued on her way, and he speeded it by adding, "Stupid trollop! After a cocked hat, are yer? Gen'lemen do it same as us, yer know, but not fer 'arf as long."

His raucous laugh followed her as she made her way upward over the green turf. A woman walking alone suggested just one thing to soldiers of any nation, she knew, but there were enough sightseers travelling back and forth the area to make her unafraid.

The day had come in with a blaze, bringing blue skies, soft breezes and the kind of temperatures she knew well. She began to enjoy the freedom and feeling of escape climbing that hill gave her. Lifting the hem of her grey dress as she stepped out she remembered how that same billowing skirt had provided shade in the desert. Had she ever lain beneath it in her underwear with Rowan and asked him such searching questions; had he ever put himself forever in her heart by confessing something he could tell no other living person? Had he ever taken her in his arms like a lover and shown her true possession? Thank God neither the Coxes nor anyone else knew about that. They would turn it into a disgusting affair that would degrade both of them.

Energetic walking gradually dissolved her anger to leave her thinking, once more, of that journey from Khunobad when she had discovered a world that made it impossible for her to accept less ever again. She did not know how long she could continue in her present employment. It was little short of drudgery for people she did not respect. They taught her nothing; she felt it could be the reverse. There was nothing rewarding about the work, no sense of usefulness. If she had not retained the tent Rowan had provided for her she would have been left without shelter by the

Coxes, and only two meals given her by the brutish Oates had shown her she would be better off buying her own food from one of the canteens put up by enterprising tradesmen for the mixed armies. But she had resisted the fact in order to save money she had put by whilst working for Lydia DeMayne. Deep inside she knew she would not stand much more of her present situation. But until a suitable alternative presented itself she had to carry on.

After the first day or two she had approached Harry Winters in the hope of being allowed to help in the hospital. But what he had been prepared to do for her when destitute in Khunobad did not apply when she was gainfully employed. Besides which, a flood of trained nurses, Holy Sisters experienced in healing, and high-born charitable ladies were providing as much feminine caring for sick and wounded as was needed now. He had been very kind, but negative. Yet Mary had thoughtfully watched the never-ending lines going down to the hospital-ships and mused that these female paragons did not appear to extend their ministrations outside the stout wooden hospitals that were being erected all over the slopes due to the news that a commission was being sent to investigate reports of appalling medical neglect. It seemed to Mary that the victims needed care outside the hospitals, where they often had to be transported miles along rough winding roads in all weathers from the front line trenches where the war was still being bitterly waged despite the apparent lightheartedness by those in the rear.

But no one could forget it altogether, because there was the everlasting rumble of heavy guns bombarding the fortifications outside Sebastopol, and return Russian fire that pounded the Allies' forward positions. The wounded from these exchanges often died from being left for hours until a waggon could be spared to transport them to a doctor, or they were forced to walk the long road to the rear, whereupon they collapsed from the effort and loss of blood. It was something that disturbed Mary, but about which she could do nothing. Surely the worthy women who had taken on the task of caring for the casualties were in a position to do so?

Hot and breathless she reached the crest of the hill and stood looking at the beautiful vista of green rolling slopes and sea as blue as the sapphires around the fatal pendant that was now at the bottom of the sea. For a moment she thought sadly of Noah, wondering where he was, and in what state. And she thought of the silver flying fish, and the evening singsongs on deck. Inevitably she recalled dancing the jig, and recognized the cause of Rowan's anger for what it truly had been.

Lost in thought she sat on the grass and wondered how she could help him. He had told her to keep away, but someone had to get near him and break down that conviction of fatality where females were concerned. Noah had once told her he wanted her to provide the sweeter side, and she had been willing to give it to him, without marriage, if he would abandon his plans to desert. All men needed it at the most normal of times, she knew, but war and other causes of stress increased that need a hundredfold, especially in a naturally lusty nature like Rowan's. According to Charles Cox he had already quarrelled with his brother and was drinking heavily. Now, a woman who had been the cause of his disgrace eight years before had apparently arrived here. It seemed as if fate was determined to break him and would not let up until he did. She prayed he would let her pick up the pieces when it happened.

A shout penetrated her thoughts, and her attention was caught by something bright green bowling along the grass within her vision. It was a silk bonnet trimmed with creamy feathers that had been taken by a sprightly breeze in that high point and was fast disappearing downhill. Mary scrambled to her feet and ran the few yards to the tumbling hat, capturing it by stepping on to one of the long ribbons, before bending to pick it up.

The sound of running feet beating hollowly on the springy turf made her look round. An officer in the elaborate showy uniform of the Scots Greys hotly in pursuit of the

bonnet pulled up in front of her with a smile, holding out
his hand.

"Very well retrieved," he drawled. "Me huntin' terriers
could not have done better."

She gave him the bonnet without a word, and he turned
away. But the owner of it was already walking toward them,
and Mary was struck by her beauty. She had thought Lydia
DeMayne unbeatable, but this girl certainly equalled her in
a blonde version of that brunette perfection. A mass of
golden hair was caught up in an elaborate style Mary could
recognize as the work of an expert coiffeur, an oval face of
great merriment was highlighted by violet eyes and a full
mouth of extraordinary pinkness that curved into an irresistible smile. But her shape, in a green silk gown fogged with
black and cream, was wholly voluptuous. Mary instinctively
knew who she was before the officer said, "The runaway is
apprehended, Lady Teale."

So this was Fanny Dennison, whom Rowan had defended
with his sword and his honour! This woman had ruined his
right to his family and his place in society. Well, she was
certainly possessed of all those things gentlemen seemed to
admire so heedlessly, and she could well imagine the boy of
twenty who had fallen so fatally beneath her spell. But had
she been worth his sacrifice? Would he feel the same way
when he saw her again?

"My warmest thanks," said the courtesan in a fascinating
gurgly type of voice that Mary immediately envied. She
might not be a lady, but she spoke like one. "Your prompt
action deserves some positive recognition."

It was then Mary realized the girl was addressing her, and
in the most friendly manner. "Not at all, madam," she said
quietly. "I'm just glad I caught it before it was spoilt. There
aren't many like that in a place like this."

Fanny looked her over speculatively. "Are you the wife of
a soldier, my dear?"

"A sergeant's widow," Mary told her, trying hard to summon up dislike for the woman and failing.

326

"I'm so sorry," came the quick sympathy. "Which battle was it?"

"It wasn't a battle. He died from the cholera in India. My regiment has only just arrived from there."

"Which regiment is that?"

"The 43rd Light Dragoons."

Fanny's face lit up. "But I met them in Alexandria. Such an impressive sight when they rode into the town like an exotic pasha's desert guard."

Mary was surprised. What had the woman been doing in Alexandria, and was there a Lord Teale somewhere? Scrutiny of the group ahead showed only several officers with spyglasses with which to study the distant Russian town. Was he one of them?

But Fanny was speaking again. "As I see no horse grazing nearby, I must guess that you have walked all the way up here Mrs . . . ?"

"Clarke," said Mary, busily working out the fact that news of the regiment's disaster at sea had either not reached this woman yet, or she was so heartless it did not count with her. No, Rowan could never have been enchanted with a woman without feeling . . . and yet she had treated him very cruelly. What was the truth about Fanny Dennison?

She gave her entrancing smile again. "I should like to offer you a seat in my carriage for the return, because you saved my bonnet so spontaneously."

"No, ma'am, really," protested the Scots Grey officer. "T'aint done, you know."

She turned her bewitching face up to him laughingly. "Ah, but it is by me, Major McDougall. *I* am not with the army." She challenged Mary. "Well, Mrs Clarke, will you accept?"

"Thank you, madam."

"*My lady*," corrected the annoyed officer. "Don't you know how to address your betters, woman?"

The opportunity to study the woman who had so captivated Rowan was one Mary would not deny herself and ruled her decision more than the prospect of her first car-

riage ride. But it was plain the three other officers who
formed her escort were no better pleased than Major
McDougall by the restricting presence of a sergeant's
widow. It was also plain none of them was her husband. So
she was up to her old game, was she?

Yet, as they made their way back along the tortuous track
and Fanny drew them all into her lively conversation, Mary
found herself liking her more and more. She was a flirt, of
course, but in such a merry way everyone enjoyed it as much
as she. Their route took them past the French lines where
officers and soldiers alike saluted the beautiful occupant of
the carriage, some with great respect, others with saucy
smiles. Mary felt no envy. She did not want a whole army
to acknowledge her; just one man.

But suddenly, her attention was taken from Fanny Dennison by something she could not believe. Walking between
the tents was a girl dressed as a soldier. No, not quite like
a soldier, for she had a full skirt over the uniform trousers,
which was what had made her stand out from the mêlée of
French grenadiers. But her shapely torso was clothed in the
elaborate colourful tunic of the regiment, and on her head
was a dashing plumed headdress. She was laughing and
chatting to those she passed, apparently not an unusual sight
to any of them.

"Lordy," she exclaimed out loud, "are they so short of
men they have women filling the ranks?"

The lieutenant facing her followed her glance and
laughed. "See that little creature, Lady Teale," he said as if
Fanny had spoken instead. "She is a *vivandière*—an innovation of the French military which I feel we should emulate.
Most of their regiments have these girls who travel with the
army to mingle with the troops and sell food or additional
provisions, but out here these valiant girls have taken to
riding out amongst their wounded after a battle to give
water, sustenance, and sometimes even wind a bandage
round an obvious wound. They gallop back and forth, apparently fearless, and one would not believe it of them from

their looks for most of them are attractive enough to make a man well merely by smiling at him."

"How very delightful!" exclaimed Fanny. "Are they officially employed?"

"I believe they are appointed by various regiments, yes."

A light laugh preceded Fanny's teasing question as to whether the Scots Greys would care to engage her to serve them in like manner. But Mary was concentrating on the distant colourful figure of the uniformed *vivandière*. There was a woman of the regiment, in the fullest sense of the word!

She was so deep in contemplation the chatter went on around her unheeded, until the slowing of the carriage drew her attention back to the woman beside her. Only then did she see the mounted officer approaching almost alongside and recognize him.

"Good afternoon, Captain DeMayne," called Fanny merrily. "I told you at Alexandria that I was bound for the Crimea, did I not? As you see, I have arrived. How is your very charming wife?"

Rowan looked at her for a long time before saying harshly, "My wife is dead, Lady Teale." Then his expressionless gaze travelled slowly over her from the modish bonnet at a provocative angle on her golden curls, to the hem of the expensive green silk gown, before taking in the fact that she had four male escorts in the carriage, none of whom was her husband. "I wish you a pleasant sojourn in the Crimea, ma'am," he added, "and trust the war will not intrude too much upon your enjoyment." With that he saluted and rode on past them toward the hills where Mary guessed he must be mounting picquet that night.

"Dear heaven, there must be some mistake," breathed Fanny in obvious distress. "His wife dead! How can that be?"

No one answered her. The officers probably knew nothing of the tragedy, and Mary was silent as she gazed behind her at the solitary figure on the horse that had survived the sandstorm with them at that time that now seemed so long ago. Rowan had given no acknowledgement of her presence, and the only consolation was that he had looked at his ex-mistress with the same expression he had worn in the cabin that night . . . as if all emotion had died along with Lydia.

CHAPTER TWELVE

The month of May had seen the arrival of great numbers of infantry reinforcements from England who, together with the newly-arrived cavalry, were drilled in the situation and strength of their enemies during those four weeks. The foot soldiers were shown plans of the complicated terrain of the area; the cavalry covered it personally in a series of sorties guided by an officer from one of the regiments that had been there from the start. Apart from the various points of vantage which had been captured then lost by both sides several times over, there were two vital aspects of that large battle area. One was the Woronzoff Road which lead from Sebastopol to the interior and passed just north of the cavalry camps at Kadikoi. The other was the River Tchernaya, also running inland from its mouth near Inkerman. The road was vital to the Russians if they were to get reinforcements and supplies in to the beleaguered fortress; the river formed a natural division between the opposing sides.

Knowing an all-out attack would soon have to be launched against Sebastopol if the war was to be finished, attention was focused on these two features. The men fresh from

India were used exhaustively for reconnaissance, piquets and patrol duty at the front line in order to rest those who had been through the terrible winter months. Day and night they watched the road and river, engaging in sharp skirmishing with their enemies doing the same thing, and constantly being called out to stand ready to repulse a possible attack. As May gave way to June such activities intensified further to protect the plans under way for an Anglo-French assault on Sebastopol on a secret date in the middle of the month. It was vital that the Russians should not make a move to break out before then or, if they did, that it should be seen and immediately repulsed.

The fact that the Russians were also doing the same in order to gain advance notice of any Allied move meant some bitter clashes between opposing patrols and piquets, resulting in further losses by the 43rd. The ironic fact of their first and only battle casualty being their very unwarlike colonel was soon forgotten when troopers began returning wounded, or as corpses. They could truthfully acknowledge their baptism as a fighting regiment.

Mary was constantly on the watch these days. She felt as inquisitive as her employers, because her gaze always subconsciously swept the camp as she passed back and forth on her tasks, or whenever she spotted returning horsemen in the pale-blue and silver of her own regiment as she hung out the washing further up the hillside. Anxiety led her to re-site her own tent so that its entrance allowed her a perfect view of that occupied by Rowan, and she suffered each time she saw him set off on patrol or piquet until his safe return.

Resisting the longing to walk past and force a meeting with him, they nevertheless came face to face on several occasions after that afternoon with Fanny Dennison, which was inevitable in a tented camp. Twice he had been mounted and with companions, and had merely nodded his acknowledgement of her. The third occasion had been quite different: At dusk she had rounded on Oates, who had slopped the food on to her plate so clumsily it had put splashes of gravy all down her skirt. He had laughed and advanced on her offering to help her remove the dress, and she had backed away with a few well-chosen words she had learnt in the barrack-block right into the path of someone walking by.

Strong hands had steadied her for a moment, then quickly dropped from her arms. It had needed only one look from him to send Oates back to his fire, and she had studied Rowan in dismay. He looked thin and haunted; even worse than on his return from Multan.

"Are you all right?" he had asked curtly.

"Yes, are you?"

"Well enough."

That had been the extent of their conversation because he had walked off at that point, leaving her yearning. If she were Fanny Dennison she could go to him, use her extensive knowledge of him to break through his self-imposed isolation. If she were Fanny Dennison she could visit him openly, draw him into social circles, re-awaken his appreciation of physical beauty. If she were Fanny Dennison she would still love him enough to help him.

During the next ten days excitement and speculation grew and, judging by the movements of weapons, ammunition and medical supplies up from the harbour to the various camps, the assault would soon be made. Charles Cox prattled constantly to his wife of all the various rumours going around, so Mary knew as much as anyone of the preparations of the massive attack that could not fail to break through the sandbagged earthworks defending the walls of the town itself. But she was relieved when it became obvious that the cavalry had little part to play in the operation, save to stand by for an improbable counterattack by Cossacks, and to form a cordon around the forward area to prevent sightseers from impeding the assault troops. The men of the 43rd might well feel disgusted at their role, but the women concerned were very thankful.

Mary had discovered a large number of soldiers' wives on her arrival. Some had been there since the start of the war, others had come out later. They lived as they could, earning a few pence from laundering and mending, often setting up in groups beneath rude shelters made of mats and mud, or anything they could cadge from the men. Some were half-wild with the horrors they had seen and endured, witless from native liquor, selling themselves to all comers for the pence needed to buy more. Many were keeping themselves and their children from fever and starvation only by the generosity of their husbands' friends, and occasionally through the concern and personal expense of an officer or his lady. A few, with some education, had become the heroines of their regiments because of their ministrations and versatility during the winter that had caused such loss and privation. These women had kept the men going despite all adversity and were universal mothers.

At first, Mary had tried to make overtures of friendship, feeling in need of it herself. But she was rejected by them all either because they regarded her as an outsider, or because she was a maid to an officer's wife. They did not regard her as a woman of her regiment, and she found no common ground with them or their way of life now. Sadly she realized she was neither one thing nor the other. She would not go back to what she had always been, yet could go no further forward. As such she was very lonely. The men she had travelled from India with had found the abundance of women of every colour, nationality and belief very time-consuming, so had little interest in the girl who had caused a sensation at Cairo but offered little other than rather fancy conversation to anyone in search of other pleasures. The only person Mary could approach for companionship was Collins, who was always pleased to see her. But she could only go across to Rowan's tent when she knew he was not there, and those times did not often coincide with the few rest periods she had.

While she worked, and often when lying awake because Rowan was on night-piquet, Mary thought about the French girl she had seen from Fanny Dennison's carriage and was full of admiration. The lieutenant who had spoken about her had said such girls were employed by their regiments. How very far-seeing French soldiers must be to use the qualities of their women so sensibly, instead of letting them turn into slatterns for want of an opportunity to be of real service.

The girl *vivandière* had so captured her imagination Mary found herself walking the long road to the French lines one afternoon toward mid-June when another rumour had sent the Coxes with a picnic-party to look down on Sebastopol one last time before it was bombarded and blown to pieces. The trip was hot and tiring, rewarded by nothing more than invitations that were easy enough to translate in any language from soldiers who saw her lone parade past their shabby tents and huts as an offer. She could not blame them. Other women did so for that reason, and she was unable to tell them why she was really there. Even so, those who tried to catch her around the waist were firmly pushed away, and the more persistent who tried to kiss her were left with a throbbing ear or ankle. Several officers sauntered up with low-voiced overtures, but left her alone when she shook her head.

Soldiers were the same the world over, she mused. Amidst the neat lines men were doing the usual things—cleaning accoutrements, shaving, having their hair cut by their fellows, clustering in groups to yarn, sprawling in the sunshine to smoke a lone pipe, writing letters home, playing cards or other simple games that needed the minimum means to play. The smell of food being cooked on smoky fires hung in the air; the familiar odour of horses wafted from the cavalry lines further uphill. It was something she had known all her life, and it made her feel lonelier than ever. All the way from Khunobad she had still felt very much a part of the regiment, and proud to be so, she now realized. But the Coxes somehow robbed her of an identity of any kind, and Oates reduced her to the level of harlot with his lewd approaches. She no longer felt part of the 43rd; just an officer's skivvy.

Then, just as she turned to retrace her steps in disappointment, her glance fell on a figure coming through the crisscross of soldiers. Her heart raced as she took in the sight of a slender girl in a tight white tunic laced with scarlet and embellished with gold buttons and braid, a short full skirt in dark-blue banded with scarlet over dark-blue overalls striped at the side with scarlet, a small white apron, and a black shako with scarlet bag and gold tassels. Slung across her from the right shoulder was a scarlet barrel with a tap at one end, and tucked into pouches in her sash were three or four metal cups. She was leading a horse toward the place where Mary stood, and there was no doubt this girl was another *vivandière*.

Mary stood rooted to the spot gazing with admiration and envy, still unable to believe the existence of such creatures. The men called to the girl as she passed, and she responded gaily to comments that were plainly not the same kind Mary had been given earlier. Then, the French girl became aware of the still figure in neat grey dress staring at her, and she smiled. When Mary smiled back she came up to the road and spoke in a high nasal, but friendly voice.

Mary had never felt so disappointed; so inadequate. She would give almost anything to be able to converse with this marvellous girl, ask her about her life with her regiment and the work she did for them. She felt a sense of overwhelming certainty that they could be real friends if only they could communicate, and the helplessness of having to stand uncomprehending and speechless made her burn with longing. Rowan would have been able to speak with the girl, she knew, and that knowledge showed the few things she had learned as nothing compared with real education.

But the French girl accepted her own linguistic limitations more easily. Pointing to her own colourful uniform she said, *"Artillerie,"* and raised her brows in question at Mary.

"Oh . . . cavalry," she said quickly.

"Cavalerie?" The girl made riding motions with a querying gesture at Mary.

"Yes, I can ride." She thought of Drummer Boy and how she had been thrown, then of Rowan saying she rode like a pedlar on a lame donkey, and felt her colour rising.

But the girl nodded approval, and introduced herself as Veronique, whereupon Mary gave her own name eagerly.

For a few minutes Veronique rattled away in her own tongue, managing with astonishing gestures and noises to convey the fact that there would soon be another battle and she would be in the thick of it. But Mary had the grace to shake her head when her new acquaintance asked her if she would be doing the same, and indicated that she would be laundering and arranging her mistress's hair. The girl smiled sympathetically, only too aware that she had no counterparts in the British army.

But there must have been something in Mary's expression that betrayed her thoughts, because the girl reached for her sash and pulled one of the little cups from it to press into Mary's hands.

"*Bonne chance, Marie,*" she said, then turned away to lead the horse back into the Artillery lines leaving Mary trembling from the encounter.

When she looked down at the cup she found it to be beautifully decorated with a small lip to allow the contents to be tipped into the mouths of men lying down. As a present, it even bettered the bonnet Noah had given her, and Mary walked back to her tent filled with such reckless-ness it made her present situation even more unbearable.

The following day it was apparent that the assault would be made come dawn, for the roads leading to the front lines were full of regiments marching up fully accoutred for bat-tle. There was a swing in their stride and smiles on their faces. Although they well knew what awaited them, each man was thankful to end the inactivity and pinned his hopes on being one of the lucky ones during a battle that would settle the war and allow them all to go home to England. An air of great excitement rushed through both British and French lines as one illustrious regiment after another made its way along the tracks in the dust of those who had gone ahead.

Mary watched the ranks of cheerful laughing men pass by,

waving to her and calling out in bravado that they would kill a 'Rooshin' for her on the morrow. She did not wave back or answer their cheery comments, too overawed by the significance of their forward movement. This was her first experience of an army going into wholesale battle and she could not share their lightheartedness. The usual daily bombardment increased more and more as the day wore on until the thunder of the guns shook even the hillside where she stood, and the sky was hung with a pall of smoke that blotted out the sun.

It was afternoon when the bugles of the 43rd summoned the regiment to form up beside their lines. Mary was ironing her mistress's petticoats on a board she had put across two boxes, and she abandoned the task to let the iron grow cold so that she could stroll to a small hillock just below her tent, where she had a clear view of the troops formed up into battle squadrons. Rowan was a squadron commander, and she saw him on Drummer Boy out in front, and felt the sombre overtones of the day even more. What would she do if he did not return? She could not stay with the regiment if he were no longer part of it.

They moved off in the direction of Sebastopol—a long pale-blue snake—and the sight of their swords dangling at their left sides had never before seemed so significant. But the sight of a lone captain with his sword worn on the right put a lump in her throat as she remembered him gasping in pain that Colonel Daubnay's orders could justifiably be broken because he had injured his right shoulder. By the time the last dragoon had disappeared into the dusk, the lump in her throat had a partner in her breast, as she thought of the French *vivandières* riding forward with their regiments. That was where she wanted to be—had a right to be.

Flossie Cox, distracted by her husband's absence at the front lines, was rude and capricious to both Mary and Oates, claiming that the dinner was 'as foul and inedible as the stew in the pots of Turkish brothels', and the petticoats Mary had ironed were so grubby and unattractive she must have substituted her own for those of her mistress. When Mary assured her they were the right ones, she was told to do them all again by morning. Trying to make allowances for the woman's anxiety over the safety of her husband, Mary took them off without a word, laid them carefully over a box in her tent ready to take back next day.

But such things as petticoats were forgotten when the assault began, with salvoes from the guns that beat anything previously heard. The empty tents below Mary seemed to mock her feelings of helplessness and loss. What was going on over to the west: were men already at each other's throats, slitting them with sword and bayonet? For the first time she realized the traditional role of women. All her life she had been in the thick of the regiment, whatever it had been doing. She had lived with it, marched with it, married into it, nursed it. It had never gone off like this leaving empty tents; neglecting her. Yet, perhaps it was she who was neglecting it. They had had to go. She should have gone with them.

By midday the empty roads began to fill again, and Mary left her stitching to run to the hillock once more. But she was stunned by the procession making the return journey. Those men who had swung confidently past yesterday were now returning like ragged, stumbling, blackened figures bearing no resemblance to the proud regiments they had been. On and on they came, piled into waggons in bleeding heaps, dangling across mules in helpless misery or staggering on foot supporting each other as best they could until they dropped by the roadside. The blinded were led by the crippled; the limbless were jerked and tossed on wooden carts. Boy soldiers were shamelessly crying, the tears making streaks through the soot of shot and shell that blackened their faces. They were all making their agonizing way to the hospitals that had been emptied in readiness for them yesterday. But they did not look like anguished victors; they wore the mantle of defeat.

Mary looked down on them and asked herself what could have gone wrong, what could have happened to a battle that had been won in spirit as these same men had marched in the other direction yesterday. Then, as she watched, a youngster in the scarlet of one of the old regiments of the line stumbled, fell, and could not summon the energy to get up again. The carts and wagons rolled past him, his shambling unsteady comrades could not heed his arm outstretched for aid. With flying feet Mary went down the slope to him, taking the hand searching for comradeship in her own.

"Rest here awhile, then I'll help you on your way," she told him breathlessly. "Rest. You're safely out of it now."

The boy turned staring eyes toward her, and some sixth sense told her they were sightless when he cried, "God bless you, Mother," and gripped her hand until it hurt. "Water, please give me water."

The resolution must have been made there and then, she realized later, but there seemed to be no more in her head than the vow to fetch the boy a drink as she scrambled up to the flat area where she and her employers had their tents pitched. Going into her own for a tin cup, her glance fell on the decorated one given her by the French girl two days before, and everything fell into place from then on. Instead of taking a cupful of water, she took up two of the full canvas buckets Oates had collected as usual, and made her careful way back to where the boy was sitting in confidence of her return.

Time flew by unheeded as she passed cups of water to all those who wanted it, walking alongside waggons to hold the vessel to the lips of those piled on to them, and keeping step with half-demented men who dared not stop for fear they would never start again. And it was not long before she saw they were also hungry, some not having eaten for twelve hours. Another return to the tents produced bread and some cold meat left from the Coxes' dinner, together with cold potatoes. Cut into thick slices, these all represented nourishment to those who were able to eat, and Mary dispensed it all without hesitation, receiving such comments as, "God bless you, ma'am", "You're an angel", or "Lor' love you, miss, you've saved me life." Not one abused her or made coarse suggestions. They treated her with something amounting to reverence.

But these men also spoke of the battle; what they had seen and endured down there where the guns were still thundering and where smoke had turned day into a semblance of night. They told of walking through a solid wall of fire that had mown down entire ranks of advancing men without leaving a single one alive. They rambled in shocked manner about carpets of red-coated men lying at the foot of the fortifications of Sebastopol, screaming in their agony as their comrades were forced to run over them in order to reach the scaling-ladders. Then of that wave falling dead or wounded to thicken the human carpet. They described the stench and clamour of that battle, the shock of discovering such strong resistance from their enemies, the fearful heat and thirst, the swarms of flies that settled on the helpless victims to crawl and buzz in open wounds. The message was clear, even to Mary. The assault had failed; it was a disaster that had cost a quarter of an army.

Although she knew it was mainly an infantry battle, Mary worried about her own regiment and the man she loved. It would surely be a miracle if anyone escaped whole from such mayhem. To those who were reasonably lucid she put urgent questions about the cavalry, but the answers were invariably reassuring.

"Och, Missy," one Scotsman told her, "the galloping laddies are well enough. They're nae but nussmaids in their bonny bright coats." Another said wearily, "The cavalry's bloomin' lucky. Sittin' on 'orses watchin' us do all the work. But best o' luck to them."

But it did not stop her from worrying as she saw the steady stream of casualties turn into a swollen river of them as the daylight hours began to haze into dusk. The killing heat of the afternoon began to ease, and Mary suddenly became aware of her own aching limbs and filthy dishevelled state. Wet with perspiration, her grey dress stained with smears of blood, her hair falling from the pins, it occurred to her that she must look as she had in the old days. But it was all to much more worthwhile purpose.

Still they came up the roads from the front line, and everyone spoke now of the English retreat as a fact. The French had broken through to take their objective, but their ally's failure meant they would never be able to hold it. The beleaguered town would survive; the war was no nearer being won.

The sinister crimson of the sunset seemed to add its emphasis to the bloody defeat of that June day, and Mary wearily continued giving water and encouraging feminine words when they were needed. There was still no sign of the returning cavalry to ease her anxiety, but her watch on the road was broken in the most unexpected and dramatic way when a flurry behind her heralded the approach of Mrs Cox in a state midway between anger and hysteria.

"What *do* you think you are doing?" she cried, seizing Mary and swinging her roughly to face her. "Have you quite forgotten yourself, girl? How *dare* you solicit for custom in this way?"

Her thoughts and mood broken so roughly, Mary could only look at the thin rat-like features of her mistress and say, "I'm afraid I don't understand what you are saying."

"Then I shall put it in plain language," came the furious response. "I do not expect my maid to play the whore by the roadside."

Mary could not believe what she was hearing. Could this woman look at her bloodstained dress and the buckets of water beside her, and really believe she was offering a tumble to men who were racked, broken and bleeding? It was so ridiculous, she did not waste time on an answer. Turning away she bent to refill the cup given to her by Veronique, before taking the few steps into the dusty road where yet another waggon was rolling past.

She never reached it. Flossie Cox was after her immediately, pulling her round again and shouting, "Don't walk away when I am speaking to you, Clarke."

"This man needs water," she said as quietly as she could

manage, indicating the pathetic pleas coming from one of the bodies thoughtlessly piled on to the waggon, several with their heads hanging unsupported over the sides.

"I need water to wash . . . and a supply of fresh clothes," came the heated reply. "It has been an insupportably hot afternoon and I have been tossing and turning on my bed without one visit from you to see to my needs."

"These men have been tossing and turning in agony this hot afternoon," Mary countered, feeling uncontrollable rage rising up in her. "Who is there to see to *their* needs?"

"They do not employ you, you impertinent creature. I do."

"You also have a pair of legs so that you can fetch anything you want. Some of these soldiers have only one left— or none at all."

Flossie Cox's hand swept out and knocked the cup of water to the ground. "Get up to my tent at once and do what you are paid to do, trollop."

"Do it yourself," Mary heard herself say. "These men are worth a hundred of your sort."

Quick as a flash the officer's lady dealt Mary a stinging blow to her left cheek that jerked her head back badly, and into that head came a recollection of a vow she had made never to let anyone hit her ever again. She stepped forward to return the slap, putting behind it all the dislike she felt for this vulgar woman and her equally vulgar husband. Flossie Cox gasped with pain and shock, covering her reddened cheek and staring at her accoster in utter disbelief. Then all hell was let loose as she let flow a tirade of abuse that ended with the promise of instant dismissal and a character reference so black she would be forced to revert to the slut she had always been. But Mary had refilled her cup and was walking toward the suffering man on the waggon. Her career as a lady's maid had ended two days ago after the meeting with Veronique. She knew exactly what she wanted to do now.

* * *

The great failure sent morale to the lowest level, and it was kept there by soaring temperatures that brought a new outbreak of cholera of a particularly vicious nature. Those encamped around Balaclava felt they had three choices—to die of their infected wounds, succumb to the dreaded cholera, or survive and endure another winter. Since there were no apparent plans for another assault, the third of those seemed more than likely. To support that belief, many of the officers who had been there from the start began packing up and going home for real or invented reasons. The soldiers had no choice but to obey orders and stay.

The Commanding Officer of the 43rd Light Dragoons was also going home. He had a valid reason, however. Poor distressed Mrs Benedict had been unable to withstand the sound of the incredible gunfire during the assault, and had wandered off into the surrounding hills, taking Rowan's silver-backed hairbrushes, where she was found by an outlying piquet of the French cavalry who had been so primed for action that one man had fired before identifying the figure in the trees. The bullet had only grazed her upper arm, but it was clear to Lieutenant-Colonel Benedict that he must sell out and take his wife home. This put Gil in command of the 43rd, and Rowan took the acting rank of major.

They soon lost fifteen troopers and another officer through cholera. Charles Cox succumbed and died between dusk and the following dawn. His wife, who had no real friends, was prostrate and inconsolable on one of the pleasure steamers, her baggage having been packed by Mary and Trooper Oates. During the violent reign of the disease that constantly plagued armies Mary had done what she could for the victims whilst planning her future course of action when she was able to pursue it.

Harry Winters had acted pessimistically when she had broached the matter with him, saying with justifiable bitterness that the last thing the British authorities considered, in his opinion, was the welfare of men no longer fit to fight. He went further to vent his anger and past humiliations over the way his own efforts to improve medical care had been rebuffed, pointing out that an untrained girl of eighteen was hardly likely to succeed where a qualified doctor holding an army commission could not.

Undeterred, Mary had then approached the new commanding officer of the regiment whom, as a captain six months before, she had nursed safely through cholera on the road from Khunobad. She felt no sense of shame in playing on his sense of gratitude in order to gain her ends. But, indebted though he was to his friend's ex-maid, Gil was equally pessimistic on the subject. Although he thought it an excellent idea to which he would give his personal support, he regretted there was absolutely no chance of official backing or recognition, and he advised her to forget it.

Mary was very disappointed in his reaction, as she confided to Collins beside his fire on that evening, when Rowan happened to be out on evening patrol.

"He was very polite; said it was a good idea," she told the little batman as she munched a slice of bread fried in bacon fat that he had given her. "But I really did expect him to be a bit more taken with it than he was. He always seemed to be a kind sort of man—more of a gentleman than some I could name but won't because it'd be speaking ill of the dead," she said pointedly. "But he didn't seem to want to stir himself one bit."

"Ah well, you've picked something of a bad time to ask him anything. He's real cut up over a letter that came yesterdee from Khunobad. I know you won't spread it around, but truth is his lady—the one what was betrothed to him last year—has writ saying she's found another. A major in the regiment what took over from us when we left. I say he's well rid of her if she can turn off a real nice gentleman like Colonel Crane when he's off to answer the call to arms. But he can't see it that way, and now he's on the same tack as Major DeMayne. Both of them was at it last night, drinking themselves under the table as fast as no man's business. Course, the Major's been like it since we got here. Always been a hard drinker, he has, but now he can

take any amount of it and not show any effects from it until
he suddenly drops down deado. It's not natural, and what
with all-night piquets and detailing himself for all the most
dangerous patrols, I can't but see that he'll crack up good
and proper before the year is out."

Mary sighed. "I don't understand gentlemen, truly I
don't. I never see . . . *saw,*" she corrected quickly, finding
it all too easy to regress in Collins's company, "troopers
being so daft over women."

"Ah well, take most of them women. Sluts they are—
present company excepted," he added hastily. "Whereas
real ladies gets themselves up simply to tease gentlemen out
of all benefit of common sense. That's the difference."

"They must be very heartless," commented Mary, thinking of Fanny Dennison's apparently warm personality.
"What pleasure do they get from seeing someone upset like
that?"

"You'd best ask *them,* girl," was Collins's sage advice.

That remark stayed in her mind, along with curiosity
about Fanny Dennison—the real person beneath the viva-
cious woman she had encountered over the lost bonnet.
Was her only aim to tease men out of all benefit of common
sense? Did she, like Lydia, *enjoy* making them desperately
unhappy? Two days later something occurred that made her
resolve to find out. The news flew around the camp in no
time, as such things always did, and Mary sat in the sweltering dusk at the mouth of her tent, looking down at the
silhouettes in Rowan's. The unbelievable had happened.
The regiment's most celebrated and brilliant horseman had
had a riding accident that had caused Drummer Boy to be
destroyed and the rider to narrowly escape death at the
hands of a Cossack patrol encountered in the hills.

Rumours were legion concerning details of the incident,
but Mary was dismayed and concerned over the cause of it,
especially after Collins's remarks on the way Rowan was
pushing himself these days. For a long time she deliberated
on what to do, then found her mind made up for her when
she saw the solution to the problem strolling on the hillside

some feet above her tent, with only a stout ageing man for company. The opportunity must not be missed. Patting her hair into place, Mary counted to ten, said, "Here goes", and set off up the hill in pursuit, determination in every stride.

Although Fanny Dennison saw her approach it made no difference to her slow stroll on the arm of the elderly man. Dressed in pale lavender-spotted muslin, with a silk sash in deep cream and a large lacy hat and parasol to match, the courtesan looked so strikingly lovely Mary had a sudden insight into why women of her kind behaved as they did. Mary herself had had enough pestering by men who wanted to use her for temporary relief and, God knew, she was not beautiful. To be born with a face and body that approached total perfection might be more of a curse than a blessing. No doubt, many men treated such women heartlessly, and who could blame them for gaining revenge when they could? Barrack-block women gave men a sharp kick where it hurt most when they had had enough. More genteel females used other means of wounding their male persecutors. They were all sisters beneath the skin.

"Madam . . . my lady," called Mary, remembering how she had been told to address Fanny. "Excuse me!"

Fanny turned her head gently, but continued her slow way across the turf. "Yes, what is it?"

"Madam, could I speak to you for a moment?"

The red-faced man beside Fanny leant forward to peer beneath the parasol and say in a querulous voice, "Eh . . . what . . . who is it m'dear?"

"A sergeant's widow, Sir Pomfret," supplied Fanny in tones designed to combat apparent deafness, and surprising Mary with her instant recognition of her. "Mrs Clarke captured my runaway bonnet one day. I think you were not with me on that occasion."

The pair had stopped to make that exchange, but Mary went no nearer. She had to speak to Fanny in private. There seemed little chance of that, for the woman in the dainty crinoline kept her hand tucked through her husband's arm as she asked Mary how she was faring in this hot weather.

"Well enough, madam," was her reply, as she realized she must make her disguised approach quickly or risk her quarry moving on after a mere comment on the hot weather. "Begging your pardon, but I was hoping you might help me over something I'm very anxious to do."

Fanny gave her irresistible smile. "If it has to do with the army I fear you will be disappointed. I have no influence in military high places, you know."

Not much, thought Mary immediately. *How many sleepy colonels' ears would willingly listen to your pleas?* "It's nothing to do with high places," she said. "It's just that I want to get hold of a horse. A little hill pony would do. I don't ride all that well." She remembered Rowan's verdict on her riding and thought honesty the best policy. "You see, I've decided to become a *vivandière* like those French girls we saw from your carriage the other day."

"What a very worthy ambition," commented Fanny with warmth. "Your regiment is lucky indeed to have women of your stamp on its strength."

"But I'm not," Mary pointed out immediately. "When Sam Clarke died, I was struck off."

Fanny frowned. "As I said, I have little knowledge of army matters, but if I hear of anyone with a hill pony to sell I will tell them of you."

She seemed prepared to resume her walk, and Mary had not yet had a chance to speak on the real cause of her approach to this particular woman. In desperation, she said deliberately, "The only way I managed to come with the regiment from India was as the maid to an officer's lady. But my mistress died—between Alexandria and here," she added, praying Fanny would read her words the way she wanted.

But it seemed she had misjudged the woman and the entire meeting, for Fanny merely expressed her condolences and then continued on her way with her breathless husband, saying as they moved off, "Are you *quite* certain this is not proving too much for you, Sir Pomfret?"

Mary stayed where she was, staring after them in great

disappointment. What could she try now? Turning back down the hill she heaved a great sigh. Well, she would not be defeated so easily—not that same girl who had nearly died in the desert but had lived. But she was halfway to her tent when she heard her name being called, and turned to see Fanny coming toward her from a spot where Sir Pomfret was in deep conversation with two other elderly men. Mary did not go back uphill to meet her. The further they were from eavesdroppers the better.

Fanny walked up to her, the lovely face full of curiosity, and came straight to the point. "You were in Captain De-Mayne's employ?"

"Yes."

"You were very discreet just now. Does that mean you know I was once a good friend of his?"

"Everyone knows *that*," she said deliberately. "It was the sort of news that went round the whole of India, including the servants. He was never allowed to forget it."

The smooth white brow furrowed as violet eyes studied her shrewdly. "What exactly is it that you want?"

"Nothing for myself, if that's what you think," Mary retorted, resenting the tone that suggested she was up to some nasty trick.

"I understood it was a hill pony just now," came the equally tart response.

"I can get that for myself . . . and I will. That was just an excuse to speak to you."

"And the true reason, Mrs Clarke . . . if that is really your name?"

"I don't tell lies," she snapped. "I leave that to my betters."

Fanny's forehead creased even further as she absorbed the meaning of that remark, the shade cast by her parasol revealing that she was no longer the fresh young creature she must have been when Rowan had adored her beyond reason.

"You are a very strange kind of girl," came the verdict. "Some education, without doubt, and with a forthrightness not often found in females of yours or any class. I doubt if you have ever been a lady's maid, for you are not servile enough. A sergeant's widow? Perhaps . . . but you are extremely young for that. Just what is your connection with Captain DeMayne?"

"He's a major now," she informed Fanny sharply, then realized she must change her manner if she wished to solicit the woman's help. "I *was* Mrs DeMayne's maid, but as we were on the march the work didn't need a trained girl. She offered it me out of kindness, so I wouldn't be left alone in Khunobad as a widow. She died during a bad storm and was buried at sea. They had only been married six months."

"So I have since discovered," murmured Fanny. Then she put up a hand to gently cover one ear. "How I wish that constant bombardment would cease. The everlasting thundering gives me the headache in this terrible heat."

"I said I didn't want anything for me," repeated Mary, not wishing to lose her listener's attention. "It's for Row . . . for Major DeMayne."

"I can do nothing for him now," was the swift response.

"But you must," she cried. "You're the only one who can. He blames himself for her death, and it's going to destroy him. You don't know half. They led him a terrible dance in India, and he's been very ill. This is more than he can take, but he wouldn't let me help. You must have heard that a few days ago he bloody nearly killed himself," she went on, emotion making her lose control of her tongue. "He's got more in him than half the officers put together, and he doesn't deserve to break his neck because he's driving himself so hard he's too exhausted to see a wall in time to jump it. He thought the world of you once. The least you can do in return is show him you were worth all he lost for your sake. I've already seen one man destroyed by a beautiful, heartless girl—he was torn to ribbons by the lash—and Rowan is now going the same way. You've got to stop him."

Fanny was staring at her with a mixture of amusement and intolerance. "You have a great deal of insolence for someone of your station, but I do believe . . . yes, I believe

Rowan has made you that way. Passion makes fools of duchesses and dairymaids alike."

"*Passion,*" cried Mary cuttingly. "That's all people like you and Lydia DeMayne think matters. Whether they know it or not, men need other things besides . . . things Rowan has never had from any female. He saved my life in the desert near Cairo. I'm going to save his now, even if it means having to beg women like you to do what I can't do myself. Go to him, please."

"You're mad! I am married now, and it would be my ruin if I were to be seen going to an officer's tent alone."

"It will be *his* ruin if you don't."

Fanny swivelled her parasol angrily. "You go. You have nothing to lose."

"I'd lose everything if I thought I could help him. But there is a reason why he will never listen to words of mine."

"And there is a reason why I cannot listen to words of yours."

Mary looked her over from head to foot. "How wrong he was. You aren't worth eight years of his life."

Fanny turned and walked away to where the husband who had given her semi-respectability was still talking to the two men. Mary went back to her tent and flopped on to the grass in the shade thrown by it, beset by the thundering salvoes from the big guns in Sebastopol. There was more than one war being fought here; more than one fortress to be stormed.

CHAPTER THIRTEEN

Across the hills there was no breath of air to ease the clammy heat of the afternoon. The clouds were so low they obscured the high points and hung above the valleys like the pall from a heavy cannonade. Way out over the sea the sky was purple and periodically slashed by fingers of lightning. They were in for a wild night, but a storm would bring some relief from the oppressive heat of the recent days. The men from India were less affected than the others, but regimental life had been adjusted to cope with it out there. At the Crimea it was not.

Rowan felt at one with the moody threatening atmosphere on that war-torn landscape as he rode back with those of his men who had been on piquet since that morning. Strictly speaking, he had no obligation to mount piquet in his new rank as Gil's second-in-command, but he continued to do so.

The sky to the south-west was now growing an even darker purple, with the lightning searing through it more frequently. The possible sound of thunder was swallowed up into the general rumble of the big guns that only stopped at night. Rowan had ridden several times to the batteries on

the heights and to those down amongst the front line trenches, where shells constantly exploded and the great black
cannonballs came sailing through the air to take off a man's
head, an arm or leg, half a horse's stomach, or just to bounce
harmlessly on the grass nearby. For years he had dreamed
of the excitement of battle; had heard old campaigners
speak of the sick nervousness, the dampness of palms holding a sword aloft, the pounding heartbeat as a man confronted his foe. They had all been fables. War was cold and
unemotional during a siege. Death flew through the air from
an unseen enemy. It was long-distance slaughter that over-
took a man as he was smoking a cigar, or consulting a map,
or relieving himself in a ditch. The glory of a charge, of rank
after rank of glittering horsemen thundering toward each
other had been superseded by an abstract grimness to wipe
every adversary from the face of the earth before they could
do the same thing. So every day that passed brought a host
of casualties to add to the thousands that had already been
lost, while the stalemate continued.

Rowan had watched the great assault fail from a safe
distance and, despite the fearful carnage from that hand-to-
hand fighting, there was no doubt the men had preferred it
to siege tactics. Morale had been very low since then, ag-
gravated by the cholera and sweltering temperatures that
made piquet work something of a test of endurance. The
men of the 43rd had even begun speaking with reminiscent
fondness of Khunobad, where there had been native grog,
native women, and even some of the wives. Oh yes, they had
longed to go to war, but they had wanted action, not routine
duties where a man might suddenly find his chum's head
rolling on the grass . . . or his own head! And he would never
see who was responsible.

During the piquet from which they were presently returning shots had been exchanged with a small band of Russians
who had suddenly crested a hill nearby and promised a fight.
But they had moved off fast when Rown had led his party
in a forward attack that had unhorsed one of the enemy,
wounded another, and caused one of his own troopers to

receive a slight injury to his left foot. What use had it been, what effect had it had on the overall situation, he was thinking dispassionately as he noticed a lone figure in a hooded cloak approaching.

Hardly had he been struck by the strangeness of any man wrapping himself in such a garment in this heat and before the storm had even arrived, than he realized the rider was not a man. The figure was very slight and was riding side-saddle. When they drew nearer he was surprised at her identity, even more so when she gave him an unmistakable invitation before veering off toward a point away from the road, keeping the hood well over her face.

At first, he intended to pass on. But the strangeness of the incident must have changed that decision for him, and he rode back to his corporal to tell him to carry on and dismiss the men on reaching the camp. Then he made an unhurried pursuit of Fanny Dennison, who had halted some yards away. She did not turn to him, so he was obliged to ride round and rein-in in front of her. They looked at each other gravely for a moment or two, each waiting for the other to begin.

Then she said, "I'm sorry, Rowan, but this was the only way I could effect a meeting without activating the tongues of everyone on this peninsular."

"Where you and I are concerned, don't you think that consideration is a little late?" he asked pointedly.

"Don't be cruel, Rowan."

He studied the milky skin touched with faint rose in her cheeks, and the eyes of such startling beauty he had once believed no man could look at them and remain free.

"It was never I who was cruel, surely."

Her golden lashes lowered as she avoided his gaze. "You do realize the jeopardy into which I am putting myself by this meeting, do you not?"

"I trust the reason for it justifies that risk."

"The reason is something that happened eight years ago," she murmured.

His horse shook its head restlessly, anxious to get back for food and a drink, and Rowan said, "It is too much to expect any service of me after all this time—and you have a husband to do your bidding now."

She raised her eyes to look into his again, and there was a hint of regret in her voice as she said, "How the years change us all. Why cannot time stand still?" At his silence she continued, "Age is the enemy of all females, you know, and those who have lived by their beauty have to replace it with wealth and position before it is too late. Sir Pomfret is too elderly and self-indulgent to possess the fitness required to maintain his conjugal rights, I am happy to say. But he fondly believes he has put an end to my amours."

"If that is a disguised offer, I fear I must decline it," Rowan said swiftly.

"You must have loved her very much."

"What?" he asked, finding the whole meeting uncomfortable.

"You must have loved your wife very much," she explained. "You always committed yourself so totally in passion, my dear. I am offering you solace, that is all."

"*Solace!*" he choked. "Here amongst the encamped armies? I can get that from any camp follower."

"Yet you do not. Why?"

"By God, do you have spies reporting my every action?" he cried, feeling her intrusion into his life.

"I have no spies—but they apparently exist. At least, one does." She held out her arms for assistance. "Do we have to conduct the whole of this conversation from the saddle?"

"This conversation is at an end, so far as I'm concerned," he said, preparing to move off.

But she dropped from her horse and walked the few steps to put her hand on his leg persuasively as she looked up into his eyes, the hood falling back from her face as she did so.

"I have been deeply in your debt for eight years. Will you not allow me even partial re-payment? There might never be another chance."

"There is nothing to repay," he said tonelessly. "None of it was of any importance."

"It was to me," she said with depth of feeling.

Then he saw the shimmer of tears in her violet eyes and was completely disconcerted. Uncertain for a few seconds, he finally dismounted to stand beside her. But she walked away from the horses, and he followed automatically until they reached an outcrop that gave them a view of the cavalry camps.

"Military men have always held an attraction for me," she said pensively. "I suppose it is the air of élan they possess, besides the dashing uniforms. I was seduced by a captain of lancers when I was barely sixteen and in the house alone. He gave me presents and my aunt encouraged him to visit. One afternoon, he sent one of his friends to conduct me to our meeting-place—except that he had no intention of coming and had passed me on to his colleague." She glanced round at him. "They were both handsome and charming, and I could not see the harm in it. As I matured the presents grew more elaborate, and my lovers more numerous. By that time I realized my way of life had become inexorably settled. I grew more selective, and the men were more discreet. Since there was no escape from what I had become I determined to make my situation as pleasurable and remunerative as possible." Her hand went out to touch his. "Then I met you at a party and would have forsaken all the others, if it had been possible."

He withdrew his hand from her touch. "Why were you not honest enough to tell me all this? None of it matters now."

"It does," she insisted. "Oh, my dear, it does! At first, I truly believed your brothers or some other officer of the 11th had recommended my generosity to you. But I soon realized you believed me to be a virgin who had been conquered by your passion."

"And so you dangled me on your string to everyone's delight and amusement," he said, recalling another who had done the same.

"No! Rowan, I swear you are wrong." She swung round to face him, and there did appear to be genuine distress in her expression. "I knew you were certain to discover the truth eventually, and I had to decide whether it would be more cruel to pretend my love had died or let you find out what I really was. The truth was, my dear, that you were the only person to treat me like a lady, so I became a lady while I was with you. That illusion was too precious to lose . . . but you paid the price of my selfishness more dearly than I could ever guess."

"That was eight years ago, and everyone has forgotten it."

She shook her head. "I have not. You were a boy of twenty, ruled by strong feelings. But a man does not change his basic character with maturity . . . and celibacy is likely to drive a man like you to destruction. I respect your grief over your bride, but you must find periodic escape from it. I am in the unique position of knowing how best to do that . . . something a camp follower would not. I once duped you into believing I was a lady, and treating me as such. Allow me to show my gratitude by now letting you treat me as a convenient whore."

He frowned at her choice of words, not liking the association with her, even now. Then he gave a slow sigh. "Go back to your impotent husband, Lady Teale. You are acting out a melodrama over nothing—and you are eight years too late."

She had turned slightly pale, but her composure did not waver as she slowly looked him over. "I would not believe her, but she is apparently right."

"She?"

"A strange creature calling herself Mrs Clarke, who asked me to provide what you have plainly refused to let her give you."

"*Mary* approached *you* and asked you to do this?" he ejaculated. "How the deuce did she know about that affair?"

"Because it was talked of all over India, including the servants, she informed me. The girl knows everything about you, it seems. She said you were driving yourself beyond all help. And so you will, Rowan, unless you let someone draw close to you."

"I sincerely trust she will not ask every female in the Crimea to offer me her charms," he murmured thoughtfully, still shaken by what she had done.

"I think not, my dear, for her present aim is to become the 43rd's *vivandière*. She is looking for a pony to ride."

Further nonplussed he said, "Dear heaven, will she never stop trying to serve a regiment that has done very little for her in return?"

Fanny gave him another calculating look. "From her determined manner I would guess not . . . any more than she will stop serving a *man* who does little for her in return."

The storm lasted for two days, bringing a halt to the constant bombardment and all movement around the camps, save for the coming and going of cavalry piquets and patrols which had to be maintained whatever the weather. The silence after ceaseless gunfire was almost eerie, and Mary sat huddled in her tent feeling peculiarly morbid. The rain came down in curtains to turn the roads into rivers of mud and saturate the canvas around her until it began to leak. Being situated on the slopes, the cavalry camps were soon being swept by a torrent rushing down into the valleys, and everything had to be raised from the ground in order to keep it dry. Mary had no bed, having always slept on a pallet on the ground, so the most she could do at night was to huddle into her cloak and perch on the wooden crate that served her as table, chair and chest. She did not get much sleep, and her spirits plunged as she shivered in the gale entering the tent from every direction, and the dampness that ate into her bones.

She had been born and bred to such conditions, but had since experienced comfort and grown to like it. She thought wistfully of the truckle-bed Sam Clarke had bought her, and the pretty curtain she had made for privacy. She remembered those days in the desert when she had lain beneath the yellow canvas in her underwear and marvelled at all she had seen and done since her barrack-block days. Isolated for two days and nights in her leaking, cramped, waterlogged tent, her sense of loneliness reached unbearable proportions. She had lost all sense of identity; she belonged nowhere. Being neither one thing nor the other had left her friendless, and the man she loved rejected her. She would give him anything he wanted if only he would let her, but he looked on her just as a constant reminder of his overwhelming guilt.

By the time she was preparing for a second night of misery, Mary's spirits had dropped so low she was telling herself it would have been better if she had died in the desert at a time when she had had all she wanted in the world beside her. Now she had lost it, along with her determination. What was to become of her now? Her brave plan to become a *vivandière* was doomed to failure. She could gain no support from anyone, and her first enquiries about a pony showed her they cost far more than she had ever imagined. There were only her savings to keep her going for a while. After they were spent she would be destitute, with three alternatives facing her—find another lady to employ her as a maid, put herself up as a prospective bride, or sell her favours and stay independent. For what? If she kept her independence the regiment would go back to India or return to England at the end of the war, leaving her behind. A passage on a ship would surely cost more than a small pony.

All through the first half of that stormy night she contemplated her future, finally succumbing to tears of despair before reaching a desperate solution. Perhaps Collins would marry her. They got on well enough together, and she would promise to interfere in his life as little as possible, whilst looking after him to the best of her ability. The longer she considered it the more attractive it became, and she finally fell asleep happy in the knowledge that becoming Mrs Collins would ensure that she remained close to Rowan.

Vivid brightness awoke her to the relief of sunshine and welcome warmth. The thunder of rain on her tent had stopped; the thunder of gunfire had resumed. Climbing stiffly from her box she squelched her way across the ground where there only remained a tiny trickle running on its downward way, and pushed open her tent-flap. A diamond world lay outside! Steam rose up wherever she looked to haze and shimmer everything in view. The sun sparkled in pools and on droplets hanging on guy ropes, tents and poles so that they looked like a myriad jewels. The grass had never seemed so green, the sky so blue, the distant sea so sapphire-clear. The hillside was swarming with uniformed men all glad to get out and stretch their legs. The bustle of a military encampment was like a warm familiar arm encompassing her, and the smell of breakfasts being cooked made Mary realize how hungry she was.

Ducking back into the tent she stripped off the dress she had slept in for warmth, and replaced it with the second dress provided by Lydia DeMayne, which she had turned into voluminous trousers during those weeks she had ridden a pony across India. The garment felt damp, but it was ironed and more presentable than the one she had on. Then she splashed her face with the rainwater that had collected in her laundrytub and tidied her hair with the aid of the hand mirror given her by Sam Clarke. She wanted to look like a good bargain when she put her proposal to Collins.

But she was not so anxious or so hungry that she did not delay in order to string up her line to hang out cloak and blanket to dry. She got no further than going outside with the rope, however, for she was halted by a sight that banished all thought of Rowan's batman. Piqueted at the head of her tent and munching the very moist grass was a small sturdy pony as near to chestnut colour as possible. Across its back was a tooled saddle with large panniers, and a cloak strap behind. She stood gazing at it for a long time as the implications of its presence began to make some sense.

"Oh lordy," she said softly, "so she did it after all."

Walking across to the animal she put her hand on its smooth neck to stroke it. It took no notice, the temptations of the succulent grass proving stronger than the touch of human friendship. But, next minute, Mary found herself burying her face against the warm hide as emotion got the better of her. Fanny Dennison would have put a lady's saddle on it, so it was Rowan's gift . . . and there was only one way he could have known she was after a pony. How could she have guessed it would hurt so much when she had asked that beautiful woman to break through Rowan's defences? This proof that it had been accomplished was almost more than Mary could bear. She remembered that time in the desert and faced the fact that a woman who had ruined him eight years ago meant more to him than she did, even after their wonderful union beneath the stars.

But, as it had done on a previous occasion, this evidence that he was quite out of her reach put fresh determination in her. Straightening up she muttered, "Stop being daft, girl, and start doing something useful. You've got the horse. Get on it and show everyone you're going to be a *vivandière* even without their support . . . and to hell with all men who are dazzled by a pretty face!"

After a week the men in the front lines began to get used to the sight of a girl in grey with a chip-bonnet in the regimental colours of the 43rd Light Dragoons riding down every day with panniers filled with the provisions they were denied whilst in the forward positions. It was not unknown for wives to take their husbands a hot meal or a tankard of ale during the spell their own regiments occupied the dangerous front trenches, but there had never been the equivalent of a French *vivandière* to sell them tobacco, candies, a piece of cheese, or the daily necessities of life. She distributed water freely to those who could not leave their posts, or to the wounded awaiting transport back to the hospitals, and the latter were often given something to sustain their hunger along with the drink of water and encouraging words.

The news spread around the British camps. Regiments leaving the positions before Sebastopol told those they passed on their way to occupy them. Infantrymen told the cavalry, who then began enquiring why the girl neglected to visit the lonely men on piquet duty. 'The Gingerbread Boys' heard these stories and were quick to claim their regimental heroine whilst investigating the matter.

Soon, one by one things began appearing in Mary's tent while she was absent from it—a beautifully fashioned barrel with a tap at one end and a shoulder strap in pale-blue, a short dark-blue cape lined with yellow, dainty black riding boots, a saddlecloth and cornsack embroidered with a *43rd* in regimental manner and, finally and unbelievably, a pair of narrow dark-blue overalls and pale-blue tunic embellished in yellow and silver. When she had made herself a dark-blue short skirt, Mary was as resplendent and regimental as the French girls she had so envied. Officially denied, she had nevertheless been publicly adopted by the men of the 43rd in a way that caused her more pride than she had ever experienced in her life.

The thrill and occupation provided by her new career as an unofficial *vivandière* negated Mary's unhappiness over Rowan and gave her a new status in the regiment. The men looked on her with respect and affection. She had more friends now than she could cope with, and if most of the British women who had come over with their regiments from England gawped at her in astonishment or malice, it did not worry her. Her normal duties of going to the provisioners to buy the things she would sell to those in the inaccessible parts of the peninsular began expanding. For an extra halfpenny she would take letters back to the men's wives or their paramours, carry packages from one regiment to the other, bring the recently-arrived newspapers to officers mounting guard, pass *billets doux* from the genteel lady sightseers on the pleasure steamers in the docks to lovelorn subalterns committed to forward duties for a period that seemed unendurable to them, or purchase expensive cigars from the captains of ships constantly arriving from England to take up to colonels who required every comfort and luxury whilst being shot at.

Of course, Mary risked being shot at too, when riding around the area before the great fortifications, and she grew very familiar with the sight of the besieged town, often wondering about the women who lived within those walls. Were they so very different from herself? Were they dark-skinned like the Indians, or paler like the Egyptians she had seen? Did they really hate the British and the French? What was it like inside that town that was being shelled day after day?

She also grew familiar with the horrors of mutilation and maiming, so that she was soon able to kneel beside half-men to give what help she could without recoiling from the sight of raw bleeding human flesh. When the next full-scale battle began she would need to be strong. But, during that month of July, there seemed little likelihood of any renewal of effort to end the siege.

Mary found her new occupation rewarding in many ways —not the least being that she was financially independent. The cooks of the 43rd were all willing to give her a meal whenever she wanted one, and a regular supply of fodder for her pony was deposited outside her tent. She made a small profit on her vending, which enabled her to buy a second hand camp-bed and a folding chair. When she placed it outside her tent to sit for a while in the evenings she invariably attracted companions who sprawled on the grass at her feet to chat.

It was not long before a new scheme occurred to her. Borrowing books from any source she could find, she began reading aloud to anyone who wanted to listen, and one of the many memorable sights of the Crimea was the girl in grey, surrounded by ever growing numbers of soldiers, reading the classics to those who would normally have remained ignorant of them. These story times became so popular, men cursed to find they must miss an installment because of military duties, and would anxiously ask their colleagues next morning to bring them up to date with fictional events.

But Mary was never so lost in her reading that she missed any activity around Rowan's tent. Fanny Dennison did not appear to visit him, so their meetings must take place elsewhere for the sake of discretion. According to Collins, his officer seemed little better and drank just as much, which suggested Fanny's consolation was in vain. The evidence caused Mary more pain than ever. The thought of Rowan taking that woman as fully and tenderly as he had taken her in the desert might have been bearable if he benefited from the emotional release. Now, she felt she had sold him for the price of a pony.

Proof that Rowan's renewed association with his former mistress was not the answer was evident when Mary came face to face with him one evening in early August, when she was wearily returning along the lengthy road she rode every day. The pestilential insects were already out in the incredibly still heaviness of air that made breathing a labour, and she was irritably waving her arm to disperse mosquitoes travelling with her when he rounded a corner at a canter, then pulled up quickly as he recognized her.

Her heart leapt. It was the first time he had deliberately stopped to speak to her since they landed—something like three months ago. But she was dismayed by his appearance. In just a silk shirt and breeches his frame looked as gaunt as his face, and those well-remembered sleepy black eyes were stony-blank still.

"Good evening, Mary," he began in that voice she still thought of as one of the most exciting sounds in the world. "If I were in uniform, I believe I should have to salute you." He was studying her so closely she sat filled with yearning for him. "So, at long last, your parent has claimed its child. You are finally home."

She forced herself out of her melting silence. "I couldn't have done it without the pony you provided."

"I agree . . . but I was under an obligation, was I not? I taught you to ride . . . at least, I *attempted* to teach you to ride. So my reputation as a horseman was at stake. Left to yourself you would have doubtless purchased some precocious showy nag with no stamina, or a vicious thoroughbred sold for a song by a cavalryman only too glad to be rid of the devil. I could not have an acknowledged pupil of mine performing equestrian delirium across the Crimea."

Finding breathing even more difficult, she managed to say, "You know I don't understand long words like that."

"I know you understand a damned sight more than is

evident," was his strong response. "And one of the first things you should have learned as a full member of this regiment is respect for its officers."

She gasped in indignation. "*What?*"

"They do not expect their subordinates or . . . or *vivandières* . . . to take it upon themselves to run their personal affairs. How dared you approach Lady Teale on such a matter?"

Feeling her colour rise slightly she said, "Somebody had to."

"Indeed?"

"You can't go on like this," she pointed out, her love for him making her voice soft. "What a lot of nonsense about respect for officers. You've had the greatest possible proof of my loyalty and my . . . respect. What are you really trying to say, Rowan? Put it in plain words, for once."

"I thought I had already done that. They could hardly have been plainer."

"And I've done it, haven't I?" she cried. "I've stayed away from you ever since." Unable to sit there on her pony while they were saying such things to each other, she slid to the ground and stood looking up at him. "But I've seen you coming and going, and I've heard what's being said by others. Your reputation as a horseman won't be spoilt by me. You can do that very well for yourself by missing a few more walls you're trying to clear."

"That was a mischance," he said unemotionally.

"Whatever it was it nearly killed you. Next time it will."

All at once the sound of bugles further down the road floated up to them to announce 'evening stables', and Mary felt full of the emotive atmosphere surrounding them in the growing twilight. Temporarily alone with him on that hillside, the moon already faintly visible in the paling sky, she felt as close to him as she had in the desert.

"Rowan, those bugles are signals to a whole army encamped around us. We're part of it, like it or not, and it depends on every one of us. All I can do is comfort and console it. But you can give it determination when it's ready to give up." She moved to stand beside his right leg, and finished telling him something she had begun that night in the desert. "You won't remember this, but you were duty officer on the night Jack Rafferty gave me a beating. You looked at me in my torn dress, fighting for breath, and told dear Sam Clarke to take me out of your sight because you couldn't stand my snivelling. I knew what you thought of me and my kind, but I didn't resent it because I understood why. The next morning you galloped past with Captain Crane, and sent mud up all over me and the only dress I had. It made me see that I was so unimportant I had become part of the background."

He was frowning now and looking more haggard than ever. "When did all this take place?"

But she wanted no diversions. "You changed my whole life by doing that. I was determined to improve myself so that I would never be seen as part of the background ever again . . . by you or anyone. You *inspired* me. You were my goal to aim for. You were all the things I wanted to be— physically brave, unafraid of anyone, confident, clever, and fighting for what you wanted against all odds. What's more, you were so very *clean.*

"From that moment on I started to copy you . . . and I still do. Whenever I think of giving up I think of that day you splashed me with mud. There's still such a long way to go, and I need you to help me get there. You once told me I had no right to feel that life had given me enough, and saved me from dying in the desert so that I could have more." She paused fractionally, then went on, "But I can't do it if *you* give up."

He looked at her for so long she thought he had travelled away from her in his mind. Then he sighed. "You should never have chosen such an unreliable subject for your inspiration, that much is obvious." He gathered up the reins prior to moving off. "I'm sorry, Miss *Vivandière* . . . but you have enough courage in you to succeed without my help." Turning the great stallion, he moved off slowly to resume his interrupted ride. "And I do not need yours. Any other creature of consolation you send to me will receive a similar polite refusal."

Mary watched him until he vanished into the shaded distance, then climbed on to her pony again and set the creature off on the downward track toward Kadikoi. The smoke from cookhouse fires was hanging in a layer in the windless air, canopying the numerous glowing dots between the rows of white tents some feet below her. Drifting up was the faint sound of men's voices as they called to each other, the clatter of buckets as the horses were watered for the night, a whinny or two from the restive beasts, snatches of music on an old concertina or penny whistle. The Army was settling for one more night on foreign soil.

Way over to the west the sea was no more than a purple mass beyond the mauve cliffs, and lights were already twinkling in Balaclava like reflections of the stars that were bright above her. The pony, sensing a rest and something to eat, began to hurry, its dainty hooves falling rhythmically on the dusty ground. Friendly shouts greeted Mary as she rode past the camps until she reached that of the 43rd.

"How about a nice plate o' broth, Mistress Clarke?"

"There's taters and beans ter spare here."

"What'd you say to a tasty bit o' mutton, now?"

She was assured of her hot meal tonight. Thanking them all Mary continued to her own tent where she settled the pony, took off the uniform of her trade and washed herself before donning one of her grey dresses. The men liked to see a neat, clean feminine figure around them. It cheered their lonely spirits.

But all through her preparation she was thinking of one particular lonely spirit, and trying not to rejoice because he had taken no other woman whilst rejecting her.

By the middle of August it became obvious the Russians were planning an all-out attack to try to break the long-standing siege before the weather began to change. Sebastopol would never survive another winter. Cavalry patrols had reported sighting movements of large numbers of enemy troops near the Woronzoff Road, and it was generally believed that the highway between the stricken town and the interior would be the site of the attempted assault.

The British and French soldiers were furious at being told to stand by for defence when they had all been kicking their heels waiting for the order to mount another attack. The cavalry were called out every morning to form up in glittering ranks ready to repulse a Russian charge, if one came, and the situation did not suit any one of them—especially the 43rd, who had dreamed so long of *making* a charge.

Rowan discussed the unwelcome state of affairs with Kit Wrexham as they led a patrol early one evening along the valley of the Tchernaya. The red-haired captain had advanced no higher in rank because he could not afford the price of promotion, and it now meant the very youthful Robin Cleaver—who had found another hopeless love to replace Lydia—was his equal. Since Lydia's death, which had occurred on the same night that Kit had mercifully shot the horse that had threatened Rowan's life, the relationship between the two had improved. There were too many bars to their ever becoming friends, but Rowan had accepted that a man whose passion was singing could also have physical courage, and Wrexham possibly recognized, albeit too late, that he had contributed toward the many problems between an overtaxed man and his capricious wife. Since Rowan no longer had strong feelings about anything, he simply saw the man he had once so resented as a comrade-in-arms.

"I cannot see what the Russians hope to gain from an attack on us," he commented as they rode slowly between the bordering heights, now particularly vivid in the glow thrown by a sun penetrating the rift through which the river ran to the sea at Inkerman—a place littered with allied bones from the battle a year before. The river itself dazzled the eyes with the reflection, making it impossible to see the far banks clearly.

"They are finished, even they must appreciate, and it will merely be an unforgivable sacrifice of their troops' lives."

"There's such a thing as national pride," Kit pointed out, separating briefly from Rowan to avoid a pit in the ground. "Would you give up without a last fight?"

Rowan looked across at the man dispassionately. "In an army pride, whether national or personal, has to be put aside for the greater demand. If a strategic victory can only be gained by wholesale slaughter, then so be it. But if all that will be gained by it is a saving of pride, would you condemn thousands of your countrymen to death to achieve it?"

The other glanced at him, eyes narrowed against the sun. "That's an unexpected comment from a man of your background. I always believed you held a different philosophy."

"Mmm, so I did," said Rowan, guiding his horse carefully between potholes. "But human poses are mere illusions, and the world goes on regardless of them. Look at those hills, for instance. Men have anguished, bled, and lost their minds there during the past year. But the hills will stand until eternity, and none of it will have mattered one jot."

Kit fell silent, and the group of dragoons rode steadily on sweeping the area with keen glances that wishfully put enemies wherever they looked. They did not expect to see anything. All military attention was on the road crossing the heights above them, and it was typical of the ill-luck of the 43rd that they should have been ordered to patrol the river instead.

By the time they reached the limit of their patrol area the sun was blood-red and fully in their eyes if they looked toward the sea along the river. They turned and approached the banks of the river to give the horses a drink before returning. The animals were grateful and walked into the shallow ford with heads down, while the men squatted on the bank to scoop up the cool water and dash it over their faces.

Just when Rowan became aware of their approaching attackers he could not afterward remember. But it was probably a combination of several senses that warned him seconds before danger had become a fact—the sound of rustling movement, the smell of overheated horses, the sud-

den awareness of something that had not been there a moment before. His head jerked round and his eyes tried to
adjust to the half-blindness of the setting sun as he stared
at the opposite bank. Then his heart jumped. There looked
to be a mass of grey-clad Russians on dark horses that melted
into the background of the shadowed hillside behind them,
so that it was impossible to tell just how many there were.
All he was sure of was that his own group was well outnumbered.

"*Kit,*" he called sharply. "Across the river, man."

All Maurice Daubnay's insistence on drilling to perfection bore fruit in the following minutes, for the men of the
43rd were leaping into their saddles as the horses still drank,
pulling the animals savagely round to form battle ranks, and
drawing their swords almost as one. Even so, their enemies
were on them before they could gain dry land, and that
red-flushed river ford became a scene of satanic proportions
with churning, foaming water, rearing horses, writhing
thrusting men and steel blades that were crimson with blood
or the sun's rays.

There was no time for thought. Each man had to defend
himself with desperation against the vicious slicing blades of
a crack Russian cavalry regiment well-seasoned in battle. Yet
there were still instances of heroism to save another, neglect
of personal safety to avenge a fellow, unspoken comradeship
in that ultimate moment of danger. The silent valley now
heard the thrashing of hooves in running water, the grunts
and hoarse cries of men in conflict, the shrill screams of
battle-horses, the rasp of steel on steel, the commands of
officers pitched to the heights of tension.

Rowan felt completely clear-headed and unafraid as he
took on any man who challenged him. In that mêlée in poor
light, his sight was so acute he easily distinguished foe from
comrade, and his natural brilliance with a sword finally
brought honourable rewards. That warrior's blood he had
always recognized running through his veins leapt to the
challenge it had so long been denied. It was as if his whole
life had been designed to meet this moment, and he slashed,

parried and sliced with the skilful grace and strength of the born fencer. Men fell away from his lethal blade that had once so nearly sliced across his own throat; others turned into death-riders as their faces lost all recognizable features.

Completely conscious of his own men as well as Russians falling around him into the water where they quickly drowned even though not mortally wounded, he shouted at his dragoons to fall back. Kit Wrexham, a few yards away in the thick of things, cast him a shocked glance over what he thought was an order to retreat. But that one moment's lack of watchfulness was his undoing. A Russian sabre caught him low across the neck, and he went down into the water to be dragged through it as his horse bolted.

Those who could gradually retreated to the bank leaving the ford full of bodies, some of which were threshing in agony. But the Russians made a bold dash across the river with swords upraised, looking like satan's horde in the deepening red of sunset, and the men of the 43rd prepared to receive their steel with their own. Rowan felt that distinctive satisfaction of seeing no man flinch from facing death, and he called out encouragement in the moments before rank met rank.

It began all over again, and he took on any who ventured within range, receiving no more than a cut on his right arm as he obeyed the instincts of generations of fighting De-Maynes. Then, through it all, he realized they were standing their ground resolutely. Those dragoons around him were as staunch and steady as any cavalrymen in the British Army, and he was glad to be amongst them. They obeyed his every order without question, and met these renowned adversaries without a hint of awe. 'The Gingerbread Boys' were up with the best.

Then, incredibly, the Russians dropped away, began to turn, and returned in ragged groups to the water. When his men made to chase, Rowan halted them sharply. It was pointless to lose further lives for a few Russian ones, and in the water were wounded men unable to defend themselves in a further fight.

It seemed to be all over; they had beaten off three times their number. The enemy horsemen were grouping on the opposite bank and starting to ride off toward the hills. But Rowan's blood heated rapidly as the stragglers reached the far bank and one man left in mid-stream brought his sword viciously down on a man in the pale-blue of the 43rd who was struggling to dry land despite a left arm hanging uselessly and running with blood. The victim dropped again, his face in the water, and lay still while his killer urged his horse to splash through the ford toward others who were moving —one being Kit Wrexham.

Commanding four of his men to go forward on foot to collect their wounded, Rowan spurred his horse into action, galloping full pelt at the Russian slaughtering helpless men as they floundered in the river. The enemy saw him just in time, and turned to counter the blow designed to kill him outright. But he was trained to fight instinctively and put up the accepted parry, little realizing his opponent was fighting with the left arm. He died with his attempt at defence meeting no more than air, and Rowan reined-in to dismount and run to Kit, believing it was the end of the matter. Yet, even as he registered the fact that the other officer would never sing again with that throat wound, a shout alerted him to the fact that the few remaining Russians were preparing to avenge their comrade's death.

There was no time to mount again, so Rowan faced them on foot as they edged their horses back into the water, four to his one, and sure of victory. But they, too, had never encountered a man who fought so skilfully with the left hand, and superior numbers counted for nothing against cuts and thrusts they could not ward off with regulation swordplay. Aware of activity behind him as the wounded were carried to safety, Rowan was soon surrounded by men who had no defence against his unorthodox attack, whereas he had always fenced with right-handed men and had built his skill on that well-known array of tactics.

Sweating, panting and aware of the cold water filling his boots to impede his movements, Rowan nevertheless gradually drove his assailants backward until they were all up on the far bank and growing bloodier by the minute. Through the sound of his own laboured breathing he heard a shout telling him their wounded were all safe, and he was just working out his best strategy for retreat, when movement to his left took his attention momentarily. It could have cost him his life if a sharp Russian command had not stilled his four battle-scarred opponents as they made to move.

Emerging from the gathering dusk was a Russian officer of similar rank to himself, who saluted Rowan and said in French, "I honour your courage, sir, but it has cost you your freedom. Both sides have withdrawn after the battle, and you are on the Russian bank, are you not? By the rules of war, I have the right to make you my prisoner."

CHAPTER FOURTEEN

They took Rowan to where they planned to bivouac for the night. The man who had relieved him of his sword and who plainly commanded the half-regiment was courteous and considerate, as were the other two officers. But Rowan was stunned. A prisoner of the enemy! How could it have happened? He had crossed the world to fight these men: a few moments ago he had been cutting and slicing at them with the intention of killing as many as possible. Now he had been surrounded, disarmed and forced to ride with them up into the hills as their captive. A De-Mayne taken alive and unwounded in battle! It had never happened before in the history of the family.

On arrival at the Russian bivouac Rowan was glad of the presence of the officers. The troopers looked a fierce unpredictable group, and there had been stories of scant mercy for anyone who fell into their hands. He was in the constant company of one or more of his equals, however, who questioned him eagerly on his unique skill with the left hand that had confused them all. Conversing in French whilst eating a hot dinner of very poor quality, the Russians were intensely interested in English life and his years spent in India, a country of some fascination to his captors. Lounging on blankets and cloaks spread on the ground beside the camp-fire, they treated Rowan more like a guest than a prisoner.

But the illusion was shattered when they settled for the night, and the senior officer said, "As a gentleman of honour, do I have your word that you will not attempt to escape, Major DeMayne? I have no wish to submit you to the indignity of a guard, or any form of restraint."

He could not sleep. The mention of some form of restraint had re-awoken memories of another night beside a camp-fire with a group of alien men who had waited until he had closed his eyes, then seized and bound him. They had also appeared friendly and generous—so much so he had allowed himself to trust them enough to sleep. Admittedly, these three officers were cultured aristocrats of the western world, albeit his enemies, but the ordinary Russian soldiers looked like prospective cutthroats. If his three escorts also slept, what was there to prevent a bayonet being quickly drawn over his throat, or a knife plunged into his heart? Earlier this evening he had been prepared to die fighting, but being murdered whilst a prisoner was a dishonourable death. That thought kept him company as he lay wrapped in his cloak on the hard ground of that foreign hillside he had travelled so far and so momentously to reach. Had it been worth the long tortuous journey?

The Russians were astir before dawn, and Rowan was soon made aware of their intention. The attack, instead of coming on the Woronzoff Road, was to be launched against the unsuspecting French and Sardinians along the River Tchernaya. Rowan felt so helpless. He watched with growing fears as more and more Russians joined their detachment until a massive force had assembled to sweep down into the valley. It suggested a major battle afoot. Knowing that his allies would be taken mainly unawares, it was a great strain for Rowan to watch and be powerless to warn them.

The Russians set out while it was still dark, and his captor appeared before Rowan to explain that he was obliged to send him off to Sebastopol in the charge of a corporal.

"I cannot spare an officer whom you are entitled to have as an escort, Major DeMayne, but Voblinsky is a reliable man who will take you to my regimental headquarters in the town. You will find some of your countrymen there, so you will not feel too strange. Regrettably, my subaltern has a lame charger which will have to be substituted for your fine stallion. In the coming battle he will need a horse that is fit, and you will be adequately served by a beast that is fit for no further action other than the slow return to Sebastopol." He gave a courteous salute. "My apologies, sir, but war is war."

Corporal Voblinsky might have been a good reliable man, but he apparently had no trust in the word of a gentleman. No sooner had his comrades ridden off than he bore down on Rowan with a length of rope, with which he tied his hands behind his back. Then he helped his prisoner to mount a grey gelding, and secured the loose end to Rowan's foot. That ensured that he could not run even if he jumped from the saddle. The sensation of being bound and helpless filled Rowan with reminiscent apprehension, and sweat broke on his brow as they set off across an empty range of hills wreathed in pre-dawn mist.

It was extremely uncomfortable as well as humiliating to sit in the saddle with his arms forced behind him and with no means of control over the horse. Luckily, it was docile in its lameness. But Rowan's strongest thoughts were for those unsuspecting men down in the valley who had the additional enemy in the mist that would cover the Russians' approach until the last minute. How would the battle go? Would initial surprise win the day? Had the Russians enough men in Sebastopol to break out from the siege and join up with their comrades to turn the tide of the war?

The din of the unseen battle soon added its emphasis to such thoughts as artillery salvoes began to shake the ground they covered. Between the heavy thunder of the big guns, Rowan could hear the lighter rattle of rifle fire and the shouts of men in conflict. In his mind's eye he was back in the river on the previous day, remembering his own natural steadiness, skill and power of command under pressure. He remembered that feeling of rightness, of true fulfilment, as his sword had met and deflected others.

In a flash, he knew his brother Monty was wrong as far as he was concerned. His own entry into the army had not been governed by family tradition, a sense of inherited defence of honour, an unavoidable obligation to his noble name. The blood of a natural warrior was in his veins. It was what he was born to do; had always known he must do. But he knew now it had nothing to do with the colours or regimental insignia a man wore. Yesterday he had defended his troopers, had fought for those men he led. The 43rd was his regiment, and he had been fighting for it, too. He realized he wanted no other, coveted no other uniform—now, when he was powerless to serve them any longer.

It took most of the day to reach Sebastopol, because a roundabout route to avoid British or French patrols had to be adopted. During that journey Rowan was given only one drink of water by the Russian, nothing to eat, and had been allowed just one short halt, during which his hands had remained tied as he lay on the grass. By the time they passed through the outer defences of the Russian town he felt ready to drop. The August heat had been intense throughout the day, and he had been unable to mop away the sweat that ran down his face, or ease the tightness of his shako. His eyes burned and his entire body ached from being forced to stay in the saddle for so long in an unnatural pose. But he straightened up with an effort, as they progressed past Russian soldiers manning the massive earthworks, who stared at him, some in curiosity, some in aggression.

Despite his physical pain, shock at the sight of the legendary town took all other thoughts from his mind. From up on the hills, Sebastopol had appeared to be a sprawling collection of white-walled buildings comprising the normal harbour community. So must it once have been. There remained but a shell of a town. Perhaps he could be excused his feeling of shock, not having been at the war from its start, but he now witnessed the results of the year-long constant bombardment of a town under siege. It was then he learned another aspect of warfare—the courage of an enemy. The soldiers and citizens of Sebastopol had suffered privation, misery and suffering equal to those who besieged them, but they had not yet surrendered.

The houses were gutted and collapsing; trees were charred, blackened and splintered; gardens and squares were pitted with shellholes and torn up by military traffic constantly passing through. The streets were full of fragments of shells and round-shot, broken glass, splintered beams, tattered curtains, useless ruptured furniture and large pieces of crumbling masonry. Amongs' all this lay the dead and wounded victims of that day's bombardment, helpless to move from the skulls, skeletons and putrefying remains of past victims. The stench filling the air was made more terrible by the hot, still evening air. Vermin ran everywhere Rowan looked, even worrying at bodies not yet cold. Those few civilians moving about the town looked emaciated, broken and almost sub-human. The soldiers looked little better.

As his horrified gaze took in all these details Rowan realized the attack of that morning could only have been an insane attempt to fool the Allies into believing the war could run into a second winter. These people were beaten to their knees, and he was filled with admiration for their pluck and spirit that had kept them from waving a white flag long ago.

They finally reached a group of small buildings just beyond the huge main barracks, and Corporal Voblinsky left Rowan while he went inside a single-storey place with a corner gone from the roof. After some minutes there was the clatter of boots, and a monocled lieutenant came out with Voblinsky on his heels. But the young officer pulled up short when he saw Rowan, and turned on the NCO.

"*Merzevets! Durak!*" he roared, and began delivering kicks to the man's body with amazingly agile feet until Voblinsky was on his knees in supplication. Then he abandoned the astonishing business to approach Rowan and salute with great respect before helping him to dismount.

"A thousand apologies for your unforgivable treatment by

this vile dog," he said earnestly in French. "He shall be posted to the front trenches in the morning. We are not barbarians, Major, and accord our prisoners—even those of your ruffianly rank and file—the most humane treatment. Tsch! Tsch!" he exclaimed in vexation as he undid the rope, "the villain shall be broken of his rank, in addition. Please, come inside, sir."

It was so painful to move his arms forward, Rowan left them lying back against his hips as he walked stiffly into the shell-blasted headquarters, wondering somewhat lightheadedly what his own men would think if he started kicking them to their knees. When offered a chair he said he would prefer to stand for a while, but he gratefully accepted several glasses of vodka, which then increased his light-headedness and feeling of unreality. Twenty-four hours ago he had been riding beside Kit Wrexham along the Tchernaya, telling him nothing was of any importance. Could he truly be a prisoner in an enemy town and finding that captivity was suddenly of the *utmost* importance?

"What of the battle this morning?" he asked anxiously. "What of the assault on the Tchernaya?"

Lieutenant Nevikoff frowned, apparently feeling it impolite of Rowan to enquire on such a subject whilst drinking his captor's vodka. "We were repulsed," he said shortly. "But it was a bitter meeting. The Tchernaya was piled high with the dead, and the water was red with the blood of defender and attacker alike, according to the report just in. Now, there is nothing left to do but defend Sebastopol to the last man." He tossed back his vodka and stared broodingly at Rowan. "You could have taken the town last June if your commanders had not been so cautious. You and I might then have lived. As it is . . ." He shrugged. "*Alors*, I intend to make the most of the days I have left, and so must you, sir. Make your peace with God, for in Him you must find your protection."

With his brain fuddled by his ordeal that day and vodka on an empty stomach, Rowan took a moment or two to understand his meaning. "Are you saying that you undertake no responsibility for my safety during captivity?"

The junior man nodded. "Regrettably, Major, the defence of our stronghold will take every Russian's full concentration. You will have to fend for yourself—as each one of us will have to do until the end comes. Let us pray it will be merciful."

In the small airless cellar that served as a prison cell Rowan spent the next few days in company with six infantry officers who had been captured during the abortive assault in June. They were all classed as walking wounded, and therefore not entitled to hospital treatment, but the foul conditions in that cellar along with poor, insufficient food had reduced them all to a state of weakness and fever that grew more serious with every day's captivity. As officer prisoners, they had been given by the Russians a captured drummer-boy, no more than a child, to wait on them. But the lad was now in a worse condition than any of them, and lay in a semi-comatose state most of the time, shivering in the dampness of that place the sun never reached.

Rowan was appalled and several times made attempts to see Lieutenant Nevikoff to complain. But the uncouth guard at their door always poked him in the chest with his bayonet when he tried to pass, and understood only Russian. So he did what he could to cheer the spirits of his fellow captives by telling them brave lies about the assault to be launched shortly that would free them all. To the frightened little drummer he gave most of his own meagre rations to keep up the boy's strength, and took his mind off their plight by telling him wildly-exaggerated tales of India. He realized the lad began to regard him with something approaching worship, but made no attempt to discourage it because it gave the poor little fellow a reason for courage of his own.

Rowan's morale was naturally higher than those who had been in that cellar two months already, but he was deeply worried about their chances of survival. He knew there were no immediate plans to storm Sebastopol, and found the constant dimness and enforced confinement very difficult to accept. Having always been free to move around, and possessing a nature that was happiest when active, he was dismayed at the frightening sense of something amounting almost to panic that beset him from time to time. Maybe it stemmed from that time he had come to find himself helplessly bound and unable to escape from a red-hot blade that had seared and cut his flesh mercilessly. That same sense of being unable to run from the inevitable had him breaking into a cold sweat and feeling distressingly ill whenever he was weak enough to let his thoughts dwell on underground confinement.

Each dawn the deadly bombardment began, and continued until evening, shells and round-shot descending to turn buildings into ruins, ruins into no more than rubble-filled craters, until it seemed the town would be flattened completely; wiped from the face of the earth along with those human souls within it.

All through that first week of imprisonment Rowan racked his brains as to how he could reach Nevikoff, or some officer of even higher rank to complain, and his chance came on the eighth day. Soon after the daily shelling commenced, their cellar was rocked by a massive explosion nearby, and an existing crack in the wall widened into a cleft broad enough for a man's body to penetrate. Being the only relatively fit man it was unanimously decided that Rowan should be the one to risk breaking captivity to do what he could on their behalf. But he had to school himself to wait until the cessation of shelling that day, since their situation would be even worse if he were killed by an Allied shell.

Emergence from that foul-smelling cellar was like being born again, and he leant against the wall outside for a long time just feeling the exultation of wide spaces and the beauty of a distant sunset that suddenly appeared like a glorious wonder of nature that had never taken place so dramatically before. So many times in the past he had been thankful for the relief of sundown, yet now he had not seen the outside world for a week he mourned the passing of daylight that would put him back into darkness.

But the scene outside was probably better shrouded by night. Another week had caused further devastation and slaughter. The stench was equally vile; the state of those picking their way through the ruins as weak and emaciated as his comrades in the cellar. Common sense had made him abandon the jacket and shako that proclaimed him an English dragoon major, so that in just soiled shirt and dark trousers he passed for a citizen of Sebastopol, the fast-growing black beard giving him the necessary ruffianly look for that beleaguered community.

But relief at being free to walk about was momentarily dimmed by the sight of the myriad glows of the British camp-fires up on the surrounding hills, and such was the stab of yearning to be back up there he forgot the purpose of the evening as he gazed at the silhouettes of soldiers moving around preparing for supper. He had crossed half the world to fight on their behalf, yet was powerless down here as a prisoner of the enemy. Up on those hills one of his brothers had died a stranger to him, the other had served with valour before honourably retiring. DeMaynes never fell into the hands of the enemy; they would sooner fall into the hands of death.

A group of rowdy soldiers passing by brought him back from such thoughts, and he remembered his mission. But his gruff enquiry for Lieutenant Nevikoff brought an equally gruff response from the Russian corporal outside the headquarters, accompanied by arm waving which Rowan took to mean that the subaltern had gone to the forward defences for a spell. Something about the further damage to the building and the disorganized air around it dissuaded him from pursuing the matter. It seemed unlikely that anyone would care about the plight of prisoners, and he would risk being shot for evading their guard. Feeling that the others depended on him, he moved off into the darkness formulating a different plan. Stronger than the rest of them, he could use that escape route to make secret excursions into the town to get supplementary food and glean the latest information on when to expect the attack.

So, during the following ten days, all those desperate attempts to prove himself in India paid unexpected and priceless dividends. Expertise at beggarly disguise, the ability to master languages quickly and experience at survival in conditions of hunger and squalor all made Rowan highly successful at moving around a hostile town at dusk and stealing whatever he could lay his hands on without arousing suspicion. With a few essential words of basic Russian, a naturally filthy unkempt state after days of cellar living, and an assumed ambling gait, he went unnoticed by Russians who would never have believed he was an aristocratic British officer. Another advantage of his past was that he could stomach any manner of disgusting mess that would keep him alive, while those he looked after were sick and plagued by dysentery when they forced themselves to eat unspeakable items that would nevertheless have sustained them.

Rowan soon discovered that the hospitals were overflowing and without supplies to the extent that only those needing amputations were carried there in a vain hope that they might be saved. The other wounded were cared for by any good Samaritan or the Holy Sisters who wandered the streets during the shelling, often becoming victims themselves. So, when two of his companions became dangerously ill—one of them being the little drummer-boy—there was nothing he could do but watch them die and then drag them out through the cleft so their bodies would not further increase the stench of that cellar.

Even though he had the relief of knowing he could squeeze through that cleft to escape the confines of his prison, the captive state tormented Rowan more and more as the days passed. The idea that he had dishonoured the family name yet again gave him little peace of mind, and each evening when he set out on his scavenging his gaze turned to those beckoning camp-fires on the hills. The 43rd was up there; he longed to be with it. How wrong he had been to imagine nothing mattered any more. His place with his regiment meant more to him than he allowed himself to accept, and the feeling that he had let them all down rooted itself so firmly in his mind rational reasoning was put aside in favour of it.

The urge to escape was constant. He had given his word not to attempt to do so that first night because his captors had placed no guard over him. The situation now was different. He was no longer under an obligation of honour. He took to haunting the harbour, seeing the ocean stretching away in the distance as a possible route to freedom in a small boat. But it would be impossible to get five skeletal men that distance even if he managed to steal a vessel. Of course, there was a man-made causeway across the narrowest point, but it simply lead to isolated Russian territory where there would be nothing to eat at all and no shelter available. Heavy-hearted, he always turned away and went back for another unendurable day of captivity, knowing he could not abandon the dying men.

August passed into September, and still the Allies delayed. Raking the distant hills with his gaze evening after evening Rowan despaired. What were they doing? There was a weakened demoralized enemy in a shattered town. Surely his own army must realize it could just *walk* in now. Had they abandoned the idea of an assault? Did they mean to blast to pieces the town and people of Sebastopol, then ride away counting the job well done?

The first week of September seemed to bear out that suspicion as the bombardment increased to such ferocity the cellar was constantly shaken by tremors, and became so unstable the inmates feared it would collapse on them. Then, on the sixth day of the month, they found no guard on the door and realized they had been totally abandoned. Feeling considerably weakened himself by this time, Rowan used what strength he had to carry his companions from probable burial alive to a crater in a nearby park, from where they had an excellent view of their countrymen moving about on the heights outside the town. It did not ensure their safety—no place was safe from the shells—but they had the illusion of freedom and were relieved of the dread of the unknown that had pervaded that cellar.

That night was particularly starry, but Rowan was the only member of that sickly fever-ridden group able to find any joy in the sight. He thought again of the desert, and the awesome peace of isolation. He thought of a girl who had given him what he had sought and never fully found in any other female, and he knew, for the second time, that he was not happy to die. There were still things he would leave undone—but such different things. The Crimea had not neutralized him, as he had thought. It had made him see clearly things that Mary, in her simplicity, had seen from the start. For a while that night he felt close to her, and was almost content.

Daylight dawned to reveal that two more of his companions had slipped into death during the night, and the remaining three were so ill they could keep no sustenance down long enough for it to do any good. Filled with anger, Rowan left them, determined to find a doctor or nurse to alleviate their condition. The Sisters of Mercy spoke French and so did the doctors, but he knew in his heart what they would say to his request. Three-quarters of the population was in need of medical help; it was an impossible task.

He passed unremarked through the devastated streets, walking slowly and with a great deal of effort. His shattered nerves jumped when a Russian gun fired the first salvo of the morning with a crack that almost split his eardrums. The daily exchange was soon under way, and the streets around him grew alive with the scream of red-hot missiles, the roar of explosions, and the continuous pattering of metal splinters that scattered to fall on everyone and everything in the area. People vanished before his eyes, walls folded up to collapse at his feet, the earth opened just ahead of him, yet he was so near his destination now he did not even break the slow rhythm of movement as he changed direction or stepped over obstacles. Twenty yards from the hospital he heard a louder whistling scream, felt rather than saw the approach of something dark, then became caught up in a pressure stronger than a cyclone that lifted him off his feet, took away his power to breathe, and flung him into the blackness of night during day.

News of the capture of the 43rd's most distinguished and colourful officer raced through the British camps the minute that patrol rode in with their dead and wounded across the saddles. The belief that Rowan DeMayne had been so broken by his wife's death that he was no longer the man he had once been was firmly refuted by the report of his extreme gallantry during the attack, culminating in his single-handed defence of the wounded in the river which had led to his unfortunate capture. The hero of the 43rd had undoubtedly proved himself once more.

Those who knew him declared he had nine lives and would be discovered with a girl on each knee when they marched triumphantly into Sebastopol before long. But even Gil grew pessimistic when the chestnut horse, Charade, came into camp riderless and bearing cuts after the battle at the Tchernaya the following morning. The slaughter at the river had been so great it was impossible to identify a number of the casualties, and they had been buried in mass graves recorded only by the fact that they had not answered the roll-call afterward. Would one pale-blue dragoon coat had been noticed amidst that bloody massacre of French, Sardinians and Russians? Unless the 43rd received official notification of his capture and survival—a procedure that was taking longer and longer these days—it would have to be assumed that Major the Honourable Rowan DeMayne had been killed by his captors or his allies during that unexpected ferocious battle on August 19th.

When Mary had ridden into camp that evening and heard about the instinctive return of Charade to the regimental lines, she had gone straightaway to Collins. The little batman had been unashamedly in tears and unable to tell her what she wanted to know. Gil agreed to see her, but he wore such a grim expression her heart missed a beat. It was very hard to stand in that tent with Rowan's possessions around to remind her so strongly of him, but she had faced up to grief before and knew she might have to do so again.

"Colonel Crane, is there any official news of the Major?" she asked quietly.

He shook his head. "His men only witnessed his capture last evening, Mrs. Clarke. Lists of prisoners are exchanged after battles, or once monthly between times. But you must appreciate it is a long business, and we cannot expect anything for some time yet."

"Where are prisoners taken?" she asked next, trying not to be upset by the sight of Rowan's spare uniform hanging on the rope across the tent, the clean silk shirts beside it, and the pile of handkerchiefs embroidered with the Drumlea coat of arms that he had told her about during one of those intimate moments before each had been aware of the love they could not acknowledge.

Gil pursed his lips. "Into Sebastopol initially, then back into Russia. But I will be frank with you, Mrs. Clarke. The town is so near to falling, I cannot see the Russians bothering with the transportation of men taken now." He must have seen her expression, for he added hastily, "I do not mean to imply that their care of new prisoners will be in any way neglectful."

"Sir, I was born into this regiment, and I know soldiers as well as anyone," she told him. "They will share their last crust with a lost child, a starving mongrel, or any man worse off than themselves. But I have been every day to the front lines where the guns are trained on Sebastopol, and from what I have seen of our bombardment there can't be many crusts left there to share."

Rowan's friend looked uncomfortable and indicated a canvas chair. "Please sit down." Then he added when she was settled, "You say you know soldiers well. Major De-Mayne is a soldier of the very finest quality with a reputation for courage you must know well, for you had evidence of it in the desert outside Cairo. He has survived deprivation on many occasions, and the most barbaric torture. I think you should not consider how many crusts there might be left in Sebastapol in connection with an officer such as he is."

She smiled then, although it was somewhat wan. "He's more than likely to have the daft notion of giving up his share to someone even weaker than he is."

Gil smiled back. "That sounds about right."

"Collins is piping his eye because Charade came back all cut and lame. The men are all saying the Captain—oh lordy, I keep forgetting he's a major now—they're saying he must have been killed at Tchernaya. But I know that stallion, sir, because he was with us in the desert. If Row . . . if the Major's body is down there in the river, Charade would've stopped by it. That animal came back here to find his master. I reckon them . . . *those* . . . Russians took the horse for themselves," she continued, fervour making her forget her speech temporarily. "That means he must've escaped into hiding somewhere, and he'll turn up here soon. Can you warn patrols to be on the lookout for him?"

The fair-haired man fingered his moustache uneasily. "I think you cannot fully understand the situation, Mrs Clarke. Major DeMayne would have given his word not to attempt to escape."

Mary stared at him dumbfounded. "Why ever would he do something as daft as that?"

"Because he is a gentleman of honour," came the soft explanation that silenced Mary with its reminder that the man she loved lived by a set of rules she found inexplicable.

There was an awkward pause, and Mary got to her feet wishing she had not approached the man who was Rowan's friend, and who must understand him better than she ever could. But he detained her with a kindly smile as he complimented her on the work she was doing as an unofficial *vivandière*.

"You are a credit to the regiment, ma'am, and strong proof that our authorities should give their approval to the institution of such persons as yourself in official capacity. I have said all along I would give you my personal support. If there is any assistance you need, pray do not hesitate to inform me."

"Yes . . . thank you, sir, but the troopers look after me well enough," was her subdued reply before she turned her gaze resolutely from the sight of Rowan's cut glass decanter and went from the tent.

She walked back up the steep slope to her own tent deep in thought, seeing nothing of the purple velvet night around her. She had been so sure of the significance of that horse returning, it was now very difficult to accept a fact that highlighted her own social limitations. Then she turned impetuously to go where she knew she would find Rowan's horses tended by the groom who knew them well. But the man gave her no cheer when she approached Charade in a strange attempt to be close to its missing owner.

"Doan'ee go too close now, Mistress Clarke," he warned swiftly. "Upset and nervy'e be. More'n likely 'e'll kick out if you goes up to 'im. They's nasty cuts. They'll be given' 'im jester's jiggery, make no mistake."

"Oh," said Mary flatly. "I thought he'd know me well enough by now."

"So'e does, right 'nough," came the assurance as the man in vest and overalls got up from the box where he had been polishing harness, and came toward her smoothing his thick moustache. "But you think 'ow 'tis when you'm sick and doan care to be fussed. That's like 'e be now. Even the Major'd 'ave to go careful like with 'im in this state."

The impulse was too great to be resisted. "Where do you think he is, Mr Bates?"

"Ah now, there you 'aves me," he began, rubbing his back to ease it. "Could be that 'e's down in that Chernayer, drownded with all they others . . . or mayhap 'e's in Serbasterpol under lock and key." His doleful face screwed into an expression of contemplation. "Either way it doan look too rosy, do it? I mean, the way they guns is sending merrygig's message day after day into the place, doan seem likely there'll be much left there afore long."

Sick at heart Mary shook her head. "No, not much."

"On t' other 'and," he continued, "I never knowed the Major not to come out of a scrape. I 'eard you was there when he come back from Multan. Any other genleman would've give up arfway. Not so the Major! E'll be back, right as ninepence, same as 'e brung you out of the desert when we was all certain sure you was both lost." He put a comforting hand on her arm. "Doan you worry 'bout 'im, Mistress. What you needs to do is carry on normal, and give us the next bit from that there tale you'm reading of a night. Is that pore young genleman going to get 'is rightful due from that there miserable grandfer, I wants to know."

Mary gave a smile. "There's still half a book to read. But I expect he'll win in the end. They usually do, after suffering a lot first."

The man gave her an artful wink. "There you are, you've jest give yourself the answer to what you come 'ere to ask."

That thought stayed with her while she read the next installment of the current book to those men clustered around her an hour later, but it was a fight not to let her gaze stray to the lights in faraway Sebastopol harbour. When they had gone she gave up the fight, and sat staring through the entrance to her tent and longing for Rowan with painful intensity. He had told her to forget all he had said and done to her, but she could think of nothing else and would never forget it for the rest of her days. He had taught her so much, had been her inspiration . . . and he had been so very wrong when he said she had enough courage to continue without it. Maybe she could be with him in sight every day, even at a distance. But if he went from the world she would not wish to stay in it. She had few illusions. Mistress Clarke, *vivandière* was beloved by the regiment. But when this war ended and the 43rd went home, there would be no need for her services. If Rowan was left behind to lie with all those who had fallen here, she would want to lie close to him.

With only a slight sense of shock Mary realized what she was contemplating, and why. The one thing Rowan should never have taught her was the sensation of true love. Jack Rafferty had been no more than a rough friend who had expected little more from her than she had from him. Sam had been a very dear companion from whom she had learnt that rapport it was possible to find with a man. But Rowan had peeled away the layers of invulnerability and touched that very tenderest of coverings with fingers that had been exquisitely expert. Once exposed, that willing surrender could not be covered again. She knew the desire to please and arouse, understood the hurt of rejection and the pain of suppression. Jealousy came too readily now. Caring was too anguished. One glance from sooty-dark eyes could turn night into day; one sentence in those caressing velvety tones could set her heart leaping; one sight of that impressive figure passing by could transform her mood.

But even worse was the physical longing she suffered. Until that night in the desert she had believed the thrust and tumble of sexual union a ritual any woman could well do without. Rowan had proved it could be so unexpectedly wonderful it gave her little peace. Just once, yet her body still felt the pressure of his, her skin had never forgotten the enticement of his hands, and her blood throbbed through her veins in memory of a mouth that had searched and found the response she had never dreamed possible. Jack Rafferty's possession of her had been meaningless. It was to Rowan that she had given herself for the very first time, and knew she could never let a man touch her in that fashion again. Better by far if she ceased to exist here if Rowan never returned.

As the days passed she watched for a staggering figure to come into the camp, despite Gil's words on escaping. Whilst doing her work at the front line trenches she asked if anyone had seen movement between the enemy fortifications and their own position that would suggest a wounded man was trying to make his way to safety. Each day she witnessed the continuous lambasting of Sebastopol that sent up clouds to hang over the city, and her heart was slowly breaking. He did not return, and no one could surely still be alive in that shattered port.

Three weeks after Rowan had been captured Mary had

her first ray of hope. The long-awaited order to storm the
great outer defences of the town set the endless snaking
columns of troops marching along the dusty tracks once
more, to reach the forward positions. This time they would
succeed; this time the Russian defenders would be driven
back to wave the white flag. By tomorrow evening they
would all be carousing inside Sebastopol, looking up at their
own camps in triumph.

The troops all shouted such things to each other, but a
brown-haired girl in dragoon uniform thought of only one
thing as she packed her saddlebags with strips of cloth, small
pads of wadding, some bottles of antiseptic lotion, fruit and
goats' cheese in place of her usual supplies. By tomorrow
evening Sebastopol would be occupied and prisoners freed
—if any remained alive.

At dawn on September 8th Mary was on her pony riding
to the forward positions as usual, with her water-barrel full
and extra canvas bags of it tied to her saddle. The animal
made slow progress under the extra weight, but she knew
there was no need for haste. The wounded would not start
coming in for several hours yet. To the daily clamour of
bombardment was added the distant sound of rifle-fire and
men's shouts as the first waves of red-coated troops flowed
down the hill carrying their scaling-ladders.

Mary could not slow her quickened heartbeat at thoughts
of what the day would reveal. Everyone who knew him
maintained that Rowan would somehow survive as he had
in the past. But he had had a reason to survive on those other
occasions. She alone knew he no longer cared.

Her arrival at the trenches increased the speed of her
pulse even further, for no one could remain immune to the
import of that scene. The entire green hillside was covered
with waiting regiments in a kaleidoscopic pattern of scarlet,
dark-green and tartan as infantrymen, riflemen and high-
landers moved about restlessly awaiting their individual orders to go. The smoke from the guns gave the morning a
misty unreality, and Mary felt the soldiers must know ten
times her own apprehension at what the next few hours

might hold. She looked at the faces of men from an island homeland she hardly knew and saw tension, excitement or impatience on their features or in their eyes. But there was no sign of fear. It was a marvel to her that they could be on the brink of death, maiming, unbearable agony, yet not be afraid, as she would surely be.

Her gaze travelled ahead of them down the slopes toward the enemy fortifications, where scarlet dots were running pell-mell through the rain of death, falling here and there, or vanishing altogether as the earth erupted beside them. Further on there were other scarlet dots inching their way up the grey-brown walls of the earthworks on ladders that were invisible to the naked eye, only to drop like stones as Russian riflemen at the top picked them off one by one. Each one of those dots was a living human soul who had loved ones, problems and heartaches as she had, Mary mused sadly. Yet each was answering the call of duty without visible fear.

A bugle-call rang out; another wave of scarlet dots rippled its way in the wake of others on that slope to eternity and, watching them, Mary suddenly had the answer to something that had plagued her for some time. Battle was hideous, agonizing, completely unnatural. Men who lived their lives prepared for such sacrifice must have something to offset it. No longer did she wonder at the passions aroused by women like Fanny Dennison and Lydia DeMayne, for she now saw clearly that they offered the complete escape from horror—sweet perfume that drove the smell of blood from the nostrils, beauty replacing bestiality, soft voices that nevertheless drowned the screams, physical ecstasy to counter physical agony.

Mary Clarke, *vivandière*, might well bring cups of water in their hour of need, but she was all part of warfare. It was not weakness, as she had supposed, that was caused by a pretty face. It was a subconscious search for absolute beauty to counter this kind of depravity. If a man was expected to face this that was presently before her, surely he was entitled to the perfect antidote!

Unexpectedly came the longing to be beautiful, scented and highly-practised in the art of pleasing a man. Rowan would never have shut her from his life then. But, immediately on the heels of that conclusion, came the fact that he had recently refused Fanny Dennison's solace, and had been very unhappy with Lydia. Perhaps the Mary Clarkes of the world were needed just as much.

Proof was soon available as stretcher-parties began bringing in the wounded. Others stumbled back dazed and tattered. Some, who were no more than untried boys, gave way to their panic and ran back to safety, their tears mingling with blood from the cuts they saw as major wounds. Initial confusion with those waiting to advance soon abated as they saw the flags marking the ambulance stations, and rallied to them. In a very short time it seemed that the casualties outnumbered the fighting-troops in reserve.

Mary was kept busy, going amongst those lying under the hot sun with their part in the long drawn out war over for the present. The white apron she wore grew redder and redder with blood, and so did her hands as she raised a helpless head for a drink, gripped the hand of a dying man, or tried to staunch a wound that was pumping life as the victim awaited the hard-pressed orderlies.

"*Water, water!*" ... "*help me, someone*" ... "*Where are you, Mother?*" ... "*this pain, I can't stand this pain.*" The cries rose up around Mary, mingling with the ringing sound of the 'Advance' on regimental bugles, the encouraging shouts of officers as the next assault wave set off, the growing rattle of rifle-fire, the shudder and roar of the great cannons, the whistle of Russian shot and shell, the baritone tremor as they landed too close for comfort, and the far-off indescribable noise of hand-to-hand conflict.

The smoke grew so thick it was difficult to see more than ten yards ahead. It set men coughing and demanding more and more water; it clouded the confused scene so that the waiting ranks were uncertain when to advance, or where their own officers were. The returning wounded could no longer see the rallying-flags, and often wandered downhill again into the fray without knowing.

The midday heat grew to bring swarms of flies attracted by the smells of sweat, vomit and blood, and increasing numbers of wounded were piled into waggons that rumbled off along the tracks, raising dust to further obscure the scene. The number lying on the grass had spread into a great scarlet pool around the various rallying-points.

Mary's own supplies quickly ran out, so she unhesitatingly joined the squad of orderlies under the charge of harassed doctors, who accepted her without question in a situation that was fast becoming overwhelming. Doubts began to arise: the unacceptable began to be pondered. Why was the casualty rate so high? Why were so many coming back before they even reached the enemy? The cacophony of distant bugle-calls was now so confused it was impossible to translate the progress of the battle.

The delirious mutterings of those who had stumbled back through the pall of smoke, faces blackened and uniforms half blown away, could not surely represent the truth? They spoke of total massacre of officers so that the men were leaderless, they rambled crazily about ditches full of dead, and scaling-ladders being pushed away from walls so that those on them fell on to waiting Russian bayonets. Some claimed they had been ordered back before they were half-way there; others that Sebastopol contained a veritable army of secret reserves with an endless supply of ammunition. One or two even claimed British prisoners had been held at gun-point on the bastions to take the bullets while Russians fired from behind them.

Mary heard that tale as she went amongst the demoralized men, and it was nearly the end of her. Exhausted, filthy, appalled at the cost of this last battle to win a war, and fearful over what she might have to face by the end of the day, it was practically the last straw. Nightmare visions of Rowan being torn apart by British bullets while his body protected one of his captors blotted out the mental sight of those she tended, so her ministrations began to be abstract and automatic.

"Ere, missus, there's no need for tears," chided a warm voice in front of her, and she returned from those terrible mind pictures to see a dark-moustached fusilier before her.

Wiping her hand swiftly across her cheeks she tried to smile. "It's just the smoke."

"Pesky stuff," he agreed. "Gets in me lungs real bad. Bin coughing somethin' terrible, I have." He put his hand on her arm, and his eyes were full of softness as he added, "This is no place for a little maid like you. But you're a real trooper, an' no mistake."

She knelt beside him quickly to tip water between his lips, asking as she did so, "You've been down there. Is it true they've got prisoners up on the walls at gun-point?"

"And more," he declared between sips. "They've even got dead men lining the ramparts, being shot at until they fall apart."

Horrified and feeling some kind of madness stirring inside her, she nevertheless fought to continue. "They say there's a secret army inside there."

The man closed his eyes and seemed to be almost asleep as he murmured, "We'll never take it. That place'll stand for another winter . . . and we'll all be dead by then."

The madness was rising further and further. She could think of nothing but that strong proud body that had taken hers with such gentle possession, now being propped up lifeless as a target to be blasted into no more than an obscene mess of blood and bones. She dashed away further wetness on her cheeks to no avail. It kept coming despite her attempts to smile encouragement. But the man was not looking at her, anyway, as through the din and roar she heard the bugles in frenzied regimental chorus. *Retreat! Retreat! Retreat!* At that point, the man before her gave a strange gurgle and regurgitated the water, along with half his lungs, into her lap.

The madness now reigned. With a terrible cry she tugged the apron frantically from her waist, and got to her feet driven by something beyond her control. She ran, and as she did she finally understood Rowan's mental torture at Multan. To contemplate another's agony was more than the mind could stand. He was down there somewhere being torn apart alive by bullets, his body was being used as a shield until it fell apart, he was being thrown from the ramparts on to waiting bayonets.

She ran through the mêlée of troops that were now uncertain whether to go or retreat, she continued to run against the tide of broken-hearted exhausted men making their way uphill after yet another failure, and her progress went unremarked because she was just another figure in uniform; another soldier in a futile bloody battle. The bugles deafened her with their message, and she was sobbing in her anguish. All around her was the only kind of life she had ever known; the only family and the only friends. But they were deserting her at her hour of greatest need. They were coming away and leaving him there; they were turning their backs on him and shutting their ears to his screams of agony. They were leaving him without solace at the end, without recognition of his courage and loyalty.

Her head now rang with the strident notes of bugle-calls, thundered with the roar of guns, throbbed with the madness of her need to reach him. Still she ran, the downward slope increasing her pace until she was carried forward in an uncontrollable progress through the stragglers in scarlet jackets, who were absorbed in their own misery. The great earth ramparts grew ever nearer through the blur over her eyes, and still her exhausted legs ran—one small figure in the pale-blue and silver of the 43rd Light Dragoons advancing on the enemy.

Then something hit her in the chest, knocking her off balance to sending her rolling head-over-heels, the straw bonnet Noah had bought her being wrenched off in the process. Burning pain spread through her shoulders and arms as she came to rest on her back staring at the sun. Momentarily she was back in the desert after being thrown from Drummer Boy. Soon, Rowan would be there kneeling beside her with water and declaring his need of her.

But the madness left her, and she knew where she was. Drummer Boy had been shot after falling at a wall, and its master did not care about anything anymore. Rowan would not come this time . . . or ever again. Her tears redoubled because she had not managed to reach him after all. She would not care that she was now dying, if he had been beside her as he had been in that desert.

CHAPTER FIFTEEN

There was the sound of shouting, wheels rumbling over cobbled streets. Heavy gunfire was continuous. It seemed to be nearer than before—or twice as loud. At first, he thought he was in the cellar, because of the darkness and the incredible weight pinning him down. It must have collapsed as he had feared, and they were all trapped beneath the rubble. But, as he lay fighting for the breath that the pressure on his chest tried to deny him, he recalled leaving the cellar and carrying his companions away from such a danger. Where, then, was he?

It was impossible to move anything save his eyes, and they were now growing accustomed to the dimness. Rolling them so that his view of the surroundings was as comprehensive as possible, he saw nothing clearly other than a chink of brightness to his extreme right that suggested clear blue skies and sunshine. Yet his body felt chilled and wet as if he had been lying out in the rain. The moisture was running slowly across his face still, and he was so thirsty he put out his tongue for it. Then he almost choked. He was lapping up blood!

Terror images flitted through his mind. Had he been

bound and tortured? Was a girl now about to be sliced apart? What new ordeal must he be prepared to face? There was a nauseating smell pervading the place he was in and the wetness of his body was of a sticky thick variety. More blood? Desperately he tried once more to move, but the weight on his legs and chest was far too great. So, while he tried to control his thoughts into cohesive progressions that would solve the frightening mystery of his situation, he lay with his gaze fixed on that tiny patch of blue that represented freedom. Slowly he recalled carrying his companions from the cellar to an open crater, then finding two were so ill he had vowed to get medical assistance for them. The bombardment had begun and he had had to dodge explosions and holes in the streets. Then he remembered the loud whistling sound, the blast of air, the sudden darkness.

He took some moments considering all that as the blood continued its thick path across his face, then felt his pulse begin to thud heavily as he reached the only possible conclusion. With his skin beginning to crawl and a rising sense of panic thickening in his throat, he rolled his eyes again. The panic doubled. It was not rubble half-burying him. It was human bodies! Fighting to hold on to his control he squared up to the truth. At the time of that explosion he had been very near the hospital, and he knew from his frequent sorties through the town that it had a yard where the dead were put in a great pile to await burial, which never took place until the yard was overflowing. Then the victims were placed in mass graves provided by shell-craters, and covered with a thin layer of anything that would constitute interment. He must have been taken for dead by those clearing the streets and piled into the yard with other victims of the day's bombardment. The blood over his face and body might be his own or that of several others.

Retaining iron control in what he realized was a hideous situation, Rowan faced the fact that he could remain in that pile for days, until he starved to death or went mad with the horror of it all. He could even be interred alive, his faint cries going unheard against the tumult of warfare. Everything in him cried out against such a fate. Was this to be his inglorious end? Was it for this that he had exultantly read the order to proceed to war, and ridden with it in his hand into the midst of an elegant ballroom? Had he dragged a delicate, unsuitable, selfish girl half across the world so that he could perish unremarked, unmourned and unfulfilled? Was it to lie in an unmarked mass grave with his enemies that he had saved another girl from the relentless sands of the desert?

Why do you always feel you have to do more than anyone else? You're just a man, like they are. The wisdom of innocence; the innocence of simple wisdom. Mary had lived all her short life with the philosophy he had only now acquired. It had taken forcible surrender and twenty-one days of captivity to bring home to him the truth. Now fate had decreed he would never live by it.

Rolling his eyes upward for a sight of that tiny fragment of blue sky he gazed at it with yearning sadness. Somewhere out there on the distant hills a little *vivandière* of the 43rd Light Dragoons would be giving water, food and comfort to the wounded, holding the hand of a dying boy, writing a last message to a loved one in England, or easing the last moments of the ruffianly soldiers she knew as her only family. He had sent her out of his life when she was the only worthwhile woman in it. He could never now invite her back where she belonged, at his side. Those fine distinctions of honour, those ridiculous airs of inexperience Monty had mentioned, had put seemingly insuperable barriers between them. Only when it was too late could a man see how easily they could be demolished.

As he continued gazing at that small patch of sky, he suddenly knew he *must* tell her. In order to do that he must somehow do what he had done once before. Just over a year ago he had dragged himself back to Khunobad with a vital message . . . one that would save men's lives. Now he had a second message to deliver. If he did not return with it he would have a third female life on his hands.

Yet the will was stronger than the flesh. It was totally impossible to move beneath that grisly pile. Knowing his

only hope was to stay awake and rational until the Russians
came with more dead, or to begin the burial process, his
anguish of mind threatened that hope as he lay in the midst
of that hill of corpses. Time passed unrecorded save for the
fact that he could no longer stare up at the hope provided
by that glimpse of sky, for the sun was well up and blinded
him. It must be noon, or later, he estimated. The heat was
growing insupportable; the stench almost suffocating.
Breathing was more and more difficult as the weight against
his chest seemed to worsen by the minute.

The roar and thud outside was now deafening, and
seemed twice as concentrated. Then it was as if a sudden
cyclone had hit him when some power greater than human
effort had the imprisoning bodies shifting and sliding in
grim cascade that sent him tumbling helplessly downward
away from sunshine and freedom. Yet, when he finally came
to rest, his control snapped enough to set him laughing
wildly. The blast from an explosion had rearranged the dead
so that the one living soul was no longer trapped. He had
been thrown free; he could now move.

Shaking and bewildered he got to his feet very slowly. To
escape he must now climb a slope that must be thought of
as no more than an ordinary hill if he was to get to the top
sane.

It was strange, he realized afterward, that he took it for
granted that he was soaked in the blood of others and not
his own as he made that grisly climb. Had it been otherwise,
he still would have reached the top, the power of fear overriding the pain of physical hurt. Incredibly, once at the top,
he immediately forgot where his boots rested as he took in
the scene before him.

The hills rising outside Sebastopol were covered in running figures—scarlet or green-clad men spread out in ranks.
British and French troops in great force clearly visible
through the drifting smoke of gunfire. Bugles were filling the
midday air with strident commands, standards were fluttering in the breeze as rallying-points and rifle-fire provided
non-stop chattering as a pale echo of the cannons. Rowan's

heart leapt. At last, the long-awaited assault! He *would* return, without a doubt—along with his victorious countrymen who would pour into the town before long.

But, as his vision adjusted to the brightness and his head cleared of the swimminess produced by his recent buffeting, the joy slowly melted away. The running figures were going uphill away from the town; the bugles were all sounding the 'Retreat'. The unpalatable facts stared him in the face. His own army was being driven back!

Scanning the foreground, the defeat was all too evident. Rowan could see clearly the top of the great defences where Russian soldiers were massed to fire down into men on scaling-ladders. That the ladders were there was evident when he saw red-coated invaders appear momentarily over the brink, having defied bullet and bayonet to get that far, only to be knocked backward, run through or beheaded by an officer's sabre, to fall again out of view. As an accompaniment to the scene, Rowan could now clearly hear the shouts and screams of invader and defender alike as they were locked in hand-to-hand combat, his own countrymen surely knowing they could only die or be taken captive now the rest of the army was in retreat behind them.

Helplessly he watched the returning troops being mown down, shot in the back—the most humiliating wound for any soldier—and he shared the heaviness of their miserable failure. Even so, they were returning to freedom, and he had to remain a captive of the Russian army that appeared to be inviolate. Lieutenant Nevikoff had stated that Sebastopol would be defended to the last man, and that event now looked as far distant as ever.

It was only at that point that Rowan glanced down and realized he was standing on a face that had eyes staring at him in deathly outrage. Violent shaking beset him to start him slithering down that inhuman hill, where he stumbled to a partial wall and began to be sick. Then, as he sank involuntarily to his knees with weakness, fear put him back on his feet to stagger away from the hospital lest he should be taken for a corpse again and thrown back on that heap.

His progress was limited. A surge of blood down his right cheek revealed that it stemmed from a deep gash in his head, and movement had produced a violent pain in his ribs. Trying to ignore both he lurched no more than twenty yards before giddiness turned day into twilight, then total darkness as he felt himself falling.

It was still dark when he opened his eyes. Thankfully it was only the darkness of night. His head thudded with pain when he moved it, and nausea washed over him. Putting his hand to the gash he discovered it was surrounded by a thick sticky mass in his hair. He was relieved: loss of blood must have been responsible for his faint. He should now be able to walk without falling if he took it slowly.

The September night must be well advanced, he decided, because it was cold in the thin shirt, and trousers that were stiff with the blood of others. As he shuffled along hugging himself for warmth he glanced up at the hills. Here and there a faint glow was visible, but the Allied armies had settled for sleep. A sense of terrible desolation swept over him. Would he ever get back where he belonged?

For a brief moment his tired brain told him all he had to do was slip through the defences in the darkness, and climb those heights. He could be amongst his colleagues by morning; back with the 43rd. Back with a girl who had shown him the real priorities of life. Then he recollected that he had left helpless men in a shell-crater yesterday, and came to a swaying halt. Endeavouring to think straight he tried to work out where he was and how best to get back to them. Looking around he saw the dark bulk of the hospital to the rear and right. If he returned to it he would be better able to judge directions.

There was something more compelling to take his attention however, and he stumbled toward the glint of water in a nearby ditch. Bending to drink the foul outflow from the town brought such a pain in his ribs he gasped involuntarily. But all else was driven from his mind next minute, when he grew aware of a familiar sound. But it was a sound he did

not expect to hear in the darkness of a Sebastopol night. He
lifted his head in growing curiosity as the sound grew louder
and louder.

Then, because of the curve of the street, he suddenly
found himself in the path of a group of people dragging a
waggon. They either did not notice his kneeling figure, or
did not care that he was there, for he was pushed aside with
such force he fell at the roadside. There he stayed, propping
himself up on his hands as he watched in dazed incompre-
hension while the rumble of wheels on cobbles increased
further.

The waggon was the first in a long procession that came
out of the night, lurched past his feet, then vanished into
the darkness again. Each cart was laden with as much as it
could contain and accompanied by dark, shuffling, silent,
shawl-wrapped figures who gave the appearance of ghostly
nuns on a midnight pilgrimage as they passed. Still they
came, on and on through that chilly star-filled night until
Rowan thought the whole population of Sebastopol must be
on the move. The truth then hit him like a bolt of lightning.
They were going. The Russians were deserting their beleaguered town and taking everything with them!

Climbing to his feet he leant against a crumbling wall as
the import of what he saw penetrated his weary brain. The
civilian people of the port were being sent out under the
safety of darkness across the bridge of boats, and that could
mean only one thing. The military defenders of Sebastopol
must have intelligence that the Allies were due to renew
their attack, and knew it would be successful this time. The
fight to the last man was about to take place with the dawn,
and his own countrymen would swarm into a town peopled
by the dead.

With his senses slowed by the past three weeks, it took
several minutes for the full implications of that conclusion
to set him forward in search of his former fellow-captives
whom he knew were helpless to move in more than a crawl.
He must find some place for them all that would give the
greatest chance of survival in the coming assault that would

surely wipe Sebastopol from the face of the earth before it
ended.

There was no way he could cross that purposeful stream
of weary, defeated people, so Rowan let himself integrate
with them, gradually moving from right to left of the column as they drew near the hospital. No one took any notice
of him, each being intent on quitting the home town that
had held out through shot, shell, snow, ice, disease and
despair for over a year. Luckily they all moved at a slow
dragging pace that allowed him to stumble along fighting
the pain in his ribs, without being overrun, and he successfully emerged from the human stream by the hospital yard
where he had so recently been thrown with the corpses.

It was not recollection of that that made him halt for a
moment, it was the sound of cries and moans coming from
within the building itself. He had learnt enough Russian to
hear the desperate pleas for help, the cries for water, the
pitiful begging for someone to come to their aid now they
had been deserted and were certain to be massacred by the
barbaric French and British.

Breathing hard Rowan moved forward to the entrance,
mesmerized by the chorus of the doomed within, and more
confused than ever at what was happening. The stench
alone should have prepared him for what he saw, but it did
not. There were no neat rows of beds with orderlies moving
between and doctors tending the dying. It was more like a
charnel house. Filthy blood-soaked men lay everywhere—on
straw, the bare stone floor, shelves and broad window-ledges
—many on top of each other. The whole place was littered
with filth of every kind and rats ran freely over everything.
The air was filled with the sounds of agony and helpless
degradation as the dying and dead lay locked together in
gruesome embrace. There was no one to hear that anguished
chorus save those whose voices united in it.

Rowan asked in his limited Russian where the doctors
were, but his question drew mass attention to his presence
as a living, walking source of help. A hundred voices begged
him for water, food, ease from pain, solace whilst dying, the

last rites for a comrade, the removal of a corpse that was preventing movement.

"We have been abandoned. They have gone. They have left us to have our throats slit by British soldiers. Lord have mercy on us all!"

Stunned Rowan turned away and shuffled back outside. Doctors deserting a hospital? Were they all being pressed into duty on the outer defences, to fall in the last stand? It was unprecedented; inhumane! Doctors were not fighting men. The town would never be saved by putting guns into the hands of surgeons.

What he saw on his return to the street told him an incredible story, however. In the darkness it was just possible to see that the procession still snaking its way through the cobbled streets had changed in nature. The waggons were now piled high with military equipment, the rumble of wheels was heavier as guns were dragged past, and the shuffle of feet had been replaced by the firmer tread of soldiers who could not forget their marching pace even when exhausted and starving. He stared at the phantom force as it made its way to the bridge of boats leading to the Russian interior. There was to be no stand to the last man after all. The army of Sebastopol was slipping away too!

He was still staring in shocked disbelief when the night around him roared and thundered, making the ground beneath his feet shake as the darkness became suddenly illuminated by vivid orange light. With heart thudding Rowan turned instinctively and saw a conflagration at the far end of the town where a succession of smaller explosions was sending up an eruption of flames, debris and flying sparks of fire to shower the surrounding area. He swallowed convulsively finding his throat unbearably dry, and his eyes narrowed in instinctive distress. A defeated army was deserting its stronghold and destroying its arsenal as it went. His warrior's soul cried in protest.

But the protest soon died as another tremendous roar rent the air, closer this time and flooding the street he was in with a carmine glow that revealed the fear and panic on the faces of the vanquished troops. Reasonably organized departure turned into a desperate selfish flight to get away from the succession of destructive explosions that were a hundred times worse than the shelling they had endured for over a year. Magazines had plainly been mined, and continued to bang and spit fire long after the first charge had gone off. Supplies of ammunition that could not be transported were being destroyed in gigantic pyrotechnic displays that became uncontainable in a matter of minutes.

They were confined to the far end of Sebastopol at present, but Rowan had no doubts that every fort and military building in that town had explosives attached to slow-burning fuses already alight. This was borne out by the growing stampede of Russian troops frantic to reach the escape route before they were overtaken by self-destruction. The silent snake of night-shrouded figures had turned into a stumbling, pushing, noisy riot of men bathed in hellish light.

It was only then that Rowan realized his own danger. Before long this town would go sky-high, along with everyone left in it. Finding sudden strength he set off toward the place where he had left his comrades that morning, finding his way easily by the red light that illuminated the streets between the frequent flares of bright orange and yellow as tongues of flame billowed out from ruins well alight. The noise of that night had become incredible. Subsidiary explosions went off in shattering succession, fires grew in size and roared as the breeze fanned them, terrified humans raced to safety, and red-hot debris showered down on to the cobbles like lethal round-shot. With the pain in his ribs burning as if with the fire around him, he reached the crater to stand for a moment or two almost double to ease it. The spot was deserted.

There was no way of telling where they might now be if they were, indeed, still alive, and Rowan felt there was no more he could do on their behalf. Even as he thought it he was almost thrown off his feet by the biggest explosion yet. Night was turned into bright yellow day as the magazine and nearby fort rose up into the sky, blasted apart by the force of its own stacked gunpowder. When the flaming pieces descended, those that fell on other buildings set them aflame also, so that the whole surrounding area soon resembled a suburb of hell, extending rapidly to where Rowan stood numbed and irresolute.

Imminent danger restored his mental powers to the extent that he realized his only hope of escape was to head immediately for the track through the outer defences by which he had entered so many days ago. If he delayed, the fort defending that sector of the town would be sure to go up and block the narrow cutting through the earthworks. He made to move off in that direction, but some irresistible sound stopped him. It was a girl screaming. In an instant, he was back in that place near Multan where the night had been lit by tongues of fire, and he had let a girl die so that he could live to return with a message.

The sound had him spinning round, but he could see no girl anywhere. Frantically his gaze searched the street that had been filled with rushing soldiers a moment before. There was a different fleeing horde now. Rats by their thousands had been driven from burning buildings in squeaking terrified streams, making it appear as if the grey cobbles were heaving up and down before his eyes.

The scream came again, and he was able to locate it. Next to the hospital was a small annexe of some kind that had barred windows. It looked no more than a store, or a pump room of one storey with a flat roof. That roof was starting to flame in the far corner where burning debris had landed and caught the top of wooden shutters. The scream had come from someone inside that doomed building. Rowan looked back at the track that was his only route to safety, then began a stumbling run.

It was not toward freedom, however. He had let one girl die, and destroyed another in order to ease the mental guilt of it. This one must be saved, whatever the cost. However, it was not a girl, but a very young man on the edge of hysteria who was clinging to the bars at the window, screaming to be saved from incineration alive . . . and his cries were in English. He was coherent enough to answer Rowan's husky demands and tell him there were ten of them, all wounded and weak from lack of food, who had been abandoned for the last two days when the hospital staff began packing up to leave.

Giving a swift reassurance Rowan went round the building looking for a door, and found it at the end that was ablaze. There was a heavy bar of wood through two iron holders, and the metal was already almost too hot to hold as he began to manhandle the log free. He was dreadfully slow because the stabs in his ribs with every movement made lifting such a weight very difficult. But the cries from inside were growing in urgency as they realized help was at hand, and they drove him on when he flagged.

Letting the wooden bolt drop to the ground Rowan tugged at the door, discovered it opened inward and gave it a push just as a blazing shutter dropped to the earth beside him no more than inches away. What he saw inside was even more daunting. Apart from the youngster clinging to the bars over the window, the other prisoners were in no condition to stand, much less walk to safety. They lay on straw scattered over a floor covered with their own filth; a group of skeletal bearded creatures with the wildness of near-insanity in their eyes.

It was no more than a flash impression, because Rowan's attention was caught by the sight of a loft above them that contained sacks of supplies which had been set alight by the fire in the corner over the door. Once they really began to blaze the loft would collapse on those beneath, along with anyone trying to get them out. Yet there was no other thought in Rowan's mind than a girl he had deliberately failed to save, as he went into that stinking place, speaking briefly but confidently in English and French to the mixture of soldiers who seemed half out of their minds.

The night turned into a total roaring inferno as he struggled in and out of that building, coughing and retching in the smoke and feeling his strength gradually ebbing with the effort of carrying one helpless man after the other into the open. By now the inferno was also outside. Half Sebastopol appeared to be on fire, the deserted streets resembling pathways to Hades as they were illuminated by the flickering reflections of flames licking a broken town. Every so often a fresh explosion set the earth trembling as the forts and arsenals were systematically blown, the satanic crimson pall over the ruins deepening further.

He lost track of time and reality. The fire that threatened to engulf him was the camp-fire of dark-skinned men in white flowing robes; the agony in his ribs was due to the raw bleeding wounds caused by the knives; the thundering explosions were the echo of blood pounding in his head as they drew the terrified girl toward him; the burning of his skin was the anguish in his mind as he forced himself to join their laughter.

How many lives would it take to repay hers? One, two, three, four . . . ? No, there were still some left. How many for Lydia? One, two, three, four . . . ? Two remained, but he could no longer see them. Flames were everywhere he looked. The doorway had vanished; the building itself had vanished. There was nothing more than a camp-fire crackling and burning before him. The screams had stopped. Now he was free to go. Yet he knew the ordeal was not over. Somehow he had to get back with the message. Men's lives depended on his getting back.

He set off. His skin had been burnt off leaving raw bleeding flesh; every step was agony. He was mad with thirst. He had done it before, he could do it again. Thunder! Roll after roll of it! He turned bleary suffering eyes toward the sound and knew it could not be real. Crimson water; crimson sky. Black ships that suddenly flew apart into black fragments, or disintegrated in a second to vanish beneath that blood-red water. Far in the distance, stark against the hellish night, a long black ribbon of movement winding upward on to hills that swallowed everything up in its normal starry darkness.

There were no ships in India. He was giving in to madness. He must remain rational; it was essential to get back with the message. *They are called ships of the desert. Noah*

FORGET THE GLORY 411

told me that. The echo of that familiar voice came to him as he turned and continued. Ships of the desert, that was what they must have been. But why did they suddenly fly apart and sink? It was a mirage. *A what?* came that voice again. *Pictures of the mind!* He smiled at her. She was all he had ever wanted. That was the message he had to deliver. No, it concerned men's lives.

He fell and did not want to get up again. But he knew he must. He had let a girl die so that he could return. She must not have suffered in vain. Yet, as he struggled upright he told himself they had asked too much of him—of any man. He would never do their vile work again.

Peering through the blur over his eyes he saw the ships once more, broken and aflame on a pool of blood. He must fight the onset of madness or he would give himself away as an Englishman. Forget the ships; the town of fire. Forget the thunder and the agony. Forget the glory. Just deliver the message. English soldiers' lives were at stake—and those of French soldiers. He could not understand that. Why Frenchmen?

He fell a second time. The mule must have wandered away somewhere. Unable to stand again he began to crawl toward the large mass ahead of him. Surely it was the cantonment gate. Or was it Khairat Singh's palace? Either way, he was almost there. He *had* returned. But he had let a girl die in order to do so. It was too much to ask of any man. That thought was in his mind as his distant destination suddenly rose in the air in a myriad pieces, and the roaring in his ears increased the thundering in his head to unbearable proportions. But he cried out in a native tongue so that he would not betray himself as redness took over the earth.

The exhausted demoralized armies settled for the night on the heights above Sebastopol knowing the attack must be resumed at dawn, at whatever cost in lives. No one had believed it could fail again, and fertile imaginations now turned the Russian defenders into an army of invincible men who had an endless secret supply of reserves reaching the port through tunnels·running beneath the very hills on which they were encamped.

When, at around midnight, a gigantic explosion shook the ground and filled the night with thunderous sound, the tense nervous troops stumbled from their tents believing they were under attack. But alarm soon changed to stunned awe as they saw Sebastopol bathed in a fiery glow and watched with an unbearable mixture of sadness and anger as sections of the town blew sky-high one after the other, ending with those ships remaining in the harbour.

What had it all been for, they asked themselves. Why had thousands died by sword, sickness and extremes of weather? For what reason had boys agonized and been sundered only yesterday? What had anyone wanted with Sebastopol anyway? The men of the 43rd recalled their long arduous journey that had taken them across ocean and desert, through cholera, heat and thirst, and devastating storm in order to reach the Crimea. By dawn, Sebastopol would be an empty ruin. There was no victory, no *glory* in this! Why had they come?

The Russians had gone leaving their enemies a shell of a town, piles of unburied dead, hospitals full of the dying, half-savage, abandoned patients, and groups of tattered, decimated prisoners too delirious to know they were now free. Scouts were sent to the silent defences at the very first signs of dawn to ensure that what remained had not been mined, and set to go off when they entered. The bulk of the Allied troops watched in a mood of bitter anticlimax from the hills they had occupied for so long.

One of the officers sent ahead to reconnoitre came across a bizarre figure dragging himself along just outside the defensive earthworks, apparently heading for the Allied camps. Bearded, filthy, covered in blood, and seemingly half out of his mind, he was muttering wildly in some language other than English, French or Russian. His clothes were torn and singed, his hands were covered in burns and blisters, there was a severe gash in his head, and his torso was covered in the most terrible scars the officer had ever seen. He would have passed by, nonetheless, if the creature had not gazed up with pain-filled eyes then gasped in English—and very cultured English, "Eight men. By the hospital—north side. Stretchers . . . get stretchers!"

The news soon reached the 43rd Light Dragoons, who reclaimed their irrepressible hero with great excitement. They had come to war to cover themselves with glory and been thwarted. But Rowan DeMayne had ensured them and the regiment lasting fame. Even the officers found themselves rejoicing to a man. Feelings of resentment and envy had long since passed; they had been through too much together for such self-indulgent refinements. What was more, they had all felt deep regret that he had been lost to them down by the Tchernaya whilst defending a regiment they had all believed he held in contempt. They now knew he was wholeheartedly one of 'The Gingerbread Boys', and news that he had survived captivity and the devastation of Sebastopol to return as he had from Multan banished depression and anticlimax at what everyone saw as an empty victory.

Gil went to help bring his friend in and was appalled at his condition. Only something tremendous could have driven him to keep going as he had. Indeed, although Gil probably knew him better than any other man, it was only those scars across his torso that identified the wretched figure from thousands more like him as Major the Honourable Rowan DeMayne.

They were bringing him up the hill on a stretcher when Gil rode up to positively identify him. But he had no intention of letting his friend be taken to one of the hospital huts that were overflowing with grisly sights. Harry Winters could tend Rowan in his own tent. The doctor came speedily, tut-tutting over something that had happened before. He put ointment on the burned hands, washed and dressed the headwound, then bound the scarred torso to support obvious broken ribs.

"He's lucky to be alive," was his emphatic conclusion. "If he goes on like this, he'll never see thirty."

Gil shook his head, smiling. "He'll be the youngest colonel this regiment will ever have one day. I'll wager he'll make a finer one than I ever will. Under his command the 43rd will fill their standards with battle honours." Sobering slightly, he added, "What's more, the proud family that turned its back on him will be honoured more by him than any other member."

"If he lives long enough."

"He will . . . so long as he stays clear of females," said Gil with personal bitterness. "They appear to cloud a man's judgement to a disastrous degree."

But females appeared to be the overriding concern of his sick friend when Rowan awoke that evening and seemed reasonably lucid for the first time. After greeting Gil in subdued tones, he said, "Fetch Mary. I *have* to see her."

Gil was puzzled. "Mary who?"

"Mary Clarke, damn you!"

He frowned. "*Mary Clarke?* Do you mean Mrs Clarke who used to be your servant? Sorry, old fellow. She'll be unable to nurse you. Poor little thing was shot during the assault. The Russians must have taken her for a trooper, in that uniform. I have to say I've revised my views on *vivandières.* I gave her my personal support for the venture, but you can see where it has led. We cannot have our women being shot at. I went to see her in the hospital—I felt I should, you know, for we have all grown extremely fond of her—but she was sleeping. Winters said she had little chance. Pity. She was a fine example of the spirit of a regiment, and more credit to us than the average trooper's woman."

Gil realized he was talking to himself, for his friend appeared to have travelled somewhere out of reach as he stared at the roof of the tent with eyes that were blacker than they had ever looked before.

Rowan lay consumed by grief. It was his final punishment. He had not atoned for those two lives by saving eight men after all. Mary had had to be sacrificed so that his everlasting guilt would be to live with the knowledge that he had destroyed her also. He mourned her loss with a depth of despair that seemed likely to remain for as long as he lived. Yet there was no question of drawing a sword across his throat. That was weakness, and she had shown him true strength. He would go on because that was what she would want. Everything he did from now on would be for her.

Men came in and out of the tent to see him and wish him well—young Cleaver, who had coveted Lydia, Kit Wrexham with his throat bandaged and speaking in no more than the whisper he would ever be able to manage, Southerland-Stewart, who had lost his wife on the journey and was on the brink of marrying the widow of a French officer. Several officers of the illustrious 11th Hussars came to congratulate the young brother of two of their own notable past members. They pressed him to transfer to his family regiment, but he declined saying that the 43rd was the only regiment for him.

It was a long night, and Rowan slept toward dawn to dream of burning water and burning ships in the heart of a desert. In the midst of the flames stood a young girl in dragoon uniform, with her arms held out appealingly to him. He awoke to find tears on his cheeks, and a visitor beside his bed. She looked as beautiful as the first time he had set eyes on her, and he still thought she seemed more of a lady than many high-born females he knew.

"Are you not compromising yourself by coming here?" he asked from his pillow.

Her smile was still irresistible. "Even you, my dear, must be rendered incapable after what you have been through."

"It was good of you to come, Fanny. News travels fast— even to the wives of elderly incapable statesmen on ships in the harbour."

"No, Rowan, Gil told me of your return."

"Gil?"

Her merry eyes twinkled. "He was jilted by his Sophie and needed consolation."

"Gil?" he repeated incredulously. "He is learning to be

human at last." Then he thought of all he had seen in Sebastopol; all the misery and suffering on this Crimean soil, and said wearily, "Thank God for women like you, Fanny. Never cease to be what you are. Society might look down its long nose at you, but you are more honest, more generous than all those staid creatures who condemn you. I once believed you to be a lady . . . and so you are, my dear, and always will be in my eyes."

She seemed deeply affected by his words. Her soft hand closed over his bandaged one lying on the blanket. "You always were the most ridiculously romantic man I ever knew."

He moved his head on the pillow. "I have no more illusions. I have finally come to terms with life."

Her violet eyes were misted with unshed tears as she said, "I think you have not, Rowan. There is one more thing you must do, and that young girl is dying for lack of it. She was more than a servant to you, that much I deduced from the start. You have to tell her, before it is too late."

His heart jabbed painfully as he took in the meaning of her words. "Before it is too late? Are you telling me she is still alive?" Struggling to sit up he demanded thickly, "Tell me the truth, for God's sake. Gil said . . . I understood she had not survived the battle."

Fanny moved to support his body in the sitting position, saying into his ear, "The wound was severe, but not mortal. She believed you lost, and did not want to live. When she heard Sebastopol being destroyed she gave up even the tiny shred of hope that had kept her alive. I was with her but a moment ago. She is slipping away fast, Rowan, and did not even know I was there. If you care—and I swear you do— only you can save her."

He had been through too much for such simplicity. "You have it wrong," he managed with difficulty. "I am the one who destroyed her—as I destroyed the others. If I had not given her a pony she would not have fulfilled that . . . that ridiculous desire to serve a regiment that did nothing for her in . . . in return. I cannot save her. I have done nothing to save any woman I have ever known."

Her arms closed round him from behind, and her cheek rested on his shoulder as she whispered, "You are so wrong . . . so very wrong, my dearest Rowan. Eight years ago you sacrificed your honour, your family and your brilliant career to save the name of a courtesan you believed to be an incomparable female. Mary Clarke told me once that I was not worth eight years of your life . . . but she is, Rowan. Give her just eight minutes of it, eight hours or eight years— however long it takes to convince her that she really has something to live for. I suspect you owe her that much."

Gil told him it was madness; Collins wrung his hands and predicted an instant relapse. Nevertheless they helped him to dress in shirt and breeches the minute Fanny left. With his hands so bulkily bandaged he knew it was out of the question to ride up the long hill to the regimental hospital, so he begged a ride on the back of one of the waggons rattling past, as Mary had on so many occasions.

It was just a hut like all the others, but the windowsills and verandah resembled a garden. Bunches of wild Crimean flowers tied with ribbons and decorated with frills lay everywhere, interspersed with tiny baskets of fruit or pots of preserves from England. As the waggon rolled past, two men in the pale-blue and silver of the 43rd were handing a fresh posy to one of the orderlies, before walking away grave-faced.

Rowan dropped to the ground filled with dread. Did the floral tributes indicate that he had arrived too late? Limping into the hut he came upon Harry Winters, who looked at him in exasperation.

"Really, this is a great deal too bad! I cannot be responsible for your recovery if you ignore my advice. I distinctly . . ."

"Where is Mrs Clarke?" he asked curtly. "What are all these flowers arranged here for?"

"Mrs Clarke?" repeated the man with too much on his

mind. "Ah, she looked after your wife on the journey, didn't she? The flowers, and the other gifts, have been brought by officers and men of the regiment—of all manner of regiments here. She is regarded as one of the heroines of the Crimea. Newspapermen have sent home reports of her courage and humanity, and many a British heart will mourn the little soldier-girl struck down amongst those she succoured."

"Mourn?" he rasped. "You mean she is gone?"

Harry Winters shook his head. "When I looked in a few minutes ago she was still hanging on, but . . ." he frowned, ". . . I don't fully understand it. The wound is responding to treatment, and there is no physical reason for her severe condition. One must suppose all she has seen and heard here has been too much. She is, after all, a girl of less than twenty. Battlefields are no place for females. I would not expose my own daughters to such an experience. But, of course, she is a remarkable creature not to be compared with the average young female. It will be surprising if she does not become a legend along with all the other extraordinary aspects of this terrible affair."

"Where is she?" demanded Rowan urgently. "Surely she is not with the men."

"Naturally not," came the terse reply. "I have put her in a small store at the end of the hut. It is not ideal, but the hospital is overflowing and there is not . . ."

Rowan walked away hearing no more of his words and feeling none of his pain now. He went in fear, unable to shake off the conviction that he had brought about her fate and was powerless to save her. The tiny room was almost filled by the bed which was surrounded by flowers, as if she was already a corpse awaiting interrment, and the girl lying there looked so pale and lifeless he halted in the doorway, filled with dread. Then he saw the faint rise and fall of her breast.

He sat beside the bed for a long time, holding her hand in his bandaged ones and silently willing her to live. In some strange way he attempted to transfer to her that iron determination he had himself adopted on two occasions when death had been hovering greedily, and to send some of his own bodily strength into her slender frame through the linking of their hands.

"Mary," he eventually whispered. "Mary Clarke, you must not believe the world has given you more than enough and be happy to die. There is a whole lifetime awaiting you. Come back to it. Come back, I beg you."

He repeated it over and over again, growing more and more desperate as time passed on a day that was unnaturally quiet without the sound of big guns. Noon came and passed, yet still he sat holding her so that she would not slip away. When her lashes gently stirred and finally lifted, he was so tired he almost failed to notice.

"Rowan?"

It was little more than a whisper, but it set his heart thudding with hope. "Yes, I'm here."

"You . . . came back?"

"Of course. You, of all people, should have known I would."

She was too weak to say any more, but those unremarkable, yet infinitely honest, eyes told him all he wanted to know. He leant forward so that she could not fail to hear his next words.

"I came back to tell you I was wrong. I thought I must and could live without you. My days in Sebastopol showed me the truth. I love you, little Mary Clarke, in a way I've loved no other woman in the world. I will not let you go again—ever. No, don't look at me that way. Of course it won't be easy. There will be snubs, insults, and doors closed in our faces, no doubt. But I have spent the last eight years of my life trying to erase them, only to have war show me such things are of very little importance against love and suffering. As for you, in a few short months you have risen above all that to win the affection and respect of every man here. You will do so again wherever we go. We are two of a kind, Mary. The only family and friends we need are 'The Gingerbread Boys' . . . and I mean to make you their Colonel's Lady one day."

Her lashes flickered, and the fingers held in his moved slightly. It was an effort, but she managed to breathe, "Me, the Colonel's Lady? That's daft."

"Let's have one thing straight from the start," he told her, his voice husky with relief. "Where my wife is concerned, *I* shall decide what is 'daft' and what is not."